TROUBLE THE SAINTS

TROUBLE
THE SAINTS

ALAYA
DAWN
JOHNSON

A TOM DOHERTY ASSOCIATES BOOK
NEW YORK

TROUBLE THE SAINTS

Copyright © 2020 by Alaya Dawn Johnson

Edited by Miriam Weinberg

A Tor Book
Published by Tom Doherty Associates
120 Broadway
New York, NY 10271

www.tor-forge.com

Tor® is a registered trademark of Macmillan Publishing Group, LLC.

The Library of Congress Cataloging-in-Publication Data is available upon request.

ISBN 978-1-250-17534-2 (hardcover)
ISBN 978-1-250-17533-5 (ebook)

Our books may be purchased in bulk for promotional, educational, or business use. Please contact your local bookseller or the Macmillan Corporate and Premium Sales Department at 1-800-221-7945, extension 5442, or by email at MacmillanSpecialMarkets@macmillan.com.

First Edition: 2020

Printed in the United States of America

0 9 8 7 6 5 4 3 2 1

For Elizabeth Jones Johnson,
who I met before I could remember.

And

For Lillian Wayne Prillerman Fogg,
who warned me.

SAINTS CAME IN

Seven. That's what we're starting with.

I woke with the dream late on a Thursday night, sometime in July.

It's a good one, as far as sevens go. The angel joker for the zero, plus seven of spades, that's seven, clean as the air you breathe. Well, cleaner, if you breathing in Harlem.

"Tell me," the dentist said while he lit my cigarette. He was using the lighter Dev gave me after I'd dropped mine in the Hudson, the one I kept by my bed still. I blew a shaky plume that scattered in the crosswinds of the fan and the raunchy East River musk slinking through my open window.

"Was I in it?" he asked when I didn't say anything. The dentist was nervous, which made me laugh a little, considering, and he eyed the holster hanging easy and louche on the post of my bed.

"Nope," I said. "But Vic was."

The dentist squeezed my shoulders. He was looking at me like anyone might, or at least anyone who heard that Victor's angel had, at last, been given her second dream. Like he was working out which runner would take his numbers on the day, hour, and minute of my death.

You get the hands with a dream, a dream that runs true. In

Harlem, we might throw a party or we might keep it real quiet—
sometimes that extra dose of juju doesn't go over well with the
neighbors—but we always play the numbers. The dream that gives
you the hands never fails, they say.

Well, what the Lord giveth he can taketh the hell away.

You get a second dream, you *and* your uncanny hands better play
the numbers, so your widow can pay for your casket.

"Victor came up to me in the Pelican with Red Man just behind
him. He said, 'Here's a job for you, Phyllis LeBlanc,' and then I was
standing next to him in this long white dress. I had on my holster,
but there were two severed hands in it instead of my knives. And
then Red Man pointed to me and said, 'You killed that man!' Just
like the end of some Charlie Chan flick. Can you believe it? As if
that would surprise anyone, let alone Red Man."

The dentist didn't laugh. "And then?"

"A wind blew through, a hot wind, and it was so bright and blue I
could hardly see. Just Red Man's silhouette like a halo. He lifted his
arms and said, 'Don't fail us.' And then I heard—someone's voice.
Calling my name. That was it."

"Don't fail?" Now the dentist laughed. "Have you *ever* failed at
killing someone, darling?"

My heart puckered like an old wound. "No."

"Are you sure it was really . . . *that* kind of dream?"

My hands still ached from the memory of it all. The last time
the dream came down I'd been ten years old and my easy knack
for throwing darts had become, overnight, the uncanny force that
makes folks slide away from you at church but come up to you after
to ask for their numbers.

They said we had saints' hands, called us jujus and witches and
confidence artists. You believed or you didn't; no matter to the
hands. They were our latter-day flood—or our plague—descended
upon us after Emancipation. Ever since we moved north, the extra
had run in my family: my great-uncle could tell a card just from
touching it and my great-great-grandmother could pick up lightning
in a storm. Mommy used to say that there were fewer of us in every

generation, so she didn't know why the dreams had struck two of her three children. I think she wanted to believe that it wasn't her fault. Especially after my brother died.

Especially after I went downtown.

But now—I hadn't done a job for Victor in nearly seven months. I'd told the man who gave me my past that I was thinking of a different future.

He hadn't said no.

This little number in the first position, it's the past sticking its fat nose into your present business. Might even be a good thing, but see these cards? They could mean some trouble just as easy. Those spades got sharp edges and no one likes a joker with a knife.

"It was," I said, soft, "*that* kind of dream."

1

"Oh, Phyllis . . ."

It had been Dev's voice at the end of the dream; just his voice, warning me against nothing I could see; just his voice, pushing me awake, and away from him, again. He had only ever called me Phyllis in extremity: mortal danger, orgasm. I wondered which it would be this time.

"Christ," said the dentist, jamming his cigarette into my silver ashtray and getting another. "Christ, where's that lighter? I hate even thinking about Red Man, and you have to go and dream about him . . ."

"He's not so bad. Not like Victor."

The dentist flinched. "You know what they say, the things he's done. You just like him because he likes you . . . you and that snake girl, what's her name—"

"Tamara," I said, not for the first time. The star of the famous snake dance at the Pelican Club was my best friend in the city. Lately, because my life has not tended to kindness, she'd also been Dev's girl. But my own lover couldn't bother himself to remember the name of some Negro showgirl.

I leaned over the dentist to take another cigarette too, but instead he caught up my hand and gently traced its scars. I hated when he did that, though I never stopped him. The dentist's hands were chapped with alcohol and smelled like rubber, while I rubbed mine with shea butter every morning. But his had done nothing worse than pull teeth and fix caps for Victor and his men. He found my scars to remind me of the necessary distance between us, the dentist and the hatchet girl.

"Are you going to take the job, if it comes?"

Was it disgust that flattened his tone? Or indifference? My heart shuddered uselessly, but I kept steady and kissed behind his left ear, the way he liked. He groaned.

The dentist was my bargain; the dentist I could keep.

It was easier to move through the world with him on my elbow than alone, when the doormen were more suspicious of women of my complexion. Unlike most white men of my acquaintance, he rarely let a bad word escape his lips about Negroes or even any other group. Besides, he was handsome enough and in possession of an understanding wife. For those qualities, I overlooked his other lapses as a lover—an aversion to cunnilingus, the ghoulish whiteness of his teeth, the faint but clinging scent of antiseptic. My dissatisfactions were, I knew, the inevitable neuroses of his profession, and considering those of my own profession, I was inclined to anticipatory forgiveness, hoping to get the same gold for myself. If I lost him, I wouldn't have an easy time finding an old man half so nice; not at thirty-five, with my first grays wiggling out of my lye-made hair, and the scars that only Dev might have loved.

"How long has it been since the last one, darling?"

"Months," I said, not wanting to own the number—seven—which felt too long and too short. I took a breath before answering the other question. "They're bad people, you know, that's all Victor gives me. Murderers and rapists. Real scum. When I signed on with Victor, that was our deal. That I'd be more than a hatchet man. That I could make the world a better place."

By killing people? You really believe that. I could hear Dev's voice in the silence; the dentist only nodded.

"Russian Vic's angel of justice. His holy knife." Pronounced carefully, like he was reading it from a book.

My fingers locked. Most people called me that first thing—Victor's angel, sometimes of justice. But only a few, the ones who had known me longest, called me his knife.

"Where did you hear that?" I asked.

The dentist looked out the window. "That—I mean, the Hindu

bartender—Dev, right?—called you that once. Stuck in my head. Sounded more biblical when he said it, though."

To Dev, there was no such thing as holy violence. I hadn't quite believed him when he first said so, not even when I let him take me from the city. He told me about karma and the weight of our past and present lives, but I only felt it long after.

These days I avoided Victor, I refused jobs, I worried alone because I could not add to my ledger, and I could not bury my knives. But Red Man would visit soon. The dreams the hands give don't lie. I had to choose, one more time.

I could go back to Harlem, to the shabby familiarity of the old apartment complex at the corner of 130th and Lenox. Move in with my sister Gloria and her husband Tom and their kids. Red Man would find me there but he'd leave me alone if I asked. I wouldn't have Dev, and I wouldn't have the knives, and I wouldn't have everything I hated and loved about being Victor's angel of justice—

Gloria loved me, but she wouldn't open her home to a murderess, not even her sister.

"Aren't you afraid?" the dentist asked.

For a jittery moment, I thought he had read my mind—or seen my ghosts. Lenox Avenue, the tony apartments on Sugar Hill around the corner, afternoon number runs for Madame Stephanie and the Barkley brothers, the barber shops and the stoops and the rent parties and buffet flats that lasted till morning, the sex and the poetry. Policy slips like numbered confetti in the silk purse bound tight by my garter.

But the dentist only knew Phyllis LeBlanc, not Phyllis Green.

"Afraid of the second dream," he said when I just stared at him.

My voice cracked on a laugh. "It's just a superstition. I know someone with the hands in—uptown—who's had four." Most white folks had either never heard of or didn't believe in the hands, but the white men in Victor's service all believed, or at least were good at faking it.

The dentist made a very sour smile. "Or Russian Vic, who's had, what is it now? Seven?"

This was a bit of a joke, too dark and too dangerous to make at any other hour. Victor claimed he had the hands, but no one quite believed him. He would make announcements out of his dreams, listing out his visions of those who had betrayed him. You learned to fear those, if you wanted to last.

The dentist fell asleep and I stayed awake for a little while longer. Ten years ago, I had walked away from the happiest life I would ever know for the sake of a pair of hands. And now, if I had dreamed true, Red Man would bring me another. I wondered if I could make a different choice.

A little before 6 a.m.—an hour I made a point of never seeing from a vantage other than the night before—I woke again. It was the dentist, this time, his insistent hand on my shoulder. I started to complain, but even in the pallid dawn light I could see the whites distinct around his irises, and felt the urgency in his grip. He tried to speak.

"A lady," he finally said. "On your stairwell."

I grabbed my holster and stumbled out of bed. My eyes were still foggy, but my hands were singing. *This time, this time,* they said and I told them not to get their hopes up; I was through with the justice racket.

But still, I ran out in an old teddy and bare feet and took a holster with four sharp knives, eager for whatever had scared my lover so.

I pushed open the fire door. It was heavy with a body's weight, and I thought the woman might already be dead until she slid down three steps and groaned. Her face looked worked-over: cut, bruised, crusted with dried blood. Livid welts circled her wrists, about the width of Victor's preferred rope, but her limbs were free. A gun bulged from a pocket of her skirt.

I climbed over her and squatted. "Now who the hell are you?"

I pushed back her hair—dirtied and gray—from her forehead— bloody—and studied her features, which a few thuggish fists had done their bit to rearrange. I didn't recognize her. The woman started moaning again and shaking her head back and forth; she would come to soon and I didn't like the look of that gun. I pulled it from her pocket and a crumpled paper with familiar writing spilled out onto her lap.

Victor. My pulse sped. I checked the stairwell again, but saw only the dentist peeking nervously around the door.

"What's this about, darling?"

"Shh." I swatted at his voice.

I read:

> *Phyllis, meet Maryann West. I know you haven't worked on my word alone yet, so Red Man will be by to give you the details later, but I wanted you to get a chance to meet your next job. Thought maybe it would whet your appetite. She's done some very, very bad things, dollface. More than enough for my angel. Don't you like her? Don't you miss it? This isn't the job for turning me down again, baby. Weren't we great together, once? I miss you.*

I put my head between my knees and counted to ten. My hand already held a knife; it jumped with each breath. I didn't remember pulling it.

"Phyllis?" said the dentist from the doorway.

"Oh God," whispered the woman, whose name was Maryann West. She pushed herself away from me, fell down a few more steps and lurched to her feet. Above us the door slammed; the dentist's heavy gallop receded. *Coward,* I thought amiably. The woman lunged for the gun and I let her, at first because Victor's threat filled my head, and then because I got curious about what she might do next. She fumbled with the catch. I watched this, judged the opportune moment, and leapt. She only had time to squint before I slashed her trigger finger and tugged the piece gently from her grip. Maryann West screamed. It echoed in the stairwell and grew into something eerie, hideously familiar.

My guilty burden, momentarily suspended by an unholy joy, reasserted itself.

For fifteen years, I'd killed almost every time Victor asked. Was it any wonder he wanted my uncanny hands back at his disposition? If I refused this time, I wouldn't be his angel anymore. I'd just be Phyllis from 401 Lenox. Phyllis, who went downtown and came back haunted. Phyllis, alone and probably dead.

Oh, goddamn Victor—he could have knocked this woman off easy as you please, no mess about it. He didn't *need* me to kill for him. But he wanted me, which was worse.

"What have you done?" I asked Maryann West. "What's your mortal sin?"

Sometimes their confessions made it easier. She glared at me with furious, frightened, swollen eyes. "Are you going to kill me finally?"

I should have said no, but I tossed the five-inch knife from hand to hand, frightened her because I could.

"What did you do?"

We locked eyes for a long moment. Then the woman turned around and walked slowly down the steps. She didn't look back once, even when she stumbled. Braver than a lion; I admired her and loathed myself and prayed she would get out of town quick, before I could catch up. A muffled sob echoed from four stories below, then the slam of a fire door.

I took the gun and the note and staggered back to my apartment. My lover was long gone; he hadn't even bothered to shut the door behind him. I found my cigarettes and my lighter by the bed, then sat by the window to smoke. I sucked the first cigarette down fast. When I went to light a second, my thumb caught on the circle that Dev had scored into the chrome with a fishhook (*This means it's yours,* Dev said, and I said, *It's lopsided,* and he had smiled, slipped it into my coat pocket, took my hand, and told me it was time to run again).

I flipped the lighter in my right hand, balanced it on my fingertips one at a time, then on my knuckles: tricks that marked me just as much as the knives.

The world didn't hold so many of us, and often the juju was about as useful as a nickel at Tiffany's. But Dev was different, not just because of his dusk-brown skin and aura of beatific serenity. Dev's hands, his knack for feeling threats, made him a good gin runner and a reliable bartender to have at the Pelican. He could even lend the service to whoever he was touching—but he had stopped telling me about my threats early; it must have felt like bailing out the *Titanic* with a spoon.

Dev only started working with Victor after I left him. After Red Man came to find me in that little house on the river and showed me the pictures of Trent Sullivan's victims. All those bodies, young and old, women and men, all races, bound in a grisly fraternity by their missing hands.

"Victor asked for you especially," he had said.

I had known Dev would never forgive me if I killed again. But I had pretended that he might, and I left.

2

After two more cigarettes and some burnt coffee from the percolator that an old lover had left behind and I always meant to replace, I called Gloria.

"I thought I could take Sonny and Ida to the park for a few hours. Give you a break. Is Tom around?" Tom didn't like me, though he tolerated me for Gloria's sake.

"There's a new ship down at the yards so I've hardly seen him for the last week. You all right, honey?"

"Oh, I'm fine. Cut. I just haven't seen my favorite niece and nephew in ages."

"And your favorite sister?"

I smiled and unspooled the phone cord from my fingers. "You betcha."

"Well, if you got nothing better to do, you know those kids would love to see you."

So I put on my yellow day-dress, the one that looked all right but wouldn't give my old neighbors cause to think I'd got uppity from my years downtown, and headed out.

Outside, I checked for Red Man, but I didn't see him. My apartment building was in the middle of East 63rd Street—not an office block—and this late in the morning I could see everyone on the sidewalk and the street easy and clear. Not yet, I thought, relieved, and headed to Lexington. I sat down at the counter of my local milk bar to eat four thick slices of challah still warm from the ovens in back, soft with butter. Late nights, they kept the borscht on the stove and I liked to eat it, thick and beet-red, with a heel of stale challah in those still hours before sunrise, when my hands smelled like French-milled soap and hard water; like lavender and someone else's blood.

There were a few soldier boys on the A train, already in uniform, duffels on the seats and bodies in energetic motion, pacing the car and swinging from straps when the wheels struck up sparks against blind curves. They were black, young and handsome. Called up, I guessed, in Roosevelt's peacetime draft, though they didn't seem unhappy about the prospect of killing themselves on the other side of the world. One of them smiled shyly at me just before the City College station and asked if I'd like to get a drink with him and his friends before they got their deployment orders.

"We're only here for a week, ma'am," he said. "My friends and I are up for a swell time."

He had fine, even teeth with a little gap between the front two that reminded me of my brother Roger, dead almost fifteen years. I wondered how I looked to him, reading alone on that car, that he would invite me to share one of his last nights before heading to war.

"Where you gonna go?" I asked, wishing for a useless moment that I were young enough to have a good time with them, because then I'd be young enough to have never met Victor.

"Minton's," he said, quick. "And there's this place my buddy Jerry knows, some mobbed-up joint, with a bird name, down in the Village . . . Jerry, what's that club called, the one with the snake dance?"

"Pelican," his buddy said, swinging over to me on the straps, all ease and good looks and unconsidered strength. "Ain't segregated, and they got the best bebop in the city after Minton's according to my uncle Joe, who plays tenor sax at the Savoy, so he oughta know. But *this* here cat, you know, he hears 'snake dance,' and all he can see is titties—uh, sorry."

"Jesus, Jerry," my admirer muttered, and elbowed his friend hard in the ribs.

The third recruit poked his head between the two of them and smiled. "Hello, miss," he said. "What these two fools trying to say is, we'd be real happy to see you at the Pelican if you'd like to find us there."

"What'd you sweet boys want with an old lady like me?" I said.

"Old lady!" Jerry crowed, and the peacemaker kissed my hand while my first admirer just shook his head and said, "I wouldn't mind you for *my* old lady." It was silly, and I was a fool to get my head turned by half of what they said, but I wasn't on this train with a knife in my bag because I was wise, or good, or did what was best for me. So I told those fellas I might just see them at the Pelican that night and waved goodbye when they got off.

I was still smiling when I got to Gloria's, and she froze with her hand on the knob. The fissures radiating from her downturned mouth traced a map that I remembered from our mother's face, and probably for the same reasons. Gloria, the golden eldest, had never given our mother the grief that poor Roger and I had. I wondered if Gloria even recognized the ghost that stared back from her mirror, late nights.

"Phyllis," she said, with heavy meaning.

"I can't be happy?"

She rubbed her neck. "Depends on what you're happy about."

"Nothing bad, Glory. For heaven's sake. You gonna let me in or should I go back home?"

To Gloria—and Dev—my seven months would be a drop of virtue in an ocean of sin, but I'd already started to feel the quiver of something different, something old but newly growing. I felt it in my hands when I held my knives, those old hurting things, which gave one kind of power and stole another away. I waited for the day the two of them would see the change in me too, but in their eyes I was still the same old girl, Victor's aging knife.

"Come in, baby," Gloria said, and embraced me. We couldn't save Roger, but Gloria had saved me a dozen times over. Not enough for her peace of mind, I knew that, but enough for me to feel the debt, which was love, for the rest of my life.

Sonny and Ida were in the kitchen, Sonny running scales on his clarinet and Ida practicing a dance I was afraid might be a jitterbug. She stopped as soon as she saw me and ran straight into my open arms.

"Aunt Pea!" she said, "Mommy told us you'd take us to see the bear!"

"Bear?" I said to Gloria, over Ida's shoulder.

Gloria shrugged. "The Central Park Zoo. I told them you might not have the time—"

"Definitely the bear," I said, and put Ida down. "And the merry-go-round and ice cream, too."

This roused Sonny from his meditation of escalating flats and we all headed down the stairs and onto the street, which shimmered with the sticky heat of late July. Mrs. Montgomery was sitting on the stoop, playing gin with her sister, Miss Reynolds—who always insisted on being called "Miss" no matter how many gray hairs she pushed under that church hat on Sundays, because she never married, and she wasn't ever gonna be anyone's missus. They tutted when they saw me and carried on for a while about how long it had been since I'd shown my face around these parts.

"But you're looking good, child," pronounced Mrs. Montgomery, after I had duly begged their pardon for forgetting to visit. "That downtown life still treating you all right?"

I fiddled with the hem of my skirt. I knew what they were asking. Ida kept quiet around her elders—Gloria wouldn't have anyone calling her children ill-mannered—but she was squeezing my hand to say that she wanted to go already and didn't care about what these aunties were going on about. Sonny, though, Sonny's chin twitched and he held the rest of him very still.

"Oh, it's all right, Mrs. Montgomery. Enough to live on," I said, as though she'd just been asking about money.

"Well, at least you come back sometimes. I remember when you were just a girl, collecting all the numbers for the building—when I hit that time I remember you came running to tell me before anyone else had seen the mutuels! That boy we have now, he's little Ronnie's kid, Ronnie from Holiness—"

At this, Miss Reynolds interjected in a sotto voce that the whole block could hear, "He's become Mohammedan now, Lord knows what we're coming to—"

Mrs. Montgomery, who had lived with her sister all their lives, just kept going: "The kid's all right, but he isn't as fast as you were, Phyllis. Takes his good time at Walker's bar before he bothers to come around here for the payouts."

"You ran numbers, Aunt Pea?" Sonny said, suddenly.

The sisters stopped talking, and glanced up at the building.

Gloria Green Perkins, dedicated missionary at Abyssinian Baptist, didn't approve of playing policy any more than she approved of the rest of her younger sister's extralegal exploits.

"Not really, Sonny," I said, "I just collected for the building."

"Well," said Miss Reynolds, after a silence that bagged like the waistline of an old dress, "the rents up here are higher than ever and the jobs scarcer than hen's teeth. I can't blame you for getting out, since you can. But at least you haven't forgotten us, Phyllis."

I blew out a laugh. "It's never a good idea to forget where you came from, and I never could besides."

I said my goodbyes and headed out before the sisters could incriminate me with any more reminiscences. I'd done more than collect numbers back then, and they both knew it. Back when she ruled Sugar Hill, Stephanie St. Clair, Madame Queen of Policy, had offered a lot of opportunities to a young Harlem girl willing to bend the law and pin it with a knife.

Ronnie's boy ran past us as we waited at the bus stop; he was just a few years older than Sonny, but he'd found himself a suit for that skinny frame and a good wool cap so he looked more than half-grown, sharp pleats and padded shoulders around a tender middle. He was flushed and grinning, and I figured that someone on his rounds had hit and he was putting in extra for his ten percent. I remembered days like that: even when the hit was for five dollars, it felt good to think you'd had your part in their bit of luck. And your own. The ones like the Reynolds sisters, who knew I had the hands and believed in them besides, always wanted me to touch their slips before I passed them to the bank.

While we waited I pulled the lighter from my pocket and did a few of the tricks that Ida loved: whipping it through my fingers, tossing it in the air, and balancing its thin edge on the bony ridge in the back of my neck. Ida clapped.

"I wish you could teach me how to do that, Aunt Pea," she said.

Sonny, twelve to Ida's ten and older than the world, put his hands in his pockets. "Daddy says you shouldn't."

"And why shouldn't she?"

He puckered his lips at his sister and said, hesitating on the first syllable, "'Cause it's unnatural and devil's work."

Ida stamped her foot. "Sonny! Thomas Perkins, take that back!"

My hand froze with the lighter between my pinky and middle finger, precariously balanced, and without the slightest chance of falling. I contemplated Sonny, still a head shorter than me but with a look in his eyes like his father's. Would the day come when Sonny treated me with as much formal wariness as Tom Perkins? I forced my fingers to move again, slid the lighter smoothly down the back of my hand, and let it drop into my bag.

"I'd think it's a slow day if the devil has time to bother with my little tricks," I said. "Ain't you ever seen a juggler before, Sonny?"

Sonny shook his head slowly; the solemn, considerate boy I'd always known, now torn between his father and his aunt. But I wasn't stupid. I knew who would win that battle, and who should. So I would steal the time I had, dance with his childhood affection with all the skill in my uncanny hands, until age and time and disillusion took him from me.

The bus came, and I handed the nickels to Sonny and Ida so they could drop them in the box themselves. We sat on the bench in back, where we had the better view of the city as we lumbered down Amsterdam Avenue.

Ida wouldn't leave well enough alone. "Is it unnatural that you're good at the clarinet, Sonny, huh, now is it? Is it unnatural what Art Tatum does on the piano?" I loved her for defending me, but I wished she would stop.

"Daddy says it's different. Aunt Phyllis has something extra. Some juju. "

"You sound like a fool, Sonny," Ida said.

"You're the fool! Daddy says it's dangerous to have that juju, 'cause other folks want it and they'll kill for it. They'll take her hands. I bet that's what happened to Uncle Roger."

I was so surprised that I could only stare. Ida started to cry.

"Is someone gonna take your hands, Aunt Pea?"

I pulled her onto my lap. "No, honey, no. Sonny's just wrong, that's all."

Sonny sulked and stared out the window. I'd had no idea he knew the first thing about Roger, though I should have guessed. Family secrets have a way of getting out. And stealing hands—rumors like that had circulated my whole life, but mostly nothing came of it. There weren't a lot of us and most didn't broadcast what we were. Even if it was possible to steal our power by taking our hands, it wasn't easy.

But a decade ago a man named Trent Sullivan had tried, and bringing him to justice had nearly destroyed me.

Tom Senior and Sonny were right about one thing: it was no blessing when the hands paid their visit. My father had long gone by the time my dream came down; Mommy had to deal with me and Roger on her own. Dad had the wandering itch, as Mommy liked to say, and unlike her, he was light enough to pass when the urge struck him. It struck him one too many times, until she divorced him and told his disapproving Sugar Hill family she wouldn't wait around for him, or anyone, anymore. How they smacked their lips when our dreams came down! They spread it up and down that our saints' hands were Mommy's punishment for getting above her station. When Sonny turned ten, Gloria started sleeping badly, waiting for him to wake up with a dream for the numbers, an ache in his hands and an overnight talent for something that before had been merely ordinary. After his twelfth birthday she'd started to relax. But now she had Ida to watch, and wonder, and protect, if it came to that, from Tom Senior's attempts to pray the devil out of her.

I kept Sonny and Ida close to me at the park. Gloria was just a shade too dark to come here without the police following close behind and making nasty comments. Sonny and Ida were dark enough, but they were children, and I had a better chance of getting them in and out before they realized why their mother never came to the park with them. Though Sonny probably did already. He was too smart to enjoy the ignorance of childhood, which I grieved while I loved him for it. I dreaded the day he would see me for what I was.

We walked slowly through the bird pavilion and then the bear den. I'd thought we might enjoy ourselves, that Sonny would forget that sticky issue of my talent and Ida would gawk at the sea lions and the grizzly bears, but maybe there was never any chance.

A pair of white boys, no older than sixteen, watched us from beside the bear den. They clearly thought a lot of themselves in their high-waisted oxford pants and low-slung bowler hats. The sandy blond one even kept his hand near a bulge in his left pocket, his fingers twitching like a nervous dog on a leash. Sonny noticed them, but when he looked at me with worry creasing the skin between his brows, I smiled faintly and shook my head. He relaxed—I could still give him that. Ida noted none of this exchange. The grizzlies squatting in existential boredom by their cerulean concrete lake had captured all of her wide-eyed attention. I looked back at the white boys, whose twin gazes still followed us like blue jays through exhaust. The sandy-haired one flexed his hand. His companion spat, generously.

"What's the world coming to," Blondie said, in a voice that had broken last week and still bled from the wound, "when we can get a family of black devils strolling Central Park just like they was decent?"

Ida's shoulders stiffened. Sonny's hands clenched. "Stay with your sister," I told him.

Blondie and his brother here probably imagined themselves big hustlers. I doubted they'd have even made soldiers for Dutch Schultz, let alone Russian Vic. That had to be a BB gun in his pocket. Still, almost anything could kill, so long as you aimed it right. I loosened the two-inch knife strapped to my left wrist, let it peek out below the cuff of my summer blazer. Then, before any fuzz could see and ask questions—as bad for my people as dime-store gangsters, New York's whitest—I bent down, picked up a likely rock, and threw it at the bulge in his pocket. A pop like a firecracker went off against his hip—a BB gun, lucky for him, but at that distance would still hurt like the devil. The dark-haired one stared at me, slack-jawed, while the other cursed and hopped on one leg. I wondered, with a vague sort of pricking in my fingertips, if using my hands to *hurt* was much better, morally speaking, than using them to kill. Should we have just walked away?

"Ida, Sonny," I said loudly, "let's get ice cream. I don't see nothing much of interest around here."

They didn't object. The grizzlies had lost their fascination.

"You're the best, Aunt Pea," Ida said, smiling again over a pistachio ice cream as green as summer grass. "You sure showed those boys. I wish I could bring you to school with me just once."

Sonny looked at her sharply. "God didn't create us to raise one above the other with unnatural gifts."

Sonny's voice, his father's words. If I'd wanted to argue with Tom Senior, I'd have gone to Gloria's for dinner. I sighed and took Ida's hand.

"Don't pick fights, Sonny, for your sister's sake if not for mine."

We were silent on the bus ride back uptown. Plenty of time for me to think about what Sonny had said. I remembered old Widow Baker on the second floor, who had a knack though she didn't have the hands: she'd died last year at the age of ninety-three after hitting the numbers an astonishing seventeen times—though she always played for pennies, so the payout was never much. Once, while I waited for her to finish reading the cards and fill out her last slip, she said something to me that never left: *Your hands are like the numbers, aren't they, Miss Green? A little luck the Lord gives us to let us get on top, just for a bit, even though they got all the power.*

Now I considered the kind of creature I had made of myself with the Lord's luck, in the service of what I'd always considered to be the greater good. An angel, they called me. Some kind of holy beast.

3

Red Man was waiting when I got back home, his back against my door and his hat tilted over his forehead. Between that woman on my stairwell and mobsters in the hall, it was a wonder that my neighbors hadn't reported me to the super. But then, my neighbors generally had the good sense to ignore anything unusual coming from my apartment.

I stepped over him to put a steady key in the lock. I could keep my head in a gale—you had to, in my game. One way or another, something would give. Red Man had another job for Russian Vic's knife.

"You could have waited inside," I said.

"Wouldn't be polite," Red Man said, and levered himself upright in a surprisingly fluid motion for one so thick and tall. I had reason to know his remorseless strength, but his muscle was padded everywhere by an inch of soft fat, so that he sometimes put me in mind of a corn husk doll with sturdy stitching and inflexible limbs. He might have been handsome if he put his mind to it; his wide face and moon eyes had intrigued me when we first met, before I understood the stoicism in him, and the cruelty carefully deployed in Victor's service. We respected one another, and we kept the considerate distance of two of Victor's most valued possessions.

"Can I get you something?" I asked when he closed the door behind him. "I can put some coffee on."

"Do you still have any of that bourbon Vic gave us for Christmas?"

I laughed and shook my head. "Why the hell not," I said, and headed for the liquor cabinet. Red Man made himself comfortable on the chaise in my living room, an old deco piece that I'd lifted from the effects of one of Victor's deceased generals. Ghoulish, maybe, but Barney had died of a heart attack, not a knife, and his good taste couldn't do him any more good where he'd gone. Red Man, who knew its history precisely, stretched out those long, thick legs and waited with a smile for me to serve him.

I poured two stiff fingers in two glasses of heavy crystal and chipped two spears of ice from the block to drop in each.

Red Man clinked the ice against the rim with a meditative swish. I pulled up a chair, spread my knees wide, and waited.

"Usually take it neat," he said, after a moment.

I shrugged. "It tastes better this way."

"The way Victor likes it."

"Yes."

"He once crippled a man for making his with soda. The bartender before Dev . . . Mitch, remember him? Stabbed the man's hand through with a steak knife. With none of your artistry, Phyllis."

He smiled a little, mostly with his eyes. He could be unsettlingly gentle, and I liked him, even when he scared me. After all, I sometimes liked myself, too.

I took a chill swallow of liquor I didn't taste. "Lucky Dev is more careful." Dev had circled around for years, doing the odd run and then disappearing, before he settled into the bartender job. I remembered it was '35, when DA Dewey's investigations had all of mobbed-up Manhattan shooting slugs at their shadows. Victor got taken in, but he had always been meticulous about covering his tracks; he offered up a few lieutenants to the gods of criminal justice and walked away with a vagrancy charge. Afterward he was happy to take on Dev, a refugee from Dutch Schultz's sinking ship—for his discretion as much as for his hands.

My ice rattled against the edge of the glass. A natural enough response, for someone else's hands. I looked down at the offending member—left—and it stilled. A memory of the ache that had passed through it this morning returned, and settled in the twists of my intestines. Was this it, then? Were the rumors true? The second dream had come, an oracle of the imminent desertion of my only power?

I looked back up at Red Man watching me, face like a portrait.

"What's the job?" I asked.

He raised his eyebrows slightly, which communicated a certain reserved sympathy. But he wouldn't answer before he was ready. "You know, Tammy was after me all morning to read my cards."

"Was she?" I said. Tamara always treated Red Man like a beloved younger brother, as though she didn't know precisely what he was. It was enough to give a girl goosebumps, like you'd watch a fool sitting on a flagpole.

He nodded. "And I told her Vic wouldn't have any of his people playing numbers with his bank, but she insisted. Said the numbers were for more than stealing old widows' pensions in Harlem."

I laughed out loud. "She said that?"

He raised his glass and I lifted mine in response. "You know our Tammy. At least she keeps it quiet when Vic is around."

"At least."

I poured myself another shot. The booze was washing out the fear, or at least my awareness of it, and my hands were steady again, steady as they'd been since the luck had touched them twenty-five years ago.

"So, what's the number, Walter?"

"Six, two, and seven. Tammy said the cards were solid, but I should exercise caution in love. Recommendation to play."

"Sounds good. We could always bet with Lucky Luciano's bank." I said it just for the reaction; Red Man's lip curled at the name of Vic's biggest competitor in the Harlem numbers racket, now that white men had busted up the black banks of my youth.

"You could."

A shiver twisted up my spine. "You have a job for me," I said.

"Victor has a job," he corrected, amicably. "But you weren't surprised to see me, were you?"

"I had a special delivery early this morning. You didn't . . ."

Do it? I wanted to ask, but stopped because a shadow crossed his face and his lips drew back, ever so slightly, from his teeth.

"No," he said, shortly. "Tell me."

"Maryann West. That's what the note called her. She was beat bloody and I let her get away. Why the devil didn't he just kill her and leave me out of it?"

"Victor likes to play."

He did, I knew that well enough, but it surprised me every time when Victor dared play Red Man. The tie between them was decades old and thick with debt. It seemed that they scared everyone but each other. Red Man reached into his leather satchel and pulled out a thin manila folder. The picture clipped to the front of the file was of a white woman in her late forties, gray hair unflatteringly cropped, with squinting eyes that might have been hard, or sad.

"She looked a bit different this morning," I said.

"But you let her go."

"I don't kill anyone on just Victor's say-so. And not in my own damn home. Which Victor knows."

"Oh, he knows. He could get a dozen of his men to bump this lady off, but you, you need reasons."

"He wouldn't want me if I didn't."

Red Man hesitated. "You're very sure of that, Phyllis?"

My pulse jumped. "The whole point of making me an angel was to mete out justice. Which means I get to choose."

"It's a nice place you've made here, Pea. Nice furniture. Nice neighborhood. You have a good life, and Russian Vic made it for you."

"We have an arrangement. That doesn't mean he owns me."

His smile, his kind moon eyes, they stopped me cold. "Doesn't it? Victor wants this done, and he wants his knife to do it."

I crunched the ice between my teeth and sucked in a sharp, bourbon-scented breath. "What if she says no?"

Red Man considered this; at least, he set down his glass and turned his gaze from me to the lacquered Chinese screen separating the parlor from the dining room. He steepled his fingers over the gentle curve of his belly and took a deep, soulful breath. I wanted to agree so badly I could have vomited acceptance on my shoes. I would kill that woman, crime unknown, just to avoid learning who I was without judgment in my hands. But I wanted the other path more.

"You know my name," he said.

I frowned. "For a while now, Walter. What's your point?"

"Point is," he said, "no one uses it." He addressed this to the screen's jade dragons, breathing gold fire. I couldn't read his face. "Even you call me Red Man same as everyone else down in the Pelican. I'm past minding, these days. But my name is Walter Finch, and for a long time, you and Dev were the only ones who had bothered to know it. Now Tamara does, of course." He shook his head with a faint smile. "You ever wonder why I took my time finding you two all those years back? I waited as long as I dared. Because I thought, maybe they *can* get out. I thought knowing my name meant something. I thought we might be the same that way, for all you like pretending you've never been north of 110th Street. But you!" He laughed, and looked at me. His face was tired and angry and hopeful, a spring of emotion conflicted and deep, a sensibility with which I had never credited him.

"I could have killed you myself for wasting that chance—I hadn't realized that you *liked* it."

I took a startled, hiccuping breath. He looked like Red Man, lounging with casual menace on my dead man's chaise, but he was right, that was just a name other people called him. I had believed what I wanted, because it was easier, because calling him "Red Man" with white folks helped them dismiss my thick lips and stiff hair.

"And you don't like it?" I asked. "Good bourbon, money, power? You've fooled a passel of people if you don't, Walter."

I watched him make a decision; he swung his legs around to the floor and faced me. "I liked it for a time. The same as you. Victor saved my life—no, I won't tell you the story—but it was at the very beginning, when he was just a jumped-up runner. We built this empire together. And then I fell in love and I had children and one day I realized I was still only what I had always been: the muscle, the dirty right hand. But it's too late, now. And I want my children as far away from this business as I can keep them, which means I stay right here. I have to be Red Man so they can be something better." He paused, and bitterness veined his next words: "Victor won't let me be anything else."

"Children," I said, too stunned for coherence. "No wonder you didn't want anything to do with me when we met."

Red Man—Walter—smiled again. "I was flattered, Pea. I don't talk about my family, though, you understand; I'm telling you this now to answer your question. You ask me what Victor will do if you say no—I know what he'd do to *me*. So I say yes. But you? You lose this place. You lose your money and your power. You probably have to leave the city. But you don't have a husband, you don't have any kids that I know of. You don't even have Dev, this time." I flinched; Walter saw it, but was kind enough to pretend he didn't. "You say no, that's the end. Victor won't ever take you back. But he might let you go."

I thought of Gloria and the kids. Victor knew a lot about me, but I'd changed my last name and pretended for him as much as anyone that I had sprung, off-white and fully formed, from a smoky stage in a Times Square club.

Victor was a hard little knot of a man, and had been as long as I'd known him. He'd had all his own teeth back then, in the good old dry days of Prohibition. If he didn't speak or smile or reveal himself with any other telling gesture, you might have even fooled yourself into thinking him handsome.

But Victor had been born ugly, with tastes for violence and vulgarity and opulence that distracted, but did not hide, that essential core. I won't say I was fooled by him, but I was twenty when we met—fresh-faced, full of my own beauty, new enough to passing to be more thrilled than exhausted by it. And then Victor taught me to kill. It was easy, deadly easy, that first time.

It only got hard later, when the slip slip of knives into vital arteries started to wriggle like spiked minnows in my own veins. It had started to wear at me before Dev. Five years had meant a lot of kills in Russian Vic's service. But Dev changed me, or he had at least changed how I saw myself.

At its easiest, love is a blanket; at its hardest, a black mirror—it isn't just your flaws that show stark against that high-yellow skin, it's your ghosts.

"Not even Dev," I said, and pulled the lighter from my pocket.

"He still watches you, you know. Every night you're there."

"He watches Tamara."

"Everyone watches Tamara."

I flicked the lid on and off.

"Out of curiosity," I said, "what did she do, Victor's job? Who is Maryann West?"

He opened the manila file to reveal the pictures inside. A dead white man slouched against a stack of crates on a concrete floor, his jeans stiff and dark, blending with the bottom half of an untucked flannel shirt. On the right of the image, dark columns of police officers' legs threw stark, looming shadows across the floor and the body. A roll of police tape fluttered, unattached, in the corner. The photo was clean, well composed, its beauty easy to miss in the visceral horror of its subject matter. Walter had an artist's eye, which some would say was wasted. I appreciated it today, because he had framed the shot to draw attention to one particular detail.

The man's arms, crossed over his chest. The ragged stumps of his wrists, where the hands had been hacked away.

"I dreamed about them," I said, faintly. "What does Aunt Sally's dream book say about severed hands? Six, six, six? Maybe I should play."

"You dreamed?" Genuine surprise in his voice, maybe even concern, but I was far away.

"Second dream, you know what they say."

"Just rumors."

"And that's what some white folks say about the hands, too."

He paused. "Not Victor."

"No." I pushed the folder toward him. "This isn't one of the old photos? It looks just the same."

I'd destroyed my life to avenge these murders. I still had nightmares of Trent Sullivan; the sound of his girl pounding her hands bloody on the bathroom door while I struggled with him on his bed, killing as a parody of love.

"It's new," Red Man said, just as soft. "Body turned up five days ago. And Victor says that Maryann West did it."

So it was happening again. The rumors that even Sonny knew had spawned another believer. My second dream was true.

"Does it work, Walter? If they're going to kill us for our hands, do they at least get something from them?"

He brushed a finger across my right wrist. "Whatever they get, Pea, it's never enough."

4

I wore my best dress and my best knives and careful makeup, so I thought I might pass for twenty-five in the dim, smoked light of the Pelican. I hadn't said yes, and I hadn't said no. I was still Victor's knife, for as long as the hands held out, or for as long as I could bear to use them.

The Pelican was a different world on Friday and Saturday nights. Then, Victor was in it to make money, as much as possible. We had a line like any other club, and men in dark suits to take your measure and pronounce you worthy. It was always integrated—Victor made a point of that—but the strange weekday crowd, the anarchist syndicate meetings and the Yiddish one-act operas and Japanese-inspired poetic dance plays and French expressionist cabaret that Tamara had spent the last two years curating, like some kind of demented talent manager who never quite got it through her head that the Pelican was a verifiable, bona-fide, bodies-in-the-dumpster *mob joint,* and who through sheer conviction had made everyone else play along until her mad vision had become as real as my knives—that world dimmed to muted pastels when the Long Islanders and Upper East Siders descended upon the Village with their wide sedans and straining billfolds. Those nights, Tamara still put on her tasseled pasties and twirled them with a python named Georgie around her neck, and she smiled, because she knew that as long as she did this job, Victor would keep letting her have her way the other five nights of the week. It suited him to court that air of dangerous exoticism, to let his white clients, both over and under the table, gawp at us and fear us. Even me—though he didn't know it.

I walked past the line—checking for my boys in uniform—and smiled at the man behind the velvet rope. He must be new, or moved up from some other grunt detail, because I didn't recognize him. He recognized me, though. The blood drained from his face. If I'd said "boo" I swear he would have fainted. He stumbled forward and unhooked the rope.

"This way, ma'am," he said.

I smiled as kindly as I could, though it was clear he couldn't tell. I walked through the doors, a little sick of the kind of woman they must imagine me to be, and by my own design.

In the twenties the Pelican had been an old Russian cigar club, and Victor had retained the mahogany paneling and leather walls while adding a few judicious modern touches: geometric glass chandeliers trimmed with chrome, Chinese silk curtains, and a gleaming zinc bar lit from behind, so that its rows of bottles glowed gold and green and amber. The stage was catty-corner to the bar, with a dozen round tables in between, but on nights the crowd wasn't elbow to elbow the barman had as good a view as anyone of Tamara's jungle dance. At ten, the place was bumping but not full up. I smiled at the regulars and noted the faces that meant Victor was here already—not on the floor, but behind the false bookshelf in the corner, which led to his office.

On stage, Charlie was going at it with his swing band, playing that new bebop jazz that was catching like brush fire in the Harlem clubs, but was unusual in a downtown joint like the Pelican. On Wednesdays, Charlie got up on the Pelican's stage to play with a little five-piece, wreathed in marijuana smoke like clouds. The Village's most dedicated hepcats came to pray, close their eyes, and shake their heads and shout in scatting tongues. He called that bebop too, but on weekends he played the down-tone version. Even then, the jumpy drums and circuitous, laddered chords made for hard listening and even harder dancing. I caught a few strains of "Tea for Two," but his French horn veered off as soon as I had them, layering and riffing. Victor let Charlie have his way until eleven, enough for the Pelican to maintain its reputation for the avant-garde, but not enough to put off the paying white customers who came to enjoy big band swing and a beautiful girl dancing with a snake. Tamara wasn't out yet. I wanted to talk to her, but she was as likely to be with an admirer backstage as she was to be alone, and the thought of putting off some amorous white boy who thought he was playing with fire was enough to make me feel old as Gloria looked this afternoon.

My feet took me to the bar without my asking and I leaned my back against it, watching for the dentist or my three soldiers, anyone to distract me from the barman shaking martinis just four feet away. Dev filled two glasses from shakers in either hand—at once showy and economical. One of the appreciative gentlemen bit off his olive and asked him what he thought of Hitler's chances in Russia.

"Wait till winter," Dev said. "It seems to me we'll be in this by then, one way or another."

"I'm thinking of enlisting, before my number comes up. Wouldn't mind flying against those Japanese Zeros."

"I've heard from a few who are doing that. At least you get a choice, they say."

"That's right—though are you likely to get called? You don't sound American."

Dev shrugged. "My mother's British, but I got naturalized years ago. I'm as liable as you. But I'll take my chances. Don't think I'd care for army life."

I tried not to listen, or at least to pretend like I'd gone judiciously deaf, but at this I turned my head, surprised into laughter at the understatement. He didn't even eat meat.

Dev flicked a glance to the side at the same moment and our gazes snagged and held, a burr on clean cotton, until I thought some warm answer flashed inside him. Then he ripped me with a shrug and waved a greeting to Tamara, just come from backstage.

"The usual, sugar," she called, shaking the bangles on her arms like maracas as she danced through the crowd. They cleared a path to get a better look; in high-necked satin or a grass skirt, Tamara always commanded attention. She was an earth goddess come to vibrant life, with brown skin, glossy hair, an ass like a naked peach, and eyes like the bottom of a well. My resentment of her had only managed to last a weekend; sure, I had known from the start how she fascinated Dev, but he hadn't been mine for a long time now and there was something about Tamara—the way she cared about everyone, the way we listened to one another—that had made us fast friends without me having hardly any say in it. Dev watched her face as he lit her cigarette.

"Well, that's better," she said, and, catching sight of me, "Sugar! Gorgeous as always, where have you been? Are you drinking? Of course you are. Make that two French 75s, Dev. Have you tried one, Pea? They're my new favorite. Our Dev's a genius."

This flow of uninterrupted, low-throated chatter was accompanied by a peck on both of my cheeks, French-style, which I bore with a smile and a small shrug in Dev's direction. Tamara admired no one more than the dancers of the French avant-garde, Isadora Duncan and Josephine Baker; she had no time for the fluttering weightlessness of the traditional ballerina.

She reached into a well-concealed pocket and pulled out a small blue hardcover, scarred with water and the multicolored mold of several continents. She pushed it across the zinc bar to Dev. A book of poems by Sarojini Naidu, who I had only heard of because Dev had mentioned her to me in an unguarded moment three years ago, after Charlie had played until dawn and the ten of us left weren't so much standing as draped over tables and one another, buffeted by clouds from sweet spliffs whose spent butts crunched beneath our feet like roaches. His gaze intent upon Tamara, tears or sweat rolling down her cheeks while another man kissed up and down the soft inside creases of her joints, Dev had lifted his soft voice like an axe beside me and swung down:

"Shelter my soul, o my love!
My soul is bent low with the pain
And the burden of love, like the grace
Of a flower that is smitten with rain:
O shelter my soul from thy face!"

I caught my breath, hard. "What's that?" I had managed.

He told me her name then. "An Indian nationalist and poetess from Hyderabad. They say I met her when I was younger, but I don't remember now."

Tamara had been with us for just a few months then, but I knew: not that he wanted her, because everyone wanted her, but that Dev would have her soon enough.

"I confess," Tamara said now, smiling at her lover, "that poetry still ain't exactly my bag, but there were two or three I swear I . . . well, I don't know if I liked them, but they made me want to dance."

Dev lifted the book, gazed at the smudged and blackened gilt on the embossed cover. *The Golden Threshold*, I read. His eyes met mine for a fraction of a breath. Then he smiled at Tamara and hid the book beneath the bar. "I think that's even better," he told her. "You should dance it one Thursday night. Isn't that something they're doing in the Irish theater these days?"

Tamara nodded while her gaze shot beyond us, glowing distantly with calculation. She could not stop, our Tamara. With Victor she had found something better than a safe haven or a sugar daddy: she'd found someone who gave her power. Sure, Tammy had to sell a lot of herself, piece by piece, to keep it. I could tell her what the view was like from fifteen years in Victor's back pocket. But like I had once been, she was still too young to care.

She was the mistress of the Pelican's off-nights, the goddess of our integrated Village oasis, the bleeding heart of an artistic mecca that privileged the iconoclast and stylized and generously syncopated. She could be thoughtless in her majesty, she could even be cruel, but I knew the sweetness underneath it all: she fed the alley cats with scraps after closing, no matter how many times Victor told her to stop. She bought everyone drinks and cadged everyone's cigarettes, in a proportion dependent on which member of her extended family currently occupied her spare bedroom. Her family, it seemed, was uniformly parasitic, and none as amiable as Tamara, who yet loved them all as genuinely as I had to suppose she loved me, or Dev, or those yowling cats behind the Pelican. She danced like an earthquake and she sang like a bullet, and some nights my heart felt bruised and overripe just to look at her.

I had never been that young, that beautiful, that good.

Tamara swam back to reality and shook her head to see me there. In a lower voice, not one for show, she asked me, "Everything all right?"

She squeezed my hand and I wished Dev would hurry with those drinks just so I'd have something else in my throat. "Got your cards on you, Tammy?" I said, hoarse.

She was surprised. "I always do. But you don't usually want to hear what they say."

Tammy had a way of reading not just the numbers, but your future from a regular playing deck. Even old Widow Baker had used her cards to play policy, but Tammy claimed the numbers carried your fate on their backs like firewood. She said an old conjure woman from Baton Rouge taught her the trick when she was living in Brooklyn, but you never knew with Tamara—she'd bet her life on those cards, but she liked stories, too.

"I had a dream. A second dream, Tammy."

Dev finally handed us our drinks. She left hers sitting on the bar. "As soon as I'm done here, we'll go back to my place. I'll light some candles, burn some incense, and do a layout in three sets. The cards speak clearly in threes."

"It's the hands, I swear it is. They want something from me, or they're calling me to account, but for what? I haven't done a job, Tammy, not for months, so why now—"

She put a finger on my lips. "Don't you worry, sugar, we . . ."

She trailed off and tipped her head, looked through me as though I'd faded out in front of her. I turned around and saw that my fellas had come after all, the three of them fine as new pennies: shoes shined, uniforms pressed, and hair smooth and stiff with the combined efforts of Murray's pomade and a boar-bristle brush. I waved and they hurried over, but I didn't have any illusions about my own appeal beside Tamara's. What surprised me was how Tamara was staring at them—particularly my admirer from this morning. She took her drink from Dev without so much as a glance in his direction, and tossed it back like Romeo took his poison.

"Tammy?" That was my admirer, taller and broader than his friends, with the gap between his teeth.

Tamara shook her head, not in negation, but as if she'd been sleeping and wanted to clear the fog. "My God, my God, Clyde, what the devil—you got some nerve—oh, you're looking . . ."

She would have dropped her glass if I hadn't caught it for her, neat and easy. Jerry and his friend didn't see it—they were too busy ogling Clyde, who had wrapped his arms around the best-looking girl in the city while she bussed him hard—but Dev did. He touched my hand. I shorted out.

He was the raw current and I the badly insulated wire; the room seemed to flicker and dim around me, leaving only my scarred hand and his fingers—darker, smoother—resting against my stark metacarpals. I heard his voice, faint and crackled, but it took two shaky breaths for the meaning to reach me and by then I knew that I'd betrayed myself.

"Someone's looking for you," he repeated slowly. Behind us, Tamara and her long-lost beau were talking over each other, discovering between them the story of how they'd come to meet in a clip joint years after leaving the small Virginia town where they'd met. Dev and I might as well have been alone.

"Must be Victor." I pulled my hand away, so he couldn't tell me any more, and drank the French 75, which at first tasted faintly of champagne and then of nothing at all.

"Victor?" For a moment I thought he'd touch me again, but Dev reached for a glass instead and poured himself a shot of that good bourbon. "I couldn't tell . . . I don't know that it felt like him. Are you two on the outs?"

The false bookshelf fell back into its recess and Victor walked out, his arm slung around the dentist's shoulders, and Red Man a few paces behind them. I wondered what business the dentist had with Victor, but I didn't care enough to ask. Victor spotted Tamara, lips locked with her soldier boy, and gave the smallest of frowns.

She would hear about this later—Victor liked Tamara to at least tease availability on busy weekend nights. Certainly Dev knew better than to kiss her in public.

"Not on the outs," I said, watching them, "he just wants me to do a job."

"And you don't want to?"

I started to answer, and then realized that I couldn't. After all I'd done, what should my *wanting* have to do with my yes or my no? I didn't trust myself anymore and now the hands had sent their second dream, their warning, another round of their dangerous luck.

"I've been asking myself," I said, "what you would do."

I hadn't known this was true until I said it. It surprised us both. Dev rested his lips on the edge of the tumbler.

"That might not work as well as you think, Pea."

Walter said that woman was murdering people like Dev and me for our hands. Stopping that evil was a pure and fiery purpose, and I craved it with the flat desperation of any junkie six months, three weeks, one night clean.

"I haven't done a job in seven months."

Dev started. The wrinkles spread like stars around the corners of his eyes and he leaned forward.

"How about that," he said. "Six months more than you managed for me."

"I didn't . . . back then I still thought that justice . . ."

"You thought it was worth the karma."

"Victor won't let this one go."

His gaze flicked over my shoulder, to Victor's usual table. I didn't turn around.

"Another French 75?" He pulled out a clean glass before I could respond. While he busied himself behind the bar, he said in a low, conversational tone, "Who is it now?"

"Some woman. Maryann West. Red Man—Walter says she's—" I stopped short. How to explain without invoking the memory of everything that had gone wrong between us a decade ago? The day Walter tempted me with Trent Sullivan and his stolen hands; the night I left Dev to kill and the night he found me too late. Dev had waited until he washed the blood away to make it gently, perfectly clear that he wanted nothing more to do with me.

"Maryann West?" Dev repeated. His hand trembled as he filled my glass.

"Don't tell me you know her?"

Dev shook his head once, an emphatic negation. "What does Victor say this woman did?"

And here we came to it. I felt as though I had waited months for this moment and now I only wanted to hide, or kill something. "The hands," I said to my drink. "It's happening again, Dev. She killed someone like us."

His breath caught. "Now, see, that's curious, Pea. Because the Maryann West that I know used to be Trent Sullivan's girl. You'll remember him—the fellow you murdered on his bed while his girl-friend screamed herself bloody in the bathroom?"

We stared at each other, long and hard enough for Charlie to finish his set with a tumble of notes. People jostled us, called for drinks, but Dev still stared and I couldn't catch my breath. Maryann West was Trent's girl? Impossible. Wouldn't I have recognized her voice? But regret had amplified and distorted those screams in my memory. If she was really Trent Sullivan's girl, it wouldn't be a coincidence.

But after so much time, why would she commit the same crime that got her lover offed? For the first time in fifteen years, I wondered: had Victor always told me the truth?

"How do you know her?" I asked.

"Two G&Ts, Dev!"

"Hey, what sorta whiskey you got?"

"Trent used to work for Victor. You had to know that."

I had to know? I started shivering.

"Walter didn't tell me."

"And since when has Walter told you everything?"

Everything important. Hadn't he?

"You gonna make that drink or what?"

"Hold on one minute, Charlie!"

"Aw, Christ."

"Do you hate me, Dev?"

His expression stripped me; bleak and remorseful and entirely closed to the possibility of hope. "I've never hated you, Pea. I—I just couldn't stay."

What are you? Dev had asked the first time I ever saw him, blood sticky on my arms while I heaved in an alley. A break in the clouds let the moonlight through and I saw his eyes, dark and knowing. He saw a girl covered in blood in a New York alley, and he never once thought to ask if it was hers.

A knife, I'd said, and he walked me home.

Dev's fingers brushed the back of my hand and closed on empty air as I propelled myself from the barstool.

He called after me, and I ignored him. Tamara, watching this, pulled away from her new man and angled herself so I couldn't pass her.

"Did something happen?"

"Oh, everything's swell, Tamara. But I'd leave me alone right about now."

She flinched, but rubbed my shoulder. "You know, Pea, there was a broad over by the door just now, giving you the oddest stare."

"I've got to—really?"

Tamara glanced at Clyde. He nodded at me. "White lady. Older. Busted up, like her old man's got a nasty temper."

This night was trying to unravel every awful feeling I'd ever had coiled inside me. Maryann West was here. And if Dev was telling the truth—

I had to find her and talk to her, before Victor noticed. The crowd had grown thick while Dev quietly skewered me from behind the bar. I wiggled my way through it, looking everywhere for Maryann and not finding her. I angled for the door, and might have made it if not for the hand that fell on my shoulder.

"Looking good, dollface," a familiar voice said. "What's your rush?" Russian Vic had the voice of a newscaster, nasal vowels pressed into service of staccato sentence fragments. He dangled subjects like fishhooks, and baited them with implied interrogatives.

I pivoted on the ball of one foot and engaged a smile. "Fresh air," I said. "I hate smoking in this press."

"Red Man said you never gave him an answer. So you're gonna . . ."

"I'm going outside," I said, firmly. "And I just found out about this job today. Our deal from the start was that I get a choice, Vic. Remember that."

Victor looked back at Walter, sprawled across a chair and surrounded by a two-foot radius of free space. "They may call you my angel," he said, conversational, "but you remember this: you're my knife. A knife's edge gets dull, well, you have to . . ."

I stepped backward. "Go outside, Victor. You have to go outside. We'll talk about this later."

Victor had a shock of silver-gray hair and more than a dozen silver teeth to match. He'd had all his own teeth when I met him, but it seemed the dentist gave him a new one each year. He grinned, and all that silver flashed. "Sure we will." His soldiers were all convinced he had saint's hands for detecting disloyalty, but I—like my dentist—figured he was lying. I'd never known a white man with saint's hands.

If I could have sprinted through that crowd, I would have. No one scared me quite like Victor. Not because he was ruthless—if anything Red Man was better known for his artistry with violence— but because I had been trading on his power for years too long.

I reached the door without any sign of Maryann West. Out on the sidewalk I could breathe again. I pulled out a cigarette with jittery relief. I flicked Dev's lighter on and off, on and off, struggling to regain enough control to go back inside.

Victor might kill me.

Seven months didn't matter to Dev at all.

Someone's heels clicked on the sidewalk. I turned to see Maryann West walking straight toward me. She'd cleaned up since this morning, but it still hurt to look at her. She squinted and stopped five feet away.

"I need to ask you something," I said.

"Fuck you," she said.

As she reached into her pocket someone else sprinted up behind me, someone who was screaming my name in a voice completely different from the one that had said *I just couldn't stay*.

Dev pushed me. I thought that was why I had fallen until I smelled blood, which was familiar, and felt it on my hands, which was also. I tried to grip my knife, and then tried again, even though by now the pain had started and I knew the blood for my own.

"Phyllis," Dev said, like he had back then, a note low and joyous that gave meaning to the silence around it. He stilled my hands and pressed his jacket to my chest.

There was something in his face I needed to understand. Not the horror or grief, which anyone might feel while holding the dying woman they once loved, but something beyond it, or before it.

"Why?" I asked, and shook.

"Shh," he said, "Pea, stay still—"

"Why work for Victor? Why stay?" I trusted him to understand the rest. Why stay in my world after I'd rejected his? Why watch me and let me watch him for a decade while we slept with other people?

He cursed and looked up and said something that might have been a prayer. I blinked, which seemed to take a very long time.

"I'll tell you later," he said.

"Tell me now."

"You're not going to die!"

"Why stay, Dev?"

I focused on the whites of his eyes, very bright and wide as the sky.

He whispered, "I'm an informant," and so it wasn't the bullet that killed me, after all.

Two.

After I died, I saw a light, blue and barrel-vaulted, with a tunnel at the end of it.

A little less than common. Three plus eight is eleven: a one and a one. Add that up and you have two.

That dark artery demanded attention, smug with its complication and its vice, but I turned to lines that pointed to a cloudless sky, and I waited.

The tunnel told me that *we don't have beds, try Harlem Hospital,* and *what the hell are you insinuating, the poor woman's as white as you are*—but the tunnel should have known I didn't care, that this train don't see no white or black, no, this train. And yet the light, all uniformity and grace, seemed content to watch instead of offering its embrace. There were people in it, old men and women, speaking in tongues that had crossed an ocean and died on foreign soil. They wore no chains; in this place they raised their hands.

At my back, the tunnel's pulse grew stronger, so that I felt its broken heart, and where a bullet had ripped through its chest.

It sang me a song I'd forgotten, about how a knife and a mystic liked to sit together in the grass beside the river when half-blown dandelions would catch his eyelashes and her flyaway hair. Silent for an hour, he would turn to her and, smiling, trace the V of cotton curls on her neck. Phyllis, he'd call her, sweet pea, all he ever needed to say.

And so, unwilling, I turned from the light.

Knives, knives, knives, wherever you look. But here, you got a heart and your lover does too and a spare one besides, to patch up the ones you've broken between you.

5

And then you're twenty-one. It's that dinner, Phyllis, that dinner we won't let you forget. Victor's invited you to some sort of parlay between him and the Barkley twins, heads of a smaller Harlem numbers bank. You know the Barkley brothers. You spent the summer of '23 collecting single plays for them on 130th Street, between Lenox and Seventh Avenue. Bo Barkley had called you "Yellow Pea" and taught you memory tricks so you wouldn't get caught with the incriminating strips under your garter. He liked our skills but he didn't want to use you for them. Back then, you saw the value in that.

Bo recognizes you, though he plays it off. He doesn't need no oracle to see what you're doing, dressed up real fine, your stiff hair bobbed short, among all these white mobsters. He sees the knives you haven't bothered to hide, strapped to the inside of your wrists, and his eyes say, clear as your mommy's: "What do you think you're up to, Phyllis Green?"

Victor and his gang only know Phyllis LeBlanc, nominally white and creole if pressed. The day they find Phyllis Green is the day they make her go for a swim in the East River. You know this, so you break Bo's gaze and pretend to get a good look at Vic's new place. Victor has bought this old gentlemen's club in the West Village, the kind of joint filled with old Russian men smoking Cuban cigars and playing poker for pennies. He said he was going to make it the neatest blind pig in the Village. The Pelican, he's calling it, a long bird that can hunt in high water. Tonight the place is half-gutted, an open surgery of exposed pipes and brick walls and thick beams they had to clear of cockroaches. But he has a table set up near the back, where he says his office will be.

Victor brags that his mother has made you all a real Russian home-cooked meal as you sit down. You're across from Red Man, who looks bored in that way he has, so that no one around him can so much as slouch. You and Red Man are the same, though back in Harlem they like to say you *pass* and Red Man doesn't pass for anything but terrifying. He's part Cherokee and not particularly red, but different enough that folks have to mark it somehow. His real name is Walter Finch—you asked the first time you met—but it's hard to call him plain Walter at times like this, when you are all tight and wired with violence.

The Barkley brothers are in their fifties but look twenty years younger, especially now, impeccably tailored in wide-legged and high-waisted suits of blue and sage green. They have matching silk in their pockets and Bo has a feather in his hat. Quentin and Bo aren't identical, but it's hard to tell when they're tricked out like a matching set. You don't get very far in the Harlem policy racket without a keen sense of style. Something that Victor, sadly, lacks. But then, white men always get twice the reward for a quarter of the work.

Which is why, it turns out, he's invited them here tonight: Russian Vic's had a good look at the money that "Negro pool" brings in, with its thousands of penny bets a day, and he wants in. The Barkleys have a respectable bank but it isn't as big as Madame Stephanie's or Casper Holstein's. Victor wants it for the numbers, then, but also for the hookers, which it turns out is Quentin's side of the business. You didn't know that.

You feel, for a moment that is not nearly long enough, as young as you are.

After Mrs. Dernov has served you all her dumpling soup and scurried out like a rat from a sinking ship, Victor places his hands flat on the table with a force that startles everybody.

"So here's how I see it. You fine brothers keep a percentage and run the operation, and I take my cut for protection. I also get my pick of the girls to set them up down here. There's always a market for the mulattoes . . . I believe you people call them high yellow?"

You think—you're not sure—that he glances at you as he says this. Just for a moment, a barely malicious slide across your freckles and wide nose, but it's enough to make us clench and ease the knife from the left wrist holster. We're ready to defend, but you've always been careful, and Victor's gaze is now steady on Quentin and Bo. They are silent with outrage and fear. The brothers don't have the experience to play with Vic, and he knows it. The numbers might be illegal, but they've never been mob business. Until now.

"Your cut," Bo says, at last, in his best white-people voice. "And how much would that be?"

Victor fishes out a dumpling with his fingers and drops it in his mouth whole and chews, smiling all the while. Red Man shifts, very slightly, to his left. The knife slides the rest of the way out of your holster before you realize it. We know, even if you don't, how this will end.

"I'm feeling generous," says Russian Vic, around a half-chewed mouthful of stewed pork and beef. The brothers haven't done more than sip the broth. "Let's say . . . fifty percent? That seems . . ."

There is a moment, in the airless gap left by Victor's dangling verb, in which you think you won't need us. Bo is too clever to fall for Victor's jawed traps. Then Quentin speaks for the first time all evening:

"Outrageous. That's extortion, not protection."

Bo glances sharply at his brother and puts a restraining hand on his shoulder. "My brother means to say, that we'd like some time to consider your terms, and perhaps negotiate a little, no offense intended for your generous offer."

Vic slides his greasy fingers into the broth again, puts another dumpling into that gaping maw. And you know. Victor never eats so much as before he gets to killing someone.

You look at Bo, straight at him. "Run," you whisper.

He stands, he manages that much, but Quentin won't budge, and so is an easy target when Victor nods and one of the men standing behind them shoots Quentin in the shoulder.

"Now, is *that* outrageous enough for you?" Victor says. "Because I can do more."

Quentin roars; there's no other word for it. He rocks the table as he pushes himself upright and Victor's soup bowl spills over.

"We came here," Quentin pants, clutching his arm, "in good faith. In good faith! We run a clean business—"

"Aside from the hookers and the numbers," Victor says, very mildly. He picks a dumpling, split and leaking, from his lap. You swallow and feel every unchewed morsel of meat and dough in your stomach rise like the Euphrates.

Bo tugs again on his brother's good arm, but he hasn't taken his eyes off Victor. "We agree," he says, and you hear every dirty curse he doesn't use behind those soft words. "Now let us go home."

You take a breath to speak into the silence that stretches across the table, but Red Man puts a finger on your knee, soft as a moth, and your voice falls away. You have a sudden vision of Bo as Jesus in an awful white man's parody of the Last Supper, his brother on one side and his greatest enemy on the other, a man who would sup with him and then kill him, a man who has placed himself beyond God, beyond all covenants. The deal Victor's offering them is an insult, and he knows it. He also knows they have no choice but to swallow the shit he's serving them and thank massa for allowing them even half of the empire they built. After all, a black man's labor is only his until a white man decides he wants it.

Victor breaks the silence. "Sit," he says. "Sit, please. You haven't finished your soup." He smiles. It's the first time you've seen that smile, though you will mark it more often over the years. It's a smile that will grow sharper the more metal he folds into his jaw, but even now the holster of the five-inch knife is warming in your left palm. You keep your hands ready. We gave them to you for this kind of danger, after all.

But you don't use our gift—that power. You're terrified of that moment you defend them and Victor and Jack and the Body and every other white man at that table turns and sees Yellow Pea. Red Man already does, but you've always known that your colors are safe with him. So you wait. And we judge you for it, Phyllis, we make the first red mark in your ledger. Not for your first half-dozen kills, not even for pretending to be one of them, but for when you denied us our purpose, stilled our power and allowed great evil to pass on by.

The Barkley brothers sit. They don't speak, though Quentin grunts occasionally as his blood soaks his fine suit jacket. What a waste of good tailoring, you think. We don't judge you for this. We all cope in our own ways.

"Now," Victor says, "I think we ought to make that split sixty-forty, what do you . . ."

"We agree," Bo grits out.

"Good!" Victor says. "Let's shake on it and you can be on your way." He stands and reaches across the table to Quentin's bloody right hand. Quentin yelps in pain when he catches it, which turns into a scream when Victor yanks him hard across the table, spilling the rest of your dinners into your laps. Vic pulls out his gun, a nickel-plated Colt .45, and smashes it three times across the back of Quentin's head. Bone crunches like wet popcorn. Quentin convulses for a few seconds and then goes still. He is dead. Just like that, one of the finest numbers men in Harlem is dead and you did nothing to stop it.

Bo stands just where he is, unmoving, in shock. "Quin?" he whispers. "Brother?" But you know Bo knows he's gone. "We had a deal," he says.

Victor makes a show of wiping the wrong end of his gun. "Well, we do, but then you goddamn niggers just had to get up your noses. Now that won't do. Won't do for people to think Vic can get disrespected by a pair of know-nothing niggers."

You and Bo flinch every time he says the word. Beside you, Red Man is as still as glass.

"So let's say that your brother here is a . . . lesson? And you go back home about your business?"

Bo nods, nods again, looks at you—just for a second, but he does it, because he knows what you are and he is witness to your silence—and says, "Like hell I will, you ofay devil."

His bullet grazes Victor's neck. It's the only one he has time to get off: first Jack, then Victor, bring him down with five body shots.

Victor walks around the table. Somehow Bo is still breathing.

"Red Man," Vic says. His voice is shaky, like he's just climaxed.

"Yes, Vic?"

"Tie him up. I want to take my time."

You end it, then. Take us up when it's too late to do much good and sink a three-inch knife precisely into Bo Barkley's temple.

"They agreed," you say, before Victor can spit something out past his rage.

"And I changed my mind, angel. I don't appreciate rogue knives. Never know who they might cut?"

"Someone is going to notice they're gone. They're respected businessmen up in Harlem, how do you expect—"

And Victor, he just waves his hand. Lucky for you, his rage has passed.

"They're just a pair of niggers in nice suits. Police wouldn't do a thing even if I asked them to. Now somebody get me a goddamn bourbon. You do it, angel, you know just how I like it."

And you do.

The hands that hold our gift chip ice as good as they throw knives.

The rot settles in, then, settles in for good, but power is a fine perfume.

You won't smell it for years.

"She's waking up. Can you hear me, darling?"

I heard the dentist first. I wished I couldn't. I took a breath and then attempted, with some small success, to push the air through rough vocal chords.

"Good girl, Phyllis. Open your eyes, that's it."

Victor was here, too. He was no harpist in heaven, and I discovered an ache, in and among the others that had gathered in celebration of my unexpected return, because he had bothered to come and that meant he still intended me to be of use to him.

I squinted up at the two hovering faces—one dark-haired, one crowned with tarnished silver—and thought of many questions, none of which I could, or would, ask.

The dentist rubbed my fingers between his hands, warm and treacherously comforting. "Darling, they say you'll be all right."

"Whoopee."

Victor frowned. "The woman who shot you . . ."

I stared at him.

"Recognize her?" he tried again. "Your job, angel. That mark you didn't want to kill nearly killed you. *And* got away. Think you ought to . . ."

I couldn't help it: "Kill her?" I raised an eyebrow, since I couldn't even manage to tilt my head.

He shrugged. "When you're healed up. Red Man will look for her till then. My angel needs . . ."

"A trip to the country?"

Victor grinned like that was a good joke. "Revenge, dollface."

"Crickets, Victor. Clean air. A whole lot of nothing to do, that sounds good right about now. Shit, I hurt."

The dentist squeezed my hand. "Should I call the nurse? You can have more morphine."

"Outside, Marty. Your gal and I have something to discuss."

The dentist's head left my field of vision and a door closed softly. I grimaced, and Victor caught it. "Bit of a limp fish, that man of yours."

"Not in bed."

That made him laugh. I'd been good at that in the old days, when he and I had spent years building the legend of Victor's angel of justice. I'd reveled in the messy grit of it; I had killed with the passion of the newly converted, and the vision of a Harlem girl unexpectedly divested of obscurity.

"Get healthy, Phyllis. Get strong. But then you're going to kill that woman, 'cause no one's going to talk about Victor's angel the way they're talking now. You're *my* girl."

"Your knife," I said.

His smile was crooked, fond. "With the killing edge."

"What if your knife got lost, Victor?"

He rested a veined hand on my collarbone, where the bandages began, and traced its length. "I'd look for it. This doesn't have to be complicated. We've done pretty well by each other, over the years."

My hands jumped.

"There's a copper out there who wants to see you."

I squinted at him. "What's the matter, they stopped taking your money?"

"When someone gets gunned down on Bleecker, forms gotta get filed. You don't know anything, right? Didn't even see the dame?"

"Where's Dev? Or Tamara? They saw her."

Victor gave me a long look. "Not an integrated hospital, Phyllis. Have to save the family visits for when you get out of here."

I wondered what he meant by that, just like he wanted me to. A hundred blunt needles, iron-hot and intermittently electrified, bored into my right side. Disordered with pain, I nearly called his bluff—*so my great-grandmother was a slave and my grandaddy was a sharecropper and sure as shit I grew up in Harlem, Victor, I've always been your Negro angel*—but that wasn't how we played the game. Flat on my back in a hospital bed wasn't the time to change the rules. And I remembered—or someone had reminded me—of a dinner, an ambush, and the forgotten Negro blood that had baptized the Pelican.

Someone knocked and opened the door. The cop—young, and not one I recognized, which meant he might be one of Commissioner Valentine's rotating army of squeaky-clean recruits—nodded at Victor and pulled up a chair.

"Just a few minutes, ma'am," he said. "You can wait outside if you like, Mr. Dernov."

Victor smiled. The cop pretended not to notice. "Got places to be, anyhow. Rest up, Phyllis. I'm sure this fine officer of the law will keep his questions to the point."

The cop frowned after him. I decided he was either clean or on the take and unhappy about it. Either way, dangerous. I affected unthreatening weakness, which wasn't difficult.

"Your full name is Phyllis LeBlanc, correct?" he said.

I nodded. A little joke, that name. Phyllis Green only existed north of 110th Street. I wondered when Gloria would start to worry about me. Knowing Gloria, it would probably be two weeks before she even bothered to knock on my door, and thank goodness.

"And you were shot in the chest at approximately 10:46 p.m. yesterday night outside of the Pelican nightclub on Bleecker Street?"

"Looks like it."

He leaned so far forward I couldn't see past his furrowed eyebrows, which met in the middle. "Did you see who shot you, Miss LeBlanc?"

"I was too busy almost dying."

"You're awfully glib about something this serious."

"Oh, I'm serious as a bullet. The trouble is, one went through me. Yesterday. So if you don't mind getting to the point?"

The kid blushed purple and quickly pulled a photograph from a folder. I had schooled my expression into exhausted ignorance, and so just managed to maintain the pose at the sight, though my pulse jumped hard and I felt faint with shock and pain.

"Do you recognize the man in this photograph?"

It was Trent Sullivan, serial murderer. "I thought it was a woman who shot me?" I said.

The officer's heavy eyebrow raised at either end. He pulled out another, recently familiar photograph. "The shooter's name is Maryann West. His girlfriend." My eyes widened in surprise, mostly real. I had believed Dev, but this truth was still quietly upending my existence.

"Why would she shoot me?" I asked, because I knew very well—her screams, her fingers tearing at the door.

"This man was killed about a decade ago. Unsolved case. But the knife work is distinctive. We've found several bodies like this over the years. We're sure to catch the perp eventually. Closing in, I've heard."

I frowned at him, wondering who Victor had forgotten to pay, and why some pissant rookie cop felt comfortable threatening me with prosecution.

And then I remembered that Dev was an informant, and since the precinct cops were in Victor's pay, he had to be working for the higher-ups: vice squad, or even Commissioner Valentine himself. Which meant Victor—and his angel—could go down tomorrow, if they wanted.

I lifted my left hand with some effort and pushed away the photograph. The cop flinched at my touch, and spilled the rest of his file over my blankets. He squatted to retrieve the ones that slid onto the floor, mumbling apologies thick with unease. Even like this, I intimidated him. This pleased me. I was still enough of my old self for that. I picked up the papers nearest my hand, and was surprised to recognize them: corpses, crudely photographed (none of Walter's unsung artistry here), each twisted body missing its hands. So many. I'd never guessed that there could be so many.

"What are these?" I asked.

"Unsolved murders," he said, snatching them. "These are just the ones from the last decade." He frowned. "And if you know anything, Miss LeBlanc, you should know the law is prepared to offer leniency for information. The individual who kills with knives has committed at least two dozen murders that we know about. More than enough for the hot squat."

"Well, I'm sure that's got nothing to do with me."

He smiled, the effect ruined by his dilated pupils and shaking hands. "I'll be seeing you, ma'am."

He'd get corrupted soon enough, but for now the policeman had a new-penny shine, ruddy with self-righteousness and purpose. I saw myself in him, as I had once been. And I understood how he saw me—a woman past her prime, washed in blood, better off dead.

Alone, I closed my eyes and considered my new, clamoring questions. Victor had lied to me for a long time, that much was clear. Maybe Maryann West had killed that man for his hands, maybe she used to do it alongside her boyfriend, but I wondered about those other photographs, that morgue of bodies stretching back a decade. Trent was already dead and I didn't see how Maryann could have killed them all by herself—maybe she hadn't killed them at all. If Victor had used me to settle some other vendetta, if he had brought down the killing wrath of his angel of justice for some petty territorial dispute but told her it was for murder—

It's Victor, Trent Sullivan had said, when he had finally recognized me in the dim light of his bedroom.

We know about the hands, I had said.

But I didn't do nothing to them—

I'm here to make sure you never do it again.

And then Maryann started screaming and Trent managed to toss me against the headboard and there were no more words between us, only a great deal of blood.

I hadn't believed Trent's denial. Even when I'd wanted to drown myself in Dev's bloody bathtub, I'd trusted Victor implicitly—that he'd never send me after someone who didn't deserve it. Only his angel could bring justice, after all.

Except that he had.

"Darling? Are you crying?"

I wiped my eyes roughly. The dentist paced at the foot of my bed. He had a look I recognized.

"I just called my wife," he said. I waited. He bit his lip. "Darling, you know how much I love you, but . . . well, she's pregnant again, that's all there is to it. I can't be with you, no matter how much I want to. This might seem difficult now, but you know Victor will take the best care of you . . ."

I tried not to listen to him, and nearly managed the trick by staring at a mold stain spreading like dried blood along the ceiling tiles.

I needed to talk to Dev. All of the lies I had told myself about him ripped me every time I took a breath—an informant, a motherfucking stoolie, all those lonely years—but he might still help. At the least, he wouldn't betray me to Victor.

"Marty," I told the dentist, "congratulations to you and your wife. Can you do me one last favor?"

He cleared his throat. "A-anything, Phyllis."

"Tell Dev I'd like to see him?"

I saw him consider the propriety of telling me that the hospital was segregated, decide against it, and then just nod.

He left.

I tried to sleep, and cried instead. My tears burned like vinegar; they made me cough. I cried for a long time, until the nurse came in. She took one look and shot me full of mother morphine, lit my veins like a carousel and spun me like soft candy, round and round.

I dreamed of Dev's hand on my forehead. I dreamed of him whispering my name. I dreamed I couldn't answer.

My dream tried to speak to me. He started, "I was just a rookie—" and choked to a stop. He tried again. "You killed our key witness—how did Victor find out?—I made a deal—I made a deal to save you."

I lost his words for a while, after that.

I could only hold on to the tone of them, sandstone crumbling against granite, scraping and fragile.

"You remember—it was the last—it was the first—I've never hated the way I hated that night."

I had seen it in his eyes, hadn't I? Even in the dream, I couldn't forget how Dev had looked at me, just before he left. As if he didn't even know me, as if he had never seen me naked and covered in blood.

But I didn't want to remember that. I wanted this dream, the only way I would ever have him again. I wanted to bury myself in it. His hand on my shoulder, the one that didn't hurt. His voice as soft as Virginia cotton.

He was telling a story about India, about the farm where he grew up.

"We kept goats for the milk," Dev said. "I thought I might be a disciple of Pusan, the god of lost animals. The way they looked at me . . . But one night a wolf got through a bad mend in the fence, killed the dam and all but one of the kids. I found her, the kid. In her mother's spilled entrails. Gagging and—"

He paused. He withdrew his hand, and I wished that this were a dream where I was given to move, to touch him. "She—" he tried. "She was covered in blood. Not her own."

I knew what he was thinking. This was a dream, of course I did. Hadn't I just tried to stop myself from dredging the same memory?

"You didn't know me when you left Trent—and his girl, oh God, his girl, poor Maryann—not until you were naked in my clawfoot tub, and the water turned pink, because you said, 'It's a sunset, Dev.' And I—"

I dreamed that his breath caught like a fishing line in his chest. I dreamed that he squeezed my hand and kissed my forehead and left me there, to dream alone in that room, without him.

My next three days in the hospital unspooled with steady boredom, occasionally relieved by pain and then painkillers. I sucked morphine like a greedy child, and dreamed strange dreams about Dev. That first one in particular was so odd that for a whole day I thought it might have been real.

He was a stoolie—or a plant, depending on how you looked at it—and I found myself jerking as though newly awake every time I remembered. The Dev of my dream had said that he had been working with the cops from the very beginning. And maybe that was only pain and paranoia, the knife I wielded on myself to pay for the hubris of even dreaming that he would come back to me. But every time that molten knowledge of it burned me through, I thought, *Oh, so that's why.* Dev had always held himself apart from us, but he'd never been out of place. Maybe he had only seemed to love me, too.

At that point I asked the nurse for more morphine and tried to forget how to think.

Walter brought chocolates—promptly confiscated—and funny stories about the Pelican. I particularly liked the one about how the dentist got so ossified the night he left me that Dev had to haul him into a taxi. "Over his shoulder like a sack of grain," Walter said, demonstrating. "Wasn't too careful, either. I wouldn't've wanted to be Marty's head the next morning."

Tamara, he said, had jumped feet first in love with her soldier boy. "Lot of long faces in that club these days. Not that most of them ever had a chance."

"And Dev?" I asked, not wanting to.

"You know Dev, he's happy for her. And his heart's not as broken as he thinks, anyway."

This sparked enough hope that I asked if Dev had said anything about me, but Walter just shook his head and put his hand on my good shoulder.

We did not discuss Victor, or the woman who shot me, or what Walter might do if I got myself lost again. I did not ask him any of the questions that my rookie cop had forced upon me. After Walter left the doctor made a pointed comment about *certain types of visitors* and I stared at him until he looked away.

The next day, Walter brought me a letter from Tamara:

> *Oh Pea, my sweetest Pea, Walter says you're at some segregated hospital uptown, so I can't get in unless I pretend to clean your toilet, which, you can imagine, is not something I find myself itching to do. If I'd wanted to scrub toilets I'd have stayed in Virginia! The Pelican is still standing, you'll be glad to know. I confirmed a real coup of a show next Thursday: a Hungarian sculptor who got out just before Hitler got in—terrifying stuff, nightmare shapes rising out of rock, absolutely terrific. The Amsterdam News promised me they'll send down a reviewer.*
>
> *Unfortunately, we're also debuting one other artist—at Vic's request. You're well rid of that dentist, sugar. Marty has as much artistic sensibility as a government-employed horsefly, but Vic's got it in him to be "generous." Foreshortened doodles of horse's heads with teeth like a toothpaste model's! I know Vic made the Pelican, but sometimes I swear he did it by accident.*

Well, I don't mean to bore you with all this gossip while you can't even come down here to see it! You scared the devil out of me, Phyllis. Get better soon and get out of that damned hospital. I owe you a good reading. I've been trying, but the numbers are funny and I think it would be better if I had you with me when I laid out the cards. All I get are spades, Pea, spades and hearts and every once in a while, as if he's been watching over my shoulder, that damned devil joker.

xoxo
Tammy

P.S. Clyde sends his love!

This made me laugh and roll my eyes and mutter crossly to myself and feel better by the end.

She was wrong, in any case—Victor had known exactly what he was doing when he made the Pelican: integrated, high-minded, perfumed with reefer and the right kind of danger, the kind that kept the cops as disinclined to arrest you for indecency as for selling liquor without a license. Tamara had just refined the model to fit her own dreams. And I wasn't sure how much stock to put into Tamara's trick of reading the fates, but I was a Harlem girl who'd been visited by the hands—so I couldn't *not* believe her, either.

The next evening, I shared the lounge with one other patient up late to watch the sunset. We inmates were, in general, an early-slumbered cohort, but today frustration had goaded me into selective deafness when the evening nurse suggested I return to my bed. It seemed that Victor's influence extended a few steps beyond the extravagance of my single room; my glare precipitated a hasty retreat, and my companion—an elderly white gentleman with a broken hip and a palsy—happily co-opted my intransigence. The view was of the Hudson and the cliffs of Jersey's dockyards beyond it. The sun squatted behind the rusted boats and long warehouses, pregnant and hungry and red as the cherry squashed against the remains of my dessert. Not even Victor could do much about the food.

The river had swallowed the sun and I was wondering if those bore-holes burning down my arm might not have some kind of salutary, character-building effect—to remind me of the inevitability of my loveless death, perhaps—when the door opened.

My companion had fallen asleep in his chair, and I could not be bothered to make the awkward turn just to greet a nurse, so I looked at a tanker slowly moving upriver until Dev's head blocked the view.

"Hi," he said.

I stared at him; he pulled up a chair across from mine.

"How are you doing, Phyllis?"

I snorted. Same old Dev, caring just enough. "I'm terrific. I hear you're nursing a broken heart, but then, that's going around these days."

He smiled, acknowledging the hit. "For what it's worth, Marty never deserved you, Pea."

God, I hated him. Hated the soft fondness in his eyes, his speckled hair, the way he under-aspirated hard consonants.

"Oh, I'm sure he did." I laughed, and winced. "I'm not exactly a catch."

Dev just looked at me. "Are you tired? I'm sorry I couldn't visit earlier. I can come back in the morning."

He meant this was his first visit. Which meant the goat, the wolf, the broken confession—just a morphine fantasy.

"Let's get this over with, Dev."

"And what is this?"

"A deal. A bargain. Probably a short straw for you, frankly, but maybe for old time's sake? I need your help. With Victor."

Dev slid a look at the old man, now drooling on the arm of his wheelchair. He stood up, pushed the man outside, and set a chair under the knob to stop someone from interrupting us. I didn't say anything; paranoia was our cost of business.

"Pea," he said. "You remember what I told you?"

Did I *remember*? I wanted to laugh at him, but I was afraid something else might come out.

"That's why I'm asking."

"You haven't asked yet."

I took a deep breath. "I don't think Trent Sullivan killed those people. And I don't think, not his girl, either. That night . . . makes more sense, that way. I think Victor's been lying, using me on his associates and telling me it's justice. If that's true, I figure you might know?"

Dev's breath left him. He didn't catch it again for nearly a minute. "You never suspected."

In his grated words I recognized something of the voice from my dream. It had been a decade since I had touched Dev like a woman with a lease on his skin, but now I reached out, unthinking, to wipe watery tracks from his face. With a faint groan, he pressed his cheek into my hand and closed his eyes, though they still leaked with steady, baffling tears. I didn't understand what I had said.

"Dev, at the club, you asked me if I believed everything Victor told me . . . " My voice closed in on itself, cut off by some latent wave of shame. Hadn't I trusted Victor? It had been safer, certainly, to believe our bargain had held. To never question, or delve deeper into those flashes of unease I felt—yes, just that sickening lurch—ever since I had killed Trent Sullivan. It is difficult to get a woman to understand something that her heart depends upon her not understanding.

Desperate, I tried, "Why would he lie when he could get a dozen other men on a hit without asking questions?"

Dev's throat worked against my wrist. "You're a legend. They're all terrified of you. Whatever you thought about justice had nothing to do with that power. Of course Victor would use it."

"Of course," I repeated. "I have been very stupid. I wish you had told me sooner."

A sob cracked his throat and he wrenched himself away. He wouldn't look at me. "Tell me what you need, Pea."

"If I've been . . . if Victor's angel has just been another bag man, all this time—" I felt wide open as a swinging door. I felt unhinged. "I want to find whoever's killing people for their hands. If he just used someone else's murders as a convenient excuse . . ."

The look in his eyes. I couldn't keep speaking, not if this was what it did to him. A moth popped and buzzed against the aging light fixture. The burnished steel of the wheelchair handle glared back at me like Victor's silver jaw. Dev's wet eyes stayed on me like a lost dog's. Lost, like that dog of Tammy's, that little yippy spaniel she named Josephine or Celeste or Betty depending on the month; she cried for weeks after it ran away during a show and no one had the heart to tell her that Victor had kicked it to death in the alley.

And the world, so happily unmoored and swinging, slotted itself neatly back into place.

"Victor," I said.

"Who else, Phyllis, who else?"

Victor wanted the hands. And if the hands wouldn't come to him, then he'd do them like he did the Barkley brothers: he'd just take what anyone else got.

It was cold in here, with the sun gone. Cold as a meat factory. I shook. "But Maryann—how'd she get back into this after so much time? And what does that devil think he can do with a dead man's hands, anyway? Has it been the whole time, Dev? The whole time I've been with him? No, no, don't tell me, I can't bear—" I sat up straight, though damn did it hurt. "I have to kill Victor." My thumbs jumped, though I didn't make them.

Dev's hands strangled one another. "And then?" he said.

And then? And then you can take me away, Dev, Devajyoti, brightest one I ever knew. Our lovers have left us and our lives aren't what we thought they might be and we have been in the way of loving each other too long, I think, to stop now.

But I asked him for a cigarette. He pulled two from a pack in his vest pocket and I held my lighter ready. The scored circle in the metal pressed against my shaking fingers. I took a long drag, coughed, and lost track of everything but pain and his voice, reeling me in.

"You should sleep," he said. His arm was around my back and my head lolled on his shoulder and I shook every time I took a breath.

"I can't even hate the woman who did this to me," I said, and then the last few pieces decided to snap together. How clearly I remembered his voice in my dream. "Maryann. Trent. Was he really a stoolie?"

"He'd agreed to testify, but—" Dev jerked and then laughed, looked down at me, and wiped his eyes. "That was low, Pea."

"It was clever."

"You were awake? That whole time?"

"I was stiff on morphine, but I guess I still heard you."

He sighed, the way you sigh after a long kiss in the dark. "Ask."

"You made a deal to save me?"

"Yes. Before you killed Trent." It was like watching Dev merge with his reflection, the one in that dark mirror that I had always seen in myself, but never suspected in him. He felt sharper, fuller. "Pea, I dragged you off of Trent's body. I was a witness to a murder. Either I testified against you or I found someone better to give them."

I gasped. "Dev—you don't—the Dewey investigation?" By the fall of '35, police headquarters on Centre Street had become a charnel house for New York's most infamous mobsters. The newly appointed police commissioner Lewis Valentine and District Attorney Thomas Dewey had political aspirations and a knack for making themselves out to be real-live comic-book heroes for the press. By the time the indictments wound down, Victor had been one of the few left standing.

Dev hesitated, then nodded. He shouldn't be telling me this. I could kill him with a stray word, a glance.

I sucked on my teeth. "I always wondered why you'd get mixed up with some blustering fool like Dutch Schultz!"

He laughed softly. "Is Victor much better?"

"He has more style, at the least. But Dev . . . you came back. You're still there. Why hasn't Dewey dragged Victor in years ago?"

He looked away from me. "I've given them plenty. His midtown operations, his illegal shipments from the dockyards."

I took that in. "But not me," I said hoarsely.

"They say Victor has betrayal in his hands, but the truth is he had found a . . . way to steal it off of us."

"You mean, it's *real*? Vic can use the hands?"

"They work for him, but I don't think they like it, if that makes any sense. They play tricks on him."

"They must have told him about Trent."

Dev nodded. "But then again, I've kept his trust for these ten years."

"I have to kill him," I repeated. God, but for a second my wrists hurt more than my arm.

Dev just shook his head. I breathed him for a little while, and then the cigarette he held to my lips.

"You said you haven't done a job in seven months."

I laughed, which was a mistake. When I finished coughing, I said, "And what's it to you?"

"I've been thinking I could—" The voice from my dream. I closed my eyes, as though that would keep him here, wide open and breaking against me. "Remember those watermelon seedlings you bought in Hudson? That fancy new kind we paid through the nose for? You planted them right beside my mother's tea roses. They're regular nabobs of the garden, Pea. The oddest colors. Purple like a snowy night sky. Speckled yellow like stars."

I turned my head and rested my lips against the sharp lapel of his jacket. The cloth smelled of him, of the clean sweat of making love and weeding the garden in those amber days in the house by the river.

"What happened to the goat?" I asked.

His arm tightened around me. "She died," he said. "She stopped eating and I couldn't watch her starve to death. So I put her in my lap and slit her throat."

6

There was a story about Red Man, the kind the young soldiers liked to tell, about how he once beat a man to death for keeping back a cadillac of dope after a delivery. And when that unfortunate was holding his face together with the back of his shattered hand, crying for his mother, Red Man pulled out that little envelope and ripped it in half. A rain of glittering heroin snow settled on the blood and dirt of that hellish back alley and Red Man took out his camera, since it looked so beautiful. Then he stove in the side of the soldier's head with the steel toe of his boot.

The part about the camera was true, though I wasn't sure about the rest of it.

But this was just after I started working for Victor. That particular soldier had seen me dancing in the Times Square club and liked to shout offers for Victor's *yellow-skint octaroon* whenever he was drunk and I couldn't get away. I was passing with Victor's crew, and he would have known the danger I'd be in if the wrong person heard him. One day that loudmouth ofay worked with us and the next he didn't—years later, Walter showed me a picture of a face like uncured sausage, white powder caked in the gashes and clumped in long, wet eyelashes. *You got a knack for chiaroscuro, Walter Finch*, I said, and we both smiled.

Walter Finch was light when he picked me up from the hospital ten days after the shooting: gentle, cheerful, undemanding. He wasn't the sort of man to wear his violence on the outside, not like Victor.

Another of our quiet affinities. I, too, could bide my time with what I had to tell him. Tamara waited against the door of his silver Packard, a paisley scarf wrapped around her hair. The solvent heat and noon sun had shrunk her, or perhaps just the space she occupied; she smiled to see me, but her eyes looked upside-down with pain.

"What happened?" I asked after I had settled myself, awkwardly, into the back seat.

"Don't you dare! You can't get shot before my eyes, Phyllis, and then go asking how I'm doing! Here, you want a pillow? I made Walter bring pillows."

I bore her ministrations with detached patience; my parting drink of morphine still murmured dulcet comfort, and if I kept very still, that song could drown out the world.

"I'm so glad to see you, Pea," she said, and wiped her eyes. "I tried and tried to read your numbers, but I guess you're special, sugar, 'cause they want you to be here before they tell me anything."

She held up her familiar card deck, the faded backs, soft as old leather, with an open palm and a closed fist trapped in violet bramble.

"You want to read them now?"

She sucked her teeth. "The luck you been having, I don't think they can wait."

"Well," I said, and wondered why the sight of those cards was pricking me, uneasy, in the ribs. She spread a blanket between us and started to shuffle, the cards flying faster than a hummingbird's wings.

"But what's happened with you, baby?" I asked. "Something's wrong, I can tell."

Tamara just shook her head and shuffled even faster. She had that chipped porcelain smile she got whenever Victor spent too long backstage. I put my left arm around her shoulders. The cards spilled, the jokers and jacks and spades face up and staring.

"It's Clyde," Tamara said, "it's that fool!" She smacked the back of Walter's seat with an open palm, and let out a cry like an animal in a trap.

Walter's driving was funereal and he kept his eyes on the road, but I caught his grimace in the rearview mirror.

"Her soldier boy shipped off," he said.

Tamara moaned. "Clyde wouldn't *stay*, no matter what I said, just like last time. He says he loves me and the next breath he's promising to write. Like he ever does! So I don't care what Hitler does to him—"

She seemed ready to blow her nose on my sling, so I asked Walter for a hankie. "Tamara," I said, almost laughing and so sad I could cry with her. "Tammy, honey, what did you want him to do, dodge the draft? Get arrested? He still wouldn't be with you in jail."

"He always finds a way to leave. He's that boy, the one I fell for back in Lawrenceville. I told you."

"The actor?"

She sighed against me. "He's just so goddamn beautiful, Pea."

"I know. But he was drafted. Doesn't mean he don't love you."

"Victor could have—"

Walter must have flinched; the car jolted at the same time I interrupted her: "Don't. You might be young, but you ain't stupid. You've seen enough to know how it is. You want that for him? Someone you love?"

She bit her lip. "What about Dev?"

"What about him?"

"He runs for Victor. And I bet you he won't be getting himself killed halfway around the world in some white man's war, either. Why's it good enough for him and not Clyde?"

I closed my eyes, afraid that Tamara or Walter might read the fear there, my new and terrible knowledge of Dev's double life. He could have died anytime in the last decade, and I hadn't even known.

"Tamara, leave her be."

"It's not good enough for either of them. But at least your Clyde has the sense to know it."

This pricked her upright; she glared at me and swelled. "Won't you *ever* forgive him?"

I started laughing.

"What?" Tamara said. "Damn it, Pea, don't make fun—"

"That's what you think? Honey, if there's any forgiveness going around, I'm the one who needs it."

"Tamara," Walter said, heavily. "Leave this. Please. Let's get upstairs."

Tamara bit her lip and bent to retrieve her cards. She froze when she saw how they had fallen, all those spades face-up, pointing at me like a devil's garden, and a family of royals pulling the weeds.

"Walter, tell me you've got someone watching Pea's back."

He looked thoughtful, then nodded. "I'll put someone on the building tonight."

Tammy gave him a sour look from behind puffy eyes. "If something happens to her again—"

Walter raised one hand—a benign enough gesture—and Tammy's words turned back hard enough to bruise. "Our angel has been at this since you were a girl, Tamara. If something gets her, I promise you, she knew it was coming."

"We haven't found Maryann West yet," Walter said, just before leaving me. Tamara had gone back to the car. "But I'm hunting, and so we will. Victor wanted you to know."

I stared at him for a good while, long enough that anyone else would have blinked or shuffled or asked me what I wanted. Walter just waited like the Buddha.

I bore it almost as well, though my arm had started to hurt more than the morphine could suppress.

"What I really need to know," I said at last, "is why you're lying about this. Maryann West didn't kill those people. Neither did Trent Sullivan. Victor did. Victor *is*, I suppose, and there you are, shoveling shit for him like it's your job."

"It is. I don't know why you ever thought it wasn't. Vic never kept me around for my good looks."

I remembered what he had told me about his kids, about his wife. "Think he'd still let me get away, Walter?"

"I think you're not very safe with that woman alive, whatever Victor wants."

Walter had worked for Victor since the beginning. He had to know the sordid mob politics behind each act of supposedly angelic justice. Had he, like Dev, assumed I guessed?

"Why *did* he have me kill Trent Sullivan, all those years ago?"

Walter kept his answer for a long moment; I could see him measuring me, and then his words, on a scale whose counterweight only he knew. He smiled a Red Man smile. "Trent worked part-time as a spotter. For people with appropriate talents. He was the one who found you at that club."

Now I did sit down, hard, on my chaise lounge. I shivered. Trent Sullivan had found me at the club. Where I tossed darts at the fruit that I juggled while naked, letting the perfect halves fall down around me in circles.

Trent had known how to see us, the ones whom the hands had visited and left with their heavy luck. He gave our names to Victor. And then I had seen the photos of what happened next.

"Why aren't I long dead, then?"

"The night you and Victor met, don't you remember? You walked right up and offered *him* a deal. And he took it."

I'm sick of swinging my girls on stage. That was my voice, wasn't it? Or had been, a hundred years ago. *I can throw knives, Mr. Vic. I can throw knives and I'm willing to throw them at those who don't deserve to walk this earth anymore. You help me kill the bastard that killed my brother and I'll kill any other real bastard that you like. I'll be your angel of justice—your knife to throw.*

Vic had laughed for nearly a minute. Now I knew why. I was an ignorant girl, whose hands were the only part of me he'd ever wanted. It must have been like hearing his steak begging for its life. But he'd agreed—Victor had helped me find the bastard who'd gunned down Roger in a basement card parlor on Amsterdam Avenue. And from then on I was his. Not an angel, but a very fine knife.

"And Trent? What'd he do to deserve a visit from me?"

Walter sighed. "He was a snitch. But I'm guessing someone told you that already. You might think about that. The plans Victor has for you, now. I owe him too much. My life, still. But you don't, now, do you?"

I didn't breathe. Then I made myself exhale, slow and business-like. "I'm going to kill him."

Walter's eyes went soft. "Take it easy, Phyllis. Whatever you decide, I won't stop you."

We said goodbye; he left; I was alone. *Someone told you already.* But he couldn't know—

I considered that I hadn't seen Dev in four days.

I tried to read for a while—*Their Eyes Were Watching God, Quicksand, Persuasion,* my neglected copy of *The Nazarene,* which Gloria had raved about last Christmas—but even Hurston couldn't keep my interest for more than a dozen pages. I wished the sun away, not because I craved darkness, but because then I would have survived another day. I stared at the clock, considered the wisdom of drinking at 3:20 in the afternoon, and pulled out the latest *New Amsterdam News* and *New Yorker*—food for Phyllis Green and armor for Phyllis LeBlanc.

My phone rang at four o'clock. I'd slipped into a merciful doze, cheek pressed wetly against a cartoon of Hitler marching across Russia, but I sprung up at the sound.

"Phyllis, that is you, right?"

"Hiya, Gloria." I sank back onto the chaise. I felt glad to hear her voice, and immediately weary.

"I've called you three times in the last week! Where have you been?"

I considered. "Slow boat to China?"

She sighed. "I was worried, you know."

"You coulda come over."

"You don't like it when I do. Don't play martyr to me, Phyllis. You're my little sister, you can't stop me from loving you."

"Can't?"

"Well," she said, laughing, "if it ain't happened by now. So where you been? Having fun, I hope? A new man?"

Dev had put his arm around me, he had agreed to help. But I had hurt him somehow, and almost died in his arms; impossible to tell how much of that sweetness was nostalgia and how much was love. "It looks like I'm on the market, but not yet."

"You were seeing that 'fay dentist, weren't you? Got tired of him?"

"More like he got tired of me."

"Oh, honey. Is that why you didn't pick up the phone?"

"Sort of?"

"Then what's the rest of it?"

"I was in the hospital, Glory."

"For—for *eight days*?"

"Ten." I waited. "Glory?"

"What—what happened?"

"A bullet."

"Where?"

"High chest, right side. Played hell with my arm, but I'll be all right."

Her breath came tight through the receiver, otherwise I'd have thought she'd hung up. My throat ached, but I wouldn't beg for sympathy; that had been my deal from the start.

Finally she said, "Come here. Live with us. Ida can sleep with Sonny, and you can have the extra room. I won't lose you, too, Phyllis—Phyllis, if you had died, would anyone have even *told me*?"

"Dev would have," I said.

"You know I don't hold with what Tom thinks about your . . . talent, but sometimes I am mighty angry with the Lord for giving you and Roger that burden."

"This isn't like what happened to—"

"Roger got killed! A few inches to the left and that man you love would have knocked on my door with your ashes. Aren't you *tired*? Don't you want to stop . . . doing what you do? I know Tom and I can't offer you that downtown lifestyle, but we can offer love, honey, and safety, and Ida just adores you—"

"But poor Sonny," I said. My tears didn't show in my voice, I was almost sure. I had wanted this too badly to wish for it: my respectable Gloria, upending her whole life to save her prodigal sister.

"He'll come around. Will you? Please say yes."

Harlem felt a world away, but it was just a couple of miles. Maybe I'd had a chance before Maryann West shot me, but now nothing would make Victor let me go.

And nothing would ease my responsibility to wield my knives—one last time.

"I love you, Gloria. I love you more than anything. And if I make it out of this, I swear you won't have to worry about me again."

"Christ, sugar, make it out of what?"

"I'm in over my head. Maybe I always have been, and I just now noticed. But I'm going to see it through. Probably . . . better you not call me till it's over."

"And how will I know?"

I gave her Dev's number. And then, after a moment, Walter's.

After we hung up, I picked up my holster and played with the four-inch throwing knife—over my head, behind my back, and then into the wall behind me. I considered the advantages of my injury: I would look less dangerous than I was. I could kill with my left hand as easily as my right. I unsheathed the three-inch knife and threw it in the wall, next to the first. Two kills, sweet and clean. Do that one more time, and then walk away forever.

I wrenched the knives from the plaster. Some dust came after them and settled on the floor and the thick fringe of Turkish carpet. I didn't bother to clean it up.

7

I waited until that night. Dev didn't call or come by.

Hitler was invading the Soviet Union, had been for the past month, crossing its borders from the Baltic to the Black Sea with a flood of soldiers, hundreds and hundreds of thousands, so many that I couldn't make myself believe the numbers printed in the papers.

If Roosevelt had his way we'd be in the war the day after tomorrow.

Tamara called to check on me, and to update me on the latest gossip from the dentist's big show. I talked for longer than I should, gripped despite myself with a certain Schadenfreude at the image of the dentist earnestly standing beside his six paintings of show horses with anatomically correct smiles while the packed house thronged the Hungarian exile's sculptures of creeping death.

We argued about the war and never mentioned the men who might get killed in it. I caught myself staring at the delivery boy who brought by my paper in the morning, wondering if he'd get drafted, or volunteer, and if he'd make it out the other end. The delivery boy just held out his hand for a tip and skipped off.

The second time Tamara called, I gave in.

"Dev?" she repeated, and stopped short. "Well, I don't know that I've seen him today, sugar. I think he's tending the bar in a few hours, but you know that we've been giving one another a little more room these days."

"Did he ask you to?"

"Well," she drawled, with a certain acid knowing that made me pull the receiver away from my ear. "He disappeared, more like.

But I got his point. Is there something in particular you want him for?"

I knew Tamara always meant just what she said when she was that precise in her diction. I grimaced and changed the subject.

"How on earth did Marty get a showing at the Pelican in the first place?"

"Oh, you know, whatever Victor says, goes. I only get so much freedom over here."

"But what kind of favors could Vic owe his dentist?"

Tamara laughed after the briefest of pauses, which might have contained worry or surprise or just dead air. "Maybe he had a few tough extractions," she said.

I laughed with her, though I didn't much feel like it, and I doubted she did either. Dev wasn't around and Marty would enjoy the dubious benefits of Victor's favor, as long as it lasted. I could have told him, it never did. Tammy begged off the call a minute later, and I sat with myself for a little while. I always worked best alone.

I prepared myself: dark burgundy dress, a rack number from Macy's that I bought by the half dozen and didn't care if I had to throw out at the end of a night's work. Knife holster for three five-inch knives and two three-inch knives tucked away in my garters. Sometimes I brought more, but I wouldn't need them tonight. For this, I wouldn't need more than one, but I liked the feel of them too, and the illusion of protection that glittered in my peripheral vision when I moved with their weight through the world.

My hands twisted and ached like they wanted to send me another dream, but I knew they didn't; they were just furious and long ready for me to fulfill their true purpose. They had tried to tell me about the deception. When I'd killed Trent, I must have known—not in my head, or even in my heart, but in my muscles and bones, in the hands that had slaughtered, full knowing, an innocent man. They might yet forgive me for that, but they demanded recompense first, they demanded real justice. Kill Russian Vic, kill the white man who had stolen them and twisted them into this unnatural, deadly shape, and I might yet live to dream another true dream.

I passed Walter's man outside the door and nodded to him. Surprised, he nodded back. I wondered if he'd tail me, but he stayed on the building. Thoughtful of Walter. He wouldn't stop me, he'd said. But did I wish he would?

It felt different, this last time.

There had been an excitement before, an anticipation of glory that had counterbalanced the jittery fear of facing death. Even my last kill—some skinflint numbers banker down in Bed-Stuy, who had tried to buy me off for an amount I knew was half of his nightly take—had greeted me with that raw, fluttering edge of purpose before I sliced his throat. The edge was dull and rusted now, liable to poison my blood. I was scared, at last. Fifteen years too late, my guts twisted like flypaper at a July cookout. What had I thought my heart was made of, that it could kill and kill and stay whole? I'd stepped through that banker's steaming blood as though I were wiping my ass after a good shit, and I hadn't noticed until later the faint click of a door closing. If I wanted to kill again, I'd have to break my own self down.

The hands didn't care. The hands were decided.

On the corner of Christopher Street and Bleecker was an office building that had not bothered to tear down its out-of-code fire escape from its tenement days, a rusty ladder with short platforms beneath each window. Back when Victor bought the building someone had noted that a good shot might barely make the narrow angle from the top of the fire escape into the back office bathroom window. Victor's answer had been to board up the window; if you can't see, you can't shoot, he said. This had worked for so long that everyone seemed to have forgotten the reason the window was boarded in the first place; at least, the second to top slat had fallen to one side for months and no one had thought to repair it. The angle was nearly impossible. I had to hang from the top rung of the fire escape and wait for the precise moment when Victor finished his business, washed his hands, and leaned forward to check his hair in the mirror. When his head lined up with the missing slat, I'd throw. He'd be dead before he saw me.

It took longer to climb with one arm, and everything hurt by the time I got to the top. When I heard him in there, I'd have to climb down three rungs, hook my feet into the rusty bars, and throw. I waited. A half hour, an hour, a moon gone from fat and red against the silhouette of the West Side docks to high and bright above my head. I wondered if Dev had started his shift at the bar, and what he would think of me when he saw what I'd done. Would it count as a good deed in his ledger, just as my hands demanded it be? Or would it be yet another sin? My heart sure thought so—it turned to lead at the thought of another fucking corpse brought down to the floor by my butcher's blade, my idiot precision.

The bathroom door opened. Victor was speaking to someone, but I was too far away to make out the words, just his unmistakable cadence. I climbed down three rungs and locked my legs firmly against the metal. I'd be doing the world a favor to rid it of his open-ended questions. He took his sweet time on the pot. His long, wet farts echoed in the air between us. Around my growing terror I managed to think, well, at least I'm not close enough to smell it. Victor stood. I unwrapped my good arm from the ladder and hung there, supported by nothing more than good stomach muscles and practice. He washed his hands in front of the mirror. He moved in and out of sight, but not long enough for even my hands to land the throw. For a delirious moment, I thought he'd just leave. I thought I'd missed my chance. But he paused and leaned forward. He opened his mouth and I realized—he was flicking his nail against his silver teeth. I couldn't imagine why, but I shuddered anyway.

I lifted my favorite three-inch knife and readied the throw.

It was a tricky shot, but easy enough for me, with all my uncanny force behind it. A second passed. Two seconds. My hands chanted, *Ready, now, ready, now.* I smelled a hot wind, burning flesh, algae rotting on a distant sea. It was their breath against my ear, their fury, their thirst to make things right after all the wrong I had done.

But I couldn't, I couldn't, not even Victor.

For years, you have wasted us, betrayed us and twisted our purpose.

I drew back my arm.

Ready, now, ready—

Victor looked up; the hands howled; I dropped the knife.

I scrambled back down the fire escape. Jumped rungs, slipped against the next, swung my left arm up blindly, banged my right arm so hard that I whimpered. Feet safe on the alley floor, thank the Lord. I bent down to retrieve the knife that had fallen and clattered like gunfire on the cobbles. A block away, Victor was screaming. No words, just needling rage. His men would search this alley in a second. Carefully, I removed my sling and my holster, shoved them under a light coat I'd stashed behind a dumpster and walked onto Christopher Street, away from the Pelican. Behind me, men were running.

I didn't think Victor had seen *me*, but he'd certainly seen something. Those stolen hands of his, those shiny teeth, what did they tell him about betrayal? How soon would he know what I had been unable to do?

My guard was gone by the time I got back to my apartment building. I wondered if Victor had recalled all of his men on duty. I wondered how long before he heard that I hadn't even tried to get an alibi. *You should get out of town, Phyllis,* I thought, I did think it, but instead I went back up to my apartment and fell asleep on the chaise lounge, beside a silent telephone.

The dream came back, rushing in like water from a broken faucet. Me in that white dress, two hands in the holster instead of knives, and Victor in front of me shining like a chrome hubcap. "You killed those men," said a voice that used to belong to someone, but had doubled and tripled and repeated into a chorus who were the hands, pointing at me.

I woke up wrists aching, thirsty, blinking in a bright shaft of light from a high, gibbous moon. The light was snuffed and then resumed;

someone, I understood groggily, had passed the window. Tamara, I thought, until she crossed the Turkish carpet and I recognized her.

I had thought, naïvely, that having shot me once, Maryann West might just leave me alone.

She reeked of grain alcohol and subway muck, but her clothes were damp and her face scrubbed nearly clean, like she'd taken a dip in a fountain before coming to finish what she started. She held a gun, of course. I pictured my knives where I had left them, in their holster slung over the back of a chair three useless feet to my left.

"Raise your hands," she said. A child had drawn the bags under her eyes in eggplant-colored crayon, frown lines radiated from her mouth in charcoal gray.

I didn't move. It would take me four seconds to lunge for a knife and throw it. I had a good chance—a better one, at least, than I had point-blank from a raw barrel and a shaky trigger finger. But I just met her moonlit eyes and shrugged. If she hadn't killed me yet, she would wait a little while longer.

"You whore, raise your goddamned—"

"How are you here?"

The gun jerked. I thought of Dev—a hard, final grenade full of the shrapnel of lost years—but she didn't shoot. She said, "The door was open. And I got to wondering what on earth you wanted to ask me back there. Someone like you."

I must have forgotten to lock when I stumbled back here. Such a stupid reason to die, but maybe that was always what caught us in the end. We drugged ourselves with illusions of competence, until fallibility laughed, and knocked us off.

"I'm not going to kill you," I said.

"Because I've got the gun."

Four seconds. Better odds if her finger eased off that trigger. Shock might do it, or sympathy. Not much of the latter going around these days, so I tried instead, "Victor told me that Trent Sullivan had murdered some people for their hands—people like me. That's why I killed him. But I had wanted to ask you if Victor had lied."

The woman radiated outrage. "He said *my Trent* killed—"

It took three seconds, and hurt just as much as I thought it would. I rolled from the chaise, pulled down my holster, unsheathed a knife, and threw. It slid into her right shoulder. The gun discharged and then rattled to the floor while she clutched at the hilt.

"I wouldn't take that out," I said, panting.

She cursed and stumbled forward. "Trent saved your life. That's what I want you to know."

"Saved my life? What, he put in a good word for me? Do you know how many people died because Trent fingered them?"

She wrinkled her nose, as though it had been impolite of me to mention it. "At least they didn't feel a thing. I can promise you that. Unlike my Trent."

Maryann West reached for the gun in spite of her own blood soaking into the carpet. I lunged and pushed her back against the door. Her heart labored against my breastbone. Even with one arm, even without a knife, oh Christ, she would be so easy. One hard snap and I wouldn't have to worry about her nasty habit of trying to kill me. I tried to keep my home clean, but her blood already stained my best carpet. I could make an exception.

"Go," I said. "I won't kill you but Victor will. So save yourself and go."

"I haven't slept a night through since what you did to Trent. You ruined my life."

We were pressed close as lovers, her blood soaking my shirt, spittle wet on my face. "I'm *sorry*."

"Not yet, you're not."

She left. I knew why I hadn't killed her, but the enormity of it pushed me to my knees. I stared at the open door.

I didn't know how Maryann West planned to hurt me next, but I was sure she'd try. I couldn't blame her, I couldn't kill her, I could hardly defend myself. I had murdered an innocent man. My sins had turned my hands.

"Pea?"

Dev in the open doorway. Dev, locking it behind him before coming to where I sat on the floor. He fingered the spilled intestines of cotton fluff from the bullet hole in my chaise. His forehead shone with sweat, gathered in the furrowed skin of his frown. I touched his eyebrows, willing it away. I'd thought I was going to die ten minutes ago, and now Dev looked at me like he could swallow me up. I realized I was very tired.

"What happened?" he whispered.

"Maryann West."

"The blood . . ."

"Hers."

"But she's not dead?"

"I'm going soft, Dev," I said. "I couldn't."

I watched him realize. "Oh, Pea. It was you, then? The attempt on Victor?"

I laughed and laughed. "What attempt? I told you, I'm soft. I can't do it anymore. Even though they want me to, this time. My—I don't know—my heart?" I gulped for air. "It feels like it's cracking apart, every time I lift the knife . . ."

He held me until I stopped crying. He pulled back. "Can you stand? There's no one after you right now. Victor is rampaging but I think he'll go through quite a number of his men before he gets to you. He didn't see you."

Against my better judgment, I relaxed at that.

"How are you here?" I asked a second apparition, for the second time that night.

He blinked and rested his hand against my collarbone, so his thumb jumped with my racing pulse. "I—had a feeling," he said, haltingly, "that someone far away was thinking of me, and that they were dying, and that they had loved me for a very long time . . ."

"So you came straight here, huh?" I couldn't meet his eyes.

He smiled, with all the tenderness that only Dev could find, and kissed me. "Pea," he said, after long minutes, "you don't understand—"

But I did, enough. "Take me to bed, Devajyoti."

8

I had nearly died twice, and the second time seemed to shake loose the last of the mortar from his defenses. Dev loved me, or something like it. He slept in my bed and joy kept me awake until exhaustion bludgeoned its way through at dawn. When I woke, the sun shone noon through the windows and he stared, unseeing, at a paper in his hands.

"What is it?" I asked.

"Maryann West is dead."

I started to laugh.

"Arsenic," he said.

I stopped laughing. "You're serious."

The light gilded his sable eyelashes and the peppery stubble on his cheeks. He'd dressed, but hastily, and though I supposed Dev would always look beautiful to me, today he cast a ragged, over-drawn shadow. I sat up and stretched in the tangled sheets, and the detritus of my old life eddied beneath me, flaking already to dust. Dev cast a glance at my naked breasts, dark nipples contracting in the warmth of the sun and his presence, and shook his head with a wondering smile.

"I need to go to the precinct. She was poisoned, of course."

"Victor likes arsenic."

"When he doesn't like you," he said, and I flinched. Then, "I know. I'm sorry. This is . . . nothing is what I thought it would be. You're not what I thought you would be. But I look back on myself then and all I can think is how foolish I was."

"You were young," I said. Like Adam, I felt my nakedness now.

"I was. Yet old enough." I had five years on him, which meant Dev had been twenty when he played his pipes and took me from the city. Only youth could be that brave, or that stupid.

"I wanted you to be right about me."

"I did too, Pea."

"And now?" I started shivering.

He turned from the window and sat heavily on the edge of my bed. "The trouble," he said, "is that I wasn't right about *me*. I had no business judging you then, and I certainly don't now. All that's left for me is to atone—"

He stopped himself and took my hand. He smiled, painfully but genuinely, and rested his head on my lap.

"Pea, I won't leave you unless you want me to. It's too late."

I couldn't tell if happiness or resignation thickened his voice, but for now I didn't care. I buried my fingers in his hair. We stayed in that layered, familiar silence until his breathing eased and I could think, *He'll stay, at least a little while.* My eyes fell on that slip of paper, resting on the sill, the one that had told him of Maryann West's death.

"What I don't understand," I said, "is why Victor would poison that woman when he went through so much trouble to make sure I'd have the kill."

"He didn't have a choice," Dev said. "Maryann turned herself in to the police last night. Just after she visited you, I'd guess."

"The *police*?"

"She wanted to confess, she said. She had dirt on Victor, she said. Someone brought her to an interrogation room and an hour later she was dead. Arsenic in her coffee. One of the men on vice squad must be in Victor's pay. Valentine will have our heads for this."

"Dirt on Victor," I repeated, bemused. "Last night, she said something strange. She said that the ones with the hands that Trent had spotted for Victor, she said that we didn't die in pain, she could promise me that. How would she know that? How is that even possible?"

For a brief moment, as soon seen as gone, Dev looked haunted with pain. "It isn't," he said shortly. "But since she was the one selling nitrous oxide and devil knows what else to Victor for a decade, which he used on those he killed, I presume that's what let her sleep at night."

"But she didn't sleep," I said softly. "Not since I killed her man. She was working for Victor too? All this time?"

He shook his head. "She stopped a few years ago. Got caught stealing at her job—got fired. She was a dental assistant."

"Dental assistant? They see that many narcotics?"

He shrugged. "Dirty secret of the profession."

"Did she tell them—you—anything important?" I was thinking of her strange smile and her hint of revenge.

"I don't know," he said. "That's why I have to get there. And Pea, depending on what she said . . ."

He looked sadly at me and I understood. If she had given the police enough information about Trent's murder, I would have to run. After last night, I could no longer count on Victor's protection.

And besides, "I have to try again," I said, as though I were swallowing medicine. "I can't leave town with him still in it."

Dev closed his eyes briefly. "And your heart?" he said lightly.

"Oh, that old thing? Let it break. It hasn't been any good to me for a decade."

His hands curled to fists on the mattress.

Some strange fear entered me, then, whether for him or for myself, I couldn't tell. "What's the matter, Dev?" I whispered.

The taut anger left him as quickly as it had come. He shrugged in self-reproach and levered himself from the bed. "I'll call you as soon as I learn anything. Lock the door this time, yeah?"

I stood. His tie wedged under my right breast and my knee slid along the smooth wool of his pants as we kissed. Then I gave him his hat and he gave me a sad half smile before we said goodbye.

Tamara came by a few hours later, just banged on the locked door until I woke up from my nap and opened it without checking the peephole. Her makeup had smudged into coon eyes and she wore a slip dress that she must not have had time to change from the night before.

"Well, at least she's still alive!" she said, and then froze when she saw my carpet. "Is that . . . a bloodstain, Pea?"

"Nah," I said, "just grenadine."

I closed the door behind her and led her to the kitchen, which as far as I remembered bore no grisly reminders of my profession. Ex-profession.

"Phyllis! What is going on around here? You won't answer my calls, neither will Dev, you've got a . . . stain on your carpet and to take the cake, last night someone tried to knock off Victor! He's got the whole place locked down like the Federal Reserve, you should see him, laying hands on people and flicking his teeth and scaring the bejeezus out of everyone. He punched a hole in one of poor Marty's paintings! I swear he made the man cry. I barely got out this morning."

"Tried to kill him?" I said slowly. "Pity they didn't finish the job."

Tammy's eyes widened. "Hush your mouth! I don't like the man any more than you do, but we don't get the Pelican without Victor. And besides, he's got some weird juju, Pea. I don't buy what he's selling about the hands, but I swear he can tell when you take his name in vain."

I rolled my eyes. "Victor sure ain't the Lord."

"Course not. But he might be the devil."

"You dance for him."

"And *you* kill for him."

I put my head down on the cool Formica of my table and felt each laugh as it bubbled up and burst and hurt.

She knelt down next to me. "Pea, sugar, I'm sorry. Don't listen to me, I haven't gotten any sleep."

"Did Victor mention me?"

"He just asked me where you were. I said you just got out of the hospital, where did he think you'd be? And Pea . . . you *were* here, right? You're in no condition to go climbing fire escapes, right?"

"Of course not, Tammy," I said, and we left it at that.

She pulled out her playing deck and started shuffling, a soft flapping of moth's wings while I waited for what the numbers might tell me. She laid the cards down fast, one after another, five rows of ten, plus two at the top and two at the bottom.

"Pick two," she said. It was her other voice, resonant as a wide bell: she was the oracle now, a role I was never quite sure if she put on like her grass skirt or if it was visited upon her, like my hands.

I raised my head. My fingers tingled as they passed above the faceless deck. I let them fall and then again.

"Angel joker and seven of spades," she said, turning them over. Whatever that meant, I didn't know. She just nodded and gestured at me: pick two more.

"Three of hearts and eight of spades, reversed," she intoned. My skin prickled and my hand in the sling spasmed with a force I felt clear to my shoulder. A small sound escaped me, but the oracle didn't seem to notice.

I picked again. King of hearts. The second card I never saw because my left hand spasmed as it lifted it from the others and crushed it between fingers that no longer belonged to me. It was like a dream again, but come down during the day as a waking nightmare. I gasped and Tammy broke from whatever trance had been holding her. She pried the crumpled card from my grip and let me hold her until the force went away.

"It's the hands," I gasped. "They want something from me. They're angry with me. They're going to keep at me until they kill me, Tammy, I know it. That's why I've got to—"

"Why you've got to what, Phyllis?"

But I stopped there and she let me. Tammy had a knack for knowing what she didn't want to know.

Dev came back, at last, when it was nearly morning. I had notched the passing of the moon with memories of my kills, until its light fell on me in ribbons.

Little Ray Barry, my first, who had put a bullet through my

baby brother's left lung and left him to die; Sally Moore, a Hell's Kitchen madam who had beat one of her youngest girls to death for not wanting to go with a client; William—had I ever known his last name?—an Irish Catholic priest who I now suspected had owed Victor some money but at the time I'd believed that he blackmailed his parishioners for sexual favors. And for all I knew, he had.

And more, rotten dozens more, who greeted me like old high-school friends: half-forgotten, faces bloated and disfigured with time, some names forgotten and some names painful to the touch. I had killed them all. My hands throbbed with each memory and I wondered if I could trust them any longer. What I had always distantly feared turned out to be true: the power behind my hands had only ever been lent to me, and the lender had come to call in his bill. Maybe they could just wander off on their own, I thought, and do Victor for me, while I lay here in a bed of my regrets.

I had reached number thirty-nine—a Bowery hooker who killed her johns, and once again I wondered—when I heard the lock turn and Dev's tired footsteps in the foyer.

"You don't have a key," I said when he paused and watched me from the doorway.

He smiled and shrugged. "Did I wake you?"

"Been keeping the man in the moon company. You know in Mexico they say it's a rabbit?"

He sat down on the edge of the bed and ran his thumb across my forehead. "So do we, in India. Imagine that, some ten thousand miles apart, and we both still see the same humble rabbit wrapped in smoke."

I leaned my head into his hand. He smelled of cigarettes, stale coffee, cold stress; the lines around his mouth seemed to have deepened overnight. He was so tired he could barely sit upright, and yet still he looked at me.

"Vic is calling in everyone for a chat. His phrasing. He lights a candle and calls on Lucifer and then puts his hands on your head and chants. Says he'll catch the traitor that way, and at the very least, he's got all the soldiers and lieutenants shitting themselves. Everyone has their little secrets."

I smiled up at him, warm as a July afternoon, and he bent down to kiss me between my eyes.

"How long have I got?"

"He doesn't quite suspect you yet. I'd give it a few more days."

"And when he lays his hands on me? Will he know?"

I remembered how Vic had turned at just the moment I ought to have thrown. I hadn't made a sound; I was a professional, after all.

"Two more bodies showed up this morning. Missing hands." He couldn't get any more out.

I closed my eyes and pulled him down to me, until his head lay on my chest and his hair tickled my chin.

"I have to try again," I whispered.

His chest shook with a sob. "Couldn't you just let Walter kill him?"

"He won't. A debt, he says. The best he can do is not to stop me." He sighed.

"What, you're not even going to try to beg me to go to the police?"

"Too late for that. Besides, most cops aren't . . . Some days it seems like they're just the other side of the same damned coin."

"Valentine wouldn't like to hear you say that. He's cleaned the force right up, he says."

"Valentine's . . . a good man, from what I can tell. But political ambitions cloud one's vision."

I wondered at the stories behind that bleak sentiment, so different from the idealistic determination that had taken me away from the city back then. A wave of vertigo rolled through me, a dizzying awareness of how little we knew about the everyday business of each other's lives. And now we were going to run away? Live together? Gloria would call me ten kinds of fool for thinking it was possible, and maybe she was right.

And yet—I pressed my cheek into the crown of his head and held him so tight it hurt. Just like ten years ago, I swelled so full with love there was nowhere to displace it. I could only sit inside its permeable borders, scared and hopeful.

My voice shook. "I had a second dream, Dev. And now it's chasing me. Every time Tammy reads the cards for me, they come up all knives and broken hearts. The hands won't let me turn from this—from him. I'm the one with all those bodies on my back."

"So what's one more, you mean?"

"This one I'll take," I said. "I craved it, you know—the killing. Like dope. A hit of justice. But there's no such thing, he took that illusion away from me, though Lord knows you tried, and now even real justice feels like—even Victor is still a person. A creation unique and irreplaceable, remember when you said that?"

He kicked off his pants and slid slowly up my body until we were nose to nose on the pillow. "We were on the water, the Hoboken ferry at sunset, wasn't it? A regular date, like two civilians." He laughed. "And I came out with that? No wonder you left me."

Regret, with its unmistakable stink, spilled between us.

"Can you do it?" he asked.

"I have to," I said, which was not a yes, which we both knew.

"When it's done," Dev said carefully, "we have to leave. That's my news from the precinct. The knife you left in Maryann West matched the wounds of two unsolved murders. My friends on the job promise no one will look very hard, but it has to be soon."

Shock kept me still. I should have realized—but what else could I have done? Pulled the knife from her shoulder? She would have bled out on my stairwell. "You must have good dirt on someone," I said.

"I suppose I do, but that's not why. Or not mostly. Victor didn't always lie to you, Pea. The two they've matched to you, one was a petty dope dealer and the other a corrupt prison guard. No one was terribly sad to see them go."

Somehow, the fact that my justice hadn't always been a lie made me angrier. "Doesn't that take the cake. And you won't miss it? Your thrilling double life?"

Something grim shuttered his eyes; he busied himself unbuttoning his shirt. "No. If we can make it out of this city, Pea, I'll make it up to you, as much as I can."

I pulled him down gently and ran my fingers over the soft hair on his naked chest. His breath came short.

"Is it possible," I said, "that you are assuming blame for sins that have never been and could never be yours?"

He groaned. I slid my hand lower. His muscles trembled against my palm. "I never told you!"

I waited. My heart pounded in my ears, but the pulse by his temple jumped faster.

"I assumed you knew how Victor used you. The way he lied and stretched the truth. I assumed that you only pretended to care about justice. And I should never have assumed it, Pea, because I know you, better than anyone. And I decided that you were worse than my dreams of you, because that made it easier to live as I did. And now I know—what it has done to you, while I thought I was somehow better, or purer, or more enlightened. I let you have that sin, that bad karma, when it was *mine*—forgive—try—please—"

He broke against me. And I held him hard and I forgave him without reservation.

9

Dev left early the next morning. I resolved to finish this business, one way or another, before he returned. If this killed me, well, wasn't that all I deserved?

I would not consider how Dev would take it.

I found Walter in the basement of the Pelican, where they stored the legal liquor along with linens, extra furniture, cleaning supplies, and whatever odds no one knew what to do with. Victor never dirtied his oxfords on the basement steps, but Walter did on Fridays, when a delivery was due.

"Is that the last of it, Jack?" he called when my shadow fell across the dim room.

"Jack's having a smoke with the boys," I said. "We need to talk."

Walter turned around slowly, like he thought I might have a gun. He squinted at me, and then nodded. "Close the door," he said.

By the time I did that and came down the stairs again, he'd made himself comfortable on a backward-facing bar chair. I kept to my feet; even seated he had a way of imposing his physicality, and I'd rather look wary than cowed.

"What brings you here, Phyllis?" His tone was even, careful, and yet some curiosity still seeped through. His eyes flicked to my hand, hovering over the slit in my dress that gave me access to the knife holstered on my thigh. I should have been more wary of trusting Walter, who they called Red Man for more than one reason, but some other, wayward impulse had only ever been able to see him as a friend. "Victor will know you're here by now. He'll be wanting to speak with you."

"Lay hands on me, you mean. Two more bodies as of this morning. No wonder there's so few of us left in the city these days."

He shrugged. "Victor's angel isn't usually that sloppy."

I flexed my good hand against my thigh. "This time she won't be," I said, and prayed it was true.

Walter just watched me.

"The part I can't figure out," I said, "is why now? Why bother poor Maryann when she'd kept quiet for all those years? And what I guess is that it has something to do with that dead man in that file you gave me, the one with missing hands who you tried to pin on Maryann. He died, and something changed—but for the life of me, I can't figure out what. So I thought I'd come and ask you."

"You never told Victor," he said, "that there was a witness the night you offed Trent."

I paused, trying to determine if that was recrimination, or just observation. "Didn't come up," I said, finally.

Walter's mouth twitched. "And Trent had kept quiet about his new squeeze. Didn't occur to Victor that someone else might know what happened that night. Let alone that the witness might be one of his own pharmaceutical suppliers. But then that man—lost his hands, let's say. They could take away pain with a touch. Not just physical pain. Couldn't heal you, but those hands made it better for a while. It turned out that Trent had been keeping him on a private payroll, so to speak. He'd give the man food and money, and in exchange Trent would get his troubles washed away. I guess after her man's death, Maryann needed what was in those hands even more. She kept our friend up in the same way. So when he turned up dead they found her number in his back pocket. One of the precinct cops who went to the interview remembered her from Trent's stoolie days and made the connection."

"And that's how Victor found out what she saw? One of his own boys on the job?" I whistled.

"I suspect vice squad already knew. But they kept it quiet for their own reasons. The precinct had never been able to connect the missing hand murders to Victor before."

"So, Maryann West connects them, and now she's cooling her heels at the medical examiner's office."

"Did Dev learn that from his cop friends?"

I flinched and then tried to pass it off with a rough jerk of my injured arm, but Walter just waited.

"I have no idea how Dev found out. He has his sources, you know that."

Walter's eyes crinkled when he smiled. "You aren't a great liar, Phyllis. Your boy has been working both sides for a long time now."

And so I found myself neatly, masterfully and yet fondly, out-classed: Walter knew precisely how much I would sacrifice to keep Dev safe. I considered the utility of denial. I considered pell-mell escape, out the back door and into a safe house with Dev. I could come back to finish Victor later. But once my shock receded, the obvious conclusions asserted themselves: Dev would not still be alive, and Walter would not be telling me extraordinary truths in a basement with no witnesses, if he wanted to use the information to hurt us. But he wanted something from me.

"How did you know?" I said.

"Oh, I know almost everything around here. Victor knows what I tell him—those hands of his only work so well. Better to keep your eyes open, I told him that when he first got a taste for that sort of back-door spiritualism. But Vic—" Walter started to say something else and then laughed. The look in his wide eyes made me shiver, and not for myself.

The door above me opened, letting in a bolus of humid air that damped my skin with the scent of baked concrete. Dev's voice called, "Pea, are you down there?"

I gave Walter a wild look, my knife halfway from its holster. "Come on down," he called. "Your girl's about to pin me with one of those knives of hers, but you've always been a calming influence."

"Dev, what the hell are you doing here?"

He raised his eyebrows and jumped lightly from the middle step. "I'm sure we both have very good explanations. Maybe we could talk upstairs?"

He wasn't so crude as to look at Walter, but I caught his implication and sighed. "Don't bother. He already knows."

Dev jerked in surprise. "Well," he said. "Well, fuck. I hope Victor doesn't?"

Walter smiled in that strange way again. "I reckon he doesn't. Not unless he got very lucky with his latest trophies. Diminishing returns. The hands don't work like they used to. But Dev, you and I both know you won't be here much longer anyway."

Dev made to put his arm around me, then shook his head and dropped it back to his side. You can wish to be the kind of woman who frightens the world, and still wish to be the kind who can take comfort in her man's protection.

I took one step away from him.

"Don't make her do this," Dev said.

Walter shook his head. "You've never been able to stop her before. She's marked for it. You aren't, Dev, I don't care what your police trained you for, or even what your hands have brought you. Let Phyllis finish this business, and get out once and for all. Both of you."

Dev stared at him, jaw working. Walter's eyes were compassionate but implacable. He was right. He had toiled in Victor's shadow for a very long time. He had given cover to evil that, even now, I did not think he countenanced. He would be better at this job, with his artist's eye and crackling smarts, than Victor had ever been with other people's hands. Some twisted honor had never let Walter steal that prize himself. He'd had to wait for me, the only other killer with a will and a chance of succeeding.

"You're an artist, Walter Finch," I said.

Some kind of light, or understanding, filled the shadows between us. He bowed his head. "So are you, Phyllis Green."

The interior of the Pelican was mottled with natural light, dim in some corners and fiercely bright in strips where the sun came through the open doors. In an effort to keep the temperature bearable, heavy industrial fans circulated the air inside, but still the men had discarded their jackets and ties. The dentist looked so casual smoking in his rolled shirtsleeves with the boys at the bar that at first I didn't recognize him. I knew that he was occasionally convivial with Victor, but it surprised me, somehow, to see the local boys sharing their break with him.

"Red Man," he said, "we brought the last of it inside, but they said you were busy down there."

My old lover glanced at me and then awkwardly away. It unsteadied me to see him again, though I hadn't spared him much thought in the last week. It pricked my vanity, if not my heart, that he had left me so cleanly.

"Did you bring enough nitrous oxide this time?" Walter asked.

The dentist gave me another nervous glance. "Just what Victor asked."

"Oh," I said. Of course.

After Maryann West was fired from her job, Victor would have needed another supplier, someone with unfettered access to regulated pharmaceuticals. The dentist looked at home with the soldiers because he'd always been one of them.

Had he known what it meant, when I told him about my dream with the hands? Or did he just give the drugs to Victor and make sure to never ask questions? Tamara had known, I realized—her strange little joke about "difficult extractions." And here I had imagined that Tamara had kept herself ignorant of the ugly underbelly of her high water bird.

Victor had been sitting in the shadows beside the false bookshelf. He stood up now and waved me over.

"Good to see you out of bed, angel," he said. "I suppose you're feeling . . . ?"

"Like shit," I called amiably, and squeezed Dev's hand hard enough to crack the knuckles. "Get out," I whispered, and left him before he could respond.

Victor looked me over, messy hair to scuffed shoes, and said, "Well, can't say it doesn't show. To be expected, right, after a bullet in the chest. I expect you heard that we've got a rat among us? That some ungrateful rat tried to kill *me*? They'll regret it, I promise you. I know you were in bed all day, right, but let's just make sure. Put that knife of yours on the table there and come back to my office."

I put the knife on the table and then let Jack pat me down for any others. There weren't any. I'd only brought that one because I'd figured it would look strange if I came unarmed. Victor smiled that chrome smile and flicked an incisor with his fingernail.

"Well, then, come with me, angel. Won't take a . . ."

Lifetime, I thought, and followed him back.

Zero goes last.

Each silver tooth marked a pair of hands. A mouth full of death, in love with its own reflection.

A hard number. Two suicide kings fighting over blood and ash. A sword behind one and an axe behind the other. One has heart but the other has power—who will come out alive? Depends on how the luck is blowing. Hearts and diamonds, sugar, all that love and brute force.

He'd left a bowl of that soup on the desk. White dumplings shimmering with fat, plucked with his fingers from yellow broth. He ruminated on one while Jack closed the door behind us. He licked his fingers clean of the juice and then wiped them on a silk hankie, silver to match his tie.

"Just like my mother made them," Victor said. "The trick is in the mixture of the meat, pork and beef. Nice to see you back on your feet, Phyllis. Sadly, Maryann West won't be needing your services, but I've got a few others . . ." He smiled, and I had the hideous impression that I could see myself in his silver teeth.

You can't win, but I don't think this has been about winning for a long time now. These cards, they're talking about survival, and sometimes to survive, you've got to make a move. Even if it might kill you.

Recommendation: Play.

10

"I'm retiring, Victor."

My voice was wary, even as I scanned the room. The silver pen-knife at the edge of the desk was provocative but too obvious, and the metal was too soft to penetrate bone. The empty Russian candelabra was a better bet, if he gave me time to swing it. But I guessed that I had one chance, and so a throw would be safer. Bludgeon, then. One of those heavy glass tumblers by the sideboard would do nicely, if it struck on the bottom edge. And it would, if I threw it.

My hands had never felt stronger, more full of energy, of a sweet, heady singing.

Victor chuckled and shook his head. "This is Dev's influence, I'm guessing. You finally take him back and this is what I get?"

He stood, fished another dumpling from the broth, and popped it whole into his mouth. His cheeks bulged while he chewed; drops of pink juice gathered on the ashy hair of his mustache. He walked around the desk and over to the sidebar. As he passed I caught a whiff of something rich and gamy, like food but also like flesh. He played his game well, forcing an unbalanced move.

"Get me a fucking drink if you're going to keep yammering at me, Vic," I said. "I'd rather be back in bed, but I'll settle for bourbon."

Victor tsked. "Got a mouth on you, dollface. But sure, anything for my angel." He poured two generous shots, dropped in two lopsided spikes of ice, and walked back over to hand me one. His eyes were glassy, as though he'd been drinking all morning, but he didn't smell of liquor, he smelled of meat.

I stared at him, and the bottom dropped out. Only the most rigid control kept me from shaking. I would die, I knew it.

To kill him—to right the balance of my debt—I would have to tear myself apart and still, somehow, keep breathing.

Dev had kissed my knuckles that morning, each one separate, a saint's devotion.

I said, "I heard a funny thing this morning."

"You did?" Victor said. "A coincidence, Phyllis, since I've heard a lot of funny things about you lately, too. You left your place two nights ago, a couple of hours before that rat tried to kill me. And do you know, I just remembered—something fell in the alley before they got away. Clattered on the stones. A gun, right? But it didn't go off. And it sounded lighter than a gun, right? So what do you make of that?"

"Could have been a knife," I said blandly.

Victor crunched ice between his teeth. "Just what I thought, doll-face."

We stared at one another. I lifted the tumbler experimentally. It would do, but it would be a shame to waste such good bourbon.

"They found two more bodies missing hands this morning," I said. "Which is strange, since Maryann West was already dead."

Victor narrowed his eyes and gave me that small, hard smile that was his truest face. "Just some trash, a pair of gypsies no one'll miss. The police don't care, don't know why you do."

"I've got the hands too, Vic."

"And so you do, Phyllis. Which is strange, you know, because I have to tell you in my long experience with you people—let's be honest for a moment here and admit that it is extensive, right?—I can't say I've ever come across another white girl with the hands. Not that I'm complaining! Good to have one on staff, as it were. But you're an odd one, Phyllis LeBlanc. Singular, in so many ways."

I heard myself laughing.

So that's how he knew. How he'd always known, and kept me scrambling to hide myself. Most white folk didn't even believe in the hands. Figures that the one white man who did would decide to steal them. Like with the poor Barkley brothers, no crime was less interesting to the fine men of the New York Police Department than one acted upon a black or brown body.

"That funny?" he asked, and I lifted the tumbler, as though to toast him.

Someone pounded on the door. A soft grunt. It opened and Dev stumbled inside, sweating and wild-eyed.

"Dev? Where'd Jack get to?" Victor asked.

"Tied up," Dev said behind me. I felt that hot wind rise up. The hands told me precisely what they thought of me, and what it was my duty to finish. I, who had taken so many unnecessary lives, would finally execute their perfect justice. There was no more time. They would break me, or I would break myself. I lifted the tumbler and let it fly.

It should have hit Victor in the temple with enough force to drop a cow.

My aim was perfect. The hands did not fail me.

But Dev had rushed me the moment I drew my arm back. He slammed me to the ground just as my hand released. And so the tumbler spun out and shattered to powder against the wall, an inch above Victor's head.

I stayed on the floor, groaning. Dev had smashed into my bad shoulder. Deliberately, I knew.

When I managed to look up again, Dev was slamming Victor's head against the wall. Victor grabbed his gun, but the shot went wide, cracking the plaster above my head. Dev knocked the gun out of Victor's hand with his knee, then dragged him to the floor. I hauled myself to one elbow, then to my feet. I kicked the gun, at least, out of reach. My hands were oddly quiet; or perhaps that was merely my own heart, gasping for air. Dev had my five-inch knife, the one I'd left on the table back in the front room. Could I save him from what he'd so clearly determined to do? I could get the last tumbler from the sideboard. Hell, I could throw my shoe.

My hands spasmed. I watched the man I loved and the man I had resigned myself to murder struggling for their lives on the parquet floor, and I held myself still. I knew why Dev was doing this. And my heart, bruised and twisted but unexpectedly whole, decided to let him.

Victor shouted until he was hoarse for Red Man and Jack and Marty and anyone else. But he must have known as well as I did: no one would be here to save him. Dev lifted Victor's shoulders and slammed him with a wet crack on the corner of his desk.

"You bitch," Victor sobbed. There was blood and snot in his mustache; blood and spit dribbling from his torn lips. "You fucking bitch—"

Dev raised the knife and drove it straight into Victor's sternum. Victor screamed. He bucked against Dev, hitting him again and again across the face and chest; bruising blows made stronger with mortal terror. I knew that strength; I had stumbled away from my kills as soft as pounded meat more times than anyone still human should remember. And now I watched this violence happen to someone I loved, and I held still my hands, which could have stopped it, and did not.

It will be over soon, I told myself, because Victor and I, we are not good people.

Dev wrenched the knife from Victor's chest and brought it down again, a few inches to the right. Victor whined like a dog. He grabbed a fistful of Dev's hair with a flaccid, bloody hand and pulled down.

"Phyllis," he said, a rasp stripped of everything but hate, "I will haunt you for the rest of your life. You will never have a moment's peace. Dev, you will regret the day you ever met this nigger bitch and I'll—"

Dev wrenched out the knife one final time and slammed it—with a crying gasp—into Victor's temple. Victor slumped away from him, sodden and dead.

Dev didn't move. He knelt on his heels with his back to me, so still that I checked the rise and fall of his shoulders to make sure he breathed. I couldn't look at Victor's body; I couldn't stand my cold joy at his death, and my relief at not being his executioner.

My hands cramped once more with an awful, final pain, and then subsided.

Perhaps they were right; perhaps I had never been worthy of them.

I found my courage, held it in the hands I had betrayed and which had at last repudiated me, and knelt to face him.

"Let me take you home, Dev." *A small house, but you can see the river from the west windows and roses grow in the garden*—he had said that to me, the night we ran away.

A banked light flared in his eyes, and he seemed to see me for the first time. "Oh, Phyllis, how do you stand it?"

I pulled him to me, as close as I could with one arm. He smelled of a kill—blood and sweat and excrement—but still like himself beneath it all. We were both shaking.

"First," I said, "you wash off the blood."

THE VIEW
FROM
THE RIVER

Zero. A grifter pawning painted glass; a king of scorched desire. You like long-odd bets, don't you, sugar? Never happier than when you're struggling? And there's no struggle like being in love.

I went up to Hell's Kitchen. That time of summer it was a honeycomb of open windows and hard-baked asphalt and exposed tracks that merited its name. I was chasing another lead from another badly overheard conversation: *She's up on Galvin Ave., should be done in an hour.* None of those other conversations in the mob joint where I spent hungry nights had panned more than fool's gold. I went anyway. *That's what detective work is, Dev,* I told myself; diligence and boredom that snaps without warning, but never unexpectedly—and then you die, or get promoted.

I was thinking about that promotion. I was wiping sweat from my eyes. I was hungry and hungover because I only had enough money for food or alcohol—

—an angel in a blood-drenched evening gown staggered into the alley and vomited into a garbage bin.

"What are you?" I asked. I already knew. I was holding her around her waist while the last spasms passed through.

"A knife," she told me, and it snapped again, the way it would for the rest of my life. Because I would never really know.

A knife, an angel, a saint. Colored lips in a light-skinned face that parted to speak in tongues, in layers, in seconds and holy eternities.

The moment before I knew her and the moment when I loved her. Everything that she held in that pair of uncanny hands.

In my grandmother's temple, the goddess Kali wore a skirt of them. That's what I thought when we kissed later that night, that I could feel the ghostly brush of twenty living fingers. The hard press of a dozen dead hands stiff with rigor mortis against my erection. She asked me what I was thinking and if I hadn't known I loved her already, I would have known then, because I answered.

"A skirt of hands?" she said and laughed and shook her hips against mine. She had killed a man two hours before. I would fall in love with other women, but there would never be anyone else for me.

1

Whenever my mother writes, she asks after her roses. *Has the Angèle Pernet dodged the black spot this year? Did you try an application of vinegar in the spring, as your aunt suggested? Do send pictures, if you can, Dev.*

I send pictures, which I frame to avoid the curling watermelon vines. These sprawling, gloss-green cables lounge at the feet of my mother's prized hybrid tea roses like fat neighborhood dogs—pampered, entirely unaccountable. I avoid responding until summer is safely passed. I send a stark image of a bare frosted bush alongside an apologetic note.

I could refuse to photograph the roses my mother has not tended in over a decade. But she misses our American house, as she calls it, and she misses me. She has remarried a respectable white gentleman with whom she has borne properly white babies. Her half-Hindu son is now—to her new family and friends—an excess best forgotten. She did not forget me. Sometimes I thought the Angèle Pernet's persistent black spot was the only reason she remembered. And yet I considered refusing her requests.

I did not consider destroying the watermelon.

I did not consider photographing it.

I came to think of those strange yellow and purple globes as tea leaves and dowsing rods. I gave them minimal care. I stayed away from the River House for weeks at a time in the summer, just as a test. But they lived, year after year, and the fruit's yellow flesh was so sweet and fragrant it turned my stomach. I gave them to some neighborhood boys, who thanked me with wide eyes until their mothers called them back inside. Afterward, they refused to speak to me.

She'll come back, those vines told me. *You'll take her back. You still want her.*

I did, though for years I hated myself for it. Then I resigned myself to it. Then I killed a man so she wouldn't have to.

But she came back.

"We have aphids."

Pea's tracked garden mud into the kitchen again. Bits of leaf and straw stick out of the floating mass of hair that has changed, slowly but unmistakably, over the last month. A burn from two days ago peels on her shoulders. She frowns at the curling skin and smears dirt when she picks at it. It catches me, the sight of her. I have been sitting at the kitchen table, holding myself very still, trying not to remember. Then she walks inside and the avalanche falls. The stink of shit and his gamy dumpling soup. What he called her, the curse he laid on us, the ache in my wrist as I pushed her knife into his head—

"Dev?"

Pea touches me. The avalanche slows and settles. I look up at her brown eyes, wide and limpid as a cow's. She is still the most beautiful woman I've ever seen.

"Aphids," I repeat. She looks about to cry, and then wrestles it back down. A flashing truth, and when the glare fades all she leaves me is her curious smile.

"Tiny plant-killing monsters? Sucking the lifeblood from my tomatoes?"

"Oh, you mean the greenflies."

She raises an eyebrow. "Is that British?"

I smile. "Why not spray them?"

"With what, darling?"

She starts to lean against the table, so I intercept her muddy hands and bring them to my cheek. She winces, and then laughs. "I'm a mess, aren't I? Sorry, Dev. I did remember the boots this time."

"I was very proud of you." I reach and pluck a green corkscrew from her brown ones—a remnant of the sprawling snow pea vines she has been beating back from the damask roses. "I don't suppose vinegar would do anything?"

"You know, despite what your mother—"

"It's my aunt Rose, really—"

"—your appropriately named aunt believes, vinegar doesn't solve every gardening problem."

She kneels so her face is level with mine, and settles those lips in some hollow between my shoulder blade and neck, a perfect touch, quickly withdrawn.

"What should we do, then?" My voice is light. Sometimes she guesses how much that costs me.

A flush spreads from Pea's cheeks to her ears. Neither of us moves. We've tried to make love only once in the past month, and even then I had to stop. Everything we say echoes forward and backward, with meanings on the surface and layered in tight folds beneath. We hear them all, but our game is to pretend that we don't.

No—*my* game. It always has been, and now my hands reach for those worn-out cards even when I know I could play it differently. When I'm at last with the woman who doesn't need my tricks. Or not as many.

"Evaluate the situation," Pea says, softly. Dirt crumbles to my collar as she traces curving bone around my eye. "Seek advice. Assemble appropriate tools. Save the tomatoes."

"How is it you sound so dangerous even when proposing to save something?"

Pea's eyes get that hard look, one I used to associate with days in the Pelican. But her lips turn up and she laughs, false and knowing. "Because I was always proposing to save something, darling," she says, and strokes me, like a punch, on the cheek.

Killing eyes and killing hands. Only, those killing hands have spent the last three hours working the soil, and her eyes—

I lean in and kiss her, searching for truth and finding joy, complete and evanescent. The bloom is off the rose by the time she opens her eyes. A breath hollows out my chest.

"Let's go to town," she says, "to the general store. I can ask Mr. Craver."

Do I regret what I did for her? Taking that sin onto myself when she has so many others, so many kills? Should I blame her for it? Should I love her so much?

That n—r bitch—

I will hold Victor's ugly, dying words inside me for the rest of my life. But she might not.

"Dev?"

I wrap my arms around her and she opens against me. "If you think that old puritan has anything useful to say, of course. We will stop the greenflies."

"If you call them that, no one will have any idea what you're saying, Dev." Her words are muffled against my shoulder.

"Then translate, Pea."

I go to check the mailbox while Pea showers. I slide lightly down the steep gravel driveway. My father meant to surface it properly for the new Chrysler he had purchased the winter we moved. Then he died, and there was the end to all that. I stayed here with Mother until I went to college, then she moved to Devon and married the younger son of a peer. I became a naturalized citizen, instead.

A single letter sits in the box. Bright white, with a seal in the corner familiar to me from filing my draft card with the rest of the precinct. Back when I thought Victor could grease the wheels of any serious trouble. Back before I killed him.

I am steady and sharp as one of Pea's old knives when I leverage my thumb under the loose edge and rip along the seam. I have dreaded this for months, but I do not flinch. Our lives have taught us that much.

ORDER TO REPORT FOR INDUCTION

Following which arresting headline the president himself requests my presence at my local draft board at eight in the morning two weeks hence.

Perhaps they won't want me. My neighbors are still wary at the best of times, though they tended to tolerance for my mother's sake. Since Pea came it's been worse. Either one of us alone seems to occupy that liminal space between "acceptable" and "colored," but together we are unequivocally Not White.

We *are* unequivocally Not White, but one can get damned tired of it mattering. If they decide that I'm white enough to enlist—or if they ship me to one of the Negro units, like Tamara's boyfriend—then what will I do? Ignore them? Take my chances as a conscientious objector? Kill?

Might be it's like that first taste of whiskey: the more you drink, the sweeter it goes down.

I feel her searching for me before I hear her voice. A tug that starts in the web between my fingers and settles in my wrists. There's a scent to it as well, sweet almonds and tomato leaves, the smell of how she *feels* but not actually how she smells. Pea always speaks of the hands as though they were a separate entity, a spirit whom she no longer trusts. But I know that they are me, as much as any part of the meat of my body can be. I was ten when my dream came down, an ecstasy of holy voices raised in song, and of holy hands, soft as chrysanthemum petals, pushing me up and up to meet the godhead. My father sent me back to my grandmother's farm for the year. My grandmother told me that they were a gift, a tiny spark of divine Shiva bestowed upon me for selfless deeds in a past life. They were mine, she said, but they were mine to use well.

I have failed as thoroughly as possible the charge laid upon me. My karmic load cannot be expiated in this lifetime. What good could I do now equal to my decade of silence? To the stink and slip as another dying man cursed me, and I took it willingly, to spare my lover?

I fold the letter into thirds and stuff it into my pocket.

"There you are," she calls from the top of the hill. She slides on the gravel as she jogs down and laughs as she keeps her balance. "Any mail? More advice from Mother?"

"Neither." I lift her hand to kiss it. "You're clean."

"Dirt does wash off."

"Unlike—" I begin, and her smile doesn't slip, but still I sense her anticipation as I turn her out for the spin, "the greenflies on your tomatoes."

"You can clean anything if you try hard enough." She takes my elbow. We settle together into the silence that follows, a deepness strung with tension, perversely comforting. River Road is a half-hour walk, but we prefer that to the car.

The silence keeps for more than a mile, all the way to the abandoned Lutheran church on the edge of town. It held its last Sunday service on the eve of the Depression, shortly after my father's death. Now, only Craver seems to remember the cracked and falling stones of that old churchyard. Warped clapboard and blown-out glass is all that's left of the second-oldest German Lutheran church in the Hudson Valley. Craver showed me, once, the plot destined for his bones, at the foot of his parents' and grandparents' graves. All I can remember of it now is its austerity, two thin, lichen-crusted slabs that even then seemed cowed by the surrounding vegetation.

"They're going to build a hotel there," Pea says.

"You heard that?"

"Ellen told me."

I shrugged. "The Bobbys are always threatening the riverfront property on this side of town. Probably nothing will come of it."

"The Bobbys? You mean Mayor Bell?"

"And his son." I look away and start walking again. "Bobby Bell, the Junior and Senior. There's been a Bell in the River House since the Civil War."

Pea shakes her head. "You've never mentioned the son before."

"No." That would cut too close. She already knows about one of the deaths on my shoulders. No need to tell her of the other.

A deer buck and two does graze by the fence at the northern edge of the churchyard. The buck raises its head, heavy with late-summer antlers, when we pass. I feel the heat of its attention, smell the tender grass sweetness of its curiosity and the banked charcoal of its aggression. But I don't fear the skewering points of those antlers any more than Pea does. Not with her beside me. She pauses for a moment to meet its eyes and her look is pure Bleecker Street. The constellation of features that I would study from shadowed corners when she spoke to Victor or Walter, and that would scare me, and that I would love. A killer. I had known precisely what she was from the moment I saw her in that Hell's Kitchen alley. It was the blood, I know that now; not despite it, but because of it.

Pea turns from the buck and rubs her thumb across my forehead. I hadn't known I was frowning. She observes me, but we are as incomprehensible to one another as we are to those deer by the graveyard.

The distant report of a hunting rifle cracks our tableau. The buck and the does jump the rotting fence and vanish behind the church.

"Is it awful to hope that no one gets venison for dinner tonight?"

My laugh cracks the air as unexpectedly as that gun. "Only venison?"

"It's a sin to eat something so beautiful. Did you see his eyes?"

"So it's only beauty that arouses your pity?"

"Lucky for you! Don't make me lose all my vices. I might die from the shock."

"I'm using your zucchini for dinner."

"Are you? And what if I happened to find some steak on our way back?"

"I would watch you cook it with a great deal of disapproval."

"It wouldn't be home without it. Darling. Dev. You know I would give up meat tomorrow if you wanted—"

I put my finger to her lips, pull us back. "Not today?"

She closes her eyes. "Not all my vices."

"Nor mine."

It's never far away, the smell of blood. Beneath her skin, and beneath mine. Nothing is more beautiful than what spills out of us when we have nothing else left.

She twitches away from me. "What's that in your pocket?" The folded envelope has shifted on our walk, so that a corner of crisp white paper pokes out. I shrug and push it back down.

"A letter from the president," I say.

She laughs. "Tell him that whenever he's finished with Hitler, I could use some help with my aphids."

I cant a smile at her and walk ahead. I don't take her hand, because she would feel my pulse.

2

The general store of Little Easton is across the street from the Methodist church and next door to the bar. Which only partly accounts for Ben Craver's perpetual air of besieged half tolerance.

He regularly petitions the town council for the Lutheran church's restoration. The solidly Methodist council has always refused. Over the years, this ritual has drawn down his jowls and carved out his belly. It is of apparently small comfort that the Lutheran congregation in neighboring Hudson uniformly regards him as one of the Elect.

His company, never enlivening, has become a downright penance these last few months. He does not like Pea.

She stops for a cigarette in front of the porch. Not inside the store but technically on his property, a detail she knows perfectly well. I lean against the railing and wait for the battle to engage.

"Well, if it isn't little Davey." Craver pauses on the top step and wipes his hands on his apron.

Pea gives him a look from behind her wreath of smoke: a delicately raised eyebrow, a hard half smile. With her wide-brim hat and tailored sailor dress she looks just like what everyone in town says. A colored siren come to steal their men and their morals.

"Hiya, Mr. Craver," she says. Her voice is deeper. She's Phyllis again, Victor's angel. I don't always like that side of her, but I have always desired it.

Craver sniffs and the folds of skin beneath his jaw crumple in a chilly nod. "Miss Green. You might recall . . ."

He points to the sign prominently displayed above the open door: CORINTHIANS 6:19 NO CIGARETTES ALLOWED ON THE PREMISES.

"I ain't inside, now, am I?" Pea's Harlem drawl gets thick as molasses around Craver or any of the locals. I know why she does it. It still makes things harder for us.

"We'll come inside as soon as she's done, sir," I say.

Craver shakes his head. "Don't drop that thing on the grass. I'm trusting you, Davey."

He heads back inside. Craver was the first person in town to befriend me and my mother. If I can't make myself like him, I can't help but feel grateful to him. We wouldn't have survived those first few years without his generosity.

"Doesn't it bother you?"

I turn to her. "I had a cigarette at the house."

"No, Craver, that name he calls you."

"Davey?" I shrug. "My mother encouraged it. She said it helped them accept me."

Phyllis stubs out the cigarette on the railing, leaving an ash smudge that Craver will notice, and resent. I ignore it. She starts to say something, then shakes her head and slips the butt into my pocket with the letter. I wish the cigarette were still alight, to set the damned thing on fire.

Craver's store is large, navigable through narrow aisles packed so tightly that they feel in constant danger of collapse. He prides himself on his inventory, and despite his rocky relations with the town, no one would consider shopping anywhere else.

Phyllis interrogates a laconic Craver about the greenflies and I wander away. She can fight her own battles, that I always knew. I'm even beginning to hope that she can stop them.

As a child, these towering, mismatched shelves contained treasures that I tracked with the verve of a Robert Louis Stevenson hero. A clumsy one, it turned out. After I destroyed a purported Ming dynasty vase with a dowel, I found myself working as his assistant for a year. He refused to let my mother pay for it.

The tracery of these memories is never far when I visit Craver's, but today they feel tender and sore. I am haunted by my past self. There he is, squatting in the shadow of the cotton bolts. He's telling stories about how the good king has descended to the naraka and the brave Prince Devajyoti will make a bargain with Yama, the lord of that place, to get him out.

It takes me too long to recognize the thickness of that remembrance, the turpentine-and-sawdust scent of it. These feelings aren't entirely mine. A boy watches me from the same shadows that I used to fold around me. He is older than I was—fifteen or sixteen—and taller, but I recognize the guarded hostility.

"Hello," I say, gently.

"You're that fella who owns the rose house by the river, aren't you? You're Davey."

"Dev," I say, and think of Pea. "You must be the Spalding kid. Al, is it?"

"Alvin."

It's no shock that we know one another, though we've never met. Alvin's the only son of Little Easton's remaining Negro family. And my murky racial status has been fodder for the town gossip mill since we first moved to town.

"Pleased to meet you, Alvin." I extend my hand.

He just stares at it. "They say you're like me."

"I'm part Indian, actually."

"Your *hands*. They say you got the trick."

I've never heard that particular slang before. I stick my offending members in my pockets. "I've got *a* trick, sure. What's yours?"

He steps from the shadows. Though he seemed harmless before, even pitiable, I take a half step back. It's the way he smiles. Like a man with a gun in his pocket. I saw that too often in my detective years to not recognize it here. Belatedly, it occurs to me that he could be more like Pea than like me. The thought is terrifying.

"You wanna see? It's pretty special, but none of the eggs around here appreciate it."

He reaches for me slowly as he speaks, daring me to keep still. I step neatly aside. I don't know what knack he has in his hands, but this isn't how to find out.

"Chicken," he says. "And what can you do?"

"I can touch threats. I can tell if you want to hurt me, Alvin." Which he doesn't, I realize. But he was thinking about it.

I don't know what happened to the rest of Little Easton's black residents, but it wouldn't surprise me if the whites ran them out for just a hint of that uncanny extra Alvin and I shared. I recall what Victor had said to Pea, when he decided to drop the pretense that sustained their relationship for over a decade: *I can't say I've ever come across another white girl with the hands.* His greatest joke. In this, white people were stultifyingly predictable; if they could not steal it, they would kill it, but they would never, ever let a colored person have it.

White people in the city might not know or care about the hands, but Craver had always made sure that everybody in town knew what he had working for him in his store. I have no doubt the arrangement with Alvin is the same.

I hear Pea and Craver three aisles over, discussing nebulizers and spray attachments. I think of calling for her. I do think of it. But I lived ten years without her, and danger has surrounded me most of my life. Safety emasculates, I have discovered, far more than hazard, or pain. Safety makes me wonder where she goes for hours, even days at a time with no word. Safety makes me worry not for her, but for myself. Pea is my monster, big enough to scare off all the others. Most days, even the ones I invited myself.

"Alvin, come over here and make yourself useful, boy. The lady needs some sulfuric acid and one of the ten-pound compost bags from out back."

Alvin jerks at the sound of Craver's thin needle of a voice and pushes past me. I follow slowly. As soon as Pea sees me her expression flickers—a frown, lifted hopefully, mercilessly erased.

"A new assistant?" I ask Craver, once Alvin has thumped down the back steps.

He lifts his bony shoulders in a speaking shrug. "You know how it is, Davey. People in this town can be old-fashioned."

Craver doesn't even look at Pea. As if his reasons for cordially disliking her aren't every bit as hidebound. *Living in sin,* he has called it in my hearing, but it is Pea who bears the weight of disapproval. *Ever since Adam*, Pea said one night. *Woman, thy sin is beauty.*

That's not the line, is it?

She had kissed me gently. *Course not. A man wrote it, now, didn't he?*

"There's something strange about him," I say.

"I'm disappointed to hear that from you, Davey."

Pea leans against the shelf. "Now, why's that, Mr. Craver?"

"It's for Davey to tell you the story, not me, Miss Green."

I sigh. "The boy told me he has saint's hands."

"And our neighbors don't like that any more than they ever did."

Pea glances at me. "Is he? What sort of saint?"

"I don't"—Craver's self-righteousness snaps like a matador's cape in Pea's direction—"see how it matters."

Pea leans in. "Oh, the kid's done something, hasn't he?"

"His gift is a test from the Lord, one I'm ashamed to say most of the men—and women—in this town have failed to pass. If we have not sinned in the eyes of the Lord, we have nothing to fear from Alvin's—"

An unexpected thud bucks the floorboards. A porcelain elephant topples from a high shelf. Pea catches it without looking. Craver doesn't notice—the bag of compost has split in the fall, and Alvin stands like a conquistador above the mess and the stink. He looks too young to be so angry. Craver's wattle trembles. "Boy, what the—"

But the boy only has eyes for me. "Your worst secret, that's what I know." He takes a step forward, then another, tracking old manure and death across the paths of my childhood. "Just one little touch and I can tell you. And her."

My vision narrows to the boy's hands, as dark as my father's. Long, tapered fingers and bitten nails. Scars across his palms, ridged but neat and thin. Pea could tell me what kind of knife made those wounds, but I note the deliberation. He is going to touch me with those hands. He is going to know—everything—not even my father—

The smell of blood congealing with the dirt and the shit in the yard behind the goat pen. The sight of it, fresh spilled. A horror distilled through years of grief into something desirable, and so desired. The more I hated violence, the more its evidence attracted me. I killed Victor, and the memory of it makes me stiff and miserable at night in the bed I cannot share with Pea. I love her, even the parts I hate, *especially* those, and I have never told her. Even she couldn't forgive that.

A decade ago I met a woman covered in someone else's blood and she was my darkest fantasy come to life.

She steps in front of me, my beloved, now very far from fantasy. She pushes Alvin against the shelves.

He grunts. "I'll touch you!"

"Go ahead, kiddo. But if you touch him I'll break your hands."

"Now look here, Miss Green, there's no call to threaten the boy!"

Phyllis doesn't even hear him. She leans closer to Alvin, who gasps for air and shakes. His hands hover above her bare arms.

"You understand? Dev is off-limits."

He tries to spit in her face, but it just dribbles down his chin. Phyllis laughs, wipes it with the back of her hand. I should stop her. I am limp with relief. Alvin is as dangerous as Pea. Another monster.

There are tears tracking across the monster's cheeks. He touches Pea and gasps.

"You—"

Pea takes a step back. "You got me, kiddo?"

He just nods.

"Miss Green, I'm going to have to ask you to leave the premises! I have promised this boy's parents that I'll protect him, and I'm honor bound to do it!"

Pea turns to me and tilts her head in a silent question. "And didn't you promise Dev's mother that you would protect him?"

"Davey is a grown man, Miss Green, and Alvin is an innocent child with an important gift."

"We're leaving," she says to me softly. "It's going to be okay."

"Don't hurt him."

"It's you I—" She stops herself.

Alvin squats in the spilled fertilizer like he's forgotten how to stand. "Mother*fucker*," he swears, staring at Pea. "Who the hell are you?"

"As dangerous as you wish you were."

Even Craver has nothing to say. I follow her outside and take the offered cigarette without a word.

Three days later, Pea disappears.

She takes the car that morning into Hudson for gardening supplies, but the sun sets behind the river without a sign of her. In the swinging chair in the garden, alone among the greenflies and her watermelon, I contemplate my letter from the president.

It instructs me to report in ten days. I would rather kill myself than kill anyone else again.

Dev, I will haunt you—

The air is thick with the smells of things alive and dead. Fruiting plants redolent and desperate grow upon the casings and nutrient ash of last year's life. It isn't so unusual to feel the attraction of life's impossible struggle from its end. It could even be the root of all sexual desire. And yet I know I am a freak to feel it so particularly. It sickens me, the thought of what war might make of that.

There are ways of dealing with things like my letter. There are people I know, hiding secrets I can use. Not Walter, not after all we sacrificed to get out. He would expect an exchange of services. And if Pea learned what I'd done, she'd go back just to save me. Maybe Finn, my former reporting officer. It's been years, but we have history. He might help.

It starts to rain. Fat drops splash the page. The noise of tiny drums. I'm tempted to let them destroy it, but my hands re-fold the damp sheet and tuck it in my vest pocket. I worry about Pea, driving alone, at night, in the rain. But she might not be alone.

Rain beats on the water at the bottom of the hill. And then, the fainter sound of distant thunder. I look toward the house: dark windows, closed doors, gutters choked and overrun. I am good at solitude. I have made myself develop the talent. But it feels different now. Closer. A cold kiss of a gun against my ribs, a soft suggestion. I never deserved her. She never knew me. And she leaves another hollow space, another windy tunnel that howls to me in Victor's voice—*I'll haunt you*—every time, every time she goes.

I am alone. And then I'm not. Curiosity dances down my arms like a chill. Someone else's intense, focused curiosity. Not Pea. Whatever else I sense from her presence, the love is always unmistakable. This person wants to use me. A familiar sensation, but one I haven't felt for months. That old sense of danger pricks me, and I come awake.

The rain feels fresher, colder.

I forget about Pea.

The boy from Craver's store watches me from the unlatched kitchen window. I walk back quickly because of the rain, as if I have no awareness of him. In the vestibule I take my time with my coat and shoes, focusing on his attention and what I can learn from it. When I'm ready, I flip the light. He doesn't have time to hide, only crouches behind a chair as if it might provide protection. From me, I suppose it does. But I'm not the one he's afraid of.

"Pea's not here," I say. "Which makes you lucky."

Alvin stands slowly. He's wearing overalls like he had in the store, but they're stained dark across the chest. He drips greasy water onto the kitchen tiles. His hands are bruised. A lump squats below his right temple. I wonder what happened to Craver's protection.

"I won't touch you, I promise," he says. "You tell her that."

"Then why are you spying on me from the kitchen?"

"Because I want to talk to you."

I take a careful seat across from him. I'm still damp, uncomfortable, real because of it. "Then talk," I say.

"Bobby Junior wants to kill me."

He looks perfectly serious. In the sunroom, the grandfather clock marks the half to an unknown hour.

"Why you looking at me like that?"

"I don't believe you."

He spreads his hands wide. "God's honest truth. And you know I got good reason to know. The shit—I mean, the stuff I saw about that lady killer of yours—"

"You will kindly leave Phyllis out of this."

"Phyllis. That's not what you call her."

"And you'll call her Miss Green."

"Miss LeBlanc. Miss angel. Some kind of angel."

I wonder if I hear a car turning up the drive, but it passes without stopping. "I can believe a lot of things of Bobby Junior, but murder . . ."

"He'd kill. He and his mayor daddy. You know it."

At that I smile faintly. "I know it. But they'd never do it with their own hands. Never if they could be caught. They'd hire someone—no, and don't tell me they could hire Pea, they would never and she would never."

He had opened his mouth to say just that, I guessed, but now he nods. "All right, I won't. But he's going to kill me. And men like that never get in trouble for killing people like us."

I acknowledge the point. "So what do you want me to do?"

"Help me. You know that family, they respect you a little. They fear you a little, so even better."

"Don't you already have Craver's protection?"

He snorts. "That old man? He can't do nothing. Doesn't even want to. He'd do anything to save that old graveyard of his. He'd sell me."

"So why does Bobby Junior want to kill you? Did you touch him?"

"My mom cleans their place and I've touched her all my life. Touched them a few times too, before they decided they believed. Mayor Bell is willing to leave me be, I think, but the Junior wants me dead."

"You want to tell me what you know that makes him so eager to bump you off?"

Alvin gives me a long look, then shrugs. Looks out the window like he's waiting for her, too. "No, I don't think I do."

"But you want my help. Why? My hands? You want me to touch the threat?"

At this Alvin takes a hasty step back. "Don't think so, Davey. Not unless you want me to return the favor."

I shrug, but at least now I know: this is a move in a game. I can believe Bobby Junior hates him, but Alvin would have no motive to hide from my hands if that were the whole story. Alvin is a boy, not particularly strong, almost grown. A boy like I was, and fear makes him dangerous.

A moment. His face is a strong tree in a stiff breeze. It barely moves. But I feel something pass, an animus. Bigger than Alvin but a part of him. It threatens me, yes, but it is a knife at the throat of someone else.

"Where is she?"

I don't remember standing. I don't remember the movement of my hands, hovering over his neck. I am trying to breathe in a downpour.

Alvin fetches against the rain-lashed window. "You touch me, I touch you."

"Tell me about Pea. What do you want with her?"

Or maybe what I felt was Pea in trouble, thinking her way to me?

Alvin jerks his head—emphatic and yet ambiguous. He ducks under my arm and scrambles for the door.

"If you're worried about her, ask Bobby Junior. I saw them in town this afternoon, drinking at the inn."

We stare at each other. I am thinking of certain looks, the heat of which I avoided. I am thinking of the way that I kissed her before I pulled back, each time. I am remembering the smell of blood and the smell of saliva. The sweet peas in the garden, and the watermelon.

Alvin takes one step into the rain. "If you don't help me," he says, "you're killing me."

Without a touch. And the one thing I will never do is kill again.

3

Pea never guessed.

I wondered why I didn't feel more guilty about all the lies I had to tell, but I supposed I was busy enough trying to save her from my colleagues without bothering with the finer moral quandaries. She knew that I didn't approve of her execution of justice. She knew that I could feel her enemies when we touched. She knew, even if I didn't, that I had drowned in her; drowned as quickly as that boy I had let fall into the river when we were twelve.

Pea didn't know all of me. I certainly didn't know all of her. Knowledge, it turned out, was a red herring.

Drifting in twilight sleep all night while we pressed every possible inch of skin to the other's body, then we shifted to touch more, breathing and sweating and fucking and sleeping and waking up to find her so unexpectedly still there—that was the thing.

Leaving her, "I have work, I'll be back in the evening, at 8 p.m. sharp, no I don't care if you won't be back then, I'll wait, sweet Pea, I'll wait—"

I did wait, and I did go to work, after a fashion.

It occasionally felt wrong, how often I would watch her when she didn't know I was looking. But it also thrilled me, it made me love her more and in ways I would never be able to tell her—to see the woman whose smile to discover me beside her in the morning was as sweet as jaggery, calmly discussing knife thrusts and mob justice with Red Man or Russian Vic. That those expressions could colonize and transform the same beautiful features made her seem supernatural to me, a Kali in truth.

And when we lay together at night, that secret knowledge of her gave me a power I could only express in how much I left unsaid. The other ways I found to say it. We read each other in light reflected from unshed tears—and yes, I saw more than she did, but I didn't see enough.

I never went to headquarters. The uniformed cops were almost entirely white, and they didn't take kindly to colored rookies like me walking their halls. Though I of all people could tell if eyes had followed me there, the policy was for undercover cops to make reports in a diner two blocks away: Sal's Sunshine, integrated—at least to friends of cops—and home to the greasiest burgers and soggiest french fries south of Houston.

I always got the egg cream, and Finn always made a point to say it was his five-year-old's favorite too.

"Dev, you all right? You look sick, wrung out. You know most of that bootleg liquor they sling at the Pelican ain't safe. Might be drinking arsenic for all you know. Gotta take it easy, kid."

"Haven't been there as much recently," I said, taking a spoon of the sweet foam head and sucking until the only taste left on my tongue was chocolate and the metal tang of aluminum alloy.

Finn, older than me, but young enough to still feel the hunger for that break-or-die snap of a big case, gave me a long look over his cherry cola. He'd dumped a solid slug of whiskey in it from his hip flask, as always. Plenty of cops had kept drinking straight through Prohibition, though few with quite so much brio as Finn, who used to bring whiskey in canteens to interrogations and offer sips to the detainees. He had an ex-wife who hated him with a passion that jolted me every time I touched him in passing. I never asked him about it. We all had our dirty seams. Places an enterprising rookie cop could stick the crowbar and apply pressure. But I hadn't seen any need for it.

"So you really have shacked up with that old lady? The hatchet girl? What do they call her?"

"Phyllis LeBlanc," I said. I took a sip of the egg cream and a little dribbled down my chin. I put it down, very carefully.

"Victor's angel," Finn said, and banged the heel of his palm on the table. "Well, isn't that just peachy. Look at you, with some pretty white girl who could just as easily cut your balls off as kiss you."

She isn't white, I thought, but I did not say it, because you didn't tell your assassin lover's biggest secret to your cop boss.

"She doesn't kill everyone he asks," I said. "She's part of this system—"

"Political gestures of mob justice," Finn said, very carefully, in the way that stopped my throat, "are not the law, Dev."

"I know that."

"I'm glad you do. But while you're eating ground rations with Victor's old lady, I figure that you can help us with something. A new development."

The clock behind Finn's head read nearly 10 p.m. She'd be waiting for me. Not worried, no, but waiting. My hands started to shake again, harder.

"What development?" Whatever they were planning, I would make sure I had the cover to protect her.

"Potential stoolie," Finn said. "Odd-jobber by the name of Trent Sullivan. He won't come to headquarters, is wary of talking to any of our undercovers, says everyone knows they're cops. But you're too new for them to know, and now you're with Victor's fucking angel? Congratulations, kid, I think you got your break. Find him, talk to him, lay the groundwork, and we'll set up the sting. Think you can do that?"

"Sure," I said. "I'll let you know how it's going next week."

"And if you get a hint of the kills your old lady has planned . . ."

"She never tells me the names."

"Of course she doesn't. So let me know what she doesn't tell you."

"She's good, too, Finn."

"You'll do your best."

I got up to leave. It was 10:15. The second hand was making me dizzy. The milk and chocolate syrup and fizzy water were churning to butter in my gut. I thought of her smile when she saw me walk through the door. I thought of what I was doing here.

"Kid . . . if you think you're in over your head, we can still pull you out."

I stared at him, so full of hungers that my eyes crunched when they blinked.

"This is mine."

Finn put his hands up. Pale and fat, greasy from the fries. "Just asking."

I barely had the money for a coffee at breakfast, but I paid for a cab to her place. She opened the door before I was halfway up the stairs. In her arms I finally stopped shaking.

4

A car turns up the drive, at last. My hands sting, they touch her even before she's forced the car out of the mud.

She is thinking about me.

I haven't closed the door that Alvin left open. Water runs from the welcome mat, across the slate tiles, and laps at Pea's muddy garden boots. The rain has given way to a mist that obscures my view of the driveway. The swollen passing of the river below plugs my ears. I wait for her on the porch, barefoot and bareheaded. Wondering if she will tell me what business she had with Bobby Junior. If I have the right to ask.

Her footsteps crunch in the gravel and mud of the driveway. Then pause, then resume. The mist gives her up. Dew beads her hair and she carries muddy shoes in one hand. Exhaustion emphasizes those lines she hates around her eyes, the ones that deepen when she smiles.

"I think I can save the tomatoes," she says.

"You spent all that time in Hudson?"

I didn't mean to say that. But shame is stayed by something like desire. Pea traces my jawline with a muddy hand. And if I were who I want to be, I could kiss her now, before any more words expose us. I could grab hold of her and pull her so close our ribs settle in each other's spaces and hurt as we breathe. But she watches me with distant pity, as though through a window.

"I ran into Bobby Bell—he used to come around the Pelican a few years ago, some rich kid begging kicks from Victor. I never knew you'd grown up together."

"He's a few years older. We never talked much."

His gang used to make a game of trapping me places where I couldn't get away. They liked using my ability against me. They had their sport, they regularly beat me until I learned to defend myself. Until my skill outpaced their cruel intelligence. It only took one demonstration, carefully planned, pitilessly executed. One night in a clearing by the river. They left me alone and my mother congratulated me on *rising above the situation*.

"Dev," Pea says, almost a whisper. "Did something happen?"

"I missed you."

"Did you?"

Could she doubt it? I look more closely and see: yes. She is here, she has planted her garden, she waits for me. But she still wonders.

"Alvin dropped by for a visit," I say.

Her eyes jerk back to my face. "The boy from Craver's store? What did he want?"

"He says Bobby Junior wants to kill him. For some secret he knows."

"Did you touch him?"

"Wouldn't let me."

"Then he's hiding something. And that kid is dangerous."

"I was thinking of helping him."

"Were you, now?"

"I can take care of myself, Pea."

"Can you, Dev?" She laughs. "Can you anymore?"

The white rush of the river fills my throat. I meet her angry eyes while something inside me snaps again and again. I catch a glimmer of her fear. What astonishing, awful power. I can scare this dangerous woman, this angel and no one's knife. It is enough.

My kiss demands. It seeks aggressive, mindless domination. And she submits for a second or two. Then she bites my lip, hard. I flinch, but she doesn't let go. Blood fills our mouths. Her arms pull me so close my breastbone aches with each frantic pulse. I run my hands through her hair, I cradle her against the sensation of my own pain. The too-sweet taste of my own blood. In my fingertips, she sings of love and relief.

I lift her, she struggles, her shoes strike the wet wood of the porch. She climbs me like a wall, wraps her legs around my waist, squeezes until I am only a memory of a breath, one that she sucks from my lips as I gasp.

I push up her skirt and force my hand in that space that presses, damp, against my stomach. Her scissor grip relaxes while her hands yank my hair convulsively. My scalp burns. My gasps are a sharp relief. She moves against my hand. A pop and a shiver and then she is climbing me again, biting my ear, my neck, my collarbone, not quite hard enough to draw blood. But I want blood.

A pair of staggering steps. We fetch up against the porch balcony. I set her down. Her lips are swollen and red, like her eyes. She says nothing, just looks up at me. Waiting, again.

Because I pull away every time. Because I feel the blood that she has spilled, and the blood that I have spilled for her. I don't know if my desire is truly for her anymore or just for all of our endings.

"What can I do, Dev?" A knife in her hand. I didn't see her pull it. But then, I never do.

"Do you want me to hurt, is that it? Do you still blame me?"

The knife hovers above her left wrist, casual, deadly. If I do nothing, she will cut herself just to make me move. She will give me her blood, which she has somehow divined is exactly what I desire. My love is overmatched. She will make it easy for me.

Lightning strikes the river and throws its light between us. Her hands are delicate. Thinner than I remember, veins and muscle and bone latticed beneath what she calls high-yellow skin. A scar rings her left wrist like a bracelet; a keloid star dimples the skin between her right thumb and forefinger. I have seen, once, the last decade of scars beneath the coastline of her clothes. I hate to look at them. The body records its pain. I don't need the reminder. But she has been unmistakably marked by my years of silence.

I put my hands over hers. She moves the knife just enough, so it kisses the first layer of my skin without breaking it. Her eyes are wide and dark and wet. We wait.

I lean in to kiss her. My tongue stings where she bit it, it swells uncomfortably. I press it against her teeth and blood breaks through again, a warm demonstration. I hear an echo of Victor (*I will haunt you*), but in this moment he's just a gnat in my ear.

"Oh," Pea says, and sucks on the corner of my mouth. "*Oh*. Fuck, Dev."

The knife pricks the tip of my pinky. She lifts my hand, watches my face as she smears that trickle of blood across her lips. It goes on dark as earth.

Mortal, mortal, like that kid goat I killed when I first understood that death would come for me one day. Mortal like my father, whose ashes we shipped to my aunts in Bombay days after he had first let me try a turn in the Chrysler. Mortal like Victor, whose blood washed away as easily as Pea promised.

Everything dies, and love only makes the blood spill faster.

I yank up her skirt, she grapples for my erection, pops the tongue from my belt in her haste. I thrust outside—she's as slippery as half-cooked okra. One hand—hers?—passes it inside. I don't look at her, I just hold on. We are two mortals, whatever the rest of the world calls us. Two creatures of bones and skin and bellows and blood. Two creatures full of love, watching it drip between our fingers.

"Look, the cucumbers are ripe. How old is that smoked salt in the pantry?"

"Pea, they're still white."

They look bizarre, misshapen tumors nestled against dark-green vines.

"They're called dragon's eggs. That's how they looked on the package."

"And you bought them?"

"I met Mae Spalding in Craver's store that day. The hell-child's mom, poor thing—she told me she used to grow them. Don't be prejudiced, Dev."

I consider this. Her smile is just a twitch in the blues and browns of her sun-haloed silhouette.

"What's that, Pea? Some hopelessly naïve American aphorism? Don't judge a book by its cover?"

"Don't knock it till you've tried it, how about."

My fingers walk the waistline of her blue jeans, mine two weeks ago. "I wasn't planning on knocking them, either."

Pea doesn't laugh like someone who could even imagine doing what we did two nights ago. But she did. We did. And this beautiful, sun-lit innocence is just as much a part of her as the knives, and who they've cut.

"The salt?" she says, and slices a cucumber from its vine. I like the way it looks in her palm. It reflects a smeared curve of her plum-red lips.

"Two, three years?" I bought it in a summer market, right after Tamara came to the Pelican. I don't tell Pea that—I don't like her to think of what Tamara meant to me. And it does me no good either.

Pea shrugs. "It's just salt, right?" She cuts a stalk of the purple-green basil, fat and bowed with flowers. She's like my grandmother in this small way, knowing each plant by its rhythms and its fruit. A sightless caress of my forehead and she walks back into the kitchen. I wait in the garden. A peaceful hum descends, the kind of trilling, buzzing susurrus that passes for silence in the countryside. Beetles root in the dirt. A ladybug eats a greenfly. Violence is peace. Even here.

"Dev, there's someone on the line." Her voice wakes me, not her hand on my shoulder. She regards me at her most unreadable.

"Who?"

"A man. It sounded official. I can wait outside."

I get up very carefully. She reeks of basil, of sweet pollen and earth bitters. A maddened corkscrew just above her ear is knotted with a flower, blush pink.

"Pea . . ."

What does she think? What explanation can I give? I can only hide in the game, my second skin.

"Probably some city officer. They're not supposed to call me, but—"

"I love you, Dev," she says, her face averted. She might even know. My saint's hands only touch the frigid air of her withdrawal. She curls against the wood slats of the garden chair and tosses the knife high. She catches it without looking, but her whole arm spasms as her fingers close around the hilt and she pitches herself forward to slam the blade into the wood. She stares at her hand. A sound escapes her. It might have been a laugh.

The receiver is lying face-up on the box. "Subtle as ever, Finn."

"Calm down, kid, I didn't say anything but your name. She at least knows that, right?"

"Very funny. And you'd have told Deborah you were dodging the draft?"

"Oh, sure, I told her everything."

"No wonder she left you."

"Don't I know it." We laugh, and I wait. "Kid, are you sure about this? You know I can't pull these strings without some big favors coming due. I thought you wanted out."

"I wasn't expecting to spend my peaceful retirement in a bomb shelter."

"Our work isn't always much safer. But you know that. Hell, you're living with her."

"Christ, Finn."

"I'm not bothering you about it. Just saying. These favors . . ."

"What do they want?"

"Red Man Finch."

I take a sharp breath. "No."

"He's a killer."

"We're all killers."

"And now even you, kid. How many years did you avoid pulling that gun of yours? And then you make Victor calamari with your girlfriend's *knife*." His laughter hits me. I start to shake. It's not remembering so much as drowning. The hard wall of his skull and the soft slip of his brains. His bloody, still face. Life that had ended because I ended it. What I had let Pea do. Oh sweet Christ, the years that I had let Pea—

"Kid, you all right?"

The tide recedes. I cough and wipe my eyes. "What does vice want him for, anyhow?"

"Because we're cops and it's our job to take down criminals. Or have you spent so long undercover you think you're a gangster now?"

I grit my teeth. "I had hoped," I say, "to be a civilian."

"Too late for that, private. They know that old injun trusts you—"

"*Finch* suspects something."

A pause followed by a soft, wet sound: Finn chewing on a pencil, or a cigar. "You saying you're compromised, kid?"

Walter knows everything, and has for years. But my divided loyalties are not anything I plan to share with my former handler.

"Not compromised. But I don't have the access they need."

"Sure you could, with a bit of work."

"There has to be something else."

"Yeah, basic training."

Pea waits for me in the garden. My hot-blooded killer, my reformed assassin. I once believed in justice too. But if such a thing exists, it doesn't look like betraying Walter Finch. Luckily, he'd never be slow enough to let me.

I take a deep, steadying breath from the diaphragm. Seven in, seven out. I feel the channels of my power, my quiet hands. They play the numbers.

"They can get me out?"

"If you're more valuable on the home front than overseas, yadda yadda."

"Let me see what I can do."

"I'm in Albany now, kid. Something like retirement. You've got to call Valentine if you want this deal."

I've been in Commissioner Valentine's good graces since my years undercover with Dutch Schultz and then planted in the lower rungs of Lucky Luciano's outfit. My time there helped net Valentine and District Attorney Dewey one of the biggest victories of the century against organized crime. Now Dewey is due to resign at the end of this year and there are rumors that he has his sights on the governor's seat in Albany. What better way to drum up good press than a new wave of high-profile indictments on his way out?

Unsticking myself from that corrupt spider's web had been hard enough the first time. There were certain—questions—about my failure to bring in actionable evidence against Victor or his top lieutenants. They didn't precisely lament Victor's death, but Valentine is a rule-man if there ever was one. Calamari, as Finn so vulgarly put it, is not standard procedure in any police manual. If I go back this time, I'll be in it for life. But the police would be, if nothing else, a wall between Pea and our old world. She couldn't join me on Centre Street even if she wanted to. Walter's help, on the other hand—

"I just need some time. To see if it's even possible."

Finn sighs. "Your draft board is in my jurisdiction. I can call and tell them to defer for a month or two, for official police business. More than that and I'm risking my neck. So whatever side you're gonna pick, kid, do it by then."

"What sides are you referring to, Finn?"

He wheezes a little. "Oh, none at all, kiddo. Us police, we're pure as driven snow."

Neither of us laugh. As we bid terse farewells I imagine his grim smile, a mirror of my own.

Outside, Pea has sliced and arranged the cucumber on a plate, topped it with basil and salt.

"I'm going to town," I tell her, but I sit down on the chair she has appropriated and wrap my arms around her waist. She leans into me and I wonder, again, if she's lost weight.

"To check on that devil-child? Do you want me to come with you?"

"To talk to Bobby Junior. If I can help Alvin, I should."

"You want to help that boy who nearly—"

She grips my wrists. Her breaths tickle my shoulder, where she rests her head.

"Will you try it?" she says, after a few minutes. "It's nice with the basil."

She feeds me. I crunch into the cucumber, sharp herbs and smoked brine. I am transported as much by her fixed gaze as the flavors popping on my tongue.

We kiss briefly. A summer kiss at the start of fall. A promise of a kiss, when the draft board or the NYPD will have my neck in a month or two. The Bells might give me a third way out, if I can ferret out the truth of what happened with them and Alvin. With that kind of leverage, they might be persuaded to use their connections to give my draft card an indefinite deferment. They might, but if they aren't? What would she do, if the army shipped me off? Survive, surely.

"See you tonight," I tell her. "I love you," I tell her.

"No," she says. "Don't do that."

"Love you?"

Her smile struggles against something else, something I can't read. When it wins, it transforms her: Phyllis LeBlanc, the most beautiful thing you'll see before you die.

"Do that all you want, baby," Phyllis says. "Just don't tell me so."

5

The driveway to the River House is longer than it ought to be. Some Bell ancestor shaped it like a cobblestone question mark, dotted by the tastefully restored colonial mansion. It's a design for magazine features of iconic upstate country houses. It's a design to charm visitors and intimidate residents, but now I don't suppose I qualify as either.

A maid answers a minute or two after I pull the bell. I note her hair straightened and pressed beneath a red kerchief, her starched apron that would have been cleaner this morning. The round eyes that are sadder, and harder, but the same as her son's.

"May I help you, sir?"

"I'm here to see Bobby Junior," I say.

She just nods and shows me into the parlor. She doesn't ask my name. I wonder what Alvin has told her. Or what she's told him.

An older man intercepts her in the hallway outside as she's leaving. I recognize him more from his photos than the handful of times I have seen him in person—he is fatter than I remember. Just as full of that presence that can make an average man seem handsome.

"Mae," he says, and then something else, too low for me to hear.

"To see Junior, sir." Her eyes are on the carpet. Her back is to a large French vase, set in a niche on the far wall.

He is much taller. When he moves I can only see the back of his suspenders and shirtsleeves, and the severe sidecut of his thick slate-gray hair.

". . . didn't I tell him to let the business be?"

Mae responds quietly. I can't make out the words, but the practiced, soothing way she says them tells me enough. Mayor Bell's wife died years ago, but I'm sure Alvin's mother had learned to use that voice long before then.

"Well, tell him to get that damned coolie out of my parlor! The Astors are due to arrive in a half hour . . ."

More soothing noises. I lean back in my chair—seventeenth-century French, newly upholstered, comfortable as burlap—and pretend I don't hear a thing. The Astors must be connected to those rumors of a development project on the old Lutheran land. So: money and influence and the imminent possibility of gaining much more. Or the threat of losing it. Alvin's fears suddenly seem plausible. Mae and Mayor Bell walk away together, still talking. His hand is on the small of her back and she holds herself as tightly as a ballerina.

Five minutes later, Bobby Bell the Junior stands in the doorway. He's better dressed than his father and at least fifty percent less imposing. "I heard you'd come back."

I shrug. "I've always had the house."

"Yes. I suppose so. Listen, I hate to be rude, but Dad's got some poo-bahs coming by in a few minutes and he needs the parlor. Why don't we take a walk and you can tell me whatever you came for?"

I follow him through the hallway and into the kitchen. He leads us out by a smaller door that opens onto the gardens and a path to the river. Typical Little Easton, typical Bells. You might get in through the front door, but they remove you from the back.

"What brings you here, Davey?" he asks as we pick our way down the steep, winding trail. His tone is wary and polite. It's been the same ever since that incident with his friends by the river. After they dredged for poor Thomas.

We pause at the river's edge. "I wanted to ask you about the boy working in Craver's store. Alvin."

"Mae's little devil? Do you know his own family's scared of him? If it weren't for Craver's damned intervention, the kid wouldn't dare show his cursed hands on River Road!"

"What did he do?"

Bobby shivers and meets my eyes almost accidentally.

"We never knew he had that . . . damned voodoo . . . or whatever you types have." Bobby snaps his hands in my direction, as though flicking off a spider. "His family kept that secret. Well, can't say it occurred to us to ask, either. It's not something civilized people tend to think about. Still, Mae ought to have *warned* us, after all the Bells have done for her. And good God, even now when I think about that rout of a party . . ."

He pulls his pocket square and wipes his forehead. No longer young, the both of us.

"Party?"

"The viewing party we have up at the house every May. But Dad had this notion to raise funds for a regional declaration in favor of the war. We've got to put some pressure on Washington, after all, or the damn thing'll be over by the time we get to the front. So we hired the boy for the night to park cars and collect glasses and make himself useful—a favor to his family. The winter ended late this year, all the orchards have been struggling. Which goes to show you charity isn't always rewarded! The damned weasel revealed his little secret in the middle of the toasts! Touched Charles Yarborough and his wife, of all people, and let's just say I think Charles's chances of winning that state senate seat in September are just about shot."

"Did you provoke him?"

"Hot damn, Davey, provoke *him*? We've done everything for that ungrateful bunch of—"

I flinch, and he stops, which is more than the Junior would have done a decade ago. It has never been good to hear, but after Victor that word is a blow from a loaded gun.

I release a slow breath. "So your theory is that he risked his family just to, what? See the looks on your faces when he described Charles Yarborough's love life?"

Bobby rolls his eyes. "He's probably some anarchist, intent on destroying white civilization. Point is, what he did is beyond anything decent people can tolerate. Who doesn't have a few skeletons in their closet?"

"Let he who is without sin cast the first stone?"

"Exactly! So you can see how we can't tolerate this business with Craver."

"Not sure I follow, Bobby."

"That man is . . . what was Phyllis's charming phrase? Nuttier than a jar of peanut butter. Wacky. All these years obsessed with the dead. He doesn't like the wheels of progress so he tries to gum the works with his power over the boy? Dad calls it *escalation*."

"Well, I can forgive a man for feeling desperate when his town threatens to dig up his parents' bones."

The Junior waves his left hand, on which his Dartmouth college ring is prominently settled, despite his never having officially graduated. Mayor Bell had connections enough to remove that particular failure from the scholastic record, but not enough to stop the gossip back in town.

"Craver's always been like that, as you ought to know. It was strange enough when he took you in—now, don't take offense, Davey, you've turned out fine, but it raised plenty of eyebrows back then. Do you remember how he told the town you had a *power* straight from that constipated god of his?" He starts to laugh, but then falls silent. I can well imagine what crossed his thoughts, and my hands go clammy with memory. He gives me a brief, funny look, and turns to the river. "More fools we, eh, Davey? More fools we for not listening. But this business with the Spalding boy, it's a step beyond. It . . . it's not right!"

"And I'm sure remembering those times Alvin's hands might have brushed yours have nothing to do with it."

"Damn it, Davey, who doesn't have skeletons?"

"Craver, apparently."

"*Craver* is playing a game. He wants that dead church, no matter that it's prime real estate that hasn't been used in decades. This town stands to make millions with the new hotel."

"Probably not the Spaldings."

"They're lucky they get to keep their orchard. And if we're lucky that boy will get drafted on his birthday."

I shake my head. "You volunteering, Bobby? Since you and your dad support the war."

"Medical exemption from service. Trick knee. Besides, I'm more useful on the home front. And don't tell me you'll find yourself over there, what with your New York connections . . . Speaking of which, I don't need to tell you it spooked me a bit to see your lady in town. I expect you know she and I go back? We passed a few hours at the inn the other day? Of course you do, the way gossip goes around here. I hope you weren't jealous?"

He pauses, hopeful. I glance at him and kneel to pick a late dandelion with most of its pollen. I blow the seeds away from his face, but I can't help the direction of the wind.

"I'm afraid there's nothing much about you to provoke jealousy."

Bobby sneezes. "She doesn't, I mean, her business here . . ."

This fucking country wheat, this absolute twit—was he really asking—

"Strictly personal, Junior. As I'm sure she told you, we're both through with the New York racket. Victor's dead, and we're here for peace and quiet."

His hands tremble in his pockets. He sweats, despite the breeze from the river.

"Sorry if I offended you, buddy."

"We're not buddies, Junior. Or don't you remember Thomas?"

He jerks. But we were both thinking it; I only chose, at last, to name the ghost between us. For many years, watching Thomas die had been the closest I'd come to killing a man. Now, I could almost laugh.

"I—Davey—I mean, that's water under the bridge—" He grimaces. Back up the hill, in the River House, a bell starts to ring. "Poor choice of words. Look, I apologize, but I have to go. Dad must want me for something. What I said—don't take it to heart. I have nothing but respect for you and your lady. All right?"

To his credit, he holds out his hand. I regard it for a calculated moment and then clasp it with my own. He could be planning to kill Alvin, but he's sincere about being no threat to me. And yet, there's something else—I'm trying to trace that ominous whiff of smoke that blows between our connected hands when he pulls away and hurries up the hill. He says something to Mae by the back door, then disappears inside. I turn my back to the house, but only because I know she's coming.

She has to make sure she's alone, first.

"My boy," she says, no introductions needed. "He spoke to you."

"Yes."

"What did he say? I love that boy more than my life, but he doesn't always have the closest relationship with the truth, you understand. He makes up stories, he exaggerates. Sure, we got problems, but I don't want him going around making it worse 'cause he thinks he got to protect me."

She seems out of breath, tired. I think of the mayor's hand on her back, so sure of its right to be there.

"He says that the Bells want to kill him."

"Now, I'm sure that isn't true," she says, but she looks away as she says it. Her nostrils flare, ever so slightly.

"If you need help, I can try—"

She holds up her hand, straightens her shoulders. "Now, that's the one thing I'm damn sure we *don't* need. Any more help."

We hold each other's eyes for a moment.

"Look," she says, the word soft as a sigh, "I raised that boy right. He's got a core of iron. He knows why the Lord gave him that burden, he knows it's his holy duty to use them for good. So don't go on misunderstanding him. We got plenty of white folks around here for that."

I nod, and she seems to take this for agreement. Or maybe she doesn't have any more time. The bell starts to ring again and she races back up the hill like the kitchen's on fire.

And that's when I place the scent that I had pulled from Junior's brief handclasp. A threat, yes, but not to me.

Junior could want to kill Alvin.

But someone definitely wants to kill Junior.

————

Craver has flipped the shop sign to CLOSED when I arrive. I rattle the door until Alvin opens it.

"We're—oh. What do you want?"

"I thought I was helping you out," I say, pushing my way inside. Alvin jumps back before I can get close enough to touch him. I raise my eyebrows. "But it seems you have something to hide."

"Did you want to speak with me, Davey?" Craver has removed his dust-stained apron and run a comb through his thin gray hair. The keys in his hand open the churchyard as well as the convenience store.

"Going to the graveyard?" I used to accompany him to clean the church and the graves. A penance, like everything he did.

"I doubt I'll have much more time with them," he said. "That pair of Herods on the hill are planning sacrilege. The gravest."

Alvin snickers. Craver stops him with a look.

"There's nothing else you can do to stop them? The town council?"

"Approved it with one dissenting vote. I've appealed to the county, but you know as well as I they'll make sure to lose the paperwork. One of the Astor sons is a principal investor."

That would explain Mayor Bell's grand visitors.

Craver turns from me and walks to the window. "They tell me the old church cross will be part of a permanent exhibition of town history they're putting in the basement of the new resort. I think they meant it as a favor. The cross my ancestors brought from Aachen more than a hundred years ago, squatting next to Edwin Bell's fishing rod. By God, I'd rather see that place burn than give him the satisfaction. If I were younger, if I were as strong as you, or Alvin here—"

His back spills rage like a furnace.

There are people who don't have killing in them. Put a gun in their hands, they'll shoot their own foot to get out.

Tamara's like that. I used to pretend that I was. But Craver? Alvin? They only need a very good reason.

"Been thinking about hurting someone, Mr. Craver?"

"Why? Did you touch something with those hands of yours?" He laughs as if it were a real joke.

"Hey, Dev," Alvin says, "he won't hurt no one. Don't look at him like that."

I wonder, idly, how I looked. Has Pea been rubbing off? "You told me that Junior wants to kill you, Alvin, but now I wonder if it's not the other way around."

"What's this? Alvin, now I *told* you—"

"If Junior don't have a dozen men wanting to kill him, it ain't Wednesday. I got my family to protect."

He seems genuine, but genuine men lie. I hold up one hand. Make no motion toward him. We could answer the question easy enough, and he knows it. He eyes my open palm, flinches, and shakes his head very slightly.

"If you find some proof, let me know," I say. "But until then, I've got my own business." I could try to keep following this trail, but Alvin's right, men like the Bobbys make plenty of enemies. I need a way out of the draft. Right now Finn and Valentine are looking like a marginally better prospect than exploiting Alvin's murky relationship with the Bells.

I let myself out and leave Craver's pious lecture to mix with the open air. Birdsong. The slush of trees tossing their hair in the wind. Clean air that carries, for a moment, the aroma of bone broth and meat dumplings.

I loved Tamara for her innocence—a good enough substitute for purity.

But I would never have killed for her. And Pea, sweet Pea, Phyllis LeBlanc, Phyllis Green, Victor's angel? For her, my sins are without price.

6

Trent Sullivan was a big man, muscular and heavy. He'd been a wrestler in his college days, made a few championships, but he threw out his back in practice and it never quite came back to him. He left school and went to work for his father. Eventually his father retired and he started working directly with Victor.

He was not the best-connected man in Victor's little empire, nor the cleverest, nor the one with the least to lose.

I guess you could say Trent Sullivan had a conscience. Not that I cared at the time. He was just a gangster to me, a stoolie in it for his own reasons. I didn't have to understand these criminals, I thought, just bring them to justice.

I was—this is not a defense—very young.

I'd been looking for him since my meeting with Finn at the diner. I found him a week later. He was nursing a draft beer one Thursday night in a dark corner of the Pelican. Unremarkable, except for the way his eyes followed Pea. I don't believe in jealousy, but like the devil, it doesn't require my approval. She was five feet away from me, laughing and flirting, shining like a sharpened knife. She pretended she didn't notice me, but at unexpected moments she would turn, her skirt spreading like a fan, and catch my eyes. *I know you,* they said.

In the Bible, that meant sex. But in my grandmother's stories, that meant love.

And somehow, this big man with a long mustache and tired sheep's eyes watched her, too, with some knowledge. He gave me a slight nod when I leaned against the wall beside him.

"You're the one, then?" he said, softly.

I twirled my cocktail glass in my left hand. The pieces snapped together, no room for hesitation. Some part of me must have already guessed. "Trent, I take it. What did they tell you about me?"

"Just that you're with the angel. And that you're colored."

"Christ," I said, "what else, my address?"

Trent laughed softly. "Could use some lessons in subtlety, your folks."

"My name's Dev. I'm supposed to find out what you can give us."

He kept his face neutral, but his hand clenched around the mug. "You wacky? See where we are?" His voice was barely a whisper.

"No one's paying us any attention," I said, just as softly, to reassure him. "And we're safer here than anywhere."

"You can't know that."

"You know about saint's hands?"

Now his sleepy eyes widened and he wheezed a sick laugh. "Like you can't fucking imagine."

"I have them. And they tell me when people are threatening me, or thinking about it. And they aren't even tingling right now."

That wasn't exactly true. Pea, sitting on the bar, a cocktail in one hand and a man's tie in the other, looked as though she could hardly remember my name but she hummed warmly against my fingertips. Pea's thoughts of me weren't threats, but they were enough of something that my hands could touch them anyhow. I had never felt that with a woman before.

"Then tell me something," Trent said, after a moment. "Something you wouldn't want others to hear."

It was a clever test. "I'm working for the fuzz," I said, conversationally.

He'd been prepared for this; he only swallowed. "All right," he said. "All right. You guys promise you'll get me out? He'll kill me for this. And they say he's got the hands for betrayal."

"You'll have to work with us. But if you give us enough rope to hang him, we'll give you a new life."

"For me and my girl," he said.

"Sure," I said, blithely. What did I care about the moll of some aging stoolie? Pea was tap dancing on the bar and I was dreaming of picking her up and carrying her home.

7

The next morning I wake to a twisted cramp reverberating from my knuckles to my elbows. The light is yellow and young. The house is silent save for the creak of Pea's shutters in the breeze. I run to her room first, even while I sift through the complicated braid of threats and feelings and realize that whoever wants to kill me isn't currently in the house.

And neither is Pea.

The duvet is bunched at the end of her bed, last evening's clothes lay a trail from the window to the closet. A perfume lingers. She is drying the Angèle Pernets by the headboard, and they anchor a scent indefinable, beloved.

She's gone, hours earlier than normal, and the threat still encircles my joints, less forcefully but unmistakably. I wonder if it threatens her as well, and the thought spurs me back to my room. I hesitate, but I take the gun.

My hands can touch threats. That's easy, the sort of thing I learned that first summer after the dream on the farm in Murbad, when my only threats came from vipers under stones in my path. But following them is the last thing I ever learned. Even now I have to gather my concentration like a skein of yarn.

This takes me to the river. Footprints the size of her garden boots slide through the mud to the track that follows the southern bank. It's choked with leaves from the recent rain and perilous with gnarled roots. I used to prefer this path as a child, until the fact that Bobby Junior also lived in a house with river access made that inadvisable.

I still would rather use the road into town, but for some reason Pea went this way, and so does that fading burn of rage and ill intent.

I follow.

The river is high today, red with mud and white with the foam of spinning cataracts. It kisses the edge of the towpath, a gentle seduction. But the undertow is strong enough to drown you in seconds. I keep my eye on the steady track of Pea's boots and think. The trembling edges of an old memory: hard men with misted eyes, dredging the river for Thomas Pullman. One of the boys from Bobby Junior's gang, my old tormentors. No one ever knew why he went to the river that night. None of the other boys ever admitted that they had come out on a dare, or that Tom had fallen into the river when he tried to push me in the treacherous near-darkness. All I had done was to step neatly to one side. The river did the rest.

I pass the overgrown grass of Craver's church, the old family farmhouses nearby. Then I reach the backyard of the River House, squatting on the bank like a fat swan.

"They're real beauties," Pea says, out of sight.

Another voice answers her. "I used to call them dinosaur eggs when I was a kid."

She laughs. "There's sure something odd about them. Maybe that's why they're beautiful. That kind of unnatural nature."

A pause. Mae says, "Watch the round leaves, they ain't weeds, they're for the aphids."

"What're they called?"

"Nasturtium. Taste good too, when they flower."

I edge around the trees until I have a line of sight to the garden. Pea and Mae are on their knees in a muddy row of vegetables. They seem to be alone. But I have a hard time imagining that Mae could pose a threat credible enough to pull me out of bed. Someone in the big house above? And yet it feels like it's *here*, not a dozen yards away.

"And what's that?" she asks.

"Should be black-eyed peas, if the spider mites don't get them this year."

I wish I could say I'd never recognize the city Pea, Victor's Pea, in this woman quietly weeding another man's garden. But it's only blood that washes off. Hearts abide. Pea doesn't like mornings, but she left early enough to avoid me.

"That's Alvin, you know," Mae said, after another long pause. "What you said, unnatural nature. It's God's gift, those saint's hands. That dream came to him four years ago, nothing any of us could do about it, and still there's something uncanny about him. My poor boy. Even to me and his father, we can love him, but there's some things you just aren't given to understand."

"My mother didn't have them," Pea says, "but my grandmother did. And so did my brother."

"And you?"

She looks speculatively at her hands for a moment. Is she wondering if they will behave? There have been a few odd moments lately when her hands have spasmed and she breathed as though it hurt. Pea shrugs minutely and balances the spade, tip down, on her third knuckle, then flips it high in the air and watches calmly as it spins downward an inch in front of the other woman's face and spears the dirt.

Both women release sharp breaths. "Lord almighty," Mae says. "What you do with that?"

"I used to kill people."

Mae nods. "The city girl. They called you an angel? I've heard—Junior's let a few things slip. That's . . . well, none of my business, I know, but I say it is a shame to do evil with the Lord's gifts."

Pea slides her fingers into the dirt. "All right. But is it always evil, Mae? Killing?"

Mae stops short and then laughs. "Well. Got me there, girl. Some men . . ."

"Some men."

A pause. "You ain't going to do anything to my boy, are you?"

"Not unless he tries to hurt me first. Or Dev."

"Your man? Davey?"

A smile thin as a knife edge, but her voice oddly thick: "My man."

But Phyllis is nobody's woman. And the threat that brought me here is just ash against my fingertips. Who could have made it—the mother? Or the angel?

"My boy's got ideas, but he's got no reason to hurt you or yours. Now, the Bells, that's another story. Thank the Lord for Ben Craver, or I don't know what I'd do."

"The Bells? Not a lot of love for them in this town, is there?"

The woman presses her palms into the dirt.

"Tell me something, city angel, you ever been a maid? Cleaned a white man's house?"

The city angel moves so they're shoulder to shoulder. "No," she whispers, so I can barely hear. "No, I ain't never, but I've heard."

And so they remain for five seconds, ten. Pea's face is gilded with morning light.

Up the hill someone rings that brassy bell six times. The mother jerks, and Pea stands up, looks over, and sees me.

We walk back the way we came. She laces her hand in mine and takes us unerringly down the wooded track that was once so familiar to me. It leads to the meadow with the swimming hole and the sweet mulberry tree, where I used to hide for hours from Bobby and his gang. I haven't been back since they spent two days dredging the river to find the body of a young boy, bloated and blue.

"I found your name," she says, "carved into the tree."

"Just my initials."

She shakes her head. She hasn't combed her hair in days. The woolly curls shine rust in the sun, they stick out like spring shoots in a hedge. The lines by her eyes deepen as they look at me and then around the green. She pulls off her boots and sticks her feet in the watering hole, clear and spring-fed. I am in the grip of her, and of memories of who I was before I met her. She hasn't said a word about what I overheard. She doesn't seem to care. But she does.

"So how did you know?" I ask.

She dribbles a handful of water down the back of her neck. I swallow. "It's the sort of place you'd find, and the sort of place you'd love. You dreamed a lot when you were younger. I did too, you know. But in Harlem it's hard to find a private place. If I'd been here I'd have found you, too. Or you'd have found me. We'd have carved our names in the tree and gorged on honeysuckle and mulberry . . ." She looks over her shoulder at me, with a small, embarrassed smile. "Take your shoes off, Dev. The water's nice."

I take my shoes off and kneel behind her and pull her against me. Her sigh bows out against my sternum. Those uncombed curls catch on my stubble and tickle my lips. The clean scent of her, hair oil and garden dirt, shakes me with memory.

Thomas Pullman fell. And yes, I watched. But for Pea I killed, for her I returned here, for her I would—I am afraid that I would—do anything at all.

"If you wanted," I say very softly, "I would let you."

She turns abruptly in my arms. She kisses me with her lips and then with the cold barrel of my gun.

"You fool, Dev." Her finger is so still on the trigger I imagine the smell of burning powder. "Still think I'd do it?"

Her eyes, dark as the bottom of the sea. Her heart, exposed beneath my hands as no one's should be. I have been too much in the habit of imagining her because I know her better than anyone.

I pull the gun from her hands. I put it in the grass behind us and wipe her eyes.

"Damned fool," she says, shaking. "That's what that was? You felt something by the River House? Do you want me to kill you? Because I wouldn't, even if you asked. I wouldn't, even if you were dying anyway, even if you begged me. Oh, there's someone I wouldn't mind killing up on that hill, but it sure as hell ain't you, sweet fool."

The boys in the clearing, laughing when they thought they'd caught me again. All the people Pea killed for justice, while I knew Victor's scheme and did not tell her. Karma is both patient and inevitable. It will catch me one day. Perhaps I did hope it would be Pea who delivered me back to the wheel of rebirth.

"Someone wants to kill me," I say.

"Probably that damned boy."

"I don't think so."

She shrugs. "Then we'll find him, whoever he is. I won't let you die either, Dev."

"Is that a threat?"

With just a twist of her body she tips herself into the spring and takes me tumbling with her. The water is deeper than it seems from the edge, nearly fifteen feet of frigid stillness, rock shrouded, sacred. Pea kicks off the bottom, knocking the loose stones against one another. I stay below. Watch sun streaking past her yellow skirt, her feet treading water. I run one finger lightly over her left arch. She jerks and shrieks loud enough for its distorted echo to reach me underwater.

She's still laughing when I break the surface. She splashes water in my face while I heave for air, then wraps her arms around my neck so we both nearly go under again.

"I should do you like that," she says. "Watch, you'll be sleeping and I'll just . . ." She's kissing my eyebrows. She's never done that before.

I laugh. "I'd touch your threat, sweet Pea."

"Maybe I'd be faster."

The water is so cold and her lips are so warm. Here we are baptized, blessed, reborn. Right now, I believe. Right now, I am grateful to be alive.

She drags me to the bank.

"It will get better, Dev," she says, like she believes it.

Sometimes I don't know how we will survive each other. Sometimes the greatest violence you can do to another person is to love them.

"I know," I say, like I do too.

Victor's voice chases me through my dreams that night. He is not a restful companion, but Pea and I sleep apart. So I stay awake, and maunder. I am remembering Walter, and all the times he's saved me.

I can't go to war, I can't give Finn what he wants, I can't work for Walter and risk being the hook that drags Pea back. The Bells will never help me without the dirt that Alvin refuses to give up. Which leaves nothing. I know that.

Dawn, at last. Just barely, but the rooster chorus is pretext enough to put the percolator on the stove.

Pea's door is open. She's fallen asleep against the frame, her knees tucked under the peach satin gown. Her arms encircle her leather knife holster like the torso of her lover. She opens her eyes when I approach. They are bloodshot and painfully lucid.

"Shouldn't walk so quiet past me, Dev," she says, all Harlem swagger and West Village ice.

"What are you doing out here?"

She shrugs and then laughs. "Waiting for you, baby."

I reach down and pick her up, which makes her laugh even more.

"Dev," she says, "put me the hell down, what are you doing—"

I drop her on the bed and she stays there, breathing hard, looking up at me.

"I'll make the coffee," I say, and turn. My heart pumps too much blood, my lips sting. She'd give me whatever I needed. But I don't want to need it.

We've both calmed by the time I return with a tray of flapjacks and late blackberries from the garden.

"My God, is this a bribe? Where's the coffee?"

"You couldn't have gotten much sleep like that."

"You thief! I smelled it, did you drink it all? You did! What did I do to deserve a man who treats me so bad?"

"I made you flapjacks."

She picks one up with her fingers and takes a bite. "Persuasive." She pours a puddle of maple syrup on the plate and dunks. "Damn, Dev, can you always cook for us?"

"You wouldn't miss the bacon?"

She looks up at me as she chews. "Well?" she says. "They're getting cold."

I use a knife and fork to eat my own, which she seems to regard as the custom of a strange and savage people. She lies upside-down on the bed once she's eaten two—not enough, but I don't want to ruin the moment by telling her so. She nestles her cheek against my thigh.

"You're scaring me," she says softly.

I stroke her hair absentmindedly as I finish the last flapjack. "With my hidden culinary talents?"

"Don't make me so happy, Dev, don't take it all away."

I stay like that, stroking her, hurting just a little bit less, until her breathing evens out and I know she's gone back to sleep. I wait a half hour. Then I call Walter.

8

I met Trent on the elevated train and we rode for an hour while he sketched what he could offer us in exchange for protection. His knowledge was patchy and oddly specific. It's a foolish cop who believes that an informant is confessing the unvarnished truth, but I wondered what Trent wanted from us. He talked mostly about hunting men for Victor, men—and some women—with saint's hands that Victor could use in his service.

"And what does he do with them?"

Trent glanced again at the old man sleeping at the other end of the train car. We were otherwise alone, stuck on the tracks right before the last stop.

"I can't say."

"Sure you can."

"I don't know exactly—"

"No need to be exact."

"Listen, it's that—what do you fellas want from me?"

"We want to bring down Victor and as many of his officers as possible on charges of murder and racketeering." Finn had been very careful to drill me in this. Whatever other petty crimes wafted through the air of the Pelican (police bribery, for example) mattered very little to him.

"I can't tell you anything about racketeering," he said. "I stay out of the business side."

"Murder, then."

The train lurched forward and the old man startled awake.

"Not listening," I said, before Trent could ask.

He swallowed. "I might," he said, "know a bit about that."

"Go on."

"So does your old lady."

A flush suffused my neck. Did he think I didn't know that? I stayed up nights plotting the lies and gentle blackmail I would use to get her out of this. All she had to do was promise not to kill. All she had to do. I was—this is not an excuse—too self-righteous and too in love.

"What do you know, Trent?"

He gave me an appalling look. Like he pitied me. And then he gave me an address in Queens. He told me to go there tonight and to watch.

"It's a full moon. You'll see something."

And so I did.

9

At exactly six o'clock that afternoon a silver Packard climbs up the drive. Pea pulls a knife and then tosses it in the air just as a dark hand waves a paisley scarf from the passenger window.

"Sugar," calls a voice I had dreamed of often and still somehow forgot. Caramel warmth salty with unshed tears.

Pea runs down the porch steps, bruises her feet on the gravel as Tamara falls out of the passenger door. The strength of their embrace is all they need to say. I approach slowly.

"Hello, Walter," I say as he pulls himself from behind the wheel. He stretches his arms over his head, a gesture neither deliberately menacing nor wholly benign.

"Good to see you, Dev."

"Didn't expect you to come in person." That's all I'll say this near to Pea.

He nods. "We had reason."

We catalogue our subtle changes in the months since my precipitous departure. A few more grays salt the temples of Walter's slicked-back undercut. A certain softness in his cheeks and belly hints at a life more pleasurably lived. And mine: natural hollows edged a little more sharply with shadows and light.

Tamara holds Pea at arm's length and says, "Well, you couldn't look more country if you were holding a fishing pole, sugar, it's just fabulous to see you so well. Walter and I were so worried, weren't we, Walter? That's why we came all the way here, we left this morning. I insisted after what my cards told me—don't put that face on,

Pea, my cards have helped you out a dozen times over, even if you don't ever play the numbers."

Pea gives her a wry look. "And neither do you."

Tamara shrugs with imperial disdain. "It would be disrespectful."

"Tammy, Phyllis," Walter says, "why don't we all sit down with a bottle of wine and some dinner and have a conversation?"

Tamara slides Walter a look of exasperation and fondness. She puts her arm around Pea's shoulders.

"Pea, have you gone completely country up on this muddy hill or do you have something to wear?"

Pea's glance at me is a submerged laugh sparking with challenge. "Do I look naked to you?" she asks Tamara, who clucks her tongue.

"Do you at least have *shoes*?"

Pea puts her hand on her hip. "And a python and a grass skirt."

Tamara's laugh brings blood to my cheeks. It's the memory of what that bright sound used to mean to me, but it's the living reality, too. Walter just watches us.

"Be right back, Dev," Pea says and pecks my lips. She sounds breezy, cheerful. Her fingers press a four-point warning onto my goose-pimpled flesh. I nod slightly to show her I understand—she doesn't know I called him. They walk into the house. I love the way Pea matches her grace to Tamara's: a viper arm in arm with a bird of paradise.

"You took your time calling about that letter," Walter says.

"I called my old handler first."

He laughs. "And I see how well that went. The fuzz is a bad bargain for folks like us, Dev. Like the army."

"They didn't always do badly by me."

"And I'm sure you'll do just fine with the colored troops."

The humor does not escape us. Walter smiles with a hard-eyed flash of teeth that makes rookie runners shit their knickers. I smile back. The memory of killing Victor may sicken me, but that is a debt Walter will spend a long time repaying.

"Do you really believe in Tamara's cards?" I ask. "Did they predict something dire?"

He shrugs. "When our Tammy starts laying those cards down, something gets into her, I won't deny it. But maybe she just missed Pea."

I look back at the house. "But we should be safe here."

"You haven't told her about the draft."

I like Walter, I always have, but I haven't felt so close to violence since I hammered a throwing knife into his boss's right temple. I slap my palm into the Packard's chrome, right beside his shoulder. His gaze doesn't leave my face.

"She. Stays. Out."

"That's her choice, isn't it?"

"Not if I'm her reason for getting back in."

"And you think she will if she finds out?"

Pea's laugh spills from her open window, with a thread of words, ". . . as if you wouldn't know, all you've done . . ."

Pea with dirt on her hands, instead of blood. Pea who laughs. Pea who plays with the knives she once used to slaughter. Walter wasn't there—she *let* me kill Victor.

"You kill enough," I say, so softly that my voice is gravel, "and you wake up one morning without a soul."

Walter tilts his head. "Doesn't affect us all the same way, now, does it?"

But his throat vibrates faintly. His breaths are too deep, too steady. Walter leans against a dead man's car, but that doesn't mean he has the dead man's heart.

"Do you ever miss him?"

He jerks. Doesn't even pretend to smile. "Why the fuck would I do that?"

"You were friends, once. Had to have been some good times."

He takes a breath, lets it out. His hands go flat against his thighs. "So if I don't miss him, I'm already a monster? You imagine this matters to me?"

I don't answer.

Walter had come into that room, I'm not sure how long after. I remember his conversation with Pea.

"*He* did it?"

"Dev, baby, you gotta get up. Walter, where are the cops?"

"Taking their sweet time. Christ, it smells foul in here. Did Victor shit his pants?"

"Cost of business, Red Man."

A pause. "Yeah. I know. But that boy's a mess. Is he having some kind of fit? Why the hell'd you let him do it?"

"He's hardly a boy anymore."

"Thanks to you, Pea."

Pea had lifted my hand to her cheek. I couldn't feel much, but the warmth of her had shocked me like boiling water. I flinched away. Later, I would understand how much that must have hurt her but at the time the only one I could hold was myself.

In front of my house, far from that dirty city, Walter steps away from me and the car in one fast, fluid motion. He watches the silhouettes of the two women in the window.

"I won't tell her," he says.

"Does Tamara know?"

He shrugs. "Maybe her cards told her. But if she's guessed, she won't tell."

My hands are shaking. I put them in my pockets, not to keep Walter from seeing—of course he has—but so that Pea might not notice if she looks down from the window.

Pea and I never speak about New York. I sleep with the door locked. Every night I smell spilled whiskey and meat dumplings and the dying curse of a man I have damned myself in killing. Better mob muscle than a soldier's gun in my hands. Better Walter's service than leaving Pea with a box of my effects and bitter memories.

Pea and Tamara come back to us perfumed and city dressed. Pea has wrestled her hair into a bun and bandeau, dark blue to match the beading on a dress I'm sure I remember, but not on her curves.

"It's Tamara's," she says, smiling. She knows I already know. "But for a wonder it fits. What do you think, Dev? Do I clean up?"

She does, and I love her, and she loves me so much that she won't let me tell her so. In her own way, I could tell Walter, Pea doesn't trust me either.

We get in the car and drive to town. We're a little early for dinner at the Riverview Inn, but there's already a party at the big table: Mayor Bell and the Junior with two other middle-aged white men, sharply dressed. I peg them as the Astor investors whom Mayor Bell was so keen to please when I paid my visit. Their wives share the end of the table, in pearls and jewels that play subtle games with evening light. I watch Tamara guess the worth of these objects and deflate. Marnie, hovering by the table with an open bottle of wine, widens her eyes when we climb the porch steps. She has run the inn since I was a boy, and has never approved of me.

"Perhaps you'd like to sit inside," she says, though none of the other outside tables are occupied.

"Gracious, Marnie," Pea says, the drawl thick enough that I nearly laugh. I know what's coming and I don't particularly care. "Of course not. We'll sit right here."

She pulls out a chair from the table nearest the Bells and sprawls into it, graceful as a cat. I guess that Marnie's heard the rumors about Pea, which is why she doesn't tell her to bring her colored self inside. Tamara watches this interplay with a dawning smile.

"They know," Tamara says, sitting beside Pea. "You let them know."

"The hair," Pea says.

Tamara shakes her head, still smiling. "Not just the hair."

Walter orders wine for the table with his Red Man voice. Marnie shakes a little as she nods and hurries inside. The Bells slide glances at us. Their guests stare openly until the Junior leans forward and whispers something. Their gazes snap away from our table like a broken rubber band. There are benefits to associating with a well-known gangster. Even this far up the river.

Tamara and Walter tell stories over the meal. Old stories we all know, new ones being shaped in the telling. Their natural melancholy somehow twists into humor so sharp it hurts. Tamara is very good at this. She tells of the first time she tried dancing with the snake:

"He started going around my neck, you know, like the gaudiest necklace you ever saw, and poor old Georgie he's so slow he couldn't strangle a Thanksgiving turkey without a nap in between, but there's Victor smiling with that mouth full of silver and this python sliding past my jugular and I just start hollering. You all heard me by the bar, didn't you?"

"First time I ever heard your voice," Pea says.

"I didn't think you were speaking English," I say.

She throws her head back as she laughs. "Lord, I don't think I was either. I think it was tongues, like in church. Anyway, it stopped old Georgie. Victor just kept smiling, like he was waiting for something. And then I heard Walter behind me—remember, Walter?—and he said, 'For God's sake, girl, you gotta dance. George won't know any better otherwise.' And I stopped screaming, and I got my tongue back, and I turned right around and there was Walter, crouched a few feet away with a machete in his hand, and Victor said, well, something impolite—"

Walter twists his lips. "Give a white man a machete and he's just a man with a knife—"

"And give a black man a machete and he's got a bullet in him," says Pea.

"Well," says Tamara, "you remember how Vic liked to talk. And I said, 'If you lunatics want me to dance, play me some goddamned music!'"

We laugh, Pea most of all. "I took one look at that snake and told Victor to find another girl. You asked for the band!"

"Some goddamned music," I repeat, shaking my head. "Did he give you any?"

She shrugs. "Georgie slid off my neck like he'd just had enough of the whole affair and Victor told me I had a job."

"That's mostly how I remember it," says Walter, dryly. "But you, sweet Tammy, aren't much of a lady when the spirit takes you. Goddamned was the least of it."

Tamara blushes. The rest of us invent implausible curses while Marnie flinches in the doorway. We all enjoy it—ruining an evening that white people assumed would be reserved for their pleasure. Pea's hands relax against the table, for once free of the tension that has plagued them since we came here.

The balance of power has swung temporarily in our favor. It tastes very, very sweet.

It snaps.

Two shadows walking down the street. Both slim, one markedly taller than the other. They resolve: Alvin, with Craver. They walk silently in step. Like soldiers. Marnie doesn't have a chance. They march up the stairs and to the Bells' table. The balance wobbles once again, slips, careens wholesale off the cliff.

"Mr. Astor," says Craver to the older of the guests, a man with dye-brown hair, a thin nose, and drooping cheeks, wearing a ruby tie pin to match his wife's necklace. The Astor's gaze slides wetly. He's drunk.

"Ben Craver," says Bell Senior, smiling that smile that presages explosions. "I don't recall that I invited you here. Or your Negro boy."

Alvin stands just to Craver's right, his back rod straight and his gaze defiant. But there's a hesitancy about him. He keeps those hands in his pockets. I catch his eye, but he just twitches and looks away. Was I right? Is he here to try to kill Junior? But that doesn't quite explain Craver.

"Friend of yours, Mayor Bell?" the second man says, with a nervous laugh. "Didn't realize how integrated your little town was. I'm as much for equality as the next man, but within reason. We don't want to scare off good money when we open."

Craver takes a step closer to the two men. Bobby Senior stands. "Ben," he says, "whatever this is about, *this is not the time.*"

Alvin shifts his weight and eases his hands into the dim light. I hope no one else notices, but I reach for Pea. She tightens her hand around mine without looking away from the other table.

"We've known each other all our lives, Bobby," Craver says calmly, "but I don't think there's any sense in us having another word together."

The elder Bell has a voice tempered by decades of stump speeches. It is capable of a great volume. "Goddamn it, Ben—"

Craver drops to his knees, grabs the sharply pressed slacks of the drunken Astor.

"Sir, that land, the church's land, it is not yours to develop, it belongs to God, to the good Lord Jesus Christ who suffered for our sins—"

I assume he continues to mine this vein, but Mayor Bell's bellow drowns it. The Astor looks panicked and disgusted. He swats at Craver's upturned, tear-streaked face.

"Get a hold of yourself, sir!"

Bobby Junior grabs Craver's elbows and attempts to haul him back.

Alvin raises his hands. "Don't you touch him!"

Bobby Junior freezes. The drunk tries to stand, then falls back into his chair. Alvin reaches—for whom, for what, impossible to know. We only see his hands, those living weapons, those holy gifts, about to illuminate another man's sins.

A threat jumps from Pea's fingertips to my wrists, but she has pulled away by the time I register its faint, muddy warning. Walter stands, pushes Tamara behind him. He reaches for his gun at the same time as Mayor Bell, but only one of them intends to use it.

Pea grabs Alvin by his shoulders. The mayor shoots. The two women—already plastered against the back wall—start to shriek and the drunk man slides onto the floor.

Then I see the blood.

Not everything desired beneath night's blanket has a place in living reality. I might have lusted after the taste of my own blood on Pea's lips, but the idea of reliving that nightmare of three months ago, her blood soaking the jacket I pressed against her chest—

I go for Mayor Bell. Calmly, carefully, full of a rage that tells me precisely when he sees me, and exactly how much he will hesitate when he raises that piece again.

I grab it. Hand around the warm barrel, a sharp tug away from his trigger finger—mine. Behind me Pea says, "Well, *fuck*, Dev."

I already knew she was safe—not enough blood—but still that voice, half-appalled, half-amused, goes through me like an electric spark.

I assess the situation. Walter levels his gun at Bobby Junior, Bobby Junior keeps his piece up, the younger Astor presses against the back wall with the women. All three are quiet and horrified. Craver shivers on the floor beside Alvin and the fainting man. Alvin touches the spreading stain beneath the burned edges of his torn shirtsleeve.

"Is he dead?" I ask Walter. The man's pants are wet, and a sharp scent testifies to the reason.

Walter shrugs. "Sauced. Scared shitless."

Pea sniffs. "Walter, does anyone ever laugh at that?"

"Couldn't help myself. Tammy, how you doing?"

"Christ, Pea, don't you know how to relax?" Tamara's voice is breathy but reasonably controlled. She's getting better at this.

"Now," Walter says, "I'm going to put this down on the count of three. And then we're all going to stand up and go our separate ways. I don't know a damned thing about what's going on here, and I don't care. No one's been hurt—"

Alvin lifts his head. "That mother *shot* me!"

"Badly," he continues, "and we're going to keep it that way. Right? I see that piece you got there, kid, so don't look at me like that. Put it on the table and we all walk out easy. Agreed, Mayor?"

Mayor Bell has been unusually silent through this. But then, Walter's power is clearly his equal. He glances at his son, then squares his shoulders. "Sounds reasonable. Junior, you heard him, put that gun on the table."

"But Dad, what if that boy tries to touch us?"

"Alvin won't touch anyone," Pea says, weary. Alvin stares at her, then remembers to nod. Bobby Junior grimaces and slides his gun over the tablecloth, amid the mess of Marnie's best dinner.

"Davey, are you planning to keep that?" The mayor gestures to the piece I'm still holding like a dead snake. "It was my father's, and I know you know the importance of those sorts of keepsakes."

I slide his gun across the table. Having any common ground with the Bells makes even my rusted soul feel dirty.

Then Walter counts to three, holsters his gun, and hauls Tamara up by her elbow. Craver gets to his feet, trembling and glassy-eyed. The Bells and their guests hurry to the side of the Astor groaning on the floor. The rest of us look at one another, clear in the same understanding—better to leave before he wakes up.

"Alvin," Pea says, "come with us, will you? That needs looking after." After a moment she adds, grudgingly, "You're welcome too, Mr. Craver."

Alvin looks up at her like he's been struck with light on the road to Damascus. "You—I—all right."

Craver shakes his head mutely and walks down the steps. Back in the street, he is unsteady, shrunken, a wobbling silhouette that dances among the long shadows of the houses until they swallow him whole.

Pea explains about Alvin's saint's hands in the car on the way back. Tamara shifts a few inches closer to the window. Even Walter looks disconcerted.

"That's a powerful charge," he says, after a moment. "A heavy one. Your parents had the right idea, keeping it a secret. But I assume you had your reasons to tell?"

Alvin's expression is a tangle of desire and wonder, wrapped around that kernel of fury that has defined him from the moment we met. It illuminates him now. "I did, sir."

I wonder how Alvin would describe the events of the fundraising party, what he saw that passed beneath Junior's notice, or what Junior had chosen not to tell. But I know that Alvin would never tell me. There is a mother's ferocity in his anger. Something that he is fighting to protect.

When we get back to the house, Pea tends to Alvin's shallow graze with matter-of-fact expertise. She offers no sympathy and he watches her unflinching, dazzled.

"You've been shot before," he says.

"A few times." She tapes down the gauze she's wrapped around his upper arm. "There. You're fine, kid."

My heart bends to look at them. No matter how I met Pea, I would have loved her. I'm still falling. I can't help it any more than Alvin can, trying not to look at her as he puts back on his shirt.

"Why ain't you afraid of me like the others?"

I leave the kitchen but not fast enough to avoid Pea's response, "Because I already know whatever you could tell me, and so does . . ."

Walter is building a fire in the living room. Tamara sits in the nearby rocking chair, her knees tucked against her chest. The descending autumn has put a bite in the night air.

"I thought you two came here for a country retirement, Dev." The young wood catches. Walter leans back on his heels. "If tonight's any measure, you'd have had a more peaceful time slinging drinks in the Pelican."

"With vice squad breathing down my neck? With Pea about to go down for at least ten counts of murder one?"

Tamara's breath hitches and Walter gives her an uncharacteristically scornful look. "Get off it, Tammy. You know what she is."

"I just . . . didn't know it was so bad, that's all. All this for Victor." She shakes her head.

"Not just for Victor," Walter says softly.

The sound of running water and clinking glasses echoes from the kitchen. Walter proffers a fat, hand-rolled cigarette. Not packed with tobacco, I realize after a puff. I savor the quality and offer it to Tamara. She smiles sweetly at me and takes three hard drags before alighting from the chair.

"Got any music for that turntable?"

Pea and Alvin appear in the doorway with two bottles of wine and glasses. Already, Walter's reefer has given my perception a pleasant distance. An instability that makes everything feel worth noticing.

Tamara puts on an old Bessie Smith album of Pea's. Alvin coughs like an emphysemic old man. He drinks some wine and tries again. Walter and I clink glasses.

"We should talk," he says softly. "Give me your letter, and I'll make it my business. You can trust me with that."

"I know."

Pea sprawls on the couch by the fire. "So when you planning to tell us what those cards had to say, Tammy?"

Tamara was looking at me, but she glances away when I meet her eyes. "In a bit, sugar," she says, and drinks half a cup of wine in one gulp.

Pea and Tamara and Alvin are passing the butt of Walter's reefer. He takes another from his pocket.

"Let's take Alvin back home," Walter says. "No, stay, Phyllis. No need to trouble yourself. Dev and I will take care of it."

I look back at Pea. She meets my gaze, indecipherable and hard. A Pelican look, a Phyllis look. My response is desire, now and always.

We give Alvin a ride home. There's no hiding the old-boy exclusion of her. I only kiss her softly and promise to explain later. She grips my hand hard enough to hurt, and lets go.

Alvin gives us directions in a wandering voice that seems to emanate from the smoke filling the Packard. His house is half the size of my modest cottage, two rooms and a porch. An old tractor hulks beside a muddy pickup. A small light shines in the kitchen. Mae Spalding stands at the door. Her hair in curlers and her arms wrapped around a tiny waist.

"Alvin!" she calls. He climbs from the back seat as though from a high wall. "You all right, child? I heard things in town. I heard . . ." Reflected kitchen light flattens her expression. Her voice is strangled with fear.

"I'm fine, Ma," he says. "Dev and that angel and their friends, they took good care of me."

His voice changes when he talks to his mother. He speaks with an upward lilt, like he wishes she would smile.

"Alvin," I say, "why did you go with Craver tonight? If you aren't after Junior, and he isn't after you . . ."

Alvin freezes comically, his right foot hanging in the air six inches from the soil. "He might be," he says, finally.

"We both know that's a lie. What is going on?"

"I just want—those damn Bells—"

He stops abruptly. His mother calls him again, a soft question. Alvin walks to the porch, pauses, comes back to where I'm sitting.

"That angel," he pronounces, "she's dangerous as a fire."

Walter barks a laugh.

"And fire, it ain't evil, it just is, right? But you can *use* it for evil. You and me, what we have is the Lord's own strength. Maybe your angel is reformed, like she says. But if not, there's a greater good in this world." His cadences change to a voice older than his years, a mimicked oratory. "And if thy right hand offend thee, cut it off, and cast it from thee: for it is profitable for thee that one of thy members should perish, and not that thy whole body should be cast into hell!"

I am astonished into speechlessness. Beside me, Walter crosses his arms. "Matthew 5:30. Not very original, kid."

"The truth don't need to be."

Behind him, his mother calls once more. He starts and half turns.

"You'd give her up?" I ask, softly, nodding toward his mother. "Did she offend thee, wouldst thou cast her into the flames, and save thyself?"

Alvin's eyes widen and his shoulders twitch, as though to break free of my empty grip.

He goes to his mother and hugs her, hard.

The rain turns icy sometime after two that morning. It hits the windows with tiny sighs. Like the voices of the wronged dead. It isn't just Victor with me now. It's Trent, and Maryann. It's everyone she killed because I had kept my silence.

I wake sweating. My breath mists in the still air of the room. On colder nights than this, Mother and I would camp beside the living room fire in a nest of blankets. We could never afford to install heating. My mother's shame, but I secretly relished the closeness it imposed. The smell of pressed roses and woodsmoke. Her soft hand brushing back the hair on my forehead when she thought I slept.

Tonight a fire already burns in the living room hearth. It paints the woman beside it in planes of light and shadow.

"The sleet's killed the new shoots by now," she says, "but at least we won't have to worry about the aphids. Silly of me to keep growing so late in September."

Her knees are pulled tight against her chest. Her face is flushed with heat. A slight shiver shakes her shoulders, sharp beneath her cream silk robe. She winces and traces one of the scars on her left hand.

I kneel beside her. She looks at me sidelong and then away.

"The cards," I say.

She gives a small shrug. "You know how Tammy is when she really gets going with those things. Give the girl some black candles and goopher dust and she could make serious money as a conjure woman. Suicide kings and laughing jacks and spades and spades, I don't know. She says it means violence, coming soon. Something brutal. She says it means the past coming back to haunt us." She laughs. "'Cause that could never happen."

"Did she say anything about the hands?"

Pea levels a look at me. "Did she need to? What am I without them? Dead, or might as well be."

"They can't just desert you, Pea. They don't have a mind, or a spirit apart from yours. If you think they're judging you—"

"Oh, they already have."

"Then it is simply *you* judging yourself. The soul feels its own weight."

She takes a breath. Considers. "Some card tricks did not bring Walter up three hours from the city."

My pulse jumps. I reach out to touch her hand. She grabs me before I can pull away.

"You cannot honestly think," she says, "that I don't know how much you lie to me."

The air leaves my lungs. I knew this day would come. I knew. "You didn't before."

She squeezes my wrist hard enough to leave marks. "You must have thought I was very stupid. All those years, and I never even wondered about your story. Why the hell were you in that alley,

Dev?" She laughs. "You were waiting for me, you son of a bitch. Waiting for a killer to give to your cops. You were lying from hello."

Her stare goes into me like two hot drills. Three shaky breaths. "I never said hello."

"No," she agrees. "No." She shakes her head slowly. Lowers her eyes to our entwined fingers. Smiles, suddenly, brilliantly. "Ain't that like life, to give you your big break, a stone-cold killer naked in your bed, and you go and fall in love with her!"

I can't meet that bleeding gaiety. I can't match it.

"Poor Dev. I ruined your life, didn't I? But turnabout is fair play, I'm sure you ruined mine."

Sleet beats the windows and French doors. A log cracks in the fire, sends up a shower of sparks. I am crying. Nothing will stop it. Victor's curse was just the beginning. It's Pea's that will get me in the end. Her love, despite everything, her love.

"You knew it all. You knew about the hands—"

"Stop—"

"—about what Victor was really doing to those poor people."

"Pea, please . . ."

"Christ, how many were there, Dev? Fifteen? Twenty?"

She pauses, waits out my sobs like they're the slushing rain. How many? I don't want to know, but the answer bobs to the surface anyway. I can be as brutal to myself as to Pea.

"At the end . . . nearly thirty. His mouth was—he hardly had any of his real teeth left—Pea—"

She slaps me. "We are getting to the end of this!"

She is Kali filled with fury, with the power of death. Her skin, her hair glows orange with firelight. This is only what I deserve.

"When Walter came here that day and showed me the photos of those dead bodies. He told me they were Trent's kills. Did you know then?"

"Yes."

"But I—" She closes her eyes. "I left before you came back. I couldn't face what I imagined you would say to me. I had promised not to kill again."

"You didn't—"

"I had promised. Maybe I wouldn't have if I had known what you were."

"You did know. Even when I lied, you felt around it."

"And when you found me, after. When you found me and washed that blood away and brought me back, just so you could leave me, oh fuck you, Dev, did you ever think for a minute that I *couldn't* have known? Not then. Didn't you think to tell me? Didn't you know me at all?"

And I am run through. No comfort, nothing but this ringing guilt, and a blade to fall on. But she deserves it cleanly.

"I—decided that you knew, because—you were a killer, I had *heard* you kill him—and you are brutal and hard as diamond, Pea—it—you terrified me—I told myself I had misjudged you. To protect myself. You had lied, that's what I said—you broke your promise. So I had been wrong. So you must have known. I am"—I hold up my hand with a smile that twists around my heart—"aware of the irony."

She holds my gaze for a minute, searching. For something withheld, for one last drop of blood. Then she heaves a breath and releases it in a sob. She is trembling.

"Devajyoti, full of light," she says, and briefly closes her eyes. "They nearly shot you at dinner today." She traces my lips with her fingers. "Don't leave me for my own good. Don't hide from me to protect me. You think you owe me anything? If you think you owe me anything, give me yourself. If he had shot you, what do you think I'd have let lie? What peace do you see in me that could survive something . . . happening . . ."

The silk of her robe slides against my arms when I lift her, slips askew to bare one breast. The other presses hard against the fabric. Her breath catches in surprise.

"Do you promise?" she asks.

All I say is, "Let's sleep here tonight."

On the sooty floor before the fireplace, I slide Pea's robe from her shoulders. I see for the first time the scar from Maryann West's bullet. An ugly keloid lump of pink tissue, stretching an inch below her collarbone to the far side of her armpit. She is stoic as I take this in. There are other scars on her beautiful, naked body. But this is the only one I know.

"You told me it didn't hurt anymore."

She smiles briefly. "And you let me lie."

We can be so cruel to one another. So full of love and hate and need and almost nothing of compassion. But this I can give her—this, and my promise. I bend down, kiss her shoulder. My lips slide down its smooth, freckled expanse. I wait for her to relax. I rub my thumb lightly over her left nipple, wrinkled and erect. She arches, very slightly, over my bracing right hand. I kiss, slowly, slowly, down the length of that hideous reminder, until I understand it as part of her. A part of what I love, and of my amends.

She comes against my hand, crying out without thought for Walter and Tamara sleeping upstairs. She grips me and breathes my name over and over. It could just as easily be sweat, the salt on our skins in the dying firelight.

10

The Long Island City address had once been a supply shop for the nearby factories. But the crash had hit all industry hard. No surprise to see it abandoned out here, among the deserted warehouses. At night it seemed two-dimensional. Gray as a photograph.

I jumped the fence. I was athletic and skilled at this particular sport. The razor-topped wire only swayed. I rolled, paused in a crouch. Pressed my hands to the earth and felt for anyone listening. No one near—but faint vibrations told me that someone approached. In back, I found the window Trent had promised behind a row of depilated bushes. Grimy, dirt- and smog-encrusted, it opened barely two inches. Judging by the rusted hinges, I doubted it could be moved from that position. I peered through. About half of the space below was visible. The light had been left on. Cement floor, swept clean. Black walls on which someone had recently chalked two pentagrams. A series of symbols radiated from the points of each one in intersecting curves that reminded me of mandalas.

In front of each pentagram hung one meat hook. It seemed more ominous, somehow, that they were all clean.

"You got him, Red Man?"

Victor's voice, always higher than I expected. Tonight it seemed reedy, breathless. But Red Man was the one hauling the body. One body, but two hooks. Someone groaned.

"Coming round already?" Victor laughed. "Aren't you a good one. Should give me plenty. Red Man, lay him under again. I'm going . . ."

Red Man sighed. "To get it over with."

Victor barked a laugh. I finally saw him when he descended the stairs to the basement. In and out of my field of vision, he opened crates, placed small objects at the cardinal points beneath each hook. I couldn't see the objects clearly enough until he passed beneath the window. But that sick feeling in my stomach was recognition, not surprise. They were hands. A dozen shrunken, mummified hands.

Red Man called from the staircase. "He's coming to again. You ready, Vic?"

"Bring him down."

Victor was dragging something large and heavy across the floor. A man-shaped bundle, with short legs and hideously elongated arms. A bit of straw and cotton stuffing leaked from where the head had been crudely stitched to the torso with hide thread. The face, however, was finely worked papier-mâché over cotton batting. It had gray eyes and a brown mop of a wig and a wide, grinning mouth. Inside were four or five teeth, firmly affixed.

Even the gap-toothed smile seemed like Victor's.

He hung the effigy from a metal loop affixed to its back on the hook to the left. The procedure felt practiced. Once hooked, the figure's arms ended just before the points of the pentagram on the wall behind it. It had no hands.

Red Man thumped heavily down the stairs. He carried their captive like a baby, a lolling head propped against a sturdy chest. A black man, my age or even a bit younger. He had been spiffy before they found him: slicked-back hair and tailored vest. His jacket and shoes were long gone, but the man still had on one of his spats.

"You know I'm not staying for this."

Victor snorted. He fingered his waistband, where he kept one of his guns. But beneath the posturing I glimpsed something oddly vulnerable.

"God damn, have you got some nerve getting squeamish now."

"What I do is business. Not hocus-pocus."

"This hocus-pocus is gonna keep us in business and then richer than ever. You don't think I know how jumpy our boys at the precinct are getting with old Judge Seabury breathing down their necks?

That upstart Valentine and his so-called Confidentials are trying to make everyone turn rat, but we won't let 'em, now will we?"

"Better ways to hunt down informants, Vic. I keep telling you."

Victor turned abruptly away and stalked out of my field of vision. "Hang him, you bloody Indian."

Something sparked behind Red Man's eyes. Colder than rage. So tightly controlled it made Victor's outburst seem like a child's. I wondered, for the first time, who really had the power in that relationship.

Red Man set the man on the floor and tied a rope around his chest and shoulders. It formed a harness, which then held his weight when he dangled from the meat hook. His legs jerked and sent him tracing an oblong star in the air. He gasped and coughed, but though his eyes fluttered, they did not open.

Victor returned to the center of the room. He held a small pair of pliers and a handsaw. His eyes were glassy and blazing. The handsaw he put beneath the swinging man's feet. The pliers he handed to Red Man.

"Do it," he said. "I have the rest."

Red Man, whose name was Walter Finch, though I did not know it at the time, glanced again at the hanging man. He nodded.

"Upper right bicuspid," Victor said.

I was trying to parse the code—or was it slang?—when Red Man pressed Victor against the pentagram wall behind the straw-and-cotton man. Pressed him with one large hand over the chest. Victor gazed up at him like a lover, sick with anticipation. He opened his mouth. Red Man kissed him with the pliers. Grabbed the tooth and yanked. Victor trembled and jerked. He would have fallen down if not for the one hand pinning him like a butterfly. When it was done, Red Man pressed the bloody thing into Victor's palm.

"I'll be upstairs," he said. His gaze slid over the far wall, where I was hiding behind the lone window. My breath stopped. But he just turned his head and left. Victor, alone, shook and cursed and spit blood onto the concrete floor. Then he lit a menthol cigarette, and started to work.

The man woke in the middle of it. He screamed so loudly I thought my skin would peel. There were incantations, which Victor hurled like curses around the hole in his mouth. There were signs burned into skin and an invocation of the devil and his unholy help-meets. The man screamed until Victor broke his jaw. Then he just cried.

I stayed. That was the job. Victor stumbled up the stairs, blood-soaked and delirious. I stayed. I could no longer feel my own hands. Victor could have walked up on me with a gun and I'd never have noticed. Victor ran the water. He whistled. I stayed.

Red Man, silent, came downstairs again. He stood in front of the hanging man. The only sound was a high whine through a constricted throat. Red Man bowed his head. He might have said a prayer. And then he raised his gun and shot the man between the eyes.

He turned around when it was done. Stared straight at my window, and I stared straight back. I was nearly invisible there. He should never have seen me. I never knew if he did.

He nodded once. He lifted the dead man down.

11

We sleep together and it is relief inexpressible. It is Pea's head on my shoulder and my arm draped over her torso. It is easy.

I smell smoke. Cloying, like burning trash. My fingers twitch: a warning.

Wreathed in a happier dream, I don't heed it until my palms are burning. By which time Bobby Junior is walking with killer purpose across our living room. He releases the safety of his father's heirloom 5mm Bergmann.

Pea is half-asleep. I drag her upright and she follows me behind the couch. Not enough protection, but thankfully Junior's first shot goes wide. The bullet ricochets against the marble mantlepiece and buries itself in the wall just behind his head.

The shock of that widens his puffy eyes. "Bitch," he mutters.

Pea stares at me. She heard that vicious echo. A shiver of a ghost passing through. And we might just join him in a few moments—she's left her knives out of reach. We're both half-naked. The nearest potentially deadly object is the fireplace poker. Bobby Junior shoots again. The bullet tunnels through the couch and buries itself in the wood beneath.

"It's you," I whisper. I point to the French windows.

She blinks slowly. Bobby Junior is muttering something, approaching us again. We're only still alive because of his shaky aim, but he was raised hunting. He'll steady if we give him the opportunity.

Pea takes both my hands, kisses me hard, and pushes me away. I stand with her momentum and run.

I scream Walter's name as I hurtle for the French windows. They open outward. There's a chance I can jump through and take cover outside. I plan for it, even though I fully expect one of Junior's bullets to rip through my back.

The next three seconds pass like pebbles through water. One, I'm halfway to the windows. Two, Bobby Junior says, "Murdering bastard." I am terrified he means Pea. Three, he shoots. I drop to the floor.

Four, five, six: the vase of colored glass falls from the mantlepiece and fractures. The poker clatters to the floor. A moment later, Junior's head thuds softly against the rug.

"He didn't hit you," Pea says. She kneels, two fingers pressed against his neck.

"No," I say, rolling onto my back. I had felt her movement behind me and known it would be safer to drop in place than go for the window. "You'd had enough time."

She gives me a brilliant smile. "Oh, baby, imagine what we'd have been together."

I could tell her that I'd never have killed the people she did. But that isn't what she means. And besides—I might have.

"Bastard's still alive," she says. And then, "Turn around, Walter, let me get my robe."

Tamara freezes behind him. "Fucking hell, Phyllis, what's that white boy doing on the floor?"

"Tried to shoot us," I tell Tamara. I climb wearily to my feet. I need to sleep for weeks. To not be on the wrong end of a gun for at least a decade.

"Will he wake up, Pea?" Tamara asks.

"In a few hours. He probably needs a doctor."

Walter sighs. "You should have either killed the bastard or left him healthy enough to talk."

"He was shooting at Dev."

Tamara shakes her head in a vigorous denial of reality. "Sugar, this is *terrible*. Thank goodness we came, Walter! I *told* you something was wrong, and look, it's hotter here than the Village in July."

Walter looks between the two of us. He is, as ever, calm and impassive in judgment. I haven't been afraid of Walter for years, but his focused attention unsettles. All too often what follows is his violence, merciless and precise. After nearly a minute he inclines his head.

"Something to drink, Dev?" he says. "Let's keep an eye on the mayor's boy and see what we can work out."

So an hour before dawn Walter, Pea, Tamara, and I build up the fire again and share the last bottle from my last liquor run. Junior rests in state between us. He scowls even in unconsciousness. Pea and I take turns with the story of recent events in Little Easton.

"The strange thing is," I say, "that Junior tried to kill *Pea*. Alvin told me he was convinced Junior wanted to kill him."

"Walter, Phyllis—don't you get a funny feeling about that boy?" Tamara asks. She has slid down the couch until she is nearly recumbent. One hand rests on my thigh, her head lists against my shoulder. She sniffs the dregs of her third glass of cognac. It could break my heart to see her like this—still afraid of violence, but determined to get drunk enough to hide it.

"Alvin's afraid of something. But I wouldn't trust . . ." Pea trails off. Junior has begun to snuffle like a warming engine. His eyes roll frantically beneath closed lids.

I lean forward. "Pea?"

"Do you—" Walter says, at the same time that Pea and I stand.

"Someone's coming," she says.

We all go outside. It's a patrol car, shining white and blue in the limpid light of a new sun. I register the insignia of the state troopers instead of the Hudson patrol that occasionally passes through.

"I think, I'm afraid—Phyllis, baby, I'm going to vomit."

Pea grabs Tamara around the waist and holds her hair back while she gets sick. The state trooper climbs from the car. White, about the same age as Walter, balding though he thinks the comb-over hides it. I haven't spoken to Finn since I told him I'd consider calling Valentine.

I never called Valentine.

My old handler nods to me. His lips twist when he sees Walter, and he shakes his head. His disappointment is clear as his headlights. He won't say anything in front of Walter, he won't sign my death warrant this morning. But he won't trust me again.

"Mr. Patil, Mr. Finch."

There's no way to describe my loyalties that would make sense to him. Finn's cleaner than most, dirtier than some. But he still believes that fundamental lie—that the worst of us are better than the best of them.

"You all had better come with me." Something in his voice makes me look back at Pea. She's taken Tamara a few feet away, so she can finish her business in the azaleas. If I'm no longer an officer in Finn's eyes, I might have lost all of my leverage to protect her. His manner is cold and professional to Lower Manhattan's most powerful mob boss. The same boss that Valentine and Dewey are supposedly itching to bring down. Could they be close? My gaze meets Pea's over Tamara's back. She shakes her head. She smiles.

"What's this about?" Walter is careful, bland, his most frightening.

Finn judges his words. He shifts his weight forward, then back. "Ben Craver is in the hospital, shot and left for dead, nearly bled to death. Looks like the same someone killed Mayor Bell an hour before. That's when they called us in. No one can find his son. Our prime suspect is missing and you two were the last ones seen with him."

It sharpens the cold of the morning. I take a step back and sink into a muddy puddle. Walter lifts a hand and settles it by his side.

But Pea is at her most essential. She hauls Tamara upright and points at the house with her free hand.

"If you're looking for Bobby Junior, he's in there," says the woman I was once ashamed to love. "Along with the gun he shot at us with."

Robert Bell, the fifth of his family to serve as mayor of Little Easton on Hudson, has lost the back of his head. The gun was fired at close range. There are scorch marks around the dimpled hole on his forehead and splintered bone edging the bullet's exit. The eggshell color of his skin is mottled blue and gray around his left arm, where they say he fell.

No one imagines that any of us held the gun. But we are who we are, and we were among the last to see him alive. They assume that we must have been involved.

A reasonable assumption, in their circumstances.

"You were all in that house?" Finn repeats. He hasn't looked at me once since we arrived. "All night?"

"Until the dead man's son tried to kill us, yes." Walter's tone is particularly dry. If Finn had any sense he'd stop pushing. But he just nods thoughtfully and licks his lips. It's become personal for him. We've been here for an hour. Long enough to see the body and refuse the watery coffee. To wait on officers conversing in low voices in the hallway.

Pea straightens suddenly. "This is ridiculous," she says. "You know we couldn't have done this. Arrest us or let us go."

"Don't tempt me," Finn says. He looks at her as he would a cockroach. As if it's faintly offensive she can even speak. I clench my fists at my sides.

"As Bobby Bell Junior has yet to wake up," he says, "we only have your side of the story for what happened."

Pea raises a delicately incredulous eyebrow. "The bullets from his gun weren't enough to convince you he was shooting at us? And something tells me that they are the same bullets that got Craver. That's an unusual gun. So what are you proposing, that we somehow provoked Junior into shooting Craver and then finishing us off?"

Finn grimaces. "The boy, Alvin Spalding, was reportedly at your house as well."

Pea's face gives nothing away. She breathes just as easily. But she's afraid. "We took him back home. I don't know where he's gone."

"We think he's run. Innocent men don't do that, Miss LeBlanc."

"*Scared* men do. You can't think he shot Mayor Bell."

"We—the investigation is ongoing."

So they aren't sure. There is something peculiar about the case that he isn't telling us. Walter leans forward and taps his fingers lightly on his knee.

"That man was shot point-blank, wasn't he, Phyllis?"

Pea smiles. "I'd say so, Walter."

"He was a big man, Mayor Bell. It'd be hard for such a small boy to get close enough to a big man like that. And it was an even shot. No signs of struggle, am I right?"

I finally see where he's leading us. "But he wasn't asleep," I say. "Which means someone he trusted enough to get close."

"Which is not," Pea says, "Alvin Spalding."

I stand. "*Officer* Finn, can I have a word?"

Finn jerks. He's gotten thinner since the second divorce. His salt-and-pepper beard is now pure snow. He looks at me like he'd rather slug me. The feeling is mutual. But he nods silently and leads me out into the hallway and another interrogation room.

"You bastard," he yells as soon as he closes the door. He pushes me against the table. "You goddamn bastard! You want to announce to that pair of killers that you're a cop? That we know each other? Want to put a bull's-eye on my forehead?"

I grab Finn's wrists and swing him into the wall. Harder than I need to—it punches the breath from him. His eyes widen.

"Should have guessed . . ." He gasps. ". . . when Valentine didn't hear from you. Never would have pegged you to turn dirty, kid. Not back then."

"Life changes you, Finn."

I release him. He sags against the wall. "That it does, kid."

"I just can't—not to Walter. I don't expect you to understand. But he doesn't know a thing about you. I can still do the job."

"Too damn well. You could double-agent for the devil."

It would have been a compliment, ten years ago. Now it's thickened to shame. Not only to have committed evil, but to have done it so well.

Finn nods. "I won't arrest you all now—"

"You wouldn't dare. Not Walter. And you don't think we did it anyway."

"Not with your own hands."

"Finn. What aren't you telling me?"

He's still breathing hard. His face is flushed. He squints like he's in pain, and I regret how hard I threw him.

"Are you even an officer anymore, Patil? Or are you one of Red Man's gang?"

A familiar hand clamps my heart and then, suddenly, lets go. I say it. "Both."

He shakes his head. But he puts his hands on the table and meets my eyes. "The gun, Officer Patil," he says. "The gun that Bobby Junior used on you and Ben Craver also killed Mayor Bell."

The pieces slide into place. "The boy," I say.

"The boy," he agrees. "Access to the house. Sneaky hands like yours. Either that or we believe that Junior killed his own father."

"You'll let us go?"

"If they have anything to do with this, I know you won't tell me. And Dewey wants Red Man. One last trophy before he makes his run on Albany."

"He won't get him. You have to know that."

Finn smiles thinly. "You aren't the only good agent on the city beat, Patil. We might just surprise you."

Walter goes back to the city.

"I'll call when I've taken care of that letter," he says.

"You're a real friend."

"Vice has someone else at the Pelican. High, I suspect. I'll need you to find out who it is."

I make myself swallow. "You can't yourself?"

"I could."

He waits for me. Red Man stillness, its faint whiff of ironic detachment. I could refuse. And he could let the draft swallow me whole.

"Give me—until things calm down here," I say. He just nods and closes the Packard door.

Tamara stays the week.

Alvin stays gone.

Bobby Junior comes to and claims self-defense. He blames Alvin for murdering Bobby Senior. Says that the boy told him Craver had hired Pea to kill him and his father. When he found Senior dead, he went after us without asking more questions.

"Sounds more like revenge than self-defense," is Pea's dry response. But they only charge him with one count of attempted manslaughter. Craver might still die. Pea and I, of course, don't count.

Alvin is their prime suspect, mostly because it costs them nothing to accuse a runaway Negro boy. It would cost them a great deal to investigate a man like Bobby Bell, with the powerful enemies he had accrued in a lifetime of politics. Still, Alvin had plenty of reasons to hate the Bells. Even more to fear them. His scheme, then, had been to position us as a barrier between himself and the anger of the two most powerful men in town. And maybe we were even meant to be his fall guys. Pea doesn't believe he killed Mayor Bell. Me? I think Alvin is just as capable of evil as the two of us. I just don't know why he would have left Junior alive.

I think Pea has seen him. I think she has fed him a few evenings when she claimed to go shopping in town. She hasn't told me for the same reason I haven't told her about my letter from the president. We are holding our trouble close, hoping it goes away. But we hold each other closer.

Tamara helps Pea cook extravagant dishes and touches me too much when Pea can see, and not at all when we're alone. It's her way of being fair. She doesn't mention her man, though missing him hurts her like a bullet in the ribs.

"Pea," she says, on our last evening together. We've emptied a bottle of wine over a dinner of acorn squash and coq au vin and fresh-baked rolls. Tamara's freshened up for dinner, but Pea is still at her most country. Blue headscarf, a gingham apron that smells of vinegar from the watermelon rinds they spent the day pickling. "Pea, let's go dancing."

Pea pulls the cork from the second bottle and points it in my direction.

"Dev doesn't dance."

"Sure he does! We danced plenty of times, didn't we, sugar?"

I laugh. "I think once or twice I even did it without stepping on your feet."

We take our glasses to the salon. By the record player, Tamara selects a fast Beiderbecke number and holds out her hand to Pea.

They dance lindy, dissolving into laughter when one or the other takes the lead. Joyous in each other's presence. I had wondered how it would be to touch and smell my old lover again. But we fit, as we have always been meant to.

Pea finds and uncorks our last bottle of wine, an unknown local variety. It's thick and sweet and slides down the glass's curved side in Ws and Vs. I stare at the liquid that looks nothing like blood.

"Dev?" Pea says.

"Let me get my cards," Tamara says. Her voice fades out as she wanders out of the room. Pea takes the glass from me and drains it in a gulp.

"What do you need, Dev?"

She smiles that way she does. That self-lacerating crescent. I take her hand. Its scars, for the moment, mark nothing more than mistakes we have made. I stand unsteadily.

"Dance with me?"

Surprise and laughter and a low-throated murmur in my ear, "Don't even try to lead."

The feel of our bodies sweating and moving in rhythm. The smell of her hair when the scarf falls to the floor. I don't even realize Tamara is watching until the needle scratches the end of the record.

"You're . . . Anyone want to ask the cards something?"

She holds up her old deck wrapped in an ivory silk handkerchief, monogrammed with some old lover's initials. There's envy in that sweet face. And desire. It suddenly comes clear—it's not only for me.

We turn down the lights and share the last of the reefer Walter left with us.

Tamara unwraps the deck and starts shuffling, tossing the cards from her left hand to her right at a rapid clip. Pea watches her in silence for a moment and then snatches a card from the air. She balances it on the end of her index finger and then throws it back into the deck that Tamara hasn't stopped shuffling.

Tamara laughs, delighted. "Girl, you show off like that—" She stops. A wave of pain is passing over Pea's face and her fingers are rigid claws against her thighs. I reach for Pea but she shakes me off.

She takes a gulping breath. The force, whatever it was, subsides. "Go on, then, Tammy."

Tamara puts the cards down, half-shuffled. "And what the hell was that?"

Pea sighs. "A debt. Or a broken promise."

"Your hands?"

"I don't think they were ever—wholly—mine."

I frown. I had dismissed this, before. It was easy to pin it on panic or paranoia, her own guilty conscience. But this time—this time, for a sliver of a second, I had felt something threaten her. My hands had touched an inverted echo: bright and angry and scented with marigolds.

"And since when have they been . . ." Tamara gestures helplessly.

Pea leans back against the couch and folds her arms tightly across her chest. I watch her, but I know better than to touch. "Since Victor," she says shortly.

Tamara makes a small, high-pitched noise from behind pursed lips. "But I thought . . ." she tries. She looks at me, a little desperately.

"I killed him," I say, in a tone so matter-of-fact, it could have come from another throat entirely.

Pea's expression is murder. "Oh, did you?"

Tamara swallows. "But Pea, even if your hands are, are—"

"Turning against me?"

"That. Why would they turn on you after you *didn't* kill Victor?

When you've"—Tammy takes another gulping breath—"killed so many others?"

Her voice fades into a questioning whisper. I'm surprised she made it this far. All the time I've known her, Tamara has had a champion ability to unnotice the violence surrounding her. I don't know if it's curiosity or her love for Pea that has prompted her to, at last, acknowledge out loud what the rest of us know.

"I reckon," says my lover, with furious self-mockery, "that they wanted me to do the deed. Not our sainted Dev, now fallen, poor thing, in my low company."

I don't respond to this; it would be too cruel. I know why she let me do it. I remember how she seized in my arms at the thought of another kill. On the job, we passed around the story of a prison guard, one who pulled the switch on the hot squat. Man woke up one day and could no longer pull that lever. It did not matter that the prisoner would die anyway. It did not matter for what crime. Sometimes a human soul can no longer mete out death, no matter how justified, without destroying itself entirely.

"But there's got to be a way to stop this!" Tamara says. "Why do they want to punish you now? The man's dead, anyhow."

Pea closes her eyes. "Oh, why don't you ask them, Tammy? Lord, but you are getting on my last nerve."

A second dream had come to her back in New York. She never told me the details, but I suspect it had involved killing Victor. And she tried. Oh, maybe we had doomed ourselves a decade before, from all our terrible choices, all our flawed love. But she still tried.

I reach out to trace the tight coils by her hairline. She stiffens, then sighs and leans into my hand.

Tammy has picked up her deck again, shuffling so fast you'd think she had the hands herself. Her tongue is poking a tent in her cheek and she has the eyes of a woman whose thoughts are moving as fast as her cards. I wonder what she thinks those cards can fix, now.

She shuffles once, pulls out the top card, shuffles again, pulls out another, then another. Seven of hearts, seven of spades, nine of spades.

"What does that mean?" I ask her.

But Tammy just bites her bottom lip and shakes her head.

Pea slams her hand on the table. Tammy freezes. "It doesn't matter," Pea says, and kisses me. As exact as I am sloppy, but we are equally desperate.

"It doesn't matter," she repeats. We fall together again. Silent, blessed, purged of conscious thought.

At some point we remember Tamara. I can't tell if it's my hand or Pea's that reaches out when she gets up to leave. Pea's words bob to the surface of my turbid thoughts: *doesn't matter, it doesn't matter.* Like my secrets and my dead. Like my lingering desire for my old lover.

Tamara, one hand on my shoulder, the other on Pea's cheek. Pea's crescent smile transformed to a real one. It doesn't surprise me when Tamara kisses her first. Pea grips my hand. My knuckles twist and bunch. As if she trusts me to pull her from the rapids, but only if she holds on hard enough.

We change. No longer two and one, but three. My consciousness has crested past coherency. I am bright and dark and a series of shades in between. I am kissing Pea. I am kissing Tamara. I love. I want. I fuck. I've lost the direct object. My penis touches the back of Tamara's throat. I push my tongue into Pea's vagina and then withdraw it slowly. She tastes of lemons and grass and, faintly, of blood. It reminds me of—there's a reason why—

Our desire's shining fury. The thought dissolves. There is nothing more particular about the taste of her than the smell of her. The way Pea looks at me when I kiss along that corrugated ridge of skin.

She whispers something. Tamara smiles and pulls me down. We are both between her legs, tasting her and then one another. When she comes that first time, she kicks out hard against my hip. It might hurt. She speaks. The words separate into syllables. They dance nonsense in my head. I can see apology in her wet and dreamy eyes. I love. I want. I fuck. And here, the arm at the other end of mine. The weight on the opposing scale. The killing forces, perfectly arrayed: evil, justice, beauty.

Later, we subside. Substances unknowable flake white from our naked bodies. Tamara sleeps, curled against my side. In the hazy dawn, Pea gets a blanket. She places it gently over me and Tamara. Our eyes meet. The sentence completes.

"It doesn't matter," she whispers, and smiles—remote, indecipherable.

The curve of her spine as she leaves. The creak of the stairs as she climbs them alone.

12

That night, after more than twenty years of silence, a dream descends. My hands open like the lotus and let it in.

I dream of a river like the Hudson, but wider and deeper, trees looming on either side of its turbid expanse like rows of serrated teeth. I dream of a boat on that river, wooden, gleaming with fresh white paint. Sails the color of a sky before a storm. At the prow is an old wooden table, and on that table a body draped in white cloth. For my father, and in my childhood, white was the color of mourning, not black. But I don't dream of who lies beneath that shroud. Lights appear one by one among the trees. Flickering lights like candles. Bigger ones like torches. Their bearers remain in shadow.

Phyllis speaks from somewhere along the shore: "I will kill him," she says.

She wears white and there are three knives sheathed in her heart. She does not bleed. She holds the silver lighter I gave her years ago, with the rough circle I scored on one side. With this she sets fire to her dress. Though it burns, she merely shines in its light. Ashes bury her feet.

The river lights up the sky—or the sky flashes brightly enough to shine to the bottom of the river.

Now I can see clearly: it is filled with floating shapes. Not fish, as I first assume, but men. Hundreds and hundreds of men suspended in shallows and the deep like fish hiding from prey. They wear uniforms and they carry guns, but the bullets they fire float like eggs to the surface. They collect against the roots and grass and mud of the shore.

Alvin is there. He approaches from the woods to stand beside her. He rips one of the knives from her chest. "I will kill him," he says. Phyllis kisses the top of his head.

Craver, wrinkled white skin wrapped around a heart of limestone, crawls from the bullets in the shallows and grasps at the burning hem of Phyllis's dress. Phyllis takes a second knife from her chest and hands it to him.

"I will kill him," the old man says.

I come to her then, naked and bleeding from my feet. I'm clutching a sheet of paper in my right hand: *ORDER TO REPORT FOR INDUCTION*.

I reach for Phyllis, but she turns away from me. She jumps into the river and swims through its illuminated depths until she reaches the boat. She climbs it, naked and shining. In the back of the boat, on the opposite side from the shrouded body, grows a garden. There are tea roses, pink and yellow, and watermelons starred like the night sky in a painting by Van Gogh.

Phyllis grabs the roses by their thorny stalks and rips them from their bed of warped wood. Her face contorts with pain, but she does not cry. Her hands tear with the force, but the wounds don't bleed. By the shore, a woman screams her name—Tamara's voice, though I never see her. Over and over, Phyllis rips the roses until only petals and bleeding green branches remain.

She does not destroy the watermelons. She only picks one up, kisses it tenderly, and hurls it into the river. It explodes like a grenade.

Phyllis faces the prow of the ship, its shrouded body. She pulls the last knife from her chest.

"I have killed them," she says, and she bleeds for the first time: a dark rain between her legs.

Tamara takes the train back to the city the next day. She grips my hand on the platform as though she longs to tell me something. In the end she just puts on her smile and kisses my cheeks.

I do not tell Pea of my dream. I wonder, as she must have, if this presages my death, or another kind of change.

The following morning is Mayor Bell's memorial. It dawns winter-cold. Two state squad cars have parked alongside the hearse in front of the church. Which means Bobby Junior is already inside. The police are monitoring his movements until the attempted manslaughter case goes before a grand jury. Though Craver might never wake up, several local papers have called even that charge a political frame-up. They blame it on anarchist elements in Albany.

My mother asked me to come to Mayor Bell's farewell. To represent the family, she said. The war has made regular communication with Britain impossible. She's as safe as anyone can be, on a Devon country estate, out of the range of the blitz. But the connection was predictably terrible, and her request unexpected. I was too shocked to object.

Pea hasn't told me why she wanted to come. I didn't need to ask. Her reason appears a moment before the reverend steps up to the lectern. An eddy in the crowd of latecomers standing by the doors. It ripples outward in whispers and gasps and second glances over shoulders.

"She *dares*?" whispers a woman in front of us. I wonder how Pea plans to protect Mae Spalding, here to bid farewell to her former employer. The man police claim that her son murdered.

The pastor, unaware or pragmatic, continues his eulogy of the late mayor: "a legendary statesman," "a loving father." Even that last seems suspect. Junior's manfully suppressed tears notwithstanding. The Bobby Senior I remember ran this town like a despot king. He exploited it with a jovial immorality bred into him by generations of Bells.

Pea twists at the far edge of the pew. She fixes her gaze on the church attendants flanking Mae. For the rest of the ceremony they stand guard beside her. I assume the hope is to induce her to leave without causing a scene. If so, they are disappointed. Every time Junior darts a look from the front, she sets back her shoulders. Her gaze is righteous and direct, Moses come down from the mountain.

She sweats like a man in the desert, too. A steady stream dampens the collar and armpits of her gray dress. Twice during the service she closes her eyes and sways. But after a moment she seems to regain her equilibrium and we relax.

The recessional is "Be Thou My Vision," bloodless liturgical fare that Pea would mock in happier circumstances. One moment I'm mouthing my way through and the next Pea has sprinted to Mae's side. Mae leans against her in a half faint, eyes rolling, breath spastic.

Junior's control snaps. He barrels down the nave ahead of the pastor and rips Mae from Pea's grip.

"Leave!" He shakes her. She looks at him as if she has just woken up. Smiles slowly.

"Did you imagine you'd be welcome here? Your son killed my father! If we weren't in a church—"

He stops. Pea has a knife at his throat.

"Let her go," says Phyllis.

He lets her go. His skin breaks against the edge of her knife every time he gasps.

"Now," she says, "walk out of this church. The memorial is over and you two got nothing more to say to each other."

"No, no." Mae stands upright with unexpected energy. "I got something to say. One last thing to say."

Phyllis nods permission. She looks proud, as if she had hoped this would happen. I can't fault Mae's fury. But I don't understand the benefit of staging a confrontation at the funeral.

"This I say to you, Robert Randolph Bell Junior, who I fed and clothed and protected like my own until you made clear you weren't any of mine: there exists justice, if not in this world then in the next, and it will find you, for the Lord hath no creed nor color, the Lord keeps his scales, the Lord knows and *the Lord abides*."

Outside a cloud must break. Light pours through the south window. It paints the three in shades of ocean: cerulean, verdigris, and pearl.

Craver wakes up two weeks later. He tells the police that he doesn't remember who attacked him that night. He tells them that it was probably Alvin. Bobby Junior is cleared of all charges, and Marnie hosts a celebration in his honor at the inn that doubles as a fundraising dinner for next year's election. The architects and prospectors begin preliminary work on the grounds of the old church and graveyard. No one tells Craver, slowly recovering in the hospital.

I go to town to pick up a telegram.

TAKEN CARE OF. T SENDS LOVE.

I smile and burn it with the ash end of the cigarette that I smoke outside the hospital doors. Mae waits with me, patient and watchful. Legally, there is no reason we can't enter this hospital as freely as a white man, but Mae and I are more than familiar with the two faces of northern segregation. I promised her I would get us in anyway. I feel wary of seeing my old mentor again, but Mae deserves to say her piece and to help her son. This is a good that my hands can still do, when they have of late been merely self-serving.

"I think," Mae says, apropos of nothing, "that all this time Craver's been like that other one Phyllis told me about, the white man you killed in the city. He's just hid it better, that's all."

It's news to me that Phyllis has told Mae about the nightmare that we've been dragging behind us. I pull my jacket closer and look over at the car, parked at the end of the street, where she's waiting for us. My fingertips vibrate with the feel of her, a liminal tension.

"How . . . precisely . . . is Craver like a New York mobster?"

Mae looks at me as one would a particularly dense schoolchild. "Not the murdering and the money. But the *taking*. He couldn't have Alvin's gift, or yours, himself, so he put himself over you both instead. He made sure other white men like the Bells believed in your gift too, just so they would give him even more of what the world already gives him just for breathing."

I stare at her while the cigarette burns to the filter in my mouth. I never considered it that way.

Craver's piety has long since calcified to myth. But hadn't he ben-

efited from the fear my hands caused around town? Hadn't he made
sure that white folks who normally never spared any thought for the
power of colored people had feared us and respected him?

I drop the butt onto the concrete and put my hands deep into my
pockets.

"The receptionist just left," I say. "Let's go see what the man has
to say."

Craver's room smells like a summer wake. Lilies of the valley, glad-
ioli, hydrangeas, Ophelia and white Killarney roses at the peak of
their bloom. From his Hudson flock, I assume.

The servant of God himself is as pale as the lilies I have to brush
aside to give Mae a place to sit. But his cheeks are flushed. He grimaces when he glances at her. He has his finger on a page of a Bible
he isn't reading.

"They let you in?" he asks me. He seems offended. That's a lot
of energy, I think, from a man who woke up from a coma the day
before.

"We didn't ask permission, Mr. Craver," Mae says. Smooth as
silk stockings. She hasn't taken her eyes from his since she sat down.
"Dev has a way of not being seen when he doesn't want to be."

"I know that about him." Each word costs him. He speaks softly.
Bobby Junior's bullet caught him in the side, ripping through his
lung and skimming his liver. That he is still alive could give one
cause to believe in God. But not his God.

"And we weren't going to let this being a white hospital stop us
from seeing how you fared."

His eyes slide over the top of Mae's head and land on his Bible.
He's scared of her. He's lucky we left Pea sleeping in the back of the
car downstairs.

"They say I'll survive. A few more years."

"Jesus is merciful," says Mae, looking anything but.

"Craver," I say, "who did this to you?"

He bites a thin, cracked lip between still-sturdy teeth. "They

say"—he breathes—"that they will soon break ground on the resort. They have permission"—like fire through a straw—"to move
the bodies."

Mae is a woman all wrung out of pity. "You know my Alvin didn't
do this, old man."

He skims her face again. Gets closer to her eyes. "Of course not."

"Then who did?" I ask. "Bobby Junior? Tell the police the truth.
You can't let them string up an innocent kid for . . . what?"

"He'd already murdered Mayor Bell!" Craver pants. If Pea were
here, she would have objected. I expect Alvin's mother to do the
same, but Mae is silent—and if even she isn't sure, I don't know how
I can be. Craver catches his breath. "I could do nothing else for him.
And I have others to think of."

"You have your bones in the ground. Alvin is alive."

He is astonished. "Davey, there will come a day when all the living will be the dead, and when all the dead will become the living
in the glory of our Lord. There is no logical reason on this earth to
value one over the other. I am the only hope for salvation of two
hundred and forty-eight souls. What is one little Negro boy to that?"

A brief silence. Then Mae slaps him. The Bible falls to the floor,
a thud and spray of tissue-thin paper. He groans like an animal left
for hours in a trap.

"Dev," says Mae behind gritted teeth. "Be kind enough to leave us?"

"Davey—"

I put a hand on his shoulder. I feel as much of a threat to him as
I would to a corpse. "She won't hurt you," I say.

"Don't wait," she says, over her shoulder. Her hands rest on the
bed, right beside Craver's weeping jowls. "This might take a while.
Better to get Phyllis home."

I look back sharply. "Is she—"

"*Go*, Dev."

Craver looks like a man about to drop from a hanging tree. I don't
even think of saving him.

———

Pea is leaning against the driver's-side door when I get back to the car. She trembles, hands rigid against her sides, eyes darting. She looks sick, or haunted. She seems unaware of my presence. My heart squeezes out a few explosive beats. We have been happy, we have been true, we have been, at last, right, these last few weeks. And I had thought we might have just a little longer.

But here, she's hurting. Nothing else I can do. I take her in my arms, hold her rigid against me until she seems to recognize my skin or my smell and lets me hold her up. She murmurs something.

"What? Pea, Sweet Pea, what—"

"Don't hit him," she says, just loud enough for me to hear. "He's . . . in front of the car? I think? Be careful. Don't hit him."

I'd ask her what she means but she starts to tremble again. For an awful moment I think she's fainted. But then she opens her eyes wide and takes two steps back. She's hot to the touch.

"Are you sick?"

She looks afraid, and then angry with herself. "Don't know, Dev. Just got a feeling. Why don't you drive us home?"

I drive us home. She sleeps most of the way, her head at an uncomfortable angle against the windshield. I move her to my shoulder. She doesn't even murmur. But at some predetermined moment, close to the house, she pulls herself upright, gasps, and says: "The brakes, Dev."

A figure darts across the road a moment later. I wouldn't have seen him if not for Pea's warning.

Which she had given one second before the figure—the boy—actually came into view. I swerve, squeal to a stop, turn to stare at her.

"Pea—"

She just shakes her head. Alvin has stopped too, like a deer in the road, but relaxes when he recognizes us.

"You came from Hudson?" he asks when I roll down the window. "You saw Craver? He tell you why he set me up like that?"

"I left him with your mother," I say, "but I don't know what she'll be able to do. He seemed determined to blame you. I think you should get the hell out of town, Alvin."

The boy shakes his head. His hair is damp despite the clear, brisk day. It sprays a pair of drops on my arm. "Can't leave my folks," he says. "This ain't their fault."

"They should leave too," I say. "Before the bank forces them out."

He sticks his jaw out. "I'm going to Craver, if he's talking he might as well talk to me. Tell me to my face why he lied like that. I didn't do shit to nobody. I don't deserve this."

"You did plenty of shit to plenty of somebodies, kid," Pea says, with a smile at once ironic and fond. "But no, you don't deserve this. Dev's right. Leave town. Find our friend Walter in the city and you might just make it."

"I don't want to make it! I want it to be *right*. What good are these hands, if I can't even make this one thing right?"

Pea turns away abruptly. Alvin looks at me. "I don't want to end up like your angel."

I sit up. Angry, yes, but also a little sick. "What do you mean?"

"Glorious," he says, "but damned."

"And what the devil would you know of—"

"I've got to get myself right first," he says to Phyllis, who only watches him through lidded eyes. "Then I'll know what to do. How to be worthy of them."

He looks down, so earnest that I could shake him.

"Come by when you want, Alvin," Pea says. Her forehead is shiny with sweat, but the hand I hold is cold. "I'll make a plate for you."

He shakes his head. "Thank you, Miss Phyllis. Angel. But from now on . . ."

Pea smiles. "Cast me away from you, then, sweet boy. I hope it does you some good. I hope you can do what I never could."

Two days later she really does faint. She slides to the floor in the kitchen and bruises her hip. "Pea," I say, "why don't we go to a doctor?"

"It's nothing, I'm fine."

"But—"

"I'll be more careful. Trust me, Dev. You don't need to worry."

Her smile is a warning. But sometimes I am brave enough for her.

"If you know what's wrong, then tell me."

"You don't—this is my business, Dev."

"Don't I get to worry?"

"Sure you do. Hell, I could give you lessons. But you don't get to bother me with it."

"Pea, I love—"

"What was that phone call about a month ago? What did Walter take care of for you?"

She waits. And sometimes I am not nearly brave enough.

"Well, then," she says after a minute fat with silence. But then she adds, "I never told you that Alvin had been coming around, either."

We look at each other and then rest our heads together, gently.

"I knew about that anyway."

"I knew that you knew, baby, isn't that the strangest? I never even had to tell you."

13

Trent Sullivan had up and dusted. That's what Finn was saying, anyway. I was worried enough to hunt him down. I went to the Pelican when Pea wasn't there—she was starting to wonder about my interest in her world. She didn't suspect the truth. No, she worried that I wanted in. I tried to imagine my shape beneath her fingertips.

A junior private eye, not doing as well as he'd like. Feet on the right side of the law and a gaze straying down the horizon. We had been breathing with the other's lungs, sleeping in the other's skin, soaking sheets in the other's sweat for two months. I loved her the way Sita loved Rama. A god's love. A saint's love. But we were mortals, with hearts of wax and joints of ash. We had touched the other's smallest, hidden self, but we could only see them blurred, through murky water. I thought I saw her more clearly than she saw me.

But not enough, in the end. Not nearly.

Red Man sat down beside me at the bar. He had put his hand on my shoulder. He told the barman to make me a drink.

"Dry martini, Mitch," he said. "Fine by you, Dev?"

I nodded. It felt natural. Relaxed. He didn't threaten me. Not that I could feel. My throat still felt as tight as a bent straw.

"You know my name," I said.

"Course I do, Dev. Our best girl is dizzy for you. It's only natural for us to take an interest."

I nodded again. I should have anticipated this. He had never so much as glanced at me and I was a rookie fool for thinking that meant he wasn't looking.

"And what's yours?" My strained, far-off voice again.

I was thinking of that gentle shot in the basement. I was thinking of how he had breathed, after. He had closed his eyes.

"What's my what, Dev?"

"Name?"

Now he laughed. Short, genuinely surprised. "You know it."

"I know what they call you." Mitch gave me that drink and backed off like he'd pulled a grenade pin. I forced a large swallow past the bend in my throat. "I was wondering if you call yourself something different."

The man by my side removed his hand from my shoulder. He looked at me with no expression at all.

Thirty seconds of the thin clarinet from the stage, shouted orders at the bar, giggling girls and arch-voiced women. I thought they might be the last sounds I ever heard.

"Walter," he said. "My name's Walter Finch. And I think our Phyllis LeBlanc might have known what she was doing when she brought you home, Devajyoti Patil."

"I love her," I said, like some John in a two-penny paperback. But it didn't feel like a stupid thing to say.

"She's a beautiful killer—she has that effect on people."

"She's not a killer. She's a woman who—I want to take her away from here."

He laughed. "You do."

"The way she lives—it's destroying her."

"Now, that's just the human condition." He looked at my glass, the olive crouching in the shallows at the bottom. "Let me show you something."

He got off the stool. He walked out of the bar. I followed him. I thought he might kill me, but Finn had told me I was about to lose the case. I thought he would kill me, but if he didn't there was a chance I could leave with her. Pea, with the bloody knives and bloody hands. Pea, with the heart like a steel trap.

("Why do you love me?" I had asked her.

"You believe that I can be better than I am.")

He drove us to Midtown, to a gambling parlor fronted by a

mediocre Italian restaurant on West 43rd Street. The operation was headed by one Lefty Manusco, a well-connected subordinate of Lucky Luciano known for his connections to prostitution. The cops on this beat never could seem to get enough to shut him down. I pretended not to recognize it.

The back room was crowded with men and women elegantly dressed, politely pissing streams of money down Cosa Nostra's pockets. A fair number of these women were prostitutes. Expensive ones. You could pick them out because they never bet money and they drank with professional determination.

"Let's play craps," Walter said. I wasn't sure I knew how to play craps. I didn't say so. I recognized a man at the table. He was sliding his chips across the felt like hockey pucks. Laughing with his hand on a prostitute's ass. She didn't bother to laugh back. He didn't look up when we sat down. Then the whispers started and he did, but he only recognized Walter.

We worked in different precincts, but Finn had pointed him out to me as a fellow undercover—Benjamin Erenhart, a veteran of the narcotics beat. Friends in high places. Finn had made sure to tell me that, in case our paths had crossed.

"Who's your buddy, Red Man?" Erenhart said, as he slid the last of his dwindling pile of chips to the stickman. I didn't know how much he had started with. But for a man on a cop's salary, he looked pretty sanguine at the prospect of losing three hundred dollars more.

"The angel's new boyfriend," said Walter, his voice flat. I felt the sudden stares of everyone at the table like the warm tongue of a large dog. But I matched Walter's nonchalance. For better or worse, my relationship with Pea protected me better than any Luger ever could. And Walter had made his point: I had put myself in this world. Now he would see to it that I couldn't get out of it easily.

Erenhart's lips drew back from his teeth, like he had knocked back a bitter spirit. "Is he, now? And you aren't afraid she will knife you in your sleep, boy?"

Lefty Manusco's back room was not integrated to anyone but Walter, and friends of Walter. Still, Erenhart should have been more careful. "She's an angel of justice. There are plenty guiltier than me for her to take care of first."

The cop drew back. The working girl on his lap got quickly to her feet, tottered in her high heels, and stilled at a look from a man in a gray pinstripe suit, sitting by the bar.

"Is that right?" Erenhart said. His face was flushed. He was smiling. Then he laughed. "Better you than me, bud," he said, shaking his head. When he ran out of chips a few minutes later, that man by the bar came over and told the boxman to lend him another thousand. Walter amiably lost a hundred while I watched. He seemed to think that was enough. We left a little after midnight.

"That man," he said quietly. "Is a cop. Plainclothesman. He's at least twenty grand in the hole with Manusco. That's not counting the women. He killed one of them last year. They said it was an accident. Hell, I half believe them, but that's only because Erenhart ain't ever gentle."

"A cop?" I felt as exposed as sunburned skin under sandpaper.

Walter Finch gave me a long look. "That's what I said. The law in this town," he said, "it isn't what it used to be. Good for us, I guess."

"Good for us."

Vice squad never had been able to get a charge to stick to Manusco. Finn had known, of course. That's why he'd said what he had. I'd just been too green to listen.

A week later, Pea came home smelling of French-milled soap and old pennies. She had been crying. We fucked each other for hours, until everything hurt.

"Did you know?" Finn asked me, over another bad midnight dinner of egg creams and steak fries.

"Not until she already did it."

He lit a cigarette, blew smoke at the fries. "Off the record," he said. "Erenhart was a bastard. He had it coming. You ever meet him?"

"No."

"Better for you. Not that I hold with executions. But some of those bad eggs on the force . . . even Valentine didn't have much to say about it . . . well, your lady serves a purpose."

"I want to get her out of this. Take her upstate. I can work undercover without her."

Finn laughed. I heard the edge, but he didn't take it all the way out. Trent Sullivan had crawled from his mouse hole the day before. We were nearly ready to take him and his woman into protection. And as soon as we arrested Victor, I could leave with Pea. Walter hadn't said no, and neither had Finn. The only other person who needed to agree was Pea herself. It seemed to me like an afterthought.

I was—this is not an excuse—very young.

14

The night before the groundbreaking of the new resort, Alvin finds me in the parlor, drinking whiskey alone and staring into the fire. Pea is upstairs, sleeping. Waiting for me, yet still keeping her distance. I feel very alone, more than I have any right to, in this house with her just upstairs. But then Alvin taps on the French windows and it is with relief that I open them.

"She's not here, right?" he asks, looking around before he pulls himself over the sill.

"Sleeping," I say. "You're letting in the cold."

He gives me a hard look and then latches the windows behind him.

I taste another mouthful of whiskey. "Would you like some?" I ask. He doesn't seem as young as the last time we saw one another on the road. Rougher. Stronger, like he doesn't have time to care where he's cracking.

Alvin nods. "I need to ask you something."

I gesture to the couch, but he sits on the floor. Possibly to be closer to the fire, possibly because he's considerate of the state of his blue jean overalls.

I pass him a tumbler with a thumb of whiskey. He takes it with his left hand and holds out his right. I stare at it. Touch him, now, after all this? But I am tipsy, flushed with heat and hunched with cold, and my secrets do not seem like such a bad trade anymore.

I take his hand. It is a brief meeting. Two strands of uncanny luck sniff one another like unfamiliar dogs and separate. Junior Bell wants to kill him, but he didn't need my hands to know that. I peer at him through amber fluid, waiting for what of mine he will drag into the firelight.

"You should have left her that first time," he says, at last. "You wanted to use your gift for good. You knew what she was. Why didn't you leave her?"

"But I did."

He frowns and shakes his head. He looks down at his feet. "That ain't leaving. You watched her. You stayed in that devil's business. What did you think would happen? A righteous man has got to keep righteous company."

I just laugh.

"The rest of it . . . Don't know what you were so scared of. Think such a little thing will stop her from loving you? A woman like your angel? She was born in blood."

"As are we all," I say softly.

He falls silent. Finishes his whiskey. I pour us both more. I feel purged, my insides mercifully silent.

I watch him gather his courage. "Dev," he says, "she's got something in her that's going bad. She's sinned and sinned with them and now they're turning against her. They'll get you, too, if you stay."

"Your hands don't tell you that."

"You'd be surprised what they tell me. Leave her, Dev. Save yourself."

"Is that your question?"

He puts his head down again and presses his palms against his temples. Whatever burns him, I don't believe he really cares about Pea and my resigned compromises.

His voice, when it comes, is high and anguished. "Why not? Why not? If you save yourself, at least *one* of you survives."

I am surprised, at last.

Unthinking, I put a hand on his trembling shoulder. "Alvin," I say, "and what will I do with that survival, when I have betrayed her? What good will my hands do, when my heart has turned on me?"

After a few more minutes, his sobbing subsides. He wipes his nose on his sleeve. Takes a few shaky breaths.

"Go to the groundbreaking tomorrow. Both of you. If you see me, help me. If you see my ma—"

"Help her?"

His nostrils flare. "Stop her."

And now I'm starting to understand. "What is she planning?"

"I'm not sure. Just . . . come."

"Thank you for warning us, Alvin."

He shakes me off. He wobbles a bit as he stands and then straightens his back. "Your angel is pregnant. Didn't tell you before because I wanted a clean answer. But you might as well know now."

I don't hear when he leaves. I only feel the gust of chill air, the smoke that blows in from the flue.

I lie beside her and she makes room for me. I hold her through what might be a nightmare, or might be another dream flowing through those hands that Alvin says are turning bad inside her. A little after dawn, she shakes me awake.

"We have to leave," she says. She's been crying.

"To go to the groundbreaking," I say.

She stares. "How did you know?"

"Alvin told me. How did you?"

She takes a breath and lets it out in a laugh. "Our baby told me, honey."

I dress and follow her to the car. I watch as she straps on her knife holster. I get my gun.

"How long?" I ask.

"Three months."

"How can she tell you anything?"

"She's got something like the hands, but different. I can't explain it. Dreams don't come down for her, Dev, they're inside her. So they're inside me, too, you see? She can't stop it."

I take her shoulders and kiss her forehead gently. Then I get behind the wheel and we start racing down River Road. The trees smudge like charcoal in my peripheral vision.

"There were guns," Pea says, white knuckled. "And fire. Do you know what he's planning?"

"Not Alvin," I say. "Mae."

"Oh." Pea closes her eyes. "Oh, *goddamn* it."

She reaches for me when we park behind a line of cars along River Road.

"Follow me," she whispers.

"To hell," I tell her.

We run. A ribbon of braided yellow and blue separates the press and public. The crowd is standing and squatting and balancing equipment on the crumbling gravestones. I don't see Alvin or his mother anywhere, but I know they're here. Pea elbows her way to the front of the press, where we have a clear view of the men in the graveyard. Bobby Junior, the two Astor investors from the restaurant, the local state senator alongside three other men. Two I don't recognize, but the third is unpleasantly familiar. Ben Craver is in a wheelchair off to one side, dressed in a charcoal suit that bulges with padding. An attempt to make it fit for the cameras, I suppose. It only emphasizes the sharp bones and pleated skin of his neck and face. I haven't seen Craver since that day in the hospital, when I left him with Mae. I do not know what has brought him here, suborned by the men who have destroyed everything he ever cared about. But it scares me.

Junior, of course, is talking about his daddy. Martyrdom has been very good for business. Nothing like a small-town murder to rally the national press around an otherwise banal construction project. Craver sees the two of us. His brief smile is beatific, disconnected.

"Wait here," Pea whispers. "I'll be back soon."

She rubs the back of my neck and then runs in the direction of the condemned church. Craver watches her leave, then snaps his gaze back to Junior. He's taking questions from the assembled representatives of our fourth estate.

"Gerry Davis, *New York Sun,* I have a question for Mr. Benjamin Craver—"

"Ben Craver," says Junior with an abrupt, waxen smile, "has joined us today, as I said, in a remarkable show of support and solidarity and an attempt to help heal our community. But he is not well—"

"How do you feel about the move of the graves to First Methodist? Your opposition to the gravesite—"

"I think his presence here is a good indication that he feels that the placement of these bodies in sacred ground, where my own father has been buried not even a month ago, is a worthy compromise. Now—Ben, for goodness' sake, man, you don't need to answer—"

Craver has very slowly moved his wheelchair forward. Those of us in the front row can just make out his splintered voice. "It's all right. I can say . . . I am very pleased to be here today. I am happy to have reached this . . . accord in this sacred space. I am grateful to Bobby Bell Junior and the investors for . . . allowing me to be here."

Junior closes his eyes and flexes his hands carefully at his sides. Craver smiles with a perfect, holy cruelty. And as a fusillade of barked questions and photographic flashes obscure the strangeness of the moment, I feel it. One finger of a silk glove sliding between the veins of my left wrist. Not a direct threat, nor an immediate one, but undeniable. No sign of Pea at the old church, so I scan the crowd behind me. There's more I could do to find the source of this threat. But Pea told me to stay. I'm afraid for her—more afraid than I've been in my life—*she is pregnant*—and our child has warned her about what will happen here.

Then: Alvin sprints from the back of the church and starts across the graveyard. He hollers something that I can't make out for the roar of the crowd. *Murderer,* they scream. *It's him. Good God, where are the police?* Pea chases him just a few steps behind. I start toward her, but she waves her arms and I stop with my gun in my hand and one foot in the air.

"Craver," she shouts—at least, I think she does, I am reduced to reading her lips. The threat rolls over me again. My hands cramp. It isn't directed at me, but it will catch me if I stay. I stay. I jump the ribbon and elbow my way closer to the police surrounding Junior and his associates.

A cop intercepts Alvin and wrestles him to the ground. Pea stares at me, but she goes back to help the kid. Craver, I have to reach Craver. He's going to do something, that's the only reason he'd ever have appeared here today. I run around the back of the police cordon, vault off the sturdiest of the gravestones, and push my way between a pair of linked arms. I land to the side of Craver's wheelchair in a wobbly crouch.

"Davey," he says, softly reproving. He doesn't seem to have noticed the fracas around us. "You aren't supposed to be here."

"What are you doing?"

He blinks slowly down at me. The officers I pushed aside to reach him have grabbed me by my elbows. I hook one leg beneath Craver's wheelchair. Buy myself a few seconds. "Giving this," Craver says, spreading his arms wide, "giving us all, back to the Lord."

The gesture makes his awkwardly fitted jacket gape between the closed buttons, a little at the armpits. A moment like a sliver of shaved ice: a bundle of wires running from his armpit to his stomach, connected to a series of dark-gray cylinders.

"Officers," says Craver, very calmly, "please take this man away from me."

My left shoulder wrenches when they pull me upright. It wouldn't hurt so much if I weren't also trying to get away. My warnings sound absurd. I babble them anyway.

I worked long enough back then in Craver's store to see his storage shed, where he keeps the hunting rifles and their ammunition. And, occasionally, for when highway crews pass through, small batches of state-registered explosives. He always warned me away: *One stick of TNT has enough force to blow up half of River House, Davey.*

His comparison had struck me even at the time. *So he hates them too,* I thought, and felt that kinship.

I thought we'd come to the groundbreaking to stop Mae. But I forgot. I forgot that there are so many kinds of threats. And many kinds of strength.

An infinity of vengeance.

"Explosives," I try again, "Craver has explosives, he's going to set himself off—"

Some asshole with a federal insignia is pressing Pea's face into the grass. Alvin shivers beside her, already cuffed. One of her knives is buried in the ground a few feet away. She rolls to her side, sees me.

"It's dynamite," Alvin starts to say, but the same fed tough hits him open-handed across the back of his head.

"One more word and I'll shoot you here, you hear me? Save us the bother of the hot squat."

Around Bobby Junior and his associates, the frenzy is subsiding. If anything, the crowd presses closer. Craver watches us. Alvin's shoulders tremble.

"You killed your wife."

The voice comes from the earth. From the stones in witness of their own destruction. From the bodies whose repose Craver will guard at the cost of his own place beside them.

"She threatened to leave and expose those pictures you made her take. You buried her body in the potter's field and told everyone she had left for Vegas."

The officer holding Alvin jumps back as if he's been burned.

Alvin sits up slowly, continues: "Bobby Senior had fixed every election since twenty-four. The police and the city council helped him do it in exchange for favors and cash. Bobby Junior was meant to follow him in the last election, but he had killed a man in the city and fathered a colored child and the mayor was worried about the scandal. Bobby Junior has forced himself on ten women, and every one was a Negro who couldn't say a word about it, because he would destroy them and their families. One killed herself. He can't get it up, unless he pretends that she's unwilling, and black. Officer Fisk has two wives—"

There are two guns at Alvin's temples now, two men implacable with anger and fear.

"You shut that hole you use for a mouth *now*, boy."

"Believe me," Alvin says, so calmly he looks possessed. Not by the devil—by a divinity. "Craver has loaded himself with dynamite. He is about to—"

Someone shoots. Pea has launched herself from the ground so

quickly that I don't realize what she's doing until she's on her side in the dirt and Alvin is crying and bleeding all over her lemon-colored skirt.

I jerk against the officer holding me, though Pea is all right, I can see it in her eyes.

"Damn it, I told you—"

I mistake the sound for gunfire at first, but it's coming from the church. Explosives detonate in rapid succession. They spit smoke and fire against the milky sky. Deafened, I crawl toward Pea. Ashes and debris rain over us, they burn where they land. Alvin writhes, but I can no longer hear those wordless howls. Pea has worked her hands free somehow. She rifles through the pockets of the officer who must have shot Alvin, the one who killed his wife. He has fallen while the old church made of itself an offering. He has fallen and the remains of his brain and skull have mixed with the ash falling around us. Three more thuds that I can feel but not hear, three more mortal rains.

Pea's hands still. We look at each other. I wonder if we will die, if our child will die, before we ever had a chance to know her.

"To hell," her lips say. Then she smiles, tangles her hand in my hair, and pushes me to the ground.

I can hear the bass of the moment Craver gives himself back to God. It vibrates through the graves he has died to save. Pea has made sure I can't see. The air smells of hell, or war. Of charred flesh and charred earth and the blood that covers them both. Only my position on the ground keeps me from vomiting. My position prostrate, facing away from Craver's massacre and toward the church.

From its wreckage, a solitary figure emerges, now that there's almost no one left to witness. A black woman, slight but strong, with enmities as venerable and fierce as Craver's, better hidden. She wears a scarf over her hair and ashes on her dress.

Mae didn't threaten Craver that afternoon. But I should never have left them alone.

She sees me looking but doesn't pause. She just points to her boy and slips out of sight.

The Little Easton Massacre is the biggest news in the country for eight days. Bobby Junior survived. He ran moments before Craver detonated—the only one who, at last, believed us.

He has been a very helpful witness to the police.

Conspiracy to commit mass murder. The commission of said mass murder. Political terrorism. Destruction of property. Trespassing.

At that last, even Finn couldn't stop a bitter laugh. Pea and Alvin and I are set to spend a reasonable time in jail followed by a short appointment with the hot squat. Walter managed to get us out on bail. He has been quiet about our prospects for freedom.

"I'll say I did it all with Craver," I tell him. "I'll confess so they have to drop the charges against Pea and Alvin."

"You'd leave your kid without a father?" Walter asks.

"Better to lose a father than a mother."

A considered pause. "You could give Phyllis up. Declare loyalty to the fuzz and turn informant. They'll keep you out of the draft and I'll get her out before they can make charges stick. Wait a few years and you could be in the kid's life, at least."

"She would never forgive me."

"Of course not. But she wouldn't kill you. For the kid's sake."

I have to laugh. Oh, if only one of our hearts were hard enough. But hadn't I made my decision the moment that I knocked Jack cold from behind, the moment I grabbed Pea's knife and turned on Victor? And then that wet, putrefying silence of Victor's curse and Victor's death—there is nothing simple about survival, after giving yourself over to love like that.

Walter sighs. "I had to mention it. There's always the truth."

I'm suspicious. "What truth?"

"That Mae Spalding did it. She and Craver between them. That old mayor had let his son do whatever he wanted with her for years, hadn't he? And I think she and the mayor had been together before that. So she had killed the mayor. Thought she could get away with it. She didn't expect Junior to go on an attempted killing spree after finding his father's body. They threatened her whole family, too, so she worked with Craver to destroy them. The fuzz would leave you out of it, if they had to—if they knew the truth."

It's what Walter would do in my place, I think. He does care for people, but he hasn't become Red Man by overindulging his mercy.

"Not an option, Walter."

"She wouldn't have to know you told."

"But I would."

We visit Alvin in the hospital, after the doctors are forced to amputate the arm. When he wakes, Mae takes his scarred hand so he'll have something to do with it. That's how we discover the other reason for Victor's grisly hoodoo: there's no such thing as one saint's hand. The one that remains is just flesh. Alvin's face twists the moment he realizes. Pain or anger, I think.

But it's relief.

"It's done," he says. "I wasn't worthy of them."

"Of course you were, son," Mae says. Her eyes are red, but dry as tinder. "None of this is your fault."

I remember his cold recitation in the graveyard of sins uncountable. His profound lack of surprise. What would it do to a soul, to know the darkest kernel of every one it touched?

"We're going to get you out of here and free, Alvin. I promise."

No one in the room—all of whom are perfectly aware of what Mae has done—says anything to this. I wonder about Mae now. I wonder about the unfathomable force that gives our hands power and takes it away. If Mae had had that luck, the Bells of Little Easton would have met a sacred justice years ago. Even with her son under arrest, she hasn't turned herself in.

Alvin meets my eyes. "Matthew 5:30."

My heart's so full it chokes me. Pea frowns. I bury my fingers in the tangled mass of her hair. "Do you regret it?" I ask him.

He takes a sharp breath. "Hell, no."

The Little Easton river resort project is officially canceled after the surviving investors withdraw support. Six days later, the little they could scavenge of Craver's remains are interred in a plot just outside the sacred grounds of the Lutheran cemetery in Hudson. The ceremony is well attended by the press and not many others. Seven days later, Alvin goes home.

Eight days later, the world forgets all about Little Easton and its lethal church politics. The Japanese have destroyed some naval base in Hawaii, news that feels at once inevitable and absurd. Congress hasn't made the formal declaration of war yet, but everyone knows they will. I keep my radio tuned to the blustering outrage on the news, awaiting confirmation. A little past eight, I pull into the cold parking lot of the Albany PD headquarters. Every office light is still on, including Finn's. His secretary lets me in without even asking my name.

He has been smoking the cheap cigarettes that his second wife hated. The pall lingers above his bare head. It tries to choke me as I sit down.

"You said you had an idea," he says.

"You know I didn't do this."

"I don't think you did, kid. But you've changed since those New York days. You could be capable of all sorts of things I don't believe."

"Benjamin Craver did it."

"Couldn't have done it all alone. He was half-dead himself."

Now's the moment. Spill on Mae, solve our problems. And a part of me—the part of me that still wishes I didn't love Pea—would if I could.

"You know who helped him," Finn says, after a moment. "Give them up. Or better yet, give up your old lady. Dewey would definitely settle for Victor's angel."

So many opportunities for salvation. But there are many turns on the wheel of rebirth. If we meet again, it won't be as her traitor. I flex my hands. "You remember Erenhart?"

"The crooked cop? That your girlfriend killed?"

"You used to go to Lefty Manusco's old place in the theater district, didn't you? He'd lend you some chips on his account."

Finn just stares.

"They say even Dewey went a few times. In the old days, before his big promotion to district attorney. Well, I wouldn't know about that, but one way or another some weekends Manusco's was half cops, wasn't it? Funny, I remember back in '35, after all the goods I gave you on Manusco's prostitution ring you ended up putting everything on Lucky Luciano instead."

"Get the boss first, kid. The bit players can wait."

"That's what everyone told me. All the same, Manusco had a good racket going before Finch had him bumped off . . . a few months ago, was it? I wonder who inherited Manusco's little black books—he was famous for his record-keeping, that I remember. Now that I mention it, I don't suppose that's anything to do with Dewey's sudden interest in bringing down Finch, is it?"

Finn just stares.

"I know a great deal," I say, very carefully. "About a lot of people. I've kept quiet about it all until now. And I just need a small reason, a little bit of goodwill, to keep quiet forever."

"Goodwill?" He tries to ash his cigarette in the tray, ends up knocking the mess to the floor. We cough. "If you spill even half of that, the only goodwill you're likely to get is a sap to the back of the head."

"Funny, but I wonder if Valentine would say so. He's been commissioner for a long time. Longer than anyone else has managed to stomach the job. He's famous enough, and ambitious. If Dewey can make a run for Albany, why not Valentine, eventually? He'd just have to wait his turn. That is, if he could maintain his reputation as the 'world's best cop.' Nothing would put him on the hot seat quite like another Seabury commission, poking around the bank accounts of his reformed police force."

Finn swallows. "All he'd have to do is send you straight to Sing Sing: another dirty cop exposed."

"While the rest of the rank-and-file take to drinking, waiting for the other shoe to drop. Or do I mean black book?"

"What the hell are you after, Patil?"

"We're at war now. That changes things. You know Valentine. Duty above all. It looks good for his reputation to have officers in the ranks. We need every able-bodied man to serve his country, isn't that what they're saying?"

He leans back in his chair. Chews the dead end of another cigarette. Cautious relief has made him wobbly at the waist. "That may be."

"So you ship us off. All of us questionable cases, the ones injudicious enough to find ourselves in some mobster's little black book. Send us over there and Valentine gets a big publicity boost for his contribution to the war effort. Even better, we're no longer a liability to him. Or you could string me up as an example. That might be the end of it. But Dewey wants one last big victory as DA. He likes Valentine, but he's more ambitious than loyal. A big Seabury-style investigation of the police might be even better, as far as his prospects are concerned, than yet another gangster arraigned on charges that won't stick."

"Dewey wouldn't—"

"Wouldn't he? It would be a big deal, Finn. Bigger than '35. Probably bigger than the Seabury commission. A hurricane can uncover a great deal of old dirt."

Finn closes his eyes as though in pain. "You won't talk to Dewey?"

"Not if you drop the charges against Phyllis and Alvin."

"We need someone to pin this on."

"Craver. Let it end with him. I go off to war with the rest of the bad apples and Valentine's political path is strewn with roses."

Finn snorts. "Even easier for a stray bullet to get you in the Pacific."

"But you wouldn't order it."

"Jesus, kid, what kind of pull do you think I have?" He laughs, a little too high, a little too fast. "Or that I'd want to do it anyway, you goddamn bastard."

We arrange it. He says it might take a few days to go through. It might not work at all—Valentine still has to agree. But I know that it will. Because I can feel the hot whisper of Victor's curse. *I'll haunt you.* But I have volunteered to wade waist-deep in all the bloody hell that he promised me.

Pea is waiting for me when I get home. Knees drawn up by the fire, eyes on a book she isn't reading.

"I made a deal," I say. "I'm getting drafted and you and Alvin go free."

"That's what this has been, all this time? You were drafted?"

"Yes. And then I . . ."

"Well?"

"I had a dream. A second dream."

"You've always been this good at lying to me, haven't you?"

"Yes."

"Did you lie about loving me?"

"Plenty."

"Is that right?"

"Anytime I pretended that I didn't."

"Marry me, then," she says, after a few strained seconds.

I laugh. "Sure, Pea."

15

I saw Trent in the city that day. He told me he was worried. There were rumors that the angel was going to get someone that night. Someone who had crossed Victor.

I told him not to worry, that the angel was with me, in my house upstate. I was going back to see her right now. Trent was supposed to have gone into protective custody a month ago, but Valentine had demanded harder evidence, enough to set up a sting.

"I'm off the case," I told Trent. "But don't worry. I'll talk to my superior about you when I'm in town again."

Pea was gone by the time I got back. She had left a note. Three words.

I had to—

A line, drawn in blood, to separate the halves of my life.

—but the woman was already screaming in the bathroom. But a man's head was already thumping against the back wall. Then the body of a smaller woman. A series of grunts. A gasped question. There passed a moment without any sound at all. I panicked and shot the lock.

Pea was curled beside Trent's half-naked body. One knife was in the wall, the other buried in his chest. Her fingers slipped in the blood that coated the hilt. Her eyes were wide and black. They stared at Trent's slack and stubbled jaw.

"But tell me why you did it?" she whispered.

My erection dimmed very slightly. I pretended I didn't hear her. I opened the bathroom door and hit Maryann in the back of the head with my gun handle. She slid to the floor without even seeing me.

Pea let me drag her away from Trent—from the body. She was limp in my arms. She stared at him and asked, again, the question that I refused to hear. I collected her knives and cleaned off any places that looked like they might hold fingerprints. My colleagues would know who did this, but they wouldn't be able to pin it on her. Not any better than they had those twenty other similar murders.

I took her to the apartment that I kept in the city. Steam filled the tiny bathroom as I filled the tub. It spilled out of the little high window that opened onto the shaftway. I wondered if someone else would smell the blood. If they would know it. If they would care.

Not the way I cared.

I undressed her like a wax doll. Like my fingers were hot coals. My desire was my enemy. Pea was my enemy. The thing that she was—I couldn't love her without hating everything I had ever believed about myself. She climbed into the tub after I led her there. She flinched at the heat of the water. She lowered herself to her shoulders, then her chin.

"It's a sunset, Dev," she said to the water. She ducked her head under. The water sloshed pink over the edge. It soaked my pants, my bloodstained sleeves. I would never undress in front of her again. This was the last time I would ever see her naked.

I started crying. The tears splashed where her hair floated on the surface of the steaming water. And when she emerged to take a gasping breath, she looked at me. For the first time since killing Trent, she seemed to see me.

"What did he do?" asked the woman. "Why did I—Dev, why did Victor tell me to kill him?"

"I'm sure you know," I told the woman. Because I hadn't heard. I hadn't seen.

"But Dev," she said. She raised a hand to touch my tear-streaked face. I flinched back. "But Dev, why are you here?"

"I couldn't leave you back there. But this is the end of it."

The woman was silent. She touched her throat with one clean, wet hand. She looked at me, and then at that hand, like she hardly recognized us both. Then she was crying. "The hands," she said, "I did it because Red Man showed me . . . the hands . . . Dev, don't do this, please—"

"You know exactly who you work for," I said. And I stood up. And I left her there, a woman, a killer that I used see around town, a sweet dame with a lethal edge. But I never let it catch me, did I? I got the better end of that deal, didn't I? She was the killer—I might have loved the sight of that woman streaked with another man's blood, but I'd kept my own sainted hands clean, clean, clean.

The thing that she was—I couldn't love her—I loved her like crazy—I would shutter my heart to her, keep myself in close darkness.

There would be no more revelations. No more holding my despised pieces to the light and finding them, improbably, precious.

16

Pea's hair is wreathed in holly, gilded with snow. Wet curls fall onto her forehead and around her freckled ears. She is wrapped to her neck in a red mink coat. Beneath it she wears a dress of yellowed ivory that belonged to her mother. The candlelight dances across her face in shifting bands of yellow and blue.

"Lord it's cold out here," says Tamara, warming her hands on her third mug of cider. "We're done, right? Are we done?"

Pea laughs so hard she sways into me. The officer of the peace, having just concluded the ceremony, looks mildly scandalized.

"Sure, Tammy," Pea says. The hands gripping mine are warm and strong and so sure. She'd catch me if she could.

"Just hold on," I say. "We're not quite done."

Pea raises her eyebrows.

"We *are* married, right?" I ask the justice, just for effect. Walter and Alvin snort with laughter.

He sighs. "As the state can make you, Mr. Patil."

"Well, then," I say. I dip her into a kiss that is mostly a joke until our lips touch. We kissed for the first time more than a decade ago. Her back against a tree in the North Woods, her hair still wet from the shower I watched her take. She tasted like strawberry ice cream and cigarettes. She asked me what I was thinking. And she still wears it, that skirt of hands.

She blinks rapidly when I pull her upright amid the catcalls and whistles. Walter's camera nearly blinds us with the flash. The muscle by her jaw trembles.

"Everything all right?" I ask. She's fainted once since the massa-

cre. At least this time I caught her. It has something to do with the
baby, with the struggle of bringing into the world whatever power
that child has.

But Pea shakes her head softly. "She's fine. Let's go inside."

Pea's nephew Tom plays clarinet as we pass, a sweet "Begin the Be-
guine" that we clap to while Tamara and Pea laugh their way through
the one verse they remember. Tammy holds on to my other side to
keep from tripping in the snow, or just to feel my heat.

Inside, the women have laid out the meal they spent the last two
days preparing. The feast would overwhelm Christmas, and be equal
to my grandmother's Diwali. Roast ham and turkey and beef, vegetables from the garden that Pea had pickled and canned and frozen,
now baked and stuffed and pureed into soups and sauces and other
unidentifiable delicacies. There are collard greens and sweet potatoes and black-eyed peas mashed and fried with peanut oil. A little
apart from the rest sits a dish of yellow potatoes and a basket of
brown, bubbled flatbread. A memory of my grandmother's kitchen
here in this faraway place: potatoes cooked with mustard seeds and
turmeric and a dozen other hard-to-find spices. My favorite dish as
a child. I turn to Pea when I see it.

"I called your mother." A faint grimace passes through her smile.
"She found the recipe for me. She's put the rest in the mail, every
one your grandmother wrote down while you all lived in India. She
has ordered me to take care of you."

"Ah," I say. "Will you?"

Something fierce sweeps across those dark eyes. "Just come back,
Dev. Just come back."

"Aunt Pea, can we eat now?"

Pea lifts Ida onto her hip and tugs on one of the bright silk ribbons at the end of her braids. "Of course, honey. Walter, will you
carve the turkey or should I?"

Walter carves. I uncork a few bottles of wine to compensate for
our rapidly dwindling stores of cider. Ida asks her mom if she can
have some, since her brother has a mug. While Gloria attempts
with fading patience to explain why Ida is still too young, Alvin

offers to show Ida the family of deer that have wandered into the
backyard.

"Thank you," Gloria whispers, and Alvin smiles shyly. He seems
more reserved now. Watchful. I don't imagine his anger will ever
leave him—it hasn't left me—but he is drained of that desperate
ferocity. Relieved of the burden of the hands, it is no longer his duty
to *make it right*, only to make do.

"Shame what happened to that boy," Gloria says quietly.

"Oh, he'll be fine," Mae says. "He's a fighter, always has been."

"Like his mother?" I pass her a glass of wine. Gloria goes to join
her daughter by the window.

Mae's red eyes crinkle at the edges, but the smile doesn't reach her
mouth. "Like all of us. Not a one here that doesn't have his problems."

I wonder what Mae makes of the summary dismissal of charges
that came through a week before. Would she have let her son go
down for the murders she committed? Or would she have turned
herself in, eventually?

"And you, Mae? Are you still thinking of killing me?"

She stills momentarily. Then her chin dips. "They always said you
could tell when someone wanted to hurt you. But they say a lot of
things about saint's hands."

"Someone did, that morning I saw you and Pea at River House. I
never could figure that out—whose hatred had been strong enough
to pull me out of my bed, but only that once? But now I'm betting it
wasn't Bobby Senior."

"How would you know? Could've been. He was a big man, full of
malice. He could have fit you in."

"Did he fit you in?"

Mae bares her teeth. "Never even occurred to him. Not until he
saw the light at the end of his own gun." She puts a hand on my
elbow. "My boy had a purpose. God gave him that gift and until
those white men took it away, it was my duty to protect him however
I could. He did his best. I know he did. But he was too young . . ."
She looks away. Gets a hold of herself. "He had secrets in him he
needed to get out. Other powerful men he could bring down with

just a touch. Junior told me one of those men at the party might have hired you and Phyllis for a hit."

"So you'd have killed us, just in case? But then Pea somehow convinced you otherwise."

Her stare is straight ahead. "I would have done anything to protect that gift."

"But not the boy?"

"Them both—"

"And what were you protecting when you helped Craver turn the groundbreaking into a funeral pyre?"

"That," she says, as full of holy fire as Craver had ever been, "was to *make things right.*"

I let out a long sigh. "But they aren't, are they, Mae?"

Her eyes grow red and glassy. "The Lord giveth and he taketh away, Dev. It's better for Alvin. I know it. I just wish . . . I wish I'd gotten Bobby Junior. I wish that dream had come to me instead."

You don't, I think. But for all I know, with that deep fury in her eyes—maybe she does. Maybe the hands are a joke on all of us—just enough to make us wonder, and never enough to change.

"And now?"

"I'm done. What's happened to Alvin . . . it's long past time. Let the bank take the land and we'll move to Poughkeepsie, we have family there. We can be regular, like we were before."

I nod, but I wonder what Alvin will think. Bell family sins hurt her longer, and perhaps worse. But she was not their only casualty. And it's Alvin who guards the secrets.

In the dining room Gloria clinks her glass amid laughing cries for the groom. Mae and I share one last look, a tense understanding, and then I rejoin the others.

Pea takes my hand. "Walter's promised me a dance."

"Walter can dance?" I rub her fingers between my own.

"That's what I said!"

Gloria raises her glass for the toast. We all quiet. Pea is tense beside me. Gloria came with her husband, who has never liked Pea and doesn't seem inclined to like me any better. But she is soft-spoken and unoffensive, with a quietly moving reference to their parents and their brother, long departed. I'm astonished to realize that she is happy for us. That most of the people standing around our dining room table this Christmas Eve are happy for us—delighted, counting Tamara.

We eat until we can hardly stand, then dance until we collapse. Pea tries a lindy with Walter, who is nearly as terrible as we feared. Tamara laughs until she has tears in her eyes.

"Walter, Walter," she says, hugging him when the song is over, "I think that's the sweetest thing I've ever seen."

Walter, ever so faintly red, just smiles and squeezes her shoulder.

I dance with Gloria and Mae and Tamara and Ida. Pea dances again with Walter, then Alvin, then Tamara just for the competition. My feet throb with sympathetic blisters watching them go. Dessert comes out of the oven. We're somehow all hungry again. Ida falls asleep by her pie. Pea carries her to bed, but the rest of the family slip upstairs soon after. The music still plays. We holdouts tap stockinged feet to the rhythm as we open up bottles of a 1935 Bordeaux that Walter gave as a wedding present. We argue politics: the war, the Japanese, our tactics, Roosevelt, Hitler, when we'll all come back home.

No one mentions that I'm to be shipped with a Negro unit in a week's time; no one mentions Tamara's beau, set to fly transport runs in the Pacific. In the midst of a heated discussion over the draft expansion, Pea turns to me with something I'd call panic if it weren't so happy.

"What was your grandmother's name?"

"Kate?" I slide my hands along her rib cage. Too easy to find even beneath the aged silk and lace of her wedding dress.

"No," she says, "the other one."

The one who made me batata bhaji and poori and cool drinks with yogurt and mint and rose petals. The one who loved me when my father loved me. Before I met death. Before I killed a man. Before I learned of blood and desire and their cost.

"Durga," I say, and Pea's breath catches.

"That's her name. So you'll know when you write."

Pea's lips are stained red with wine and her cheeks are bright with blood. I kiss her softly. "Just going out for some air," I say.

Walter watches me go. Pea is saying something to Tamara, her back trembling with laughter.

The snow has stopped, but the wind kicks up the drifts. Ice stings my cheeks. It takes three tries to get my cigarette to catch. The light from inside the house is warm. Spilled generously, like their laughter. I shiver in a beaver coat and a wedding suit. I think about my daughter, asleep in Pea's womb, but dreaming. Durga, child of a family I have nearly lost.

Inside, Tamara cackles with laughter. "Walter, why don't *you* try dancing with a ten-foot python and tell me how easy it is!"

A pause while everyone considers and discards the easy joke.

My hands feel sluggish and rigid with tension. A river runs through them, wide enough for many bodies and very cold. It is a river of threats that has crossed an ocean to reach me. Men with bullets and men with tanks and men with bombs and men with sorrow in their hearts, who only want to go home.

There is the matter of a curse. I know she has not forgotten it. I hope she doesn't believe in it. *You will never have a moment's peace. You will regret the day you ever met this—*

I smoke the cigarette down, drop it into the snow. I am smiling.

Just you and me, my diamond-headed baby, here at the end. You got some-thing big to say, I know it. But what good has knowing our future ever done us? Should we struggle away from it? Or should I just turn your face to the table, easy, easy, and let our troubled hands play out?

The car began to drift off the road. Tamara grabbed the wheel, screaming.

"Stop the car, Pea, dammit, brake the fucking car!"

At least Phyllis's feet still belonged to her will. She braked while Tamara pulled them onto the narrow shoulder.

Phyllis, whose hands had at last been returned to her, fumbled with the door handle and then collapsed outside, on her knees on the frozen tarmac. She started to vomit but did not dare touch her hands to her own face. After a moment, Tamara was beside her, a warm arm and a safe voice taking her back around to the car.

"Just go to sleep, sugar," Tamara said, because she had promised herself—Phyllis needed taking care of, even if Dev hadn't said so. "It's over now."

Tamara's hands had never touched a dream as it passed through them. But she knew dreams, nevertheless, as an oracle does—from above, from the numbers. She thought of what the cards had shown her just before they left the city: sixes and kings, death and deadly battle.

She and Phyllis were going to ground in a house in the country.

Their ghosts had followed them as surely as their lovers had left them, but there was always more than one front in war.

For a moment, Tamara possessed, though she did not know it, the look of a soldier.

THEY
WALKED IN
THE LIGHT

1

"When this war is over, sugar, I'm going to Paris. And I won't dance, either—not like before, anyway. A cabaret on the Left Bank, that's where I'll go, and I'll sing in French—"

A dry voice from the back seat. "Tammy, you don't speak a word of French."

Tamara—the recently retired snake dancer notorious of a West Village gin joint, raised her chin. "Bonjour, comment allez-vous, voulez-vous coucher avec moi—"

Her companion and passenger clapped her hands. "Hope you aren't planning on saying that to *every*one you meet!"

The driver, erstwhile snake dancer, solidly Francophile if not—yet—Francophone, tried to level a quelling glare at the tired, light-skinned face in the rearview mirror, but cracked.

"Let's see how good you do, then!" she laughed.

The woman in the back—four months pregnant, recently retired hatchet girl notorious of a West Village mob racket—was smiling. In a humorous, surgical tone that always anchored Tamara's memories of her, the woman said, "But *I* am not attempting to repeat the successes of the great Miss Baker."

Tamara smiled into the mirror but kept her eyes on the road. "I will, you watch me, Phyllis Green. I'm sick of up north, sick of the damned cold. In Paris the Seine is made of lights and champagne. Here, what do we have? The Hudson? A stinking mud hole in summer, an ice floe in winter, and nothing on the other side but New fucking Jersey."

Phyllis Green—lately Patil, though she was taking her time with the paperwork—sighed and leaned back against the camel-brown velvet seats. "Ain't that the truth."

The car, a respectable 1936 Dodge sedan, did not belong to either of them, but they had claimed it, as they had claimed each other. The owner, after all, was busy driving ambulances somewhere in the hell of the European front. A little goddess on the dashboard, a brass divinity with ten arms and a skirt of hands, was a reminder of him, though there were others. Phyllis pressed her face into the upholstery, which still smelled a little of the owner's cigarettes and the cologne he would wear on police business—though she had never made that connection. She drooled as she dozed, and smiled as though she could hear him through a line. Tamara noted this, and then looked quickly away.

They stopped at a gas station just outside of Rhinebeck, and Tamara waited outside in the cold while Phyllis used the ladies' room. The attendant, a boy who put her in mind of succotash, with his carrot-red hair and string bean–green jumpsuit, frowned at them. He looked back at the older man in the cashier's booth, wondering, Tamara was sure, if the presence of at least one Negro woman in the only gas station for forty miles merited notifying management. Tamara raised her head and then, remembering, lowered it again. She studied her boots, dark yellow, hand-tooled Italian leather, probably cost more than anyone in this pit-stop town could imagine making in a year—but then, she had learned early that there wasn't money in the world green enough to make up for black skin in a white man's eyes. If she were back in the Pelican, she would have glared, she would have dared that white boy to say a damn word. But they were upstate now, far from the relative safety of Walter's gang, and Tamara Anderson knew how to survive.

"You gonna go for the change, kid?" she asked when he just stared between her and the closed bathroom door and back up at the cashier.

His eyes snapped back to her and he wrinkled his nose. "I'll give it to your missus when she comes out."

Her skin flushed and her breath got choppy. The nerve of this boy—if he *knew* the weight she had behind her, all the smiles she'd faked and truth she'd hidden to keep it there—the words were out before she could snatch them back: "Missus?" she said, wide-eyed. "Oh, but she's my sister."

The boy jerked back, surprised. He stared at Phyllis when she left the bathroom, a little paler than usual, but unmistakable nonetheless when you knew what to look for. She closed her eyes briefly and put a steadying hand against the wall. Worry flashed through Tamara, chased with remorse. The doctor had said she needed rest. And here Tamara was, playing more games?

"What you staring at, kid?" Pea asked, wearily.

The kid closed a tight fist over the bills and stammered. "You-you best be off. They—we—don't let you folk stay past sundown."

Phyllis pulled back her shoulders and touched the knife holster beneath her mink coat. She hadn't been passing on purpose, but they had both known a certain ambiguity would make this necessary gas stop safer. And it would have worked.

Phyllis did not bother to respond. They had known the danger of taking this road; the white folks up here had certain notions of "racial purity" and reputations for their methods of maintaining it. At the driver's-side door, Phyllis held out her hand and, after a hesitation brief enough that it shamed her, Tamara handed the keys over. They were in danger now; no matter what the doctor said, they needed to get out of town on the double. As they got into the car, the boy went to talk to the cashier, and their whispers slid along the cold earth like snakes. Phyllis gave her friend a small, fortifying kind of smile, and Tamara managed to take a full breath.

Phyllis turned onto US 9, sliding behind a flatbed loaded down with shorn logs and icicles that occasionally wobbled and smashed in the narrow gap between them. Not long after, a blue pickup that they both recognized from the gas station pulled up close to their bumper. Tamara cursed.

"We pay them, and those ofays decide to chase us anyway? God-damn it, Pea, I *left* Virginia because of the damn lynch mobs."

"Those fools? They ain't even a lynch two-man show. Some stooges in a rust bucket who are about to get left in our dust, that's all they are. Now, you hold on, Tammy—"

This was all the warning Tamara had before Pea swerved hard to the left and pressed the gas pedal directly to the floor. Dev had kept his old Dodge in good condition; the motor roared to meet the challenge and they shot forward. The flatbed truck was a blur in Tamara's passenger-side window, and Pea slid in front of it just before they hit a curve.

"Goddamn it," Tamara said, still gripping the door in a death vise, though Pea was slowly easing the gas. "God*damn* it," she repeated.

Phyllis shook her head. "Hysterics later, Tammy. Keep watch."

Tammy took a breath and swiveled to look out the back window. The pickup was playing peek-a-boo with the flatbed, but it couldn't get up enough speed to pass it before a car came in the other direction.

"Cletus and Junior C are still gunning for us."

"I hope not literally."

"Oh, *Christ*. Why are we going upstate again?"

"Little Easton isn't a sundown town."

"Yet," Tamara muttered.

Phyllis gave a bleak laugh. "The house is on a hill. At least we can see them coming."

"That's mighty comforting, Pea."

Phyllis kept laughing. Tamara, watching her, thought she might just cry.

You are ten kinds of fool, Tamara Anderson, she was telling herself. You are a fool made to teach other fools how to do their business. You are out here alone on the road with Pea, and instead of resting in the back seat like the doctor told her, she's driving the getaway car while you keep the lookout on a pair of murderous gas station attendants.

"You *fool*," she muttered. They weren't at the Pelican anymore. She didn't have Victor to protect her when she played those kinds of games. That silver bastard was dead, and this woman beside her had done everything but plant the knife in his skull.

"What's that?" Pea asked, her voice bright and ready, as though she could think of no greater fun than hot-tailing it out of a sundown town in a sweet ride, with her best friend by her side.

"Just laying blame where it's due." Tammy laughed a little, surprising herself. All she had ever wanted was to be safe. But here she was, cross-grain to all of her comfortable grooves. Here she was, about to die in a fiery wreck on US 9. Damn Phyllis—why had Victor's bloody knife finally gotten it into her head to try to be good? Hadn't they been comfortable all those high-flying years at the Pelican? Two queens, hearts and spades, flanking Victor's diamond king? Well, *she* wasn't about to confess what she'd done—no need to show all her cards.

The pickup did its little dance from behind the flatbed again. This time, it got some speed on the straightaway, its lights bright and malevolent in the folding gray evening.

"Pea," Tammy said, urgently, "Pea, could you give us a little more gas? I think they're gonna—"

Two deer, healthy bucks, darted into the road behind them. The truck slammed on the brakes, and the truck bed jackknifed against the cab. One of the deer made it to safety, but the other flew over the truck cab and crashed through the windshield of the old pickup. It spiraled out of control and slammed into the long end of the wide-bed.

The silence that followed could have cut glass. Pea pulled to the shoulder, turned off the engine.

"Should we check . . . ?"

Heart pounding, Tammy lifted her eyes to the rearview mirror.

The flatbed was smoking and quiet on the highway. But that wasn't what grabbed her attention. In the back seat, she saw the top of a slate-gray head, parted with an edge like a razor and slicked with grease.

Tamara choked on her own spit and spun around—but the seat was empty. Phyllis clapped her on the back as she coughed and coughed.

"What is it?"

"Vic—Victor—I swear, Pea, I swear I saw his hair in the mirror—"

She turned to the empty seat, and looked back at Tammy. "Like hell."

Tamara reached into her purse and pulled out a silver flask. "I ain't joking!"

"I don't see anything."

"He's gone now."

"What? His ghost? You can't be serious."

"Well, we all knew he used that juju, don't we? That he stole all those hands? What's to say he couldn't find a way to haunt us?" What's to say he couldn't have come back to save her? The thought ought to have been comforting, but it left her queasy. She took a slug of bourbon.

Phyllis gave Tamara a long look and turned the engine. She pulled them back onto the road. "Well, if he's back," said Phyllis, "I'll just find a way to kill him again."

This was—though there was no way for either of them to know it—an unwise thing to say. Phyllis's hands, so beguilingly quiescent these past few weeks, flexed entirely of their own accord and moved to grasp the knives in her holster. Phyllis gasped, but she could no more control them than she could kill a ghost.

They stopped it, this time. Tamara did not feel reassured. She drove the rest of the way, checking the mirror every thirty seconds. But she would not turn back—Tamara wouldn't make that mistake a second time. In the stories of the dead, that's what they said—if you heard something while crossing that river, you kept your eyes on that promised by-and-by. If you turned around, they would keep you. If you turned around, your eyes would fill with smoke and you weren't never coming home.

2

The women arrived at dusk, with flurries of snow brushing the frozen driveway up on the hill. The wind gave it an impression of shape, a smear of motion and form that lingered in their sight long after the flakes had bowed and risen and scattered. Phyllis stared in silence at the red front door, the trellis covered in sleeping vines. After a minute, the door opened.

The woman on the threshold was white, just a few years shy of what Tamara felt she could reasonably call "old," but she projected age, nonetheless—a querulous disdain that some white women equated with dignity.

"Sweet Jesus," whispered Phyllis. "Why didn't Dev tell us Mrs. Grundy was white?"

"I don't think he ever met her," Tamara whispered back. "She answered the ad in the *Gazette*."

Phyllis closed her eyes. The woman in the door tapped her foot.

"Get in, then! You're letting in the cold."

"Right," Phyllis said, laughing a little. "You deal with her."

"Me? You're the fancy lady of the house."

"I don't do fancy anymore," Phyllis said. "Besides, I want to check the garden."

The garden was a strip of charred earth littered with chunks of ice like dirty meteorites. Even the rosebushes had been reduced to a series of crooked spindles, dark gray against the lighter gray of the house's faded whitewash. Phyllis tramped through them in her city boots and Tamara cursed her under her breath before climbing the stairs. She held out her gloved hand. Mrs. Grundy looked at it like a very worthy specimen at the museum.

"And your friend?" she said. She had a funny accent—straight and clipped, like Tamara's own white-people voice. Rich white people generally spoke whichever way they wanted, so perhaps she and this newspaper-ad housekeeper shared a certain experience of judgment. Still, Tamara put her gloved hand back in her coat pocket, unshook.

"She won't be long," Tamara said faintly.

Phyllis walked through the naked roses, removing the spines gently when the branches snagged on her coat. Her movements were angular but not rigid, what Tamara would have labeled a Graham method–inflected Bauhaus style, were she still the mistress of the Pelican's off-nights, a student of the modern arts.

But she wasn't, not anymore. Now Tammy was just a girl with an old deck of playing cards in her right pocket and her heart in her throat.

Phyllis moved in a kind of prayer, a ritual invocation of the dead or sleeping earth, of the powers that saw fit to touch her and touch her baby, of the cruelty felt in the palm of the Lord, and his beauty. There was death in that dance, defiance and fear.

She knelt between the two tallest bushes and dug her naked hands in the dirt. Her mouth moved, but neither Tamara nor the housekeeper could hear her over the wind and the river. In any case, Tamara might have guessed—Phyllis was speaking to the man she had married just one month before out here in the snow, full knowing they might never see one another again. Dev had told her to sprinkle his ashes in the garden.

Phyllis hiked up her heavy woolen houndstooth skirt just high enough to reveal the green hilt of the knife strapped to her thick silk hose. The housekeeper gasped, but did not in fact speak—an interesting datum that Tamara might have noted if not for what her friend did next.

Phyllis threw her knife high in the air, caught it and slammed it into the earth. The two larger knives in her holster followed half a second later, marking the bottom vertices of a long triangle.

"Pea, are you—"

"I wasn't told about any *weapons* on the—"

"Stop, damn you! Damn you! Oh, Christ almighty, *please* . . ."

Phyllis twisted and jerked, a rag doll struggling against the living hands at the ends of her arms. She threw herself down, her torso tangled in the thorns of the roses. When she lunged again for the three green hilts that marked the resting places of her knives, her fur coat remained stuck fast in the branches. Her face was wet with tears and mucus and her throat burning with curses. When her arms moved again Phyllis uprooted part of the plant. It wouldn't survive.

It was Tamara who saved her, in the end. Tamara, whose distant oracle eyes were enough to quiet Mrs. Grundy. Tamara, running down the steps and into the garden and embracing Phyllis as tightly as she could from behind. The hands smacked her and struggled, but the body that held them wasn't as strong as it used to be. Tamara could endure it.

"Leave me!" Phyllis gasped. "Before they hurt you!"

Tamara just squeezed harder. Phyllis sighed and then tilted her head back into the embrace. After half a minute, the chokehold did its work and Pea slumped into unconsciousness.

The night Tamara decided to leave the Pelican hadn't seemed particularly notable to start.

Oh, sure, Clyde and Dev were off in the war, the cards were as mute as a dead soldier, Pea was pregnant and strange as the queen of diamonds. Victor was dead. For all that Walter was an able mob boss, he didn't have the social panache of his predecessor; or maybe it was that Tammy was mourning Vic after all, the sadistic ofay shit, who had, in spite of it all, given her free rein with the best little gin joint in the whole world.

Whatever the case, Tamara had been gloomy as she made herself up for the first Wednesday jazz night at the Pelican since the events that had led to its temporary closure and change in management. She'd had to buy Charlie four steak dinners at Frank's (Five dollars a pop! No wonder half the time they were the only black folks eating, and in the middle of Harlem.) to sweet-talk him into his grand return. Charlie played in mob joints when they wanted his music, but unlike Tamara and Phyllis, he'd just as soon leave them for something poorer and safer. The Pelican, she had cajoled Charlie, was something special, it wasn't just a paycheck, though of course she'd double his pay (she knew she'd had him then, it just took two more trips to Frank's for him to admit it).

Pea had met her that night in a cab out in front of her apartment, bundled up in a mink that Tamara didn't recognize. It wasn't Dev's style, though it might have been Walter's. It didn't seem like the kind of thing that Pea bought for herself, but you never knew these days with the new Phyllis; nobody's angel still carried her knives.

She smiled when Tamara got into the cab, but she had been impassive a moment before, not so much as a wrinkle between her eyebrows.

"Something wrong?" she asked after Tammy slammed the door.

"I just don't like this feeling," Tammy said. The cards in the band of her brassiere seemed as heavy as stones.

"What feeling?"

Tamara's lips twisted. "Things are changing feeling."

At that Phyllis's smile surfaced, more natural than before. "Things are always changing, baby."

"Not like this. Not so fast."

Phyllis just raised her eyebrows and put an arm around Tammy's rounded shoulders. There was a crowd trying to get into the Pelican, which had gained some notoriety after recent events. The police had closed the joint and Walter had paid significant sums of money to significant people to get it opened again. She had tried to thank him, but he had waved her off with a large hand and a curt, "Cost of business, Tammy. You just keep making her the kind of place that people spend money in."

She had been buoyed by the sentiment, but now all of that optimistic joy had drained out of her. Everything was changing, everyone good was gone; Clyde had fought with her again before he left and now wrote her with some farmboy actor's idea of chivalry that made her want to swim the Atlantic just to tell him where to put it. Still, some old pleasures endured. She and Phyllis climbed out of the cab right in front of the Pelican's velvet rope. Everyone was out in their finest duds, even if for some that meant combed cashmere coats and for others suits in bright colors with shoulders wide enough to sit on. Whispers followed them like eager puppies as they sailed past the line and through the swinging double doors.

Pea gave her coat to the doorman and turned to Tamara with a very hard smile, the kind that had both scared and attracted her when they first met. Now, it dared someone to say something about her dress, whose silk pleats seemed designed to accentuate the distinct curve of her belly.

Tamara's only thoughts came up in a wave of longing and jealousy and a fear so bright she squinted. What if Clyde didn't come back? What if she never had his baby?

She came out of it when Pea chafed her hand between hers, barely any warmer. "You're still fixing on that letter?" she said, quiet.

Tamara sighed. "Forget Clyde." And then, grudgingly, "You look beautiful."

She lost track of Phyllis for a while amid the laughter and admiration, the sheer rush that nights at the Pelican always gave her. This time Tamara didn't even have to keep an eye open for Victor, lurking by the bookshelf entrance to his office, awaiting his obeisance. It was Walter, instead, who put a warm hand on her back and then Charlie's shoulder and toasted competently to the Pelican's return. "It's been an interesting few weeks, but I'm grateful to see so many familiar faces here once again. Here's to another decade of the Pelican, the only place in the Village you'd find us all sharing our liquor together—entirely legally acquired, Detective, I can show you the papers in the back—" Laughter. The detective, a white man so firmly in Walter's pocket he had his own billfold, gave a terse smile and lifted his glass. "Now, let's get back to what we do best: listening to the latest bebop courtesy of the master here"—a nod to Charlie, making as if he didn't think much of the hoopla, but sucking it down like good reefer—"and sharing the funny little bits of ourselves that won't fit anywhere else on this benighted island."

Whistles and hollers, laughter and cheers and the wind chime percussion of clinking glasses. Phyllis came to her attention all at once, as though a spotlight had swerved and stilled at the edge of her sharp, freckled cheeks, the smooth curve of rose silk over her belly. The crowd surrounded her, but she held herself apart with a stillness that perhaps only Tamara could recognize as fear, even shame. Pea's eyes darted to the bar, and Tammy felt alongside her the shivering vertigo of realization, that he wasn't there, that nothing would be the same for any of them, not ever again.

A familiar hand settled on her shoulder and she jumped. He didn't feel anything like Victor, but old defenses were hard to lay down. "How are you two holding up? How is she?"

Walter pointed his chin with admirable subtlety at Phyllis, staring out at nothing, drinking a glass of something amber and chilled with two precise cubes of ice, seated like a dowager queen at the center table just as Charlie and his boys were getting started.

"She's—well, I don't know, Walter. We're fine, really—"

"That bad, huh?"

"We're fucking miserable. This war . . ."

"This war," Walter agreed.

They shared a tight smile and allowed the room to distract them. Tamara drifted from table to table, sharing jokes, sampling the best Mexican reefer, even kissing a few of the boys who asked for it. She sat at Victor's old table near the back, empty even now, out of respect or superstition, though the place was packed. *Feel it*, she told herself, *feel it, 'cause it's all yours now.* But that hazy distance held her back. It was Victor, Tammy could swear it, that old juju of his even now spreading its greasy fingers across the gleaming chrome of his precious club. She took in a sharp breath. The cards, tucked inside the band of her brassiere, were in her hands in a heartbeat. "Well?" she whispered to them. "Well?"

A simple shuffle and cut: the king of diamonds. Suicide king, axe in hand, here for revenge. She sucked in a breath. There was more, but she didn't want to hear it. Instead, she did what she should have done from the first; she went to relieve Pea from a little of the burden of her loneliness.

Pea smiled with an arch knowledge when Tammy sprawled in the chair beside her.

"Having fun?" she asked. Her eyes were going glassy. Tammy wondered how many thumbs of whiskey she'd drunk here alone tonight.

"Not even a little. You?"

"Just remembering. So, that would be a no. The cards tell you anything?"

Those eyes didn't miss much, even wet with liquor. "Nothing useful."

Pea seemed paler than usual; she wiped her forehead with a handkerchief and avoided Tamara's eyes. It was probably the baby. That child of two saint's hands was apparently able to give her mother visions, sights either inexplicable or better unexplained.

The hour got later, Tamara went backstage to ready herself. Charlie kept playing. The haze of reefer clung to walls like a soft blanket as she started her set, lifting poor old Georgie over her head like a barbell, while he seemed to look back at her reproachfully. At some point the spirit took her, and Tamara started dancing among the tables, stomping her feet to the esoteric rhythms of the bass. They felt her and she felt them, folding her into the improvisation as smoothly as that pellet of yellow color folds into white margarine. She let Georgie wend his tired way around her neck and shook so that her breasts twirled in opposite directions and the tassels on her pasties glittered in the stage lights. They all watched her, but no one hollered or even smiled. Tamara was present, at last, in this place that had been her refuge for so long. But she couldn't seem to pretend anymore. Not about Victor, not about Walter, not about Phyllis. Not about whatever she might be herself—

The trumpet swooped up and she arched back, fingertips brushing the sticky floor.

Someone was swinging from the ceiling.

A slow back and forth, like a mother rocking her baby's cradle.

The legs twitched, one foot bare and the other in a bloody boot. With a wrench of effort that her belly would make her feel later, Tamara flipped upright.

The swinging changed direction. The rope groaned against the tree limb, and the man didn't make a sound. A cool breeze brushed past; it smelled of creek mud and cut grass and, very faintly, of blood and urine.

Charlie put down his trumpet. "Is that blood?" he asked, and she was surprised, because that meant that they could all see the ghost of Pete Williams, who'd been lynched outside of town the year before she left Virginia.

A flash of silver—and then Victor sat in the empty chair across from Phyllis, lounging in a suit of narrow gray pinstripes and a navy-camel hat. He bared his gleaming teeth, said something Tamara couldn't hear, and blew a long puff of smoke. It formed the shape of a gun and discharged a billowing bullet at Pea's bowed head.

"Call a doctor! She's fainted!"

Pea was slumped against the table, her glass in pieces on the wet floor. Blood dripped down her legs and mixed with the urine that she couldn't hold back as the child turned in her belly, and saw and saw.

3

The doctor insisted on bed rest, on peace and quiet somewhere in the country. Pea hadn't even asked; Tammy had looked at her huddled on that hospital bed and told her she'd be coming along.

Now they were here, too late and too cold for second thoughts, both haunted by ghosts that had no business following them so far up the Hudson.

Tamara and Mrs. Grundy between them managed to carry Phyllis upstairs. She came to silently, her eyes so full of pain that Tamara distracted herself with fluffing pillows and spreading an extra quilt. Those hands were, for now, quiescent. Mrs. Grundy proved to be a sober and unflappable companion in emergency, and Tamara found herself grudgingly grateful for the older woman's presence. When the housekeeper produced a dark-green bottle of laudanum from her pocketbook, Tamara actually smiled. The drops, expertly administered by Mrs. Grundy, sent Phyllis into a quick and deep sleep.

"And the baby?" Tamara asked, entirely too late. She was breathing hard, as though she had finished her second stage show of the night. She did not look at Phyllis's face, but her hands, limp against the blue-and-red quilt.

Mrs. Grundy slid the bottle back into her bag with fussy efficiency and regarded Tamara for several seconds longer than necessary. "I took it through all my pregnancies, and my sisters as well."

It had been years since the last time Tamara had seen a laudanum dropper; they were generally the preference of a woman of a certain age and arthritic condition back in Lawrenceville. She wondered what other intoxicating substances Mrs. Grundy kept in that pocketbook, but she didn't ask.

"And how old are your children now?" Tamara tried instead.

Mrs. Grundy sniffed. "Twenty-five and twenty-seven, the two who survived. May our Savior grant at least one of them comes home after this war."

Tamara spared a wish for Phyllis, that she were well and here to squeeze her hand in warning and then bust out laughing when they were finally alone. Imagine—this was Phyllis's voice in her head—all of us cooped up in this house all winter, and this white lady's another one for the Club of Interminable Waiting. It explained why Dev had hired her, though.

They went to the basement, where Mrs. Grundy shoveled more coal into the stove, checked the pipes, and informed Tamara that she would return at noon to make luncheon and supper. Tamara did not attempt a repeat of the handshake, merely nodded like the highest-in-her-hat Richmond miss.

Tamara shook her head as she left. "And Mom wonders why I left the country," she muttered.

Alone, she helped herself to the pot roast and gratin potatoes that Mrs. Grundy had left in the oven. Then Tamara pulled up a chair to the potbellied stove, still warm from the remains of the fire, and pulled out her cards. Even covered by the handkerchief, they felt warm to the touch, busting for revelation.

"Sorry, sweeties," she whispered to them, "I had a busy day."

The cards, one could say, knew more of Tamara than any lover or friend. They always would—that's the fate of an oracle, to know the numbers and be known by them. The cards jumped in response to her touch, slid into elegant waterfalls and showed their bellies like lonely dogs, eager to please her after a long day of silence. The deck had belonged to her great-aunt Winnie, felled by a winter flu five years back. It was Aunt Winnie—and not the Baton Rouge conjure woman Tamara had invented to bolster her reputation—who had taught her great-niece the tricks of the cards: the shuffles, the deals, the sleights of hand, and, most important, the numbers. Aunt Winnie said her own mother had taught her, a New Orleans quadroon who sold her body to pious white men every Sunday afternoon to buy herself and her children out of slavery a few years before the war.

The role of the oracle is to see, not to change: Tammy's quadroon great-grandmother had foreseen the war and got her children as far north as Virginia before bounty hunters ripped up their free papers and sold them all back again to a Richmond plantation. Her aunt Winnie, a week before she passed, had called Tamara to her room, though she didn't seem very sick at all, and gave her the deck and the ivory handkerchief. It was monogrammed with a simple "P.," but the knowledge of what that initial had meant to her ancestor was now all locked in the earth.

The deck itself was unmarked by any identifiable branding. Its heavy satin-finish paper had yellowed with age, and the embossing on the face cards had faded to a ghostly blue, such that in the low light of the fire, the queen and king of diamonds looked like African royalty, her ancestors before they were captured and dragged across an ocean to pick cotton. The face cards weren't mirrored—the jacks and the kings even had legs like little drumsticks—and there was meaning in whether they laid themselves out upright or upside down. On the back of each card were two hands, one outlined blue and the other red, one closed fist and the other palm up. A wreath of brambles spiraled out from their central image. Sometimes Tammy read for card sharps, and sometimes just for interested boys who came to the club and passed their time with her. Some of them noted the deck, and a few of them tried to convince her to hock it. She left those schemers behind real quick. She knew the deck was a strange specimen. She felt its strangeness beneath her fingers; she didn't need some antiques collector with a magnifying glass to tell her its value. These cards had been made for the same force that animated the dreams, and the uncanny luck that trailed behind them.

She wasn't always good to the cards. Sometimes, she shied away from the dark stories in suits and numbers, and told pretty lies instead. She was good at pretty lies; no one had ever noticed but the cards, who stung her fingertips spitefully the next time she brought them out. She remembered Aunt Winnie's voice, sharp and tired, "You think you can flirt and pretend your way out of any trouble, Tammy? You have a *duty*, and you'll be old before you know it."

She grimaced and poured a glass of wine. "Well, Aunt Winnie," she said, "here I am, doing my duty, for all the good it'll do me." That word again. She tried to do good, she *tried*. But Tamara also wanted fine liquor and fur coats and long nights of jazz and conversation with anyone willing to bring a bit of themselves to the table, and why should she have had to choose between them? When Victor had offered her that chance, she took it, knowing full well what he was. And so had Phyllis—damn her for deciding she couldn't handle the life anymore.

Still, some kind of grudging loyalty had made Tamara turn in her dancing shoes, get Phyllis into Dev's old car, and bring them up here to wait out the winter. It was more than she'd done for anyone else in her life, a kindness so new it still felt stiff and scratchy against her skin. Giving a cousin someplace to stay for a few weeks was one thing; for Pea, she'd given up the Pelican, the city. She couldn't regret the choice, but faced with the stark reality of this small house with its peeling wallpaper and old-fashioned furniture and antiquated heating, she comforted herself with liquor. At least she could use her cards for good here. Someone had to; those hands needed taming.

After midnight, she poured a third glass of wine and started a very specific reading. Not for Phyllis, which Tamara had done dozens of times before, but for her hands.

She'd never thought to do that before. The oracle judged her own lack of imagination.

One card, cut, second card, cut, third card.

She opened her eyes. Seven-two-seven. The interpretation came nearly as quickly: seven of diamonds for luck, upright or in reverse, you couldn't tell with the diamonds because there were no numerals printed on the cards. In the first position, it was a neutral beginning. But then came two, an inversion, spades pointed at the earth. And then seven again, seven of hearts: luck, but also courage in reverse, hearts falling down.

The hands had begun with all the luck in the world, poised neutrally between the sky and the earth—heaven and hell, if you like, though that wasn't quite it—but over time, unused, or used for evil purpose, their destiny had been left to rot. The luck, and the power that moved it all, had turned on its once chosen vessel. The crisis embodied in the spades found its resolution in the falling hearts. They spoke of one last chance to stop the corruption, but the heart had failed the hands.

Lost, everything that the vessel had once dreamed of being.

The oracle put down the deck, though she left the cards, and the story they told, open on the table.

Tamara lifted her glass. She trembled, and the liquid splashed onto the wood. She wiped it with her sleeve, unthinking.

"The heart failed the hands," she whispered, looking at nothing, anywhere but the numbers.

She thought of Phyllis sleeping upstairs, of that dreaming child in her belly, of the hands that had once been the terror of Manhattan and now just terrorized this lonely house. Those hands still longed for killing justice, but the man they wanted to reach was already dead.

Phyllis had killed so many, killed hundreds if you believed the whispers at the Pelican. Tamara did not know the details—she had tried not to hear—but she knew that Dev had killed Victor, at the end, and he would only have done such a thing to spare Phyllis.

"The heart failed the hands," Tamara repeated, and swallowed. "Or the hands never gave one goddamn for her heart . . ."

There was more, she felt it. That baby, squatting inside Pea, drinking down dreams and spitting them up like poison. She scooped up the numbers in one smooth motion and shuffled. She laid out a star pattern. Left foot first: six of clubs. Right foot: six of diamonds. Seven of clubs and ace of spades, the left and right arms. And for the crown, the angel joker. The child herself, as close as breath. Wreathed in sixes and sevens, bound with clubs and spades. Her hands were strong, but fading. The curse had got to her. She felt the weight of the mother's hands. Smelled the blood on them, rotting, like the floor of a butcher's shop. Smelled something else, too—hair grease and Russian dumpling soup. Victor. There had been a curse, hadn't there? A curse on the father and the mother. But they were the same thing, the curse and the rot, they fed one another. The poison was choking both mother and child. They wouldn't survive it. The moment that baby tried to come into the world with her pulsing saint's hands, the power would burn them clean. The mother wouldn't survive it.

The mother—Phyllis—Pea—

How do I save her?

The answer was in the crown: the angel joker, tricky but merciful. Take it on yourself, young oracle. Bring that corruption over to you and free them both of its taint. Oh, sure, then you have to live with it: that burning anger of the saints without the hands to compensate, Victor grinning silver at you from over the breakfast table for the rest of your life, nightmares. Enough to drive you to drink and an early death. But you could do it. You could take it on for Pea's sake.

Or you could leave it alone and let that bloody legacy strangle itself.

A log cracked in the stove. Tamara jerked upright and into her body. She found herself looking through the window above the kitchen sink, the one that opened onto the garden. Just beyond her own warm reflection, she thought she saw—she might have seen—

—a silver head and two button eyes, smiling.

Mrs. Grundy woke her up with the pointed toe of one black boot, thrust gently but firmly into Tammy's lower right ribs. She grimaced against sudden awareness—the press of the noon sun against her eyelids, the chill of the kitchen floor, the acrid aftertaste of two bottles of Bordeaux and a bit of . . . ashes? Oh yes, she had forgotten the reefer. She groaned, lifted her left hand and peeled back the sleep-crusted lid of one bloodshot eye.

"What are you doing here?" she croaked.

Mrs. Grundy's thin, painted eyebrows rose to the middle of her forehead.

"I thought you were a burglar."

"Passed out on the floor?"

Mrs. Grundy sniffed. "I mistook your snoring for a saw."

Tammy closed her eyes. "Sweet Lord, tell me I'm still dreaming."

The Lord was not so kind. After a moment, she pushed herself onto her side and then upright. The room swayed once or twice and then settled into an ice pick behind her right eye.

"Are these *playing* cards . . ."

Tammy blinked hard and realized that she'd let her beauties fall every which way after that last reading—or visitation, depending on how you looked at it. She fought back nausea as she put the deck back together, counting all fifty-four cards like old friends.

"Go check on Mrs. Patil, if you please," she said.

Mrs. Grundy gave her a long look and then left without another word.

The deck secured and safe again in her pocket, Tammy staggered to the bathroom, deposited the contents of her stomach in the bowl, and splashed cold water on her face. The boiler had gone out in the night; they'd need to light it again before she cleaned the rest of her. She dared a look at her haggard face in the mirror and then looked back down at her stockinged feet.

"So now what, Oracle?" she asked herself. She'd meant it to be mocking, but the cards were with her now, and they knew a truth when she spoke it.

Her choice was a joke, a cosmic trick played by bitter ancestors. Take on the curse or let her best friend die? But it wasn't *Tamara's* fault that Phyllis had covered herself with mob justice. And it wasn't her fault that Dev had killed Victor and brought that old bastard's curse down upon them. None of this was the baby's fault, either, but it wasn't up to Tamara to save anyone. She had problems of her own. A West Village club to get back to, once this business was done. She had wanted to help Pea. She had come here because she hadn't been able to see her way around it. She loved that woman, for heaven's sake! But to take that heavy fate on for her? She was an oracle, a snake dancer, a regular girl taking shelter in the mob's long shadow, not Job.

She had tried to be good, but this was too much. Too much for anyone. The cards and whatever moved them were wrong to ask it of her.

We didn't ask for anything, that slinking deck seemed to say when she finally left the bathroom. *We just show. Maybe it's you that's asking, Oracle?*

She told them to hush.

Pea was just coming down the stairs. They took one another in: Pea bloated with that baby, pale and pinched with the after-effects of laudanum and a night spent wrestling a curse; Tamara puffy from a night on the floor, wrung out from a night spent wrestling a choice.

Pea was delighted to see her. "Slept well, I take it?"

Laughter bubbled up like last night's dinner. "Like a princess on a pea."

Mrs. Grundy looked between the two of them and flared her nostrils. "You should sit, Mrs. Patil. I wouldn't want to have to carry you up those stairs again."

Phyllis winced. "Yes, ah—I'm sorry to have been such trouble. Thank you for your assistance."

In truth, Phyllis had the best white-people voice of the three of them. It made sense: she was the only one whose survival, for a time, had depended on convincing white people to overlook her yellow skin and thick lips. Even *being* white like Mrs. Grundy couldn't compare to that brutal schooling in the ways of white folk.

"I brought another bottle of laudanum to leave here in case you're in need of it again." She drew it from her bag and put it on the table. "Well, then. Pleased to make your acquaintance, Mrs. Patil."

She held out her hand. Easy, Phyllis shook it. Tamara closed her eyes; they were burning. Her hands she strangled behind her back.

"Are those sorts of fits . . . normal for you, Mrs. Patil?"

Phyllis sounded darkly amused. "Normal? Not really. Regular? Unfortunately."

"Well. I'll just make something quick in the kitchen, Mrs. Patil. I'm sure you haven't eaten."

"That would be delightful, Mrs. Grundy," she said with an amused glance in Tamara's direction. "We'll be in the parlor."

A sick weight settled in her stomach as she followed her friend's slow progress to the parlor couch. She kept thinking: but this is *Phyllis*, this is *Pea*, the terror of the Village, the angel of justice, Victor's knife. She was a violent goddess, a creature of legend, not some poor *woman* to be brought low by a damned baby. Tamara kept churning between swooping disbelief and the hard slap of the cards until she thought she might just need to bend over a porcelain seat for the second time that morning. She swallowed hard and busied herself with making a fire. Phyllis lay against the couch, hands on her belly, breathing.

"You strike those matches any harder, you're liable to burn the whole box." Pea's voice made her jerk.

Tammy's hands trembled as she struck another. The stick flared between her fingers and let off a stench like a devil's fart. She stared at it, frozen, until the flame burned down to her fingers and she let it drop onto the rolled-up newspaper with a yelp. The paper caught and curled like a sleeping child as the flames kissed the logs and kindling above.

"Something happened."

Tammy lifted her chin, tried on a smile. "I had to choke you till you passed out and then had a good conversation with a couple of bottles of Bordeaux, but other than that, nothing really."

But she was thinking: Pea, Phyllis, Pea, that *goddamned baby*! There had to be a way out, a way to save her. She had to ask the cards again. Search until they gave her a different answer. Taking on the curse couldn't be the only way.

Phyllis gave her a very mild look, and Tamara felt naked, undone, judged and shriven.

"Well, sit down, baby. You look like you've seen a ghost."

Tamara laughed, high and giddy. "I did!"

"Victor is dead, Tammy."

Tammy put her hand over Pea's and squeezed. She tried to feel the rot, the poisoned roots that would strangle her and her child to death, but she couldn't.

She just felt love like an arrow.

4

Walter called the next morning and Phyllis stayed on the line with him for nearly half an hour. Tamara sat in the kitchen, watching her oatmeal cool beside the cards. They were laid out in her fifth set of three of the morning. Jack of diamonds, jack of spades, two of hearts. Death and death, they said. A curse that ran through gristle and bone. An oracle who could witness, or who could act. In the background, the woman who had started all of this back when Tamara was just a child in Lawrenceville discussed the bloody business as though it weren't about to kill her and her baby.

"It's the body, then," Phyllis said. A second later, Tamara mentally corrected herself: the Body, the second-most-notorious hatchet man in Victor's gang. She left the cards and went to the sink. She ran the tap.

"Baby, the body count might be *exactly* why he'd snitch—I know that. That's where he got the name, isn't it? When he hides a body, even Saint Peter can't find it? But hey, Walter, no one's perfect. And even the NYPD gets lucky once in a while."

She laughed, a laugh freer than it had any right to be, considering the subject of conversation. The sink was full of last night's dishes, so Tamara made her hands busy. A soapy wineglass fell from her stiff fingers and the stem broke clean off the base. Dregs of red wine mixed with the soap and glass and ran, businesslike, down the drain.

"Dev's hands aren't magic, Walter. He gave you what he could, and it ought to be enough. Maybe it's the Body, maybe it's Marty, maybe it's someone you haven't thought of yet—Mrs. Robinson must have seen enough to burn her eyes after all these years . . . Oh, Walter, the cleaning lady."

Tamara liked Mrs. Robinson. The woman was seventy if she was a day, but wouldn't tolerate any young do-gooder trying to help her with her groceries. She had a sinewy strength and a face so professionally straight that you just knew she could tell some tales if she had a mind to. Tamara's grandmother had spent her life cleaning other people's messes, and if you caught her on a good summer night, after she'd poured herself a fortifying tumbler or two of curative bitters, she could make you bust a gut for laughing. Grandma's white folks stories had been Tamara's favorite as a young girl, just realizing what it meant when those laughing, red-faced men passed through town in their trucks. When Mrs. Robinson cleaned Georgie's cage, she always commented on his appetite and fed him precisely one cricket. Tamara would try to tease a laugh from her, or at least some tutting disapproval, but the most she ever managed was one thin eyebrow very delicately raised, and, in tones so dry they surpassed even Phyllis, "Well, you young people keep having your fun, for as long as you can, I say. They'll knock it out of you soon enough."

Mrs. Robinson had cleaned Victor Dernov's toilet for more than a decade. Mrs. Robinson, Tamara was sure, could tell the best sort of white-people stories, ones that made you cry for laughing. Or just cry.

"I'll let you know if I think of anything," Phyllis said, after a silence. "You'll talk to them?"

Before she realized what she was doing, Tamara shut off the tap and ran into the living room. "Don't you dare!" she shouted. Phyllis looked up, at first annoyed and then alarmed.

"What happened?

"Mrs. Robinson is no rat and you know it, Phyllis Green! Don't you touch her!"

"I never said she was," Phyllis said, very carefully. Tamara thought: her knives may be rusting in the garden, but that don't make her less dangerous.

Walter murmured something on the line. Phyllis frowned and

cupped her hand over the receiver. "No, no—don't worry about it, Walter. Yes, we're doing fine. Right. Goodbye."

Tamara was breathing hard, her heart galloping like a lame horse. Her skin prickled in cold waves. She thought she might faint. She had never—what had she been thinking?—done anything like that before. She knew her goddamn business!

Phyllis reclined on that old couch like Pharaoh's mistress.

"What's got into you, Tammy?"

Tamara clenched her fists, but she had so little strength in her fingers that they slipped out again to flop against her thighs. She took a little step to the left and collapsed onto the ottoman.

"You said you were looking for the snitch, and that Mrs. Robinson—"

Phyllis tilted her head. "I doubt she is. But it's *possible*. That was my point. Walter is just looking at his lieutenants, but there's a lot more people watching."

Tamara gulped a breath. "Well, don't hurt her."

"Her son's a small-time banker in the Bed-Stuy policy racket. She's got no reason to snitch, and Walter knows it."

Her son? And then Tamara remembered a good-looking boy who brought Mrs. Robinson home some nights. He'd asked Tammy for some numbers once, and she'd teased him about betting against the bank. She turned her head to the side and shrugged.

"Well, I don't know about those sorts of things."

Phyllis looked more like Pea again to her; she gave Tamara a confused, sad smile, the kind that seemed to come at the tail end of some great pain.

"You sure about that?"

"I know what I need to, but I don't get involved."

"Don't you?"

"I'm just the snake girl! What the devil does mob business have to do with me shaking my titties on a stage?"

"Well, if you're shaking your titties for the devil in charge, baby, I'd say it does."

The rage hit Tamara so hard she rocked back with it.

"Don't you look at me like that, not you, Phyllis! You've got ghosts like a country dog has fleas, and you don't even know it! Goddamn it, goddamn it, Pea, why did you have to take it all so seriously? Couldn't you have knocked off a few baddies and called it a day? Couldn't you have run off with Dev that first time and *stayed* here in this cracker country? Oh no, but you got to be the best, don't you? Be the very best angel for the devil himself, and now where has that got you? Sick to death with a baby, your man in the war, and your devil's old ghost settling in for the winter! And now I'm supposed to fix it? I gotta clean up this goddamned mess you made? I love you, Pea, I swear I do, I never had a friend like you, but—"

Grief cut her off like a closed fist. Phyllis just stared at her, mouth open, eyes wet.

Tamara stood up, walked straight through the kitchen to the side door and out into the cold punch of winter.

To sit back and watch her die. To know she could have done something, but to choose, instead, nothing. To live the rest of her life with that most damning of proof that she had always been better at pretending goodness than being good.

She kicked a stone. It wasn't Tammy who'd spent fifteen years cutting a bloody swath through New York's lowlife. She hadn't submitted her will to a man with no more moral sense than those silver teeth Marty stuck in his mouth every year.

Sure, said Tammy's own thoughts in Pea's damned voice, but you danced for him.

The cards weren't any more forthcoming—two of hearts, five of clubs, seven of diamonds, primes, those solitary figures, accusing her: *choose her or choose yourself, Oracle, but we both know who you really are.* And then the other ghosts started crawling their way through Tamara's peripheral vision, along with old silver himself.

Her uncle Chester, who had died of a heart attack last summer, in his mistress's bed.

Great-Aunt Winnie, eyes eloquent with disappointment and re-served pride.

A light-skinned woman who reminded Tammy of Pea, and must be her great-grandmother herself, whose cards and kerchief she had kept in trust all these years.

She blamed Victor's curse, though she couldn't understand why Pea got to sleep the night through while Tamara paced the kitchen until twilight. She'd resorted to using Mrs. Grundy's laudanum more nights than she liked to admit. Was it that Tammy was the oracle to Pea's unhappy fate? Or was it the choice, that angel joker, that had the haints up in her business like a church lady at Sunday repast? She told herself she needed distraction, and so she rang Walter.

"Just checking in on my favorite place in the world," she told him, aiming for and hitting that perfect note of airy cheerfulness, though it cost her more than it used to.

"Still standing, Tammy," Walter said, dryly. "Miss us already?"

"It's not exactly the Flamingo up in here, Walt."

"I thought you hated the Flamingo. On principal."

"Well, it's certainly no Pelican! Who's on tonight, anyway?"

"Some dancer," Walter said, a little distracted. "I don't remember the details. Someone on your list."

"French or Russian?"

"Chicagoan?"

"Oh! Don't tell me Katherine Dunham found time at last? Last I heard she'd gone to Hollywood and forgotten all about us."

"It would seem she remembered. Tammy—I appreciate your interest in the joint, but you're up there, we're down here—"

"If you're too busy, Walter, you can just say so."

"Is everything all right with you and Pea?"

"Why wouldn't everything be?"

"Just a feeling."

"You got the hands now too?"

Walter laughed. "Grateful to say I've never had a dream come down. But I do know my business. You'll let me know if you need me? I promised Dev I would keep her safe. I don't make a lot of promises, Tammy."

Keep *her* safe? And how, Tamara thought, was Walter going to keep Phyllis safe from her own bloody past? "There's nothing wrong, Walter."

"But you've been seeing dead people."

Tamara opened her mouth and felt everything she had meant to say drain away. She had never felt so distant from the Pelican, from Victor's New York, from the glittering play she'd performed for herself, night after night.

"How do you know that?" she asked flatly.

"Pea told me you think that Victor is haunting her. And right before she passed out that night at the Pelican you screamed something. About a body in a tree. So, tell me Tammy, what did you see?"

"I saw Pete Williams," she said softly. Walter didn't respond, so she found herself filling that soft space he left her with her own, real voice. "He was this boy I knew growing up. We might have kissed even, I don't remember. I kissed a lot of boys. Mama didn't like it, said that I was growing up like my dad. Anyway, Pete and I didn't run with the same crowd. My mama taught literature at St. Paul's and I lived mostly with my grandma, who had her master's—the first in the family—anyway, we were that kind of family, some liked to call us uppity, but we were well educated, respectable, despite my dad. And Pete's family lived in a one-room shack down by the creek and none of them stayed in school past eighth grade. Pete might have gotten through some high school, but he dropped out to work. Something dirty. Road work or construction, I don't remember. He dated one of my girlfriends for a while, but we all said she could find someone better, so she left him. She married a dentist from Richmond . . . beat her ass every Sunday night, like it was part of the liturgy.

"Pete was a nice kid. Poor, not educated worth a damn, but kind. I think that's worth a lot more than we realized back then. But they say that he fell for some white girl—not rich, either. Some cracker girl from a cracker family that also lived near the creek, but on the other side. I don't think that she accused him—I think her family just didn't like the idea of her with a black man. Not that they called him that. Not when all those men tied him up in the back of their pickup, and drove him a couple of miles outside of town, and strung him up on that old sycamore tree whose roots must go straight down to hell, and left him there for the crows and the possums and the little black children who found him. Little Pete. He grew up short and wide, but all muscle. He must have fought. There were too many of them. So they killed him and strung him up and no, I never saw him, Walter, not until that night at the Pelican when I saw him clear as sin swinging from the rafters with his neck broke in a noose and one foot in a bloody boot."

"That's why you left town, isn't it?"

"Why would you say that?"

"Might be because I did the same."

"You saw a lynching, Walter?"

He made an indeterminate noise, something between a snarl and a laugh. "Not quite. They took me and my sister from our mother and our grandparents, gave us to one pious white family after another, stuffed us full of the white man's god and told us we had to atone for the sins of our fathers. Our skin was the sin, you understand. Our culture. My sister said if she could never go back home she would rather not be here at all. She hung herself. I ran off."

Shock kept her silent for a long moment. Walter never spoke about his childhood; he never spoke about his *life* outside of the Pelican. She didn't know the first thing about where Walter had grown up, not even the state, but she had always known he'd grown up with violence.

"I'm sorry about your sister," she said, after a moment. "Why did you ever let them call you Red Man?"

Now he did laugh. "Who could understand that better than you, Tammy? Red Man was the price I paid so my sister's murderers could never touch me again. Their insult became my bullet. And you?"

She had never liked being seen. But with Walter, it didn't feel so bad.

"I came to New York and asked around for the baddest man in the Village. That's why I stayed, even though I didn't like . . . everything I saw. But he was the whitest white man I'd ever met. He could protect me from anything. With him, nothing could happen to me like what happened to Pete. But it turns out you can't hide, Walter. Not the way I was doing. You turn around one day and the monster's dead and his angel wants to put away her knives and pay off debts . . ."

"Can she?"

She took a shaky breath. "What do I know, Walter? What would someone like me know about that?"

That afternoon, Tamara went to Pea's room and opened the curtains to let in the weak light.

Pea looked in her direction without turning her head.

"Is that really necessary?"

"You planning on sleeping through the winter?"

Pea sighed. "Sometimes she dreams about him."

Tammy's stomach gave a familiar lurch and she grabbed Pea's cold tea from the bedside table. The lavender and rose hips had gone bitter in the night, but she drank it down straight. That goddamn baby, she thought, and then stopped herself from thinking any more. "Well," Tamara said, businesslike, "I thought you might like to see this. You keep sleeping through the afternoons."

Phyllis propped herself up on her elbows. "See what?"

Tammy's smile came a little more easily now. "Just look out the window."

Mrs. Grundy came up the driveway at 3:50. As always, she appeared to have walked. Tamara and Phyllis watched in astonishment as the housekeeper proceeded to wait on the front steps, gloved hands crossed in front of her.

Phyllis scooted closer to the window. "What the devil is she waiting for?"

"Just watch," Tamara said.

"Did she *walk* from town?"

"She says that she enjoys the exercise."

"And the cold biting off her nose, apparently!"

Tammy giggled. Some easy warmth returned to her, some of her flailing rage quieted like an exhausted baby. She could not hate Pea. She could not even, in moments like this, believe that the two of them were so very different.

At precisely four o'clock, the housekeeper lifted her right hand. Her knock coincided with the second chime of the grandfather clock.

The display was all Tamara had hoped for; they shared a look and Phyllis burst out laughing.

"No!"

"Every afternoon!"

"Will you get it or should I?"

"You know you're not supposed to rush." Tamara jumped up from the bed. "Oh damn, the clock finished chiming, now she'll just use it as an excuse to moan about how those Negroes are always running late."

Phyllis started laughing so hard that she choked and Tamara thumped her slightly harder than necessary on the back. It was nearly a minute before Tamara finally made it to the door, where Mrs. Grundy waited, pinch-lipped, actually tapping her foot.

"Oh, you're here already!" Tamara raised her hand to her cheek in theatrical consternation. From the top of the stairs, a muffled snort made Tamara jump. Mrs. Grundy peered past her into the dim entrance, as though into the lair of a dragon.

"I rang the bell," said Mrs. Grundy, stiffly.

"Oh, did you?" She put on her best silly girl face, perfected these last few years at the Pelican. It was such a good face; it got her so much freedom—and love, when she wanted it—that there had been long stretches, months at a time, when she'd even believed it herself.

It did its work here; Mrs. Grundy sighed and walked into the front parlor. But Tamara noted, though she did not like to, how stiff that face had sat on her features, how hollow her voice, how empty her eyes. What, she now wondered, had any of those boys found there to love? Had even Clyde fallen for that player's mask?

Tamara closed the door and went to help Phyllis down the stairs. They sat together in the parlor while Mrs. Grundy busied herself in the kitchen. Tamara's easy mood had vanished like a soap bubble. What did it matter that she liked to play a little? What did it matter that she'd always been pretty enough to get folks to go her way? Oh, Aunt Winnie had disapproved and loudly, but she'd been an old woman, jealous of that easy power.

Phyllis gave her a long once-over while Tamara glowered. Why was this her choice? Why was this her weight, when she'd kept her head down, she'd kept her hands clean? But the cards pricked at her irritably, as did the memory of Victor, who was dead.

"What's been eating you, Tammy? What aren't you telling me? Is it the cards? You've sure been keeping them close lately."

Tamara felt dizzy, in free fall. She reached out for a distraction. "That baby probably won't be able to pass, you know."

Phyllis touched the top of her belly, somehow larger again today than it had been yesterday. "You mean Durga."

"Dev is too brown. She won't be able to do like you."

"We could say she was Indian. Or Mexican."

"Not the same, is it? Mrs. Grundy won't be shaking *her* hand, Miss High Yellow."

"She's making our meals, Tammy, and cleaning our toilets. I figure it was worth a handshake."

"It wasn't worth it to her, when it was my hand I held out there."

"So she's another bigoted white lady, Tammy. America's full of them. Can I help that?"

Tamara drove a fist into the couch cushions, which merely swaddled the force of the blow. "You don't have to play into it, either! Remember when you came back to the city after the wedding? Remember where you stayed, Phyllis?"

"The hotel?"

"The goddamn *Algonquin*. These whites up north, they might be too up their noses to put a sign above the door, but I sure as hell couldn't go through it. Pea, pitch-toed as you are, you still Negro, you still know it, and ain't none of this Miss Ann bullshit do you any credit."

Phyllis drew in a sharp breath. She lowered a hand that seemed to have sprung up like a jack-in-the-box. "So where should I have stayed? Since you're playing moral justice today."

"In Harlem, how about!"

"Oh, so you live in Harlem now?"

"I don't live in a goddamn cracker jack box named after a bunch of Indians they *also* wouldn't let through the door!"

Phyllis punched out a breath. Then another. Tamara realized that she was laughing, gasping, hysterical. She fell to her side on the cushions and gripped her belly as though the child would otherwise claw its way out of her.

"What kind of a world am I bringing her into, Tammy? What awful world?"

5

A package of letters, courtesy of the U.S. Army, arrived one afternoon toward the middle of March. There was one from Dev, four whole pages filled on both sides with his broad, loopy handwriting. Tamara's heart tweaked when she realized that he hadn't sent her anything. She didn't know why he would. Clyde had written to her, though. She kept the letter, unopened, for a day, trying to savor the fact that at the very least he was still alive.

"Well," Phyllis asked her, that second day, "you gonna open it? All we do lately is wait, I don't know why you want to go around waiting more."

"At least this way I get to control it," Tamara said. Phyllis nodded at that and put her head on her shoulder.

Clyde hadn't been native to Lawrenceville like Tammy was; he had come to St. Paul's from farther south as a student. Aunt Winnie had passed that winter and Tammy hadn't been able to shake the blues ever since; she had wanted to leave town, but she couldn't bear to, either. The cards told her to get out of the house, at least, so she went to the summer production of *Romeo and Juliet*. She sat there riveted to the seat while Clyde delivered Mercutio's dying monologue. Afterward, she just stood in the lobby while he shook hands and joked and, eventually, noticed her. *You liked the show?* he asked her. *You got a nice voice, Mercutio,* she said, and he laughed and held out his hand.

They spent three weeks together. Days sitting on the broken wall outside the malt shop, waiting for the white busboys to give them their burgers from the back door. They'd take them back to the willow tree by the stream in her grandma's yard and stay until sundown reading parts from plays that Clyde had discovered in the St. Paul's library. Then she would read his numbers and show him her best tricks. He loved her deck as a piece of art and never once suggested the pawnshop. You can love someone for the smallest things, sometimes. She'd stumble through the door at nearly midnight, and her grandma would just look at her and tell her to be careful.

And then a prominent Negro theater in Richmond offered him a part in their fall season production of *Othello*. He would play Iago, a villain, for once. *I've got a sweet face, that's my problem. Always want me for the hero.* She told him he had a big head, but he hardly heard her. He said that it was a good opportunity, that he couldn't just rot away down in the country. She told him that he had her. He kissed her cheek. *Oh, and how many times a day do you tell me about everything you're gonna do when you get to New York, Tammy? The only thing I don't know is why you haven't left yet.*

She felt crushed by the indignity of it. She had hated him for not seeing it, for thinking that a bad ending didn't change the whole play.

But even as young as she was then, Tamara had an oracle inside her. She knew the ways of pulling good numbers out of bad.

She told him to meet her by the creek in two hours and bring some wine. He loved her, she knew it better than him. But he wouldn't let that stop him. And she'd never pretended it would stop her.

She took him an hour outside of town, to a special spot by the old creek. They sat on the grass of the clearing and listened to the cicadas and drank a whole bottle of wine. The fireflies surrounded them, flew in and out of her hair. They were like buzzing green stars. They realized they could see the Milky Way. Then the clouds came in fast and the creek rose so high she wondered if they'd get caught. But they stayed and she sang to him. For the rest of her life she'd remember that. Singing Ellington in the charged air before a storm, holding hands with Clyde. The oracle part of her knew they might have a second chance because she changed the ending.

Clyde never forgot her; she'd made sure of that. The fireflies and the rain that never quite fell, singing at the top of her lungs out there where no one could hear her (*Gracious, girl! Those pipes!*)—the whole reason she had stuck in his heart like old gum for years after they lost track of one another.

She wanted him for a good long time, Tamara had thought, if he made it back. *If you can stand to look him in the eye. If you can bear the thought of being happy after you sell her down the river.*

Tamara sat up abruptly and went down to the kitchen. She couldn't—if Phyllis knew what the cards were saying—Tammy could never tell her.

Lately Phyllis had a hard time keeping anything down, so Tamara had asked Mrs. Grundy to make something sweet to tempt her. She came back upstairs with two spoons and a tray of bread pudding that was the housekeeper's first effort.

Phyllis took her time with that first bite, then smiled ruefully. "It's good," she said.

"I'm shocked," Tamara said. "You should have seen her face, as though I'd asked her to make a feast for Gluttony himself."

"And the other six deadly sins if she had a spare minute."

They leaned into one another with their laughter.

"Poor Mrs. Grundy," Phyllis said. "You can almost see her asking God what she did to deserve such indignity."

"Got stuck with two Negroes with a sweet tooth."

"Oh, you know she probably ate half of this pudding down there by herself."

"Wouldn't surprise me," said Tamara, around another spoonful.

"So, that letter you got," Phyllis said, while Tamara was laid out with ecstasy.

"This pudding tastes real good for you to go and ruin it."

"Did you open it, at least?"

Tamara nodded.

"So what'd he say?"

"He broke up with me! That . . . that raggedy-ass, two-bit actor said that I shouldn't 'go to waste' waiting on him! Like I were a goddamn apple pandowdy!"

"That can't be all he said."

"Why not?"

"Because I saw him. If that man don't love you—"

"Sure he loves me. But that didn't stop him! He said he misses me, he thinks of me all the time, *when I'm in the back of that tank, with the guns pointing to the sky and the only thing I can see are the contrails and black smudges of those Zeroes, and if my hands aren't steady it won't just be me I'm killing but dozens of our men at the front, I think about you, and I find still waters.*"

Tammy couldn't continue. Phyllis was thoughtful for a moment, or maybe just hungry. She took four full bites before she responded. "He's just young, baby. He's trying, he's got a good heart, I could see that, but he's young enough to believe he can stop you from hurting. That he can love you and not leave a mark."

"I'm just as young as that fool, and I don't believe that!"

"Well," she said, "you're a woman."

"He told the war office to send me notice if he dies."

"His remains?"

"Go to his mama, thank God."

Phyllis took a deep breath, thinking, most likely, of whatever Dev had written to her in that long letter riddled with black smudges from the censor's edits.

"You got a smoke?"

"Phyllis, aren't you supposed to be cutting back?"

"No more than five a day, the doctor said. I've only had four."

Tamara sighed, lit up one of the last in her pocket, and took a drag before handing it over. Their breath clouded the air between them, and then drifted toward the snow-crusted window. Tamara and Mrs. Grundy had barely cleared the driveway from the last storm, but Mrs. Grundy said they were due another tonight. Was it normal for winter to last so long? In her three years in the city, she'd never felt a March like this one, colder than a Virginia January. Tamara didn't want to complain. She had to seem strong enough to see this through. Phyllis would cut her in a minute; she'd send her home for her own good if it looked to her like she was cracking under the strain. And Phyllis didn't even know why. What good was it to be an oracle if you couldn't change a damned thing?

It would be okay. If the boiler broke down again she'd get Pea downstairs, in front of the fire. They could stay up half the night drinking and telling stories, playing a safe deck of cards.

Pea shifted against the pillows and swallowed. Tamara tensed, in case she had to help her to the bathroom, or a bucket.

"They've sent him to North Africa now," Phyllis said. "I can't tell what he's doing because I swear a third of that letter had black lines through it."

"Africa? What else did Dev say?"

"That his superior officers are idiots, overflowing with racial prejudice, he's working with the Algerians, but he can't say more about his duties. But at least he's been transferred from ambulance detail." She clenched her hands over her knees. "He hated that. Too much blood."

"They let all that through?"

"I knew what he wasn't saying."

"He always did hate blood. He'd even look away from the catsup they use in the theater. Poor Dev."

"Yes," Pea said, and stared at nothing in particular long enough for cigarette ashes to scatter on the quilt. She looked down, surprised, and brushed them off. "Tammy?"

"Yeah?"

"He said he'd had a strange dream and he wanted me to ask you . . . about that night backstage at the Pelican."

Tamara flinched. Phyllis took a drag and peered through the smoke. "He said to put it just like that. He said you'd know what he meant. And you do."

"It's not . . . a good story, Pea."

"That right?" Pea was breathing heavy. Her back hurt her more than she wanted to say.

Tamara went over to help her. "Why did Dev want me to tell you?"

"I'm not sure, baby. He just said it was in his dream."

Tammy stopped short. "*That* kind of dream?"

Pea laughed. "We're just drowning in dreams over here. What's one more, is that right, baby?" But she was talking to her belly now. Tammy sat on her heels, forgotten. And is that how it would be if she took on the burden? Cursed and alone, with just the cards for company? Would the taint kill her instead if she tried to have a child? Oh, she'd probably live, that was the worst of it: she'd have to live badly while Phyllis lived well. There was grace in this world but—Job himself could have told her—not much justice.

Tamara tipped her chin up. She'd tell the story, then. What of it? What was the worst thing she'd done, compared to this woman's sins? Who here could judge her?

Not Victor's ghost.

Not Victor's angel.

"It was Christmas Eve two years ago. We were at the Pelican, backstage. Drunk as three cats in a tub of gin. Well, I don't know about Dev, he could be ossified to his eyeballs and still walk a straight line. But me and Victor, we were good and tight. The place was closed for the night and we were enjoying a bottle of scotch, Victor called it his Christmas present. It tasted like paint thinner and old hay to me, but do you know I got to like it by the third snifter. It got late, I don't know, about three or four in the morning. Victor was playing with that Colt of his, the one with the nickel inlays. God, I hope they buried that with him. If ever there was a piece that could speak nightmares.

"Well, what do you know, Victor got it in his head that he wanted to test Dev. Yes, Pea, like that, he wanted to test his *hands*. He said, *We can be scientific about the matter?* And Dev and I just stared at him blank, because you never want to answer one of his questions. The only way he knew how to end a sentence was in a trap. No getting out of that one, though. He said to Dev, *So touch me,* and Dev said something rude, and Victor lifted that piece calm as you please and pulled back the safety. He said, *Am I going to kill you, Dev?*"

Tamara stopped abruptly. Phyllis moved, but Tamara hid her face. "What did you do?"

"I tried to get behind Victor, like he might forget about me if he couldn't see me. Dev didn't seem to notice. He said to Victor, *You don't know yet.* Just like that. He seemed so calm, so *sure.* You're like that too, Pea, with your knives. But I'd never really known Dev that way. It surprised me. Victor pulled the trigger and I screamed, but you know those big pistols, once you fire them everything else starts to sound like a mosquito buzzing around your head. So I was screaming, but I could barely hear myself, and Victor fell back with the recoil he was so stinking drunk and Dev just *sat there* and pulled a cigarette from his breast pocket. The bullet had put a hole in the wall a few inches to the left of his head. Jesus. *Jesus.* That's all I could say. Victor was giggling and poured himself another drink. He said, *Don't worry, dollface. I just need your man for some business. Don't start blubbering.* Then raised that gun, smooth as could be, and it was me facing down that barrel."

Tamara shuddered, thinking of it, and the rest of it. She swore for a moment she could see Victor panting and licking his lips just beyond the ice crusting the window.

"What did he want?" Phyllis said, and caught herself. "Oh. He wanted to know what Dev could tell from touching you."

Tamara's heart was racing, her palms sweaty, her neck pulsing with heat and cold. She couldn't finish it. Not the real story. Even if it was just Phyllis, who had no right to judge. She found herself straightening crooked things out, making ugly things shiny; an old, bad, habit.

"He said, *Am I going to kill her? You get one chance.* And next thing I knew, Dev pushed me to the ground and he just stood there, facing the gun. He said he knew that Victor didn't want to lose him, so he'd better stop threatening his girl. Victor seemed to lose interest in the whole thing then. He really was stinking drunk. Dev picked me up and we left."

"He let you leave?"

Tamara looked away. "Victor had romantic notions—not with you, of course. But he wanted women to be like the harem girls in *The Thief of Baghdad.* You know, gauzy as ballroom curtains with bubbly for brains. The ones who cry a lot and faint easily and are forever getting kissed by men they actually want but don't know it."

Phyllis gave a small, knowing smile. "So you made sure that's what he thought you were."

Victor had expected her to fall to the floor. He'd expected to watch her eyeliner run in dirty rivers down her face while she begged for her life and Dev's. He expected Tamara to be shocked by his violence—and she was. So shocked that she realized a few fatal beats too late just how she had betrayed herself.

"Safer that way," Tamara said. "Don't give me that look, as though you never played the angel for him."

"Did I?" Pea asked, and something made Tamara's breath stutter in her chest, made her heart ache.

"Well, I think that's why he let me—let us—go."

"Funny of him. But you never could tell when he drank like that." Pea gave her a long look, the kind that meant a hundred things she wasn't saying. "I'm tired, baby. Let me sleep."

Tamara tucked her in and brought her water and put the pillows under her back just so, all the while thinking that Dev had some nerve, asking her to tell that awful story whose real ending made her look like some regular mob girl, some cold-hearted creature who only valued her own comfort. And for what? Could he know that Victor's curse was rattling around his old house? Could he know that Tamara held his wife and daughter's fate in her soft oracle's hands?

Dev had been laid up for weeks after that night. Tamara had waited three days before she could bear to visit him. He said he didn't blame her. Because he loved her, she'd thought. But now doubt came down in a white-hot flash: had he loved her after that night?

Had he seen through her all this time, and never let it show?

She'd been so silly, so sure, so complacent about that deep, good-hearted love in him. Tamara had swanned around the Pelican, proud to have a man like him for her own. She'd felt good in the reflection of his goodness. She'd known exactly what Phyllis had lost and re-gretted, leaving him for all that violence that the angel called justice.

And now Dev might not have loved Tammy at all. He might have just stayed, out of habit or loyalty or—pity, even, goddamn him, knowing she couldn't bear an honest assessment of her character. What did he really think of her? What had he told Phyllis? What truths were permitted over that connection that time and blood and guilt and dozens of other lovers had not dissolved? Tamara had been jealous, she could admit that now, jealous of every discreet glance, of every casual conversation, of how deliberately they never so much as brushed the other's sleeve. He would sigh, sometimes, just after he and Tamara made love and she had *known* he was thinking of Phyllis and would never admit it. What had he written in that letter? What did he know about Tamara? Had his second dream come down, a warning knell from the front?

Had it told him the truth: that Pea was dying, while Tammy whistled in the wind, doing nothing, saving herself for no one?

6

She snuck into Pea's room after midnight and took Dev's latest letter from the desk. Pea groaned in her sleep, turned and then subsided. Tamara held her breath until she was back in the hallway. She went back downstairs to the kitchen to read it.

February 22, 1942
Pea—

Well, it seems that the commonwealth has claimed me, despite my best efforts. I have been pulled from ▮▮▮▮▮▮ *and stationed to* ▮▮▮▮▮▮▮▮▮. *I'm afraid this letter will reach you months from now, when no doubt my circumstances will have changed once again, but I will always write, Pea, I promise. As long as I am able.*

I wanted to scratch that last bit, but I suspect the censors will make such confetti of this letter that it would be a shame to aid those enemies of self-expression. So I will leave you with my slightly morbid, always loving, thoughts.

The air is dry here. Drier than anything I knew in Murbad. It scorches your lungs. The people wear scarves on their heads and robes down to their sandals. It helps against the heat, of course it does. This is their land, they ought to know how to dress for it. The British, however, mock the clothes and supposedly primitive customs of these people all the while swilling quinine, trussed up in their military uniforms and baking in this hard fist of a sun until they look like nothing so much as lobsters in Wolseley helmets.

Well. I doubt that will get through, but just in case it does, I will imagine you laughing.

I have not been laughing very much. The ambulance detail was very hard, Pea. Harder than I expected, and I expected a scene from the more brutal levels of the naraka. The dead did not bother me so much, not after a few weeks there. I know this sounds—well—I confront my failure of imagination. I don't know how this will sound to you, my Kali, my goddess of vengeance. But I have worked where I have for a decade.

Before last summer, I had never killed before—never killed a human before—but I knew what death looked like.

But the wounded, Pea. The blood and the screams and the splintered bone and pulped flesh and the blood—I did not imagine that there was so much blood in the world as what I saw in the hospital ████████████. *We waded through it. It stiffened our clothes. The smell never—never—left my hands. (The censors will probably be appalled that I am describing this to you with so little regard for your sensibilities. You, my angel, may tell them to* ████ *themselves if I cannot.)*

I was with the Negro unit in Europe. (I gather that Tamara's beau was posted to the Pacific theater? It's hell over there, too, that's what they say. But if he's lucky enough to get trained ██ ████ *he might make it back. Don't tell her I said that—what am I saying?—I know you won't.) They were good men. A few were even from Harlem, and one said he knew your family, Pea. Though he probably knew you from your numbers days and didn't want to spell it out. His name is Barkley, said his father passed a decade ago but that he was a well-known businessman in town. How's that for a small world?*

About to get smaller—how many of those boys I left there are alive now? The base ████████ *just after I left.*

And now I am here in the desert, aiding one set of colonizers against another set of colonizers on behalf of a new power whose colonial ambitions haven't gone past their own continent as of yet, but whom I strongly suspect of waiting to seize the pie. The dreams and desires of the ▮▮▮▮▮ *aren't even the nail clippings of a concern for any of these nabobs—* ▮▮▮▮▮▮▮▮▮▮▮▮▮▮▮ *Pea.*

I cannot tell you what I'm doing, but at least it's no longer ambulance duty. When I work with the locals it isn't so bad, but the British officers are worse than even my memory of them. It appears that having grown up does not save one from much torment. Being a Hindu—and not a servant—is more than enough to stir their nationalist bile.

Goodness, I can't imagine that any of that went through. Unless the censors are American, of course. Wave to good old Uncle Sam, Pea. The land of the free, the home of the brave. That star-spangled banner does seem to be hanging in there after all these years, doesn't it?

It makes me wonder about my hands, in fact. All of our hands. It makes me wonder about a universe that would give these people almost all of the power and then, of a moment, give a little sliver of it back. But with such a burden, it sometimes seems better to be powerless. Not quite. And yet, the hands torment you. They are obsessed with our necessary complicity. Even here, they hate what I have to do and for whom.

They would rather kill us for the greater good than let us find happiness in this lifetime.

Durga visits me in my dreams sometimes, don't ask me how. Please stay safe. I'm not sure what we are bringing into this world, but I am sure that Durga is a soul burnished by fire.

I must end this letter—they're calling me at headquarters. But I must ask—I had a very strange dream the other night— one of Durga's, I hope. It reminded me of an incident with Tamara a few years back. You should ask her about it. That night backstage at the Pelican. Though maybe you shouldn't bother. You know Tammy, she'll just lie about the bad parts.

Goodbye, my sweet Pea. Touch our Durga for me and tell her to be still and to send the bad dreams to me.

Your
Dev

Tamara didn't sleep that night. She sat in the dark in the kitchen, knees hugged to her chest, stomach churning along with her brain, thinking of all the ways that the people who she loved the most saw straight through her, and how much she hated them for it. She burned with the unfairness of it: she, who had never done anything truly *bad*, even if she'd gone knocking on bad's door, now had to tolerate the judgment of the Village's most notorious killer and her stoolie lover?

She felt hot and cold, as though she had a fever, as though shame could eat her up from the inside and leave her zombie corpse rattling around come morning. Had Phyllis known she was lying? *You know Tamara,* Dev had written, as though Tamara's untrustworthy character were an old, reliable joke. Sure, she had loved Dev—she'd certainly enjoyed being his lover—and Phyllis was like a sister to her, but those relationships had always been within certain parameters. Tamara was the regular girl, the good one, the foil against which their bad decisions stood out more starkly. It was supposed to be a fair exchange: Tamara's innocent, easy friendship for their hard reputations and checkered pasts. She made them feel better about who they had to be while they protected her from the world. But now . . . did they think, all this time, that they had been doing *her* the favor? Had they indulged her rosy vision of herself while believing that she was really just like them? And if so, why had they never told her?

Her nails had dug four half-moons into her palms by the morning. An empty bottle of wine spilled little red drops on the floor by her feet. Another wineglass lay shattered somewhere behind her; she'd seen Victor around midnight, picking at his silver teeth with a chicken bone. He'd vanished after she threw the glass. She finished the rest of the bottle direct. She ought to take that laudanum, she thought. She ought to just drug herself and drown the clawing shame in dreamless sleep. And she might have, but for the unexpected sound of someone coming down the stairs.

Tamara held her breath, but Phyllis didn't come to the kitchen.

She went to the parlor, instead. What was she doing? Pea had been sleeping all the time lately. Even with Tamara's bad habits—the cards, the wine, the relieving drops of old-fashioned medicine—she would wake up a little before noon, which was generally when she managed to rouse her friend.

But now Pea was in the parlor, building up the fire, as though it didn't cost her to move past the dreams that big-headed baby sent her. Tamara thought of going straight in to confront her, but the shame of admitting how she knew—*Stealing Dev's letter, baby, really? And this is how you plan to prove that you're better than me?*—held her back.

Phyllis picked up the phone. She dialed a number that Tamara wasn't in any fit state to guess by the clicks on the rotary dial as it went around, and when she spoke it was in a clipped, professional, white-people voice that felt shocking, given the hour.

"Yes, sorry to have kept you waiting. I'm moving a little slower these days."

Tamara sat up straighter. Phyllis had been spending a great deal of time on the phone with Walter lately. But she wasn't talking to Walter, not with that voice. More mob business?

"I'm aware of that. But we proceed on my terms or we don't at all." Another pause. Tammy thought of getting closer to the parlor, but then shook her head. Pea, of all people, would notice immediately. Better to hear half of the conversation than none at all.

"Good. Okay then, these are two men." Pause. "Quentin and Beauregard Barkley, Lenox Avenue." She let out a slow breath. "They're worth a lot. Policy bank. Twenty-eight. Yes, the same place. Finch. But I want to make sure their families are taken care of, after. Yes, I'll have the funds wired this afternoon."

Tammy shivered in front of the pot-bellied stove. There was a shiny black ring on the iron stovetop, precisely the size of Pea's old percolator that boiled over as regularly as a geothermal vent. She kept her gaze fixed on that artifact of their domesticity even as Phyllis hung up the phone and dialed other numbers—Walter, this time, just to catch up, and then her sister and niece and nephew. Tamara's knuckles ached from the force of her grip on the edge of the canary-yellow kitchen chair, yet she was not consciously aware of holding anything. She felt as though she had been cast into a turbid river, and the roaring of the water was Phyllis's voice: *they're worth a lot, twenty-eight, Finch.* A voice hard as steel and easy as a good cutting knife. An angel's voice, a Phyllis LeBlanc voice, a killer's voice. And why not? How else would she sound, ordering a kill from the comfort of the divan of her upstate country house? And yet, there was that black ring of burned coffee from a percolator that she always complained about but never replaced. Despite that mountain of corpses between them, Pea still existed, and was still—if Tammy could stomach it—her friend.

Phyllis finished the call with her sister, promising to wire more money, this time for her nephew's clarinet lessons and her niece's new band uniform. Tamara gripped the chair so tight that a bit of splinter pricked the fleshy pad of her right thumb. *This* was who had decided to judge her? *This* was the one for whom she was supposed to take on a curse and Victor's smiling ghost? And was Dev any better, staying with her when he knew just what she was? Who were they to judge the choices Tamara had made to stay alive? The cards pricked her, seemed to bend light around them from where they lay on the table. She loosened her grip on the chair and turned her attention to them with reluctance. They'd have something to say about all of this, she knew. Like Aunt Winnie, they never missed out on a chance to comment. They probably wanted to point out that Dev, at least, had more than enough right to judge her for what happened that night with Victor. But Tammy closed her eyes and closed her hands and closed her heart until all she could hear was rushing water. Safe from all contradicting thought.

Pea's voice from the doorway shocked her back into reality.

"You're not sleeping," she said, dryly.

Tammy kept her eyes shut. "And how do you know?"

The warm laugh in Pea's voice slapped Tammy across the cheeks. "The cards are out, and the laudanum is still in the cupboard."

Tammy cracked open an eye. Pea was leaning against the doorframe, her belly cradled beneath a guiding hand, her eyes red from lack of sleep, folding into crow's feet as she smiled. Her hair rose in a fuzzy halo around the front of her head, and twisted into a knotted mess in back.

Tamara could not speak. Pea would die soon. It would never stop being Tamara's fault.

Some, not all, of the laughter left those jeweled eyes. "How much did you hear, baby?"

And now all she could do was spit up bile. That baby, that damned baby and her sainted hands, why did she have to come and ruin every good thing they'd had together? "Do you think ordering the hit makes it better, Phyllis? Oh, sure, it cuts down on the laundry bills! Afterward you make sure you throw some change to the family, and you feel good and holy, I bet!"

Phyllis gave her a good look for a long time, until Tamara squirmed in her seat and realized, belatedly, that she was still just a little drunk from last night's wine. Her tongue felt thick and rotten in her mouth. She regretted saying anything and she knew if she opened her mouth again she would make herself unforgivable.

"Not so good," Pea said, at last, "not so holy. I know what I've done. I know who I am. I know my sins to the gram, Tamara Anderson. There's no feather heavy enough to balance them."

"Blood money doesn't make up for doing Red Man's dirty business!"

Pea's nostrils flared. Tamara could have sworn that she was about to laugh, though her eyes were glassy tunnels to a distant pain. "No, it wouldn't," she said, and pushed herself from the door frame. "Though money certainly don't *hurt* the family, if they're already dead." She stepped over the remains of Tamara's debauchery, made note of the letter in Dev's distinctive sloping hand on the tabletop, and rinsed the percolator of yesterday's dregs.

"Want any coffee, sweetie?"

"How many people have you killed, Pea?"

Water ran briskly in the sink. The sharp rap of the filter against the side was prelude to the click of it back into the base, and the faint squeak of the base screwing into the top.

"Depends on how you count," she said, matter-of-fact but soft about it. "Fifty-four with my own hands."

Tamara sucked her teeth, a spontaneous reaction lingered upon for effect. "Jesus."

"Got nothing to do with it, I'm sure."

She moved back into Tammy's field of vision and put the percolator on the potbellied stove.

"Did you really think it would never come back to haunt you?"

Pea looked distant, thoughtful. "Maybe I did? Maybe I didn't care? It's hard to remember, now. I'm not the girl I was, then. Nor the woman . . ."

She looked down at her belly, cupped the child between her cursed hands, and smiled.

The next day, Tamara called Walter again.

His new assistant answered the ring after three tries and promised to leave a message. He called that night, while she and Phyllis were playing gin with a set of regular Bicycle cards in the salon.

Tammy left her and took the call in the kitchen. Pea could still hear her if she wanted, but she supposed that was only fair.

"Walter, you watched Victor all those years, when he found people with the hands?"

"What, I don't even get a hello?"

"This is important."

He laughed a little. "You mean when he killed them? Yes. I remember very well, Tammy."

"Did you ever notice . . . anything that they shared? The people he killed? Besides the hands."

Walter let out one of his slow, steady breaths. She imagined his mild expression, his wise eyes and the crease between them. "They weren't white," he said. "I think one was Jewish."

"Anything else?"

"They lived their lives a little . . . outside of the stream. Panhandlers, numbers runners, Times Square dancers—apologies to our

Pea, that sort of thing. As though the hands were pushing them against the current. Almost none of them had families or even steady lovers. Dev was one of the few who actually worked for the establishment, but, well, you saw how that turned out."

"And did they ever say? I mean, if you talked to them, before . . ."

"Sometimes," he said, shortly.

"Did they ever say *what* they felt the hands wanted? Where they were being pushed?"

He held a silence again, a soft space in which she wondered if she shouldn't have asked.

"It's funny," he said at last. "Only one ever told me anything very specific. He painted walls down by the docks, was always getting chased out by police and the owners. He said that he wanted to 'make it right.' And now I seem to recall that Alvin said something similar, didn't he? It's enough to make you wonder."

"Wonder what?"

"If the dreams, the hands, might not be precisely luck. Maybe something closer to a possession."

Tamara, who had kept her silence about Phyllis's fits and her un-controllable hands, felt her throat close like a fist.

7

When she was seven years old, Tamara's best friend was Little Sammy, so called because his daddy was Samuel Senior, and his mother wanted everyone to know it. His mother was the neighborhood prostitute and Samuel Senior was a big man, more protector than pimp. Little Sammy had a dream come down when he was ten, the only one in their generation, but before then he was a little kid like the rest of them, running barefoot to the creek before their mothers could tell them to put their shoes on, fishing with bits of string and hooks they bent from old needles and chicken wire. Even then, he had a knack for the fishing line. Tammy didn't, and one day when she was trying to get a rock perch that was wiggling on her hook, the metal went clean through her hand. They took her to the town doctor, who let her drink Grandma's medicinal bitters while he cleaned and bound her wound. "Just take it easy with that hand," he had told her. But even though it hurt, she could not leave that puckered flesh alone. She would unwrap the bandage and show it off to Little Sammy and his friends. At night alone, she'd poke around the bloody edges, marveling at how the most swollen areas went white at her touch. It got infected, of course, and then her mother had to take her to Richmond for stronger medicine; her daddy gave her a whupping for it when they got back, as though an infected hand weren't enough punishment.

But Daddy wasn't here to whup her anymore—Tamara'd whup him right back if he tried—and pressing the wound of Phyllis's ugly past and ambiguous present was a torture too exquisite, too perfectly suited to her oldest needs, to leave alone. So what if she made herself sick over it? She wanted to goad Pea until one of them popped.

So she asked more questions, each more intrusive than the last: Who was the first person you killed? Who was the ugliest? Who was the richest? Did you steal from their bodies? Did you end up covered in blood? Did you hide their bodies? Did you lie to Dev? Did he really know exactly what you were up to?

At that, Pea gave her an answer dry and raspy as a cat's tongue. "Even better than me, Tammy. Don't make the mistake I did."

"What mistake would that be? Leaving him?"

Pea laughed, filled with a strange and distant delight. "Imagining that he is easy to know."

That stymied her into silence for the next day. The larger Pea got, the less Tammy could stand the sight of her. Winter lingered into the start of spring and she felt consumed with bitterness, like a root vegetable left too long underground. Phyllis should have felt it too, but she seemed impossibly content with her slow, careful movements, her long, dreaming silences, her early-morning phone calls to New York mobsters.

Tamara wrote Clyde:

> I've been thinking of a play, a kind of cross between French existentialism and surrealism, all the actors in a round standing like statues as they scream at one another. Here's the setup: two people at the edge of the River Styx. One's a killer, a real nasty piece of work. Mobster with so many skeletons in his closet he's gone and bought a few extra closets. The other's a normal sort of person, not too bad, not too good; made some compromises, sure, and maybe watched someone die, but certainly never did anything active to kill them. Here's the twist: the boatman gives them a choice. The killer can go to hell, no questions asked, hellfire for all eternity. The other can just go to heaven, and it's business as usual. Or, the regular Joe can take on a bit of that weight the baddie has in his pockets. Then both of them can make it as far as purgatory. So what does the regular Joe choose? Get to heaven, but feel

responsible for sending the baddie to hell? Or resign himself to purgatory and save the killer from eternal damnation? What do you think, Clyde? Would it work? I think you could get an audience really worked up, thinking about all of the moral angles of the thing. I might try to put it on at the Pelican next year, if I can find a writer. But I've just got one problem: I can't think of how it should end. What choice should the hero make? Does the mobster deserve grace? Does the hero deserve heaven?

Love,
Tammy

P.S. I wrote and tore up about a dozen replies to your last letter, and you should be damn grateful, because I really wanted to tell you exactly where to stick it. If you are really planning on leaving me behind, don't you dare respond to this letter. I'll be damned if I let you play me for a fool again.

If you make it back, we are going to write plays together and raise a little army of actors and singers and dancers and, sure, if one of them wants to be a doctor or an engineer, well, there's no accounting for taste, and don't you dare die over there, do you hear me, Clyde? I'm here waiting for you, so don't you dare.

She was drunk when she wrote it, and drunk when she sent it, and spent the next day brutally sober, nursing a hangover and the shakes and a bad case of regret. Mrs. Grundy diagnosed her tactfully with a cold and sent her to bed with mint tea and honey and a heavy bone broth. Pea came in and kept her company. Tammy wanted to resent it, but she held on to her hand like a sick child and breathed.

"Stopped the laudanum, did you?"

"Been sleeping . . . too much. The cards don't like it."

Phyllis nodded thoughtfully, though always before she had treated the cards and Tamara's role as the oracle as an amusing personal quirk. "And what do they do when they don't like something?"

"Jokers and suicide kings. They tell me so, Pea. And then I see Victor."

"I can see why you'd want to avoid that." Pea lifted the cooling bowl of broth from the sideboard and held a spoon in front of Tammy's mouth.

"Oh, leave me be."

"Just drink a little more. You look like Victor's been sucking the life out of you."

Tamara took a sip and then another. It felt nicer than she would ever admit out loud. She'd always wanted to be taken care of, and could never trust anyone enough to let them.

"Pea," she said, "why haven't you asked me about what happened that night?"

"With Victor and Dev?"

Tamara nodded.

Phyllis put the bowl back on the sideboard and sank down into the pillows beside her. "I thought I already had."

"But you knew I was lying."

Phyllis shrugged. "You'll get around to it when you're ready. Don't forget I know you, Tammy."

"Don't look at me like that!"

"How am I looking at you?"

"That sly little smile! You think you're wise just because you've seen more than I have? You think that you have the right to judge me? Sure, I'm not perfect, maybe I'm not the girl I always wanted you and Dev to see, but I'm not—I'm not *bad*."

She'd tore that smile out of Pea's eyes, at least. It didn't make her feel any better.

"But I am, is that what you mean, Tammy?"

She wanted to say *yes* as emphatically as the ferryman, she wanted to send her best friend all the way down the river. But her heart wouldn't cooperate. "No—not you . . . but we're not the *same*! I never killed anyone, I never spent decades living on someone else's blood . . . I'm not still *ordering* goddamned hits! We're not the same, Phyllis."

"Did I ever say we were?"

Tamara turned away. The cards were beating a tattoo against her temples, a tenderizing mallet on raw meat. They said, *Choose, Oracle, or we make the choice for you.*

The shakes had mostly gone after two days, but nightmares plagued her. Tamara felt cards bouncing and pinching her in her dreams, demanding her attention like a willful child. She didn't want to open up that yellowed ivory handkerchief. She didn't want to read the numbers and feel them inside her head, arranging themselves into patterns that she had intuited from the first moment Aunt Winnie made her cut the deck and lay down a simple set of three. But the cards had to speak and it was her duty to listen, hadn't it always been?

Aunt Winnie always spoke of responsibility, of the sacred role of the oracle. Tamara had rolled her eyes at the time. She hadn't wanted to take the cards, or the force behind them, seriously. She had just wanted to be a regular Lawrenceville girl, going to the theater on weekends to see the double feature from the balcony with her friends, ogling the St. Paul's boys who seemed to her at the time as sophisticated as Parisians. She hadn't wanted to be marked like Little Sammy, whose life after the dream came down to him had been short and firefly bright. But she couldn't resist the numbers, even when she tried. The world they opened up was *hers*, as uncomfortable as it felt sometimes. The more she had accepted the life of the cards, the more she had found what moved her—French philosophers, Irish poets, British dancers, Harlem playwrights, Shakespearean St. Paul's actors with more ambition than sense—until she found herself no kind of Lawrenceville girl at all, a philosophical exile in her own home. She had only stayed as long as she did for Aunt Winnie. After her death, only New York would do, and evil men with long shadows. Aunt Winnie would have burned her ear off with that acid tongue of hers if she had known Tammy's plans. Even dead, to be honest, it seemed to Tamara that she sat in judgment from behind the smudged eyes of the queen of hearts. Respect your elders, that's what they had told her. They hadn't mentioned it was because your elders would always be watching you, and finding fault.

By early April, the sun had started to warm the frozen earth, but winter still gripped them in the mornings and evenings. On Sunday, when Mrs. Grundy had her day off, she went down to the basement boiler herself to shovel in coal and heat the pipes that had frozen overnight. Lord, but Tamara'd be glad for spring. She'd never passed a winter so damn cold in her life. She'd go to Paris when the war was over. Every club was integrated over there, they said, none of this crass American business of sitting in the back or beneath the stairs when she was allowed in at all. When she came back, she'd teach Pea all the new post-war dances, show off all her post-war French. She wanted Pea to be at her wedding, she wanted to show her Lawrenceville, for their babies to grow up together, for them to grow old together. What did she care what Phyllis had done in Victor's service? She'd never been *her* angel—

Tamara's heart seized so convincingly that she cried out and collapsed against the stairs. "Oh Jesus," she whispered, and then, for a time, could do no more than wheeze. She waited to see if she would die, but her vision cleared and her heart kept beating and the cards, they were waiting.

They had known she would give in. She laid them out right there on the basement stairs with trembling hands, while Phyllis slumbered in what Tamara hoped was peaceful ignorance two floors above.

The cards sighed onto the wood. She laid them out in a pentagram with the head at the bottom and the heart marked at the center. This pattern was for listening, feeling the cards out. It had taken her years to learn to read so many numbers at once with their multiple inversions. But with Aunt Winnie's sharp voice guiding her, Tamara had learned to take in the pattern, to let the cards hold her, to feel the lines supporting the numbers at each point and cohering in its center.

Left foot, three of diamonds, neutral; right foot, three of hearts, upright; left hand, ten of spades, reversed; right hand, ace of spades, reversed; head, queen of hearts, upright; and heart, the suicide king himself, axe and diamond above his blue-black visage, reversed.

The oracle stared down at the numbers with soft, glassy eyes. If anyone were around to watch her (and there was, she knew that, if you were generous with your definition of "anyone"), they would have seen her hands relax their unconscious grip on her terrycloth robe, her lips part, her eyes take on a dreamy concentration particular to opium eaters and oracles. Slowly, the pattern came clear.

Threes were neutral numbers, half six, which was the number of death. But two times three made six, which meant life and danger. The diamonds represented untold wealth, the hearts unspeakable grief. They were upright, but in the head-down pentagram, what was upright was also reversed. Life and death, then, a cycle that had the potential for both great rewards and brutal heartbreak. And in the position at the feet, it meant that they wanted to move, but something hadn't quite let them yet. The hands and heart made a line of reversed cards. These were Pea's hands, full of spades that were falling to the earth. From the ace to the ten, she had been given great power and it was slowly falling away. The direction, the purpose of those blades, had been twisted. And now that corruption had reached her heart. But that suicide king didn't have to kill himself for the corruption to be reversed. Someone could take it from him: the queen of diamonds, the monarch at the head and yet behind them all, the voice of the cards that moved through the oracle who was Tamara, the voices of the ancestors clamoring in her head, *The corruption shall be burned from this earth and the way made clean! We are in the earth, we are in the trees, we are in the sky. We see! Beware us!*

The oracle shook and trembled. The cards, the luck, they roared beneath her fingers, but the oracle was gone, lost in the frozen earth, in the slow-moving sap of sleeping trees, in the feathered clouds of a dawn sky.

Above her body, a woman called her name.

Tamara opened her eyes as though peeling back an orange. She opened them as she had been, facing the closed door at the top of the basement stairs. It was open now, and Phyllis was in it, backlit by the yellow dawn light streaming from the French windows in the parlor. Beside her was Victor staring murder at the both of them.

Phyllis's hands were twisted behind her back but they surged sideways now, flailing toward Victor's chest. Phyllis cursed and threw herself back against the doorframe. Tamara pushed the cards aside and scrambled up the stairs. She ran straight through Victor and she could swear the air he occupied smelled unclean, like the butcher's shop at the height of summer. Phyllis was on her knees, one shoulder hitched against the far wall, sweat pouring down her face as she wrestled with the ends of her own arms. Tamara wanted to scream herself, at the sight of it. But she took a shaky breath and grabbed Phyllis around the waist.

"Pea, calm down! Pea!"

Pea relaxed against her, but the hands twisted and smacked the pocked and gouged floorboards that Mrs. Grundy had polished just last week. The hands were reaching for Victor, standing above them. In a fit of rage, Tamara dropped Phyllis and reached for the hands instead. They were too fast for her, of course. They smacked her hard the second she tried.

"Leave her be!" Tamara screamed. "Sweet Jesus, leave her be! Can't you see it's too late? Can't you see he's already dead!"

The hands, Pea's beautiful, scarred hands, hit her like a steel bar on the jaw and Tammy slid quietly to the floor.

When she came around, Tamara was still on her back on the warped floorboards. But someone had put a blanket over her and a pillow under her head and was icing her jaw with a block wrapped in a towel.

"Is he gone?" Tamara asked. The jaw hurt but it didn't feel broken. Her head, however, felt wrung out and stuffed with moldy towels.

Phyllis, squatting awkwardly beside her, bent forward and held out two fingers.

"Can you see me? How many fingers am I holding up?"

Tamara rolled her eyes and swatted the hand away. The earth rocked for a bit and Pea held her until it subsided. "Your hands are safe again?"

Phyllis's jaw clenched. "They're mine again."

"So he must be gone."

"Victor." Pea's voice was flat.

"Who else. Don't tell me you still don't believe me? After that little show?"

"My hands—"

"Decided to play jacks with my face. They don't seem to know he's dead. They still want you to kill him."

Phyllis closed her eyes. Her voice broke. "I am so goddamn sorry, Tammy."

Tamara swallowed thickly, past a lump in her throat as bright and salty as fresh blood. "Why didn't you just kill him when you had the chance, Pea?"

Phyllis just shook her head. "Here, baby, can you sit up? Let's get you somewhere more comfortable. I tried to carry you, but . . . well."

Between them they got Tamara to the couch in the salon and then Phyllis busied herself making a fire. The steam was just barely coming up through the pipes and the room was so cold Tamara could see her breath. She was starting to get the sort of headache that would lay her out for days. Even the firelight made her squint. And yet, seeing Phyllis so frightened and apologetic hurt her more. What were they going to do? The hands didn't care about Phyllis anymore, if they ever had. *The corruption shall be burned from this earth and the way made clean!* Tammy didn't want the way made clean, not if it had to be like this.

She started to shake again and pulled the covers up higher. "Could you bring me some tea?"

That took Phyllis into the kitchen and gave Tamara time to compose herself. She was the oracle and Phyllis was her best friend. She would use the cards and find some way out. She would understand the hands and make them yield.

Phyllis came back and handed her a mug. "Cardamom tea. I forgot that we still had a little in the pantry."

Dev used to make it for her too. Tamara breathed it in, recalling that bittersweet love, full of romantic gestures and empty of commitment. Her hands tightened around the mug, but she didn't look up.

"The cards say your hands turned against you. That you did what you shouldn't have and didn't do what you should have, and now they've gone bad."

"You get all that from a bunch of numbers?"

"Numbers and suits. It's my calling."

"It is that. Did they say there was something I could do about it?"

"No," Tamara said, which wasn't a lie, though it felt like one. If she were going to let Phyllis die like this, shouldn't she at least tell her? But Tamara couldn't bear the look in Phyllis's eyes any more than she could bear the sacrifice the cards demanded to save her. She cleared her throat.

"I mean, I didn't ask. But I've been thinking a lot about the hands, and how they work with the numbers. It sometimes feels as though the numbers and the hands are all part of the same ball of chance. The universe connects them, and we just get glimpses of where it's going."

Pea laughed. "The universe plays policy now?"

"Why not?" Tamara warmed to her theme; it felt like a way out. "It's just luck. Just a little bit of luck that gets you ahead. You know how many of us get our start in business from a lucky hit? Every policy slip is a little pebble thrown against the system. It's our people saying, we know they got it all now, but we'll get ours, too, someday. Why can't the hands be like that? But now it's not a pebble, it's a big rock. It might actually make a dent in that wall if you all throw at the same time."

"But we don't."

"But you could."

"Oh, now you're talking black liberation?"

"Dev isn't black. I'm talking *global* liberation."

"Gracious, girl, you making me tired just listening to you."

"Has that baby dreamed you anything lately?"

"Bodies. Men and women. A river of rotting meat."

8

In April the women went outside more, now that the ground had thawed and the sun came out for more than shy minutes at a time. In her eighth month, Phyllis moved slowly but with ponderous grace. The horrors of the first two trimesters appeared to have lessened, but in the absence of physical pain she grew quieter and more reflective. She looked at Tamara sometimes with a panicked despair that neither of them could answer. The baby kept dreaming, but whatever those dreams left behind she didn't share.

Tamara called her grandma. Just the sound of that voice made her nostalgic and aching for home—a home she couldn't wait to get out of when she was actually there. She and her cousins had gotten together to pay for a phone line the year before, after Grandma had sworn she'd die in that old house, no use trying to convince her to move in with Tamara's mother. They chatted for a while—the latest church gossip, the exodus of St. Paul's students signing up for the war, the new chapter of the NAACP that a young dentist and his professor wife were talking about opening in town.

"Now, I know you did not call me to talk about all that small-town business you couldn't stand when you were living here," she said. "So, out with it, girl."

Tamara smiled and imagined the fondness of her grandma's frown as she said this, eyebrows raised, lips pursed. "When you were growing up, did you know people with saint's hands?"

She sucked her teeth. "You want to know about *that*? Don't know what good it ever did them, but sure, there were about a dozen in town when I was a child. We used to whisper about getting dreams.

For a while even I wanted one, but thank the Lord he spared me that burden."

"Is it so bad to have the hands, Grandma? Who wouldn't want a little extra?"

"I sure don't! Of those dozen I knew back in the day, only one lived to see forty. And he's still with us, but Syl Freeman lives alone in that hunting shack and he don't go out much. I think he just decided to keep his head down and survive. In any case, he's the last of his kind. No one has had a dream in town for I don't know how long. Your mother would claim it's the power of the Lord over the devil's works."

She said this with such disdain—and a faint impression of her mother's cadences—that Tamara had to laugh. "You aren't buying that, huh?"

"Hell, no! Pardon my language, but your mother is just hot and bothered by that nice-looking pastor of hers. No, whatever the hands were, they didn't come from the devil. They were holy. Too holy for a human to hold them for long. All them that got the dreams would . . . they would try, Tammy. They would go to the town hall and try to vote for mayor. They would walk straight up to the lunch counter at Central Diner and sit there while the white folks worked themselves into a lather. More than a couple got themselves lynched that way. If they left town, it was more of the same. They became criminals, they hid in the woods, they joined armies, but they could not abide. They couldn't wait for their reward in heaven, they had to bring it right on down here. And they couldn't."

Tammy took a breath, slow and steady. "I hear you."

"Those old souls," Grandma said softly, "they suffered too much."

"They—who suffered?" But she knew. She'd felt them most of her life.

"Do you remember," Grandma said, "that old story about your nana? Been thinking about it lately. Funny that you called about the hands, because I've been catching myself reminiscing. An NAACP chapter here in Lawrenceville of all places. It makes me wonder what we could do with a pair of hands . . ."

"About Nana? You mean, the night they told her she was free?"
She could imagine her grandmother's slow nod, her distant eyes.
"I never told you all of it. Your nana didn't like to talk about it.
It was March. Winnie and I were young, no more than six. They'd
taken Charleston and Sherman was marching north and everyone
knew it was over. And then there was a rumor that it had happened,
Lincoln had come to Richmond and we were all free. Winnie and I
ran out with the other children, whooping and hollering. We were
young, but we knew what freedom meant, all right. At some point
the old store house caught fire. Maybe someone set it, maybe a lamp
broke, but it was burning bright. We ran for water. Everyone was
busy trying to put it out. But your nana turned around, and saw them
all lined up right on the edge of the forest. All the old slaves. The
ones that had tried to run and got themselves turned to dog food.
The ones that had collapsed in the fields. The ones that'd had the
luck to die free, or close to it. Hundreds, thousands—depending
on her mood, because you remember how your nana enjoyed elabo-
rating. But there they were, watching the fire and the new freemen,
laughing. The dead didn't speak. They were silent as a knot on a log.
But their eyes, Annie, she'd tell me, their eyes were brighter than
the flames. They flashed so bright she could hardly see. And when
they flashed, she felt the wind. It was hot and dry, as if it had blown
in from the Sahara, but your nana had been born in New Orleans, so
she recognized the salt in it, that green hint of the ocean. It knocked
her to her knees. And then that wind, it circled around her, as if it
were a dog sniffing. And for a moment, she saw. She saw that wind
as a great blue fire, coursing through the sky, boiling around her.

"And before it passed over them entirely, little fingers of it touched
the heads of three people from the plantation, and they fell into
a dead swoon. And wouldn't you know, just after the war the rumors started about the dreams, about the hands, about people with
a knack for the numbers. And for a few years during Reconstruction
it seemed that it might be working. We opened banks, we bought
land, we got ourselves elected.

"There used to be more people with the hands, child, many, many more. Then white folks—well, they couldn't abide any power they could not have. They didn't believe in the hands, but they killed them anyway. And your nana couldn't do anything about it, with just her cards and her numbers. You inherited that, you and Winnie. You don't have the hands, but you can *see*."

Tamara chewed on that conversation with her grandmother while life in the house moved as slowly and sweetly as it ever did. Mrs. Grundy baked cakes and pandowdies and soft banana puddings. Phyllis read the books her sister sent her: religious tracts and the latest bestsellers interspersed with a few offerings from Harlem's literary old guard: *The Ways of White Folks* by Langston Hughes and an anthology of short stories, *The New Negro*.

Two weeks passed and she didn't take out the cards once.

She was thinking about what it meant to be an oracle, to *see* but to be unable to act. She hadn't understood that burden when Aunt Winnie taught her the numbers. She hadn't known that what they did was connected to how people like Phyllis turned their little bit of luck between clever fingers. But while those hands might be theirs, they didn't entirely belong to them. They were possessed, just as Walter had said, but not by luck—or at least, not luck as she had imagined it to be, impartial and unpredictable.

In India, Dev once told her, people started getting the dreams after a failed rebellion against British rule called the Mutiny. In Haiti, it had happened right before their revolution. Maybe the American Indians got them earlier than anyone on this continent, in those days when the pilgrims were stealing their land and slaughtering them for sport. But in the former territories of the failed Confederacy, the dreams came down the day the slaves were free.

She could not avoid it, any more than her grandmother could. *Those old souls, they suffered too much.* What did they suffer? The million indignities of a human being sold and worked and raped and culled as property. And when they saw their brothers and sisters and sons and daughters at last freed, what did they do? They sent them a gift. Or something like it—a little bit of luck, a little bit of hope, a chance to lift the weight. It was almost enough. But the weight came back with horses and hoods and red fire. And in each generation, the hands touched fewer and fewer—while the spirit that animated them grew angrier and angrier.

Their fury was consuming Phyllis. She had killed who she shouldn't and failed to kill who she should. They were not forgiving. Not eighty years later, and the weight heavy as it had ever been.

The oracle did not feel equal to that. She did not want to confront the judgment of those implacable old souls.

But if her grandmother's story was true, if she was like her nana, like her great-aunt Winnie, then it was her duty to bear witness. And without her, Phyllis would face whatever was coming alone.

So one night, after Mrs. Grundy had left and Phyllis had gone to bed with a strangely knowing look and a warning to be careful, Tamara sat on the floor in front of the cold fireplace and unwrapped her neglected cards. They ought to have been eager, desperate for attention after so long in the dark, but they moved sluggish and heavy as she bent them into their tricks. As if they knew.

The oracle fixed the question in her mind and repeated it out loud: "Spirits of my ancestors, guardians who have guided our hands: what must she do?"

She shuffled three times more, repeating the question each time. Then she took the top card and laid it at the point of the star pattern. Queen of diamonds, the African queen, with her blue-black face and wise eyes. The ancestor. She took the next card and laid it on the point to the right. King of diamonds; one of the suicide kings, African like the queen, with his axe swinging down toward his head.

She touched the top of the next card—

—the earth growled and trembled—

—blue fire all around her—

—a crash upstairs, something throwing itself against the wall—

—the one who had fallen, the once-beloved, the now-despised, who carried on her shoulders the fury of their thousand disappointments, who could have been a savior of her people and now would never be saved—

—she called out the oracle's other name—

—called it out of love.

Tamara broke from the cards and ran upstairs, ran through the remnants of her oracle's sight, the hot wind of blue light. A fork from the tray Tamara had forgotten to take downstairs flew over her head and speared itself into the hallway wall. Phyllis grabbed the plate, broke it into shards. She was silent, tears and sweat mixing and dripping down her chin. Tamara stood there, paralyzed and useless, as her friend aimed to kill her. Tamara braced herself. But in a movement so fast it did not seem human, Phyllis jumped and twisted her entire body in the second before her fingers released. The shards shattered against the floor. Pea fell to her knees then, before the hands could find some other tool, and swung her arms against her belly.

"You want her, don't you?" she panted. "Don't you? You can't kill me just yet."

Her right hand lifted itself up, as though in peace. Or like the axe hand of the suicide king.

Then it lowered itself to the floor. Pea shuddered. Sweat dripped steadily from her nose while she hauled in rasping breaths.

The hands were hers again; her own tired flesh.

9

A second letter from Clyde arrived during spring's first bloom, that last week of April. Tamara sat on the front stoop with a stole around her shoulders and steeled herself. She figured he hadn't thrown her over after all, if he was writing again. But she worried, in any case. Would he give her an answer, at last, to her impossible dilemma?

> *Dear Tammy,*
>
> *I apologize for my last letter. I haven't been thinking very clearly these days. You'd think it was the fighting, but it isn't that so much as the waiting. You stagger back to camp and every missing face hits you, you check the casualty rolls, you sit around waiting for your next chance to get them back. The boys here are something else, Tammy. Cracking, sharp as tacks, all ready to go. I got us to put on a production of* A Midsummer Night's Dream *last week. The boys and I memorized our lines together since I only have the one copy, and the one playing Bottom was a hoot, he'd just mix it up with his own fresh language when he got the notion. He even had the white officers howling. That was a good day. His plane got shot down yesterday and he's listed as missing.*
>
> *If Toby's still alive, we'll get him back. Uncle Sam won't leave him out there. I have to believe that.*
>
> *They tell us not to write about hard things in our letters back home, but they don't know you, Tammy; you're as hard as any soldier, behind that dancing laugh of yours.*

I've been thinking about your play. It sounds terrific, solid, but I'm not so sure you've thought through all the implications of this choice of yours.

You say it's between a "regular Joe" and a no-good killer: all right, I'm with you. But then you make it sound like this regular-type person is really so convinced he's gonna get into heaven. Now, I don't claim to know much religious philosophy, Tammy, but isn't someone who is so sure they got a right to heaven just the sort of person least likely to go there? Does just avoiding bad things make you a good person? Don't you have to do good things for that? I think you get a lot more power in your third act if old Joe starts to realize that he's not going to skate through on a fast-ticket to the pearly gates just because he lived his whole life being careful. I think it means something if by being the kind of person who would sacrifice a little to give Mr. Killer a lot he becomes someone who deserves heaven, even as he is renouncing it. You see what I mean? The bind now isn't "What will I give up for this awful person who doesn't deserve anything anyway?" but "What kind of person am I, really? Can I enjoy heaven when the only way I get there is after I've proven to myself that I don't deserve it?" You see what I'm getting at? Don't make the dilemma just about the consequences of where old Joe is headed (because, let's face it, most of us have seen hell here on earth and purgatory is probably a damn sight better). Make Joe and the rest of us really squirm in our seats. Make him judge himself.

As for what he chooses at the end—depends on how you want it to go. Existentialism would leave him there, trapped in his choice. Theater of the Cruel would make him get on that boat after pushing old Killer into the river, just in case. But, hey, how about some Lawrenceville optimism, Tammy? Maybe that's another way out, or in.

If I make it back from this, you know I'm yours.

All my love,
Clyde

Tamara looked up and wasn't too surprised to see Little Sammy jog past her with a fishing pole tossed over one shoulder and a bucket of worms in one hand.

He looked just like he had right before the cops shot him down, except for the small detail that she could see the muddy ground through the outline of his bare feet. At least he couldn't feel the chill.

"Sammy?" she whispered. He looked around, as though he could hear something but couldn't tell what. Then a breeze lifted her hair and he broke apart like a dandelion gone to seed. She imagined she smelled the old creek in it, the green, rotting heat of deep summer, the grass crushed beneath her toes, the smooth, dry snick of the cards beneath her fingers back when they had told her that Little Sammy was going to die, and she had said nothing at all.

"Tammy," Pea called down from the window, "is there something from Dev?"

Tamara glanced down at the other letter that had arrived in the military packet, addressed in that familiar loose, educated handwriting.

"Yes," she said.

"Well, let me read it first, at least."

Tammy stood up like a toy soldier and climbed the stairs.

Pea was in the window seat, propped up to ease her back. She was swollen with that baby, round as a ripe berry. Just now, Tamara couldn't stand to look at her. She dropped Dev's letter on Pea's chest and turned to go.

"Are you ever planning on telling me what devil has been gnawing on your insides for the last few months?"

Tamara froze. "I'm doing my best."

"Wouldn't it be better to talk?"

It wouldn't. She couldn't. She left Pea there, so sick and fat and horrible. She left the house without a word and got in Dev's car and took a drive.

She kept going past River Road, past the new convenience store and grocery and their already-decimated racks of daily papers, past the shuttered windows of the mayor's house, and then the hasty fence that surrounded the remains of the old church and graveyard. Tamara tried not to look too closely, afraid of the ghosts of a place where so many had died. But soon she cleared the town, and surrounded by the early spring fields of the country, she rolled down the window and took a breath. The warming air smelled faintly of woodsmoke and the dung from the cattle farm nearly five miles over, which reminded them of its presence when the wind was right. The farms were bigger in her part of Virginia, and by this time of year the first shoots would already be stubbling through the earth, but she pulled to the edge of the road and trembled with the sick relief of being, at last, somewhere she understood. She and Clyde had never known a spring together, but Tamara could almost imagine him beside her, his high-cuffed pants showing that strip of ashy skin that dried out under the stage lights, as he rehearsed his lines from *Hamlet,* that passionate tenor scaring the crows from the corn: "*I am thy father's spirit/Doom'd for a certain term to walk the night,/And for the day confined to fast in fires . . ."*

She leaned across the dashboard, rubbed her cheek into pooled sunlight, and wondered if she would ever feel warm again. It was impossible, had been impossible for months, but now she had no fight left in her. Clyde had seen right through her little game, and he probably didn't even know it. *He* was the real Lawrenceville optimist, the genuine article, a good boy from down south who honored his elders and opened doors and volunteered for a hellhole of a war before he could get respectably drafted into it and honestly thought Tammy was the sweet, book-loving singer he'd fallen for all those years ago. He didn't know shit, and she wasn't even a good enough person to tell him. She'd orchestrated his love for her the way she orchestrated one of her legendary nights at the Pelican. But this wasn't a night on the town, this was the rest of her life, and it turned out she'd stopped playing. She'd loved Dev, but she'd always been playing—was it really so surprising he had noticed? He wasn't like Clyde, so country-fresh he was still cooling on the windowsill. He was good, but he was hard, too. He had to be, to survive for so long as an undercover cop at the heart of Victor's empire. He lied as much as she did, but for a noble purpose. He had seen her, and loved her anyway. Was Clyde strong enough for that?

Make the audience really squirm in their seats, he told her. Make "Joe" judge himself, even if it wasn't fair. Even if Joe never killed anyone. Joe had always been lying: to the killer, to the ferryman, to the audience. To the cards. To herself.

Tamara lurched upright, threw open the door, and ran a few steps into the crunching brown grass at the edge of the field. She sank to her knees and pounded on the earth and howled like a wounded dog.

She came back an hour later. Her hands were steady again, her eyes red, her heart hollowed out. She climbed the stairs to Phyllis's room.

Tamara paused in the doorway. Pea was sleeping on her side, a pillow against her belly, and Tamara felt something swell inside her, something like the oracle's knowledge, but her own. Tammy had agreed to come up here after Phyllis had been rushed to the hospital that last night at the Pelican, when she had nearly lost the baby. Tamara had imagined herself a Ruth to Phyllis's Naomi. She had anticipated the boredom of short gray days that folded upon themselves like crepe silk. She had anticipated claustrophobia and desperation for a decent glass of bubbly with a well-dressed man who could tell good jokes.

But Tammy hadn't anticipated the sweetness. The way Pea looked in the morning, with sun spilling that warm light across her wide forehead, settling in the valleys of her slightly parted lips, her throat, her thighs. With that pillow on her belly it looked still more mountainous, and sometimes she would hum in her sleep, and sometimes she would smile. The way they talked, like words were lumps of sugar and they were children gorging at Christmas Eve. They could talk the hands off the clock, but even the things they never said lingered in Tamara's throat like candy.

She had never loved anyone like she loved Pea. Not even Clyde. Sure, she and Phyllis had kissed that night with Dev and even now, in certain light, she didn't mind the notion of touching Pea until she came. But the love she felt wasn't really that kind—it was a blood love, a bone love, and it ricocheted off of her other loves at unexpected angles.

She couldn't—though the cards spoke in spades and sixes, though Pea's second dream had come and gone, though her hands were wild and corrupt weapons still tied to her body, though the choice they demanded of her was impossible—Tamara couldn't bear the thought of losing—

Phyllis turned over and opened her wide, clear eyes. "Well?"

"I've got to go. I'm going, Pea."

Pea closed her eyes briefly.

"Ain't nobody making you stay, baby."

She told Mrs. Grundy when she came in the next morning.

"For how long will you be gone, Miss Anderson?"

Tamara waved her hand. "Oh, a few weeks, probably."

Mrs. Grundy blinked. "Mrs. Patil is due in three weeks."

"I called her sister. She'll come down to help out this weekend."

Mrs. Grundy set her jaw and nodded. Tamara could have slapped her. Did everyone get to judge? Even this northern peckerwood? But it didn't matter, she reminded herself. That was the bittersweet pleasure of running up the white flag.

Phyllis said she understood when they said goodbye. If she did, she was doing better than Tamara, who cried on the afternoon train—so relieved to be gone, so guilty to be leaving her.

Walter picked her up from Grand Central in that silver Packard. She tilted her chin when she stepped in front of the white folks in her better fur to climb into the back seat of a better car. Walter just laughed and tipped his hat before he opened the door. Tamara caught the curious, resentful stares and smiled brighter. She couldn't be proud of everything in her life, but at least she'd gotten where she'd meant to go: a long way from Lawrenceville, from the bloody ground beneath the hanging tree outside of town.

"You look tired," he said.

She straightened her back—which had been hunched against some unconscious weight—and glared at him in the rearview mirror. "And *you* look nearly as silver as Victor."

This wasn't fair—he had a few more white hairs among the black, but they were mostly by his temples, giving him a skunky slick-back that suited his new role at the head of the operation.

He laughed. "My wife says I should dye it. I say it would look undignified."

Your wife? Tamara thought, but kept her surprise to herself. "It looks good, honestly."

"How's Phyllis?"

They were heading north on Broadway, drifting west as the sun set over the distant line of the Hudson. As they moved, streetlights flickered to yellow life down the cross streets.

"Miserable."

"What did the doctor say?"

"Her blood pressure is better. She just has to push through. No more than a few weeks left."

"And how are you, Tammy?"

She scowled. "Crummy, and I'm sure Pea already told you all about it."

"She said that Vic's still paying you visits. She said that you'd been tormenting yourself with those cards and couldn't spend any more time with her ghosts."

"Don't talk like that, Walter!" She smacked the back of his seat. It only hurt her hand.

"Talk like what?"

"Like I'm making all this up. Like I just got tired of her . . ."

And besides, were they really Pea's ghosts? Little Sammy, Pete Williams, Aunt Winnie, her great-grandmother—hell, even Victor, if she had to say it out loud. Even Victor's sad, puffed-up silver ghost.

"I could understand it if you had. Our Phyllis isn't always pleasant company."

A few more tears leaked from the corners of her swollen eyes. *Baby, what happened?* she would say, if she could see her now. "She is," Tammy said, sullen as a child. "She is to me."

"So what are you doing here?"

Her breath stuck for a moment, but she snatched it back. Her ragged nails dug into her palms. "I just couldn't stand it. She and Dev . . . they think I'm like them. When I'm not, nothing like them!"

"And the cards?"

Did he know? But how could he? She only shared that with the cards and the ancestors. The choice she was making every day, even if she had refused to own it: Pea, dead in a matter of weeks. That dreaming child, growing up without a mother. She caught a sob and strangled it in her chest.

"Don't you think they're just parlor tricks, Walter?"

"You don't."

"Well, they just tell me there's no good I can do there. I'm better back here. I missed the city!" She took a deep breath of the fishy decay blowing in from the Hudson. "Hell, I even missed the stink of it! You have to tell me everything that's happened at the Pelican. I know you've been following my schedule, but I haven't even thought about the spring season . . ."

She trailed off. Walter's shrugs were always eloquent. This one smelled of disappointment and calculated silence. She let him keep it—it always amazed her how often people would rush to fill Walter's silences. They'd say all sorts of fool things just to stop him from staring.

Walter turned down 72nd Street and then onto Riverside Drive. She rolled up the window as he smoothly accelerated. He had told her he was taking her to dinner, but she didn't know what restaurants he fancied so far uptown.

"So you're staying, then," he said, finally. His voice was flat enough to skate on.

"Pea made her choices! I'm sorry she's suffering for it now, but no one can expect me to give up my own life for hers. Christ, if you could see her, ankles fat as eggplants, back twisted like an old tree, the nightmares that baby gives her that she'll never tell me—and her hands so thick that some days she can't make a fist but she can still make a knife dance. That baby's made her a prisoner in her own body. Watching her makes me want to—want . . ."

"What do you want, Tammy?"

Bebop and reefer till dawn, dancing in her stockinged feet on sticky floors, telling stories with Pea on warm summer nights, lingering glances with Dev and long kisses with Clyde, a whole rack of babies all the colors of the earth playing in the yard behind them, secure in the love of their aunties and uncles and free, as their parents could never be, of dreams and history and hard numbers.

She pressed her cheek against the window and counted her breaths. Walter didn't speak for the rest of the ride. As they passed over the Harlem River into the Bronx she registered that they were far north, far from familiar Manhattan avenues, but she was remembering Pea and it was hard to see anything else.

He pulled in front of a house on a street so leafy and isolated it seemed impossible they could still be in the city.

"You know that Vic cursed Dev before he bit it. Probably hit Pea, too."

"Pea, too," Tamara said, balefully.

Walter turned to look at her and registered something with a short nod. She felt a jolt of fear; she hadn't meant to reveal anything. "And her hands still have a mind of their own?"

He knew about that? Had Phyllis told him during one of their early-morning calls on mob business? "They seem to," she said cautiously.

He raised his eyebrows. "Think they might be connected? The curse and the misbehaving hands?"

"Yeah, it's occurred to me, Walter."

"Yet you're still here instead of there."

"It won't do her any good if I'm here or on the moon! She and Dev killed that bastard, not me!"

This time his shrug just smiled. "You really think that Victor's ghost'll scram if you walk out on Phyllis?"

Her heart thudded like a snare drum. "I'm not like you. Or Pea. Or Dev, even!"

"Even," Red Man said mildly. "And yet you sure manage to spend a lot of time with us."

Tamara thought of that awful story that Dev had wanted her to tell Phyllis, of course she did. She remembered how Dev had looked in the hospital, bandages over his left eye where they'd had to operate. He had made her swear not to tell Phyllis. But she never would have. Pea cared so much about justice, and Tammy was just the snake girl, just the jungle dancer, just a country girl running from the sound of crows in the morning boughs of the hanging tree. What was in her hands but a pair of Greyhound tickets and the stains of all the loves she had been too scared to keep?

"So," Tamara said, just so she didn't have to think about it. "You boys found your snitch yet?"

Walter took his time about answering. "I think we have. Nice of you to take an interest in the business, Tammy."

"Like I keep telling Pea, I'm not in the business. I just wanted to make sure you didn't do anything to Mrs. Robinson. She doesn't deserve any of your business practices, Walter."

Walter smiled softly. Tamara leaned back in her seat. She should have known not to mention this. But she couldn't stand anyone to have an opinion about how she conducted herself; the faintest sulfurous whiff of it scalded her throat.

"Tammy, tell me, why do you think my 'practices,' as you call them, would be so unpleasant for her?"

Tamara swallowed acid. "I've heard stories."

"And you think I would treat a loyal, hard worker like Mrs. Robinson the same way I treat, oh, I can't imagine—some gangster? Some street runner? A stoolie?"

"I'm not saying you'd . . . hurt her exactly, but . . . well, Walter, you have to know your reputation!"

"I know Red Man's reputation," he said mildly. "It doesn't seem that you much object my business practices when they help you, Tammy. Who has been sending you money all these months?"

Tamara clenched her lips shut and didn't say anything.

"I made a promise to Dev, and I'm going to keep it. Phyllis—" he started, but then, uncharacteristically, stopped himself. He turned around in his seat. "Let's get inside. I don't want to keep Miriam waiting."

"Where the hell are we?" she said.

"Riverdale. I thought you could meet my family."

She closed her mouth. She had danced in this world long enough to know that a man's family was separate, sacred. A family was a soft target.

Walter stepped out of the car and she opened her door before he could come around. It was one thing to play chauffeur in Grand Central Station, another to do it in front of his Riverdale mansion, which was a gift she had never thought to receive.

From the outside the house seemed enormous, brick and marble and neoclassical columns framing stained and lead-paneled glass. The inside was marginally less imposing, made warm by mosaic parquet flooring in the foyer and gauzy curtains over the floor-to-ceiling windows. A white woman greeted Tamara effusively as soon as she stepped inside, touching her hand with an ease that shocked her. The woman must be Walter's wife, she must be, but Tamara couldn't quite believe a white person so willing to treat with black skin.

"You must be Tamara," the woman said, going on tiptoe to kiss cheeks. "Walt has told me so much about you."

Walt. Here the man the Lower East Side knew as Red Man, and not just for his skin, was called Walt. Tamara glanced at him while his wife squeezed her hands with every appearance of delight and his smile was wide and wondering. It transformed him, and she thought, *Nice to meet you, Walt.*

"Tamara, this is Miriam, my wife. Where are the twins?"

"Playing out back. Should I call them in?"

"No, let them stay. Tamara can meet them at dinner. What's that I smell?"

"Just some chicken and matzoh balls for the soup. Oh, and kasha and some pickles—I'm sorry, Tamara, do you like kasha? The twins can't get enough lately, but I won't feel offended at all if it isn't to your taste. I do try to keep kosher in the house."

Walter put his arm around her shoulders, and she seemed as tiny as a doll beside him. "Miriam is the best cook I know," he said.

"I'm just so happy to meet one of Walt's work associates," said Miriam. "He's always thought so highly of you."

Tamara could not imagine what Walter had told her about his work or his associates, but she was only being honest when she said she would be delighted to share their table tonight. No wonder he had guarded this space, no wonder he treasured her. Miriam was kind in a way that Walter craved. Maybe because without it, he'd be a monster. Tamara thought about the recent flood of Jewish immigrants from Europe, some of whom she had hosted at the Pelican, and what they said Hitler was doing to the ones who couldn't get out. She hoped Miriam didn't have any family back over there.

The children were Chaim and Rachel, eight-year-olds who looked more like each other than either of their parents, though she caught something of Walter in their silent, efficient appraisal as she faced them over dinner.

"So what do you do?" Rachel asked. "Do you negotiate?"

"I book talent and I dance," Tamara said, before she could hear Miriam's well-meaning explanation of her husband's negotiations. "But right now I'm taking care of a friend."

"What's wrong with her?"

"She's sick," Walter said.

"She's pregnant," Tamara said.

Rachel grabbed a pickle. "I don't want to be pregnant. I want to run the business with Daddy."

"And what does Daddy think?"

"That Rachel and Chaim can be whatever they want," Walter said, and gave her a faint Red Man smile.

Miriam brought out dessert, a pastry of layered dough and honey topped with pistachios, sickly sweet and unspeakably delicious. As the twins coated their fingers with sticky honey syrup, Tamara found herself reaching for that little handkerchief-wrapped square in her suit jacket pocket. They'd been calling her since that morning, and she felt safer bringing the cards out here, as though they would be reluctant to embarrass her in front of company.

Rachel was immediately intrigued. "Are those for betting on poker?" she asked.

Miriam's smile was just as bright, but it had a wary edge. So she certainly knew *something* about her husband's business, then. Tamara shook her head quickly.

"No, these cards aren't for betting. They're just for tricks." And fortunes, but she decided that Miriam wouldn't likely approve of that, either.

Instead she played simple tricks for the kids: a cut-to-it, half-and-half, and one she called the made-you-look, which involved switching a card they'd already picked by sleight of hand. These were, strangely enough, among the first things Aunt Winnie taught Tamara, when she began her apprenticeship. *Learning to make the cards lie is the first step to learning to make them speak,* she had said. Tamara had liked that part more than what came after. It had hurt less.

But the cards were playing with her, this time. Chaim and Rachel kept picking out the suicide kings or the ace of spades, no matter how much Tamara feathered and bridged the deck. She kept her expression light, and Miriam seemed delighted, but she wondered if Walter caught a whiff of her panic. *Death and death,* the cards were saying, *we should have been more. You should have done more. You should have saved her.* But she wasn't going back. She'd made her choice.

It was when Rachel picked the king of diamonds again, even though she was *sure* that she had buried him at the bottom of the deck, that she saw Victor grinning at the head of the long table.

The twins leaned over their plates with the sticky remains of pastry and peered at her.

"Are you sick?" Chaim asked, followed almost immediately by Rachel, more to the point: "Are you pregnant?"

She shook her head. "Thought I saw a bee, that's all."

Victor seemed aware of them, but not as focused as before. He directed a few comments to Walter as he reached for a pastry, and his words came to her like rushing water. His expression was amiable, not particularly cruel or angry. He seemed normal, like the man Tammy had tolerated for most of her three years at the Pelican. She had forgotten to be afraid of him by that Christmas Eve two years ago.

Tamara excused herself and went to the washroom. Behind her, Rachel said loudly that she must be pregnant too. Didn't pregnant women vomit? Her mother hushed her.

She turned on the tap and looked at herself in the mirror.

"Tamara," she whispered to that red-eyed girl with the puffy cheeks and trembling shoulders, "Tammy, baby, you knew you were making a bargain. You asked around town for the biggest devil to hide under."

The girl winced. Victor flashed in and out behind her. But he was blurry in the mirror, something closer to her own reflection.

"Tell him what you did, Tammy." She was doing Pea's voice, as though she were telling Pea a story.

But it felt like another haunting—a possession—an exorcism.

"That night," she said, in her own voice again, "I was drunk, and I hadn't expected it. Victor had seemed nice. There had been some shamus pawing through his office and I'd told him about it. He was in a good mood. But then he wanted to play that stupid game with Dev's hands. He wanted . . ."

She choked. The water started to run scalding into the bowl, and clouds of steam put a veil between her and her ghosts.

"Tamara, I'm breaking the door in. Tamara, do you hear me?"

That wasn't her voice. And it wasn't a ghost, either. It was Walter smashing the door with his fist, not Victor smashing Dev's face with a gun.

She turned off the water. Someone whimpered. Dev? No, her, it was her.

"Wait, Walter," she said, just loud enough for him to hear. She was sweating in the wet heat of that small room. It dripped through her hair, ruining the egg-white slick-back. Victor's ghost wavered in the steam of the mirror. A blue light was coming up behind him, a blue wind, woodsmoke and ashes, blood and backwoods dirt. It was just as her nana had always said: there beyond the flames, she saw them, the old slaves, then all the others, following: Pete Williams and Little Sammy and Aunt Winnie herself.

"What have you been doing, girl?" she whispered, just as Aunt Winnie might have. The whole line of them opened their mouths and no sound came to her, just flashes of suits and numbers sparking past her eyes with furious velocity.

You use our gift to enrich yourself? You use our gift to hide? Wake up, Oracle! Do you dream of so little? Because we dream of the children, we dream of lifting them up, we dream of changing—

The door burst inward. The lock splintered from the wood and spilled dust on the floor. Walter stood where Victor had been, where her ancestors had gathered with their terrible judgment. It felt as though Tamara were too late. Too late for what? To change, to be better, to be the woman she'd always wanted to be. The ancestors had told her and at last she was ready to listen: it was time.

Walter caught her before she fell.

"Don't let her die," she sobbed, "don't let her die. I'll do it, I'll save her, I'll take the curse."

Walter was a big man, good to cry on. He took her to his office to get herself together.

He settled into his big leather chair behind the desk. "You asked about the snitch, before."

She blew her nose, suddenly wary. "You said you found him."

"We think so. Tell Phyllis that the snitch was giving out information about old kills. Mostly incriminated fellows who are . . . no longer in the business. If it ends there, we won't have a problem. The Barkley brothers' remains were found—an old case. The family was grateful. The police passed along an anonymous donation. From 'an old friend,' they said. A cousin is thinking of reopening the bank with those funds. We won't interfere. You tell her that."

Tamara stared at him, her thoughts still too choked and sluggish with tears to make sense of his words. The Barkley brothers? Why did that sound familiar?

Phyllis, on the phone, that morning that Tamara had read Dev's letter. Ordering mob hits in her best white-person voice. Ordering mob hits—or informing on the mob? Old case, Walter said. She hadn't been ordering a death. She'd been *telling* the police where to find one of her old kills.

Tamara gasped and gulped before she could properly decide to feign ignorance. She was losing all of her old defenses.

"Don't," she stammered, "don't—don't—please, Pea is—"

Walter nodded, as though she had confirmed something. She wanted to vomit all over him. "I made a promise to Dev, I told you. I intend to keep it. He wrote to me, you know."

She drew herself up. She was better than this. She would never again be that empty-headed showgirl who turned her back on cruelty for an illusive safety. "What did he say?"

"You have a heavy weight on your shoulders, and he doesn't want to add to it. He told me to be kind." Walter laughed with every appearance of warmth. "Can you imagine? But let's be honest for a moment, Tamara. No one knows you quite as well as I do, do they? There are moments where kindness is the last thing you need."

She swallowed the last of her spit. "Like now?"

He spread his hands. "What do you think, Tammy?"

"I have to go back."

"Good," he said, "I hoped you'd do that."

"Why?"

There was a strange light in his eyes, something like the spark when he held his wife and laughed with his children, but shaded by Red Man's knowing, carefully deployed cruelty.

"You need each other."

10

Victor wanted to know how much Dev's hands could tell.

Victor didn't let them go after Dev stood up to him. He got the gun on Dev, and made Dev touch his skin and then he started saying names. Runners and soldiers Tamara knew, some hatchet boys from other gangs, a few women she didn't recognize. And after each name he asked Dev if this person or that person was a threat. And if they were, how much. She could tell, Dev's word was going to execute these people. Of course Dev hated it. He never wanted a part of that. So he just said no. Every time. He didn't even pretend.

Tamara stood there, watching. She was terrified, praying with everything in her that she could just disappear. Victor got quiet after a while. He stared hard at Dev and then, appallingly, right at her.

"He's lying, isn't he, Tammy? He's not even trying?"

Tammy closed her eyes. When she opened them, she was still there. Dev and Victor were both looking at her, expecting something, a performance that she couldn't give.

Victor's nostrils flared. "You aren't afraid for your man?"

That was when she realized how she'd gone wrong. She should have started crying, she should have knelt and begged for Dev's life. Oh, Tamara was sure scared. But as Aunt Winnie could have told her, she was scared of the wrong thing. And maybe Dev knew, because he looked at her wide eyes and said, "Go, Tammy. Leave, I'll be fine."

Victor got this funny look, like he was seeing all sorts of things in her he hadn't bothered to notice before. His voice got flat and hard. "Stay. Answer the question."

She stayed. Even then she didn't worry about him hurting her. She didn't even worry about Dev. She just worried that Victor might not take such good care of her if he got the notion she thought about anything but snake dances and Tuesday-night billing.

She babbled. Tried to say that she didn't understand, that she didn't like this game, but Victor cut her off. "Yes or no question? Is your man lying?"

And Lord save her, but she looked him straight in the eye and she said yes.

He looked sad for a moment. Sloppy drunk and sad. She knew she'd done it all wrong. He lowered that gun.

"Maybe you aren't much of a lady after all, dollface. Not very loyal?"

She knew better than to answer that dangling interrogative, but her mouth kept moving. "I'm plenty loyal, Vic. You know you can trust me."

Her mouth and her coward's heart. She wanted Victor's silver grin more than she wanted Dev's smile in the morning. Victor just laughed. Dev moved toward her, but Victor kicked him and he fell. Vic should have been too drunk to aim that kick, straight to the ribs. But violence was always one of his talents.

"You're just a dog, aren't you?" he said to Dev now, waving that gun. "A poor dog, aren't you? You trade Phyllis for this fine piece of sugar, and look, she's got as much womanly sentiment as my Colt. You're a real poor dog, making me feel sorry enough to let you go. A lying bastard who thinks he's better than me. But at least I don't have a girl that would leave me on the ground like that, you poor dog."

Dev didn't say anything. He was panting like it hurt to breathe. Tamara wanted to cry. She wanted to get down there with him and cry into his shoulder until she could stand to look at herself again. But she just stood there and tried not to shake.

"Tammy," Dev said again, "get out of here."

Victor gave her more of that funny look. She'd never seen him like that before. And then he surprised her. "You know what, take him. He might be a lying bastard, but he's a poor dog, so why don't you take him home, dollface?"

Tamara and Victor stared at one another. Those narrow brown eyes. That lingering whitewash of the smoke from his cigarillos. She was scared then. She was terrified that he could see her.

Later, Dev said that he understood, that she just wanted Vic's protection. But it was worse: she didn't want him to think of her as anything more than his pin-up girl, the curator of his better image. She didn't want to be like Phyllis. She wanted to be small enough to hide behind him.

Which was why she'd laughed. Her brightest laugh, soft as silk tassels and the calfskin soles of new dancing shoes. She knelt and lifted up Dev by his armpits and sat him down in the nearest chair. He winced. Maybe one of his ribs was already broken. He didn't say anything to her, then. He had known what she was about to do.

"I think you two must have some business to discuss. And you know I don't do business, sugar." She laughed again, pecked Victor on the cheek where his stubble burned her lips, and she left. She just picked up her mink and swung her hips like a bell clapper. Like she had no goddamn idea what she was doing. She could have taken Dev out of there. She could see in Victor's eyes that his offer was an honest one. But what would he have thought of her, after? If she weren't just the dizzy dancer? He would have respected her more. But she had never wanted his respect.

In the back alley, out of range, she heard Victor screaming, smashing in the side of Dev's face with the butt of that pistol, breaking the orbital bone. *You. Will. Tell. Me.* Victor kicked him in the side five, six times. *You poor dog,* he said, and she knew even then that she could go back in there. She could brave Victor and save Dev from the worst of it. In the hospital, they told her Dev had cracked five ribs. The day he came back to the Pelican, his face looked fine, but he still couldn't take a full breath. He made sure to dance with her in front of Pea. She didn't have any standing to object.

11

The house was swaddled in darkness, as Tamara was swaddled in memories, and neither of them sufficiently braced against the evening chill. Behind her, the lights of the taxi illuminated the driveway as it crunched down the gravel, making and unmaking the path to come until it swung out onto the road and disappeared entirely.

She climbed the stairs slowly. What felt different? She had only left that morning, but she was not the same.

Phyllis opened the door before she could knock. She did not invite Tamara in.

"Forgot your toothbrush?" She was arch, but Tamara could feel the effort it took her to keep her spine straight and her eyes cold. Phyllis wasn't the same either. Hadn't been for a long time, strange that she'd only now noticed.

"Forgot a card," Tamara lied.

"Which one?"

"Devil joker," she replied immediately.

Pea cracked a smile. "Oh? Could have sworn you'd taken him with you this time."

"He's got a habit of popping up where I least want him. So I figured maybe I'd stop running away."

"For a change."

"For a change," Tammy echoed uncertainly. "Pea. Walter says he found the snitch."

Pea's expression didn't shift, her hands didn't twitch, the soft pulse of her exposed jugular continued its steady beat, unperturbed. If Tammy hadn't already known, she never would have guessed. She was a wonder, this best friend of hers, as strange a creature as any Tammy had encountered in her literary days back in Lawrenceville or her grandmother's stories.

"That's good news, isn't it? I take it Mrs. Robinson was safe."

"Yes. Pea. That's not it. They found the Barkley brothers. He said that the family was going to take the money they came into and start a numbers bank. He said he wouldn't interfere, as long as that was as far as this goes."

Phyllis shivered. But that might have just as well been the open door, the bracing air, the encroaching night.

"Well," she said, at last. "Come inside, honey. The nights are still cold."

They went into the kitchen and Pea uncovered a pie on the table and cut two generous pieces.

It had to be pumpkin from the color, but covered in the oddest fluffy white crust, and who put crust on a pumpkin pie, anyway?

"Is that meringue?"

Pea laughed. "Would you believe I told her that it was 'very white of her' and she just thanked me!"

Tamara laughed so hard she had to wipe her eyes, probably more than the joke deserved, but it felt so good to be here again.

"And your sister?" she asked.

"Coming in two days. It was the soonest she could take off. Are you going back again, once you find your card?"

"Oh, no," Tammy said, stretching back, draping her coat over the back of the chair, settling in for good. "You ain't getting rid of me again till that baby is born."

And she would be, Tamara thought, as Pea skimmed off the meringue and then tasted it with the tip of her pinky. The three of them would make it through this; no dead ofay's curse or angry ancestor could stop them. The oracle made her choice in that old kitchen; she put her hands over the angel's—bloodstained both—and said in her heart, *I will take what you cannot bear, love, and gladly.*

They went to the river, still high and red from the winter melt. Spring had finally arrived in full: new blossoms on the trees, new bugs in the grass, and birds screeching so loud it made Tamara think the city was comparatively restful. They shared a caramel apple while they sat on the blanket. Mrs. Grundy had brought back a whole dozen, individually wrapped in waxed paper and nestled like eggs in a basket of straw. Tamara had been all astonishment and her lips brimming with thanks, but Mrs. Grundy had only given her a soldiery nod and said, "I'm glad you decided to return, Miss Anderson." Tamara had just stared at her. She supposed Mrs. Grundy had been thawing toward her for a while now, but this felt decisive. As though even this not-quite-old white lady could see the battlements crumbled inside her and the wildflowers just peeking their colors out above the wreckage. Then Tamara had remembered Pea's story and was politely overcome with a fit of coughing.

Tamara smiled again now, remembering. Phyllis was buried deep in one of her silences. Tamara might have taken it for judgment, before. She might have goaded Pea into speaking about her past, just to make her ashamed. Now, Tamara settled on one elbow and dedicated herself to polishing off the apple. She contemplated the cards, restless in her pocket. She had made the decision, but she still hadn't found a way to formally make the exchange. She supposed she should try tonight. Pea was as full as an old moon; they didn't have much time. She wiped her mouth with a sticky hand.

"Pea."

"Hmm?"

"What will you do, after the baby is born?"

Pea tilted her head slowly in her direction. She yawned. "I haven't thought much about it."

Tamara sat up a little straighter. "That's a lie." She couldn't have known. She hadn't spent these long months afraid that her life was in danger. Or, worse, that the thread it hung on was tied to Tamara's self-protective heart.

"Is it? I'm not like you, sweetie. I'm not the most . . . natural mother."

Tamara snorted, relieved. "Neither was mine, but we made do."

Pea smiled and looked back out at the river. She wrapped herself again in silence, and this time Tammy didn't dare break it. She'd nearly fallen asleep to the lullaby of kestrels and gurgling water when Pea's voice startled her back into the world.

"My God, did they tell a good lie. Look how it even got you, Tammy. You went looking for a bad white man, and you found Victor. A bad bargain from the word 'go.'"

"I found you," Tammy said hoarsely, "and Dev and Walter. Not such a bad bargain."

Pea seemed as distant as a ghost, looking back upon her life. She laughed like it hurt.

"But it's on me for believing it. That I could make myself up in whiteface and kill for them and still come out clean . . . All that power they got, and here we are just wanting a nibble. And for that nibble they take our souls."

"They can't do that. No one but God can do that."

"It's just the earth, Tammy, that takes us in the end."

"And the ancestors? The hands?"

Pea shrugged. "I only know what I've seen. And you have to admit, I've seen my share. Maybe they linger a bit, some strong souls. Some good, some cankers like our Victor. But the earth is billions of years old, Tammy. Even Methuselah's got nothing on that."

"The earth is . . . Phyllis, I don't mean to sound ignorant, but isn't a billion a million million? The earth is a million million years old? How is that possible?"

"Time has a habit of passing. And so do humans, and every other living creature on this green earth. And if they all got a soul, then the air ought to be full of them, we ought not to be able to see for all the spirits passing through us."

"God is a lot greater than the earth. If He sees fit for us to have souls, then He'll find some space for us."

Phyllis took a soft, slow breath. "Sure, baby."

"Well, you know plenty of folk agree with me. And doesn't it make it worse, if those folks you killed, well, if that was all there was to them?"

"Does it make it worse?" She sounded bleak, her voice leached of color. "That every bit of what made them a person on this earth drained away when I sliced their throats? That they had existed and then they didn't, and I'm the reason why?"

"Pea, I didn't—"

"I watched the light leave their eyes. I hauled their dead bodies, which had lost everything of dignity, cold and wet and stinking of blood and shit; they felt like nothing alive, like cold clay . . . there is a soul, Tamara, I believe that, I believe that. But it dies too."

They shared the blanket for an hour more. They didn't speak. They just watched them pass: the river, and time, and their awareness of them both.

She waited until that night, after Mrs. Grundy had left. They sat together in the parlor, listening to a new blues record that Phyllis had ordered and had just come into the post office. When the torture of anticipation outpaced the pleasure of her last curse-free hours, she got up from the couch, turned off the music, and faced Phyllis.

"I need to do something," Tamara said.

Pea considered that for a moment. "With the cards?"

"How did you guess?"

"You were different when you got back. And who knows better than I do what those cards meant to you, Tammy?"

"I'm an oracle," Tamara said aloud, for the first time in her life. She pulled out the cards and they settled into her like home.

Phyllis nodded slowly. "You want to tell me what this is about?"

"After we're done."

Pea didn't object. Where had she come by that easy trust when Tammy'd had to fight so hard for hers? Or maybe it wasn't so easy for her. Pea always kept a little back, locked away in that strongbox of her heart.

Pea stayed on the couch and Tammy knelt on the carpet across from her. She shuffled in waterfalls and bridges, more than she needed to, but it felt good, and it gave her a chance to feel the cards.

She needed to show that she was willing, at last, to make the trade. But she had never needed to speak *to* the cards before. How could she manage it?

With tricks, Aunt Winnie said, clear as the river beside her. Tamara smiled, missing her.

She found the cards she wanted and seeded the deck with them. She asked Pea to cut the deck, and made sure the card she wanted was on bottom: her old friend the suicide king of diamonds, his stubby legs flailing over an abyss. Victor and his silver smile. He should have come out of the woodwork for this, she'd almost looked forward to spitting on him personally. Still, she didn't miss him. She had Pea shuffle the cards this time and then cut again. It was a bit like dancing, it came out without her thinking too hard about it. Pea pulled out the ace of spades, just as Tammy wanted. The curse, the knives, the angel and her corrupted justice. Her vision had been pure, the oracle told them. And now for the third card, shuffle and cut: six of hearts, death and rebirth, the oracle's card and Tamara's heart, bearing them both. The power of the cards was rushing down to her now. She only had time to look up, catch Pea's eyes and Pea's hands, and say her name as a drowning man might call to the shore—

A dream grabbed her, pulled her under. It was not her dream; it was the cards, it was Durga. The child was already there, as close as a breath. A baby like a wheel, spinning in a wind of blue light. She had changed, in the months since the oracle's last reading. Her saint's hands had transformed into something else. And behind her were more wheels and more winds, turning and turning, blowing up from below in the colors of the earth. They were coming, these dreamers with their uncanny hearts and the force of ancestors and spirits and gods and old, aching hands behind them. *Rejoice!* they said. *For we will not await our own destruction. We will rise up to meet them and turn them aside.*

Is that possible? the oracle thought. Power corrupts, and power is corrupted.

No one answered her. They were all too busy dreaming.

She felt the weight of the mother's curse here. Smelled the blood on her hands, rotting.

Let me take it! the oracle shouted into the blue wind. Let me fulfill the bargain.

The blue wind paused and faced her. She felt them inside it: the ancestors, the oracles of her family, the long line that stretched to the slave ships, to old stories painted in forgotten languages. *It will be hard for you, Oracle. We have given the child a different gift.*

But I can take the curse? The mother will live?

The child and her kind will remake the world. If you accept her burden, the mother we will forget.

Relief shook the oracle, but a lifetime's caution made her pause. What has changed in her?

Look, Oracle! This is our gift: her heart.

But the oracle could see this was no gift, or no easy one. The child would grow up filled with dreams. Like fire she would spill them, before and behind her.

How can you make them bear this?

Aunt Winnie came to her as a thin note from that faceless chorus. *Because it is to be borne. The hands can no longer serve. What would you have us do? Sit idly by while the world turns against us? Our people have as much a need as we ever did; no, we have more. We have given you our hearts! Oracle, remember your duty! I taught you as well as I could in the time I had. You are to witness. You are to hold them to the path. You are to be our voice in the world of the living!*

The oracle held out her simple hands. Give it to me, then. I will bear what I must, and I will help that child when her load grows heavy.

They swept her up so that she lost sight of the babies in their wheels, rocking like buoys in a storm. It was only her and the blue. They sang a tune she would never recall, but it pierced her like a butterfly, right to the wall. It hurt, of course it did. The smell of rot was in her nostrils now, the splattering grief of five dozen souls. It flayed her and choked her and then settled, all at once, upon her heart. Like the old roots of a killing tree, it squeezed. The oracle cried out,

but she did not deny it. Then comfort, sweetly come: a soft breeze of
honeysuckles and fresh-cut clover, cicadas churning the evening air.
A strong voice, made soft in her ear: *You done good, Tammy.*

She came to facedown in the carpet, each thread in the weave
as large as cornstalks in her blasted vision. Bloody saliva dripped
down the side of her face. She was shivering too hard to swallow.
Pea got her onto the couch and under a blanket, those saint's hands
trembling like a young girl's, or an old woman's. Their gazes met,
stripped Tamara naked as a child.

"What did you do, Tammy?" Pea whispered. "I felt—something—"

Tammy laughed and then coughed for a good while. Her vision
went white at the edges, and she might have seen old Vic there,
waiting. She didn't care. She had done it, she had done it, as well as
any oracle could. Breathing again, she held Pea to her, Pea and that
dreaming child, who would live.

She awoke the next morning to the sound of Phyllis on the phone,
giving directions to some anonymous cop about where to find fresh
evidence of old murders. They looked at one another from across the
room after she hung up the phone.

"It'll get back to Walter."

"I can handle Walter. Are you sick, baby?"

"Not exactly."

"Then what is it?"

"Just some old ghosts. How's Durga?"

"She's—" Pea looked surprised, put an unconscious hand on the
lower swell of her belly. "—sleeping."

Tammy smiled as her heart squeezed to pieces.

A few days passed. The cucumbers and watermelons put up energetic shoots. She kept her cards wrapped in their silk sheath and
dreamt of where they would go when the baby was born, when the
war was over: Paris, Hollywood, Mexico. She wanted to dance again.

Word came again from the front: Clyde's plane had been shot
down, and he was recovering in a military hospital in an undisclosed

location, but which she gathered from his thespian references was near Japan in the Pacific. (*I was a dignified and potent officer, but unfortunately at the moment, Tammy, my functions aren't particularly vital, though Doc promises me they'll get better,* a riff on *The Mikado* that made her laugh.) He was vague about even the details he could have shared: he'd had surgery and he'd get better, but they didn't know if he'd be cleared to fly again. He might come home, he said. She could tell he didn't want to, but that didn't matter so much right then. She cried in relief and ran her fingers over his neat secretary's hand. He'd come back. She was almost sure that he would.

There were letters from Dev in the same military mailing. A long one for Pea, and a short one for Tamara. A block of text centered neatly in the middle of the page, without salutation or farewell:

> *Perhaps it was unfair of me to arm Pea with that old story. Were it not for the extremity of our circumstances, I never would have breathed a word of it. Understand, I never blamed you, Tammy—I just saw what you did not wish to see. I wish I could apologize, but you would smack me for insincerity—I would do it again, and gladly, for her sake. So I was unfair to you, because I cannot force your hand.*
>
> *No matter what: she has loved well, as we have loved. We live in hard times. I drown in screams by day and dreams by night, here beneath the desert's open sky. I dream of her knives in the garden. I dream of your cards. Your stub-legged king of diamonds. You called him a suicide king, didn't you? But I know the four of us well enough—though we all go in the end, we will none of us go willingly. Do you remember that book of poetry I lent you? I left it behind, along with the rest of me, so you will forgive imperfect memory:*
>
>> *"Tarry a while, till I am satisfied*
>> *Of love and grief, of earth and altering sky;*
>> *Till all my human hungers are fulfilled,*
>> *O Death, I cannot die!"*

She took out the cards that afternoon. They hadn't so much as snuffled at her since she'd let those old roots crowd her heart, but Dev's letter had left her with a scratching unease. Pea's hands were docile as two lapdogs. Clyde was safe. Even the mournful smudge of Victor's ghost did not seem, in these late days, like any great burden. Dev had written before she'd made her choice. She just needed to check. But when she rousted the cards from their slumber and laid them on the yellow Formica of the kitchen table, they muttered of old wars and new battles, of crabbed hands and tender shooting hearts. Danger everywhere. A new age—

"Yes," Tamara snapped. This pulled a long cough out of her, while Little Sammy's ghost fiddled with a bit of fishing wire on the floor at her feet. She caught her breath. "But what about *us*? What about Dev? What about Pea?"

She shuffled again. The jack of diamonds slid right off the top, upside down. *Jack o' diamonds*, she hummed to herself, *he did rob a friend of mine*. "Course he did," she muttered, sweeping up the cards in her left hand and smothering them with the handkerchief in her right. That smug little white man, what part of the world didn't he think was his?

Phyllis's sister came to visit with her children. Gloria was light-skinned enough that some would call her pitch-toed, but just dark enough that she could never have followed Pea downtown. At least, not through the front doors. For a long time Tamara had thought that passing made Pea's life easier, but now she could see how it had separated her from her family, from the world she belonged in.

Gloria had married a man who hated Phyllis for that and other reasons, who had given more than a drop of that resentment to his oldest child. Sonny sat on the farthest edge of the porch all morning, his gaze fixed on a book whose pages he turned only occasionally. The youngest was running around the yard, hunting flowers which she had declared she would weave into a wreath for her aunt. Tamara was helping Ida, though it had been fifteen years since her last spring garland. Better to run barefoot across the soft grass than sit by and endure that at once awkward and intimate conversation between Phyllis and her older sister.

"Tom will be gone for months at a time if he takes the promotion," she heard as Ida gleefully uprooted the crocuses from the garden.

"Does he want to?"

"He says it's for the war. He wants to do his duty."

Pea didn't say anything to that, which was its own response.

"Ida," Tamara said, tugging her elbow. "Why don't we keep walking? I don't think your uncle will be happy if we take all his flowers."

"Uncle Dev won't mind," she said, with admirable perception, "but Aunt Pea might."

They went down to the river and a little ways along the path that the spring rains had nearly washed out. Sonny joined them five minutes later, while they were squatting in a patch of clover, looking for luck.

"I don't know how to braid a wreath," he said. He held his book, *The Ways of White Folks* by Langston Hughes, in both hands, like an offering. It was one of Phyllis's—she must have given it to him.

"It's okay, Sonny," Ida said, very kindly. She took the book from him and settled it against a raised tree root. "We can teach you."

Tamara's first wreath broke and fell apart. Her fingers were clumsy creatures with anything but the cards. Ida laughed. "Look, Aunt Tammy, even Sonny's got farther than you!"

Tamara laughed with her. "You want to make me one too, Sonny? It'll be our secret."

He smiled. "Nuh-uh. You gotta do your own work, Aunt Tammy."

She turned her head up to the dappled light coming down through baby green leaves. She smacked her hand against her thigh. "Where'd you get that mouth on you, boy?" she cried. "Why, I have a mind to—" She tickled his stomach. He pinned her to the ground and tickled under her arms and they all fell to shrieking, there in the copse by the river.

A half hour later, they started back up the hill. Ida ran ahead, eager to show off her wreath to her mother and her aunt.

"Aunt Tammy," Sonny said softly. "Is my aunt all right? She looks . . ."

Tamara stopped short. What had he seen? The lingering effects of the curse? Her bloated fingers, her wandering gaze? But they'd made the two-hour drive to the doctor the week before.

"It's been a hard pregnancy, that's all. She's fine now."

He looked down at his hands. "She used to play with those knives for me, when I was real little. My dad made her stop. He yelled at her and said it was dangerous. But it wasn't, was it?"

"The only dangerous thing was who she played with them for, Sonny. She loves you."

He nodded hard. "I know."

They came up over the ridge, back into Pea and Gloria's line of sight. Ida had already given Pea her wreath, which was wide enough to drape across her chest. Tamara's was a meager enough offering, a single-strand dandelion chain that was all that had survived the destruction below. Pea took it with a smile and bestowed it with deliberation upon Gloria. Her sister blushed.

"Oh, for heaven's sake, Phyllis . . ."

Sonny stepped between them and turned to Tamara. "Kneel down," he said, imperious as a king among his suit. "You're too tall for me to reach."

"Sonny!" his mother hissed. "I know I taught you better than that!"

But they were all laughing, even Gloria, as Tamara knelt on the damp grass and bent her head for a crown.

She felt that sooty curse, even now. A weight that was not her own, a vise around her heart. But she did not feel burdened. If you can share your joys, you can share your troubles too.

Gloria and the children went back to the city. Phyllis and Tamara stayed in the garden, rationing cigarettes between them and drinking the champagne that Walter had left them straight from the bottle. They were laughing hard enough to drown out even the crickets.

Pea was telling one of her rare stories about her mother, who had died when she was just twenty-three.

"So Rob stumbles off the elevator at, oh, it had to be two in the morning. Drunk as half a bottle of whiskey can make him, real stinking tight. And I know Rob a little, but Mommy babysat him when she was fifteen so he's always coming around to say hello to 'Miss Judy'—never mind Mommy got married *and* divorced a decade before. She was always Miss Judy to Rob. So he stumbles off that elevator and heads straight to our door. I'm watching through the peephole. Mommy tells me to mind my own business and I tell her a drunk and disorderly in our building is everyone's business."

"She smack you?"

"She just laughed and let me stay."

"And then?"

"Rob knocks on the door. Well, he starts just calling her name, but when she don't open he starts knocking. Then he starts hollering again, so Mommy opens the door just to get him to shut up. Rob's so drunk, he nearly falls over. He's holding his arms out just like this, like he's holding up a wall. 'Miss Judy,' he says, 'how ya been doin', Miss Judy?' Mommy says, 'I've been fine, Rob, but I think your mother won't like you getting home so late, so how about you turn around and go back there now?' He nods, like he thinks this is a fine idea. But then he's holding the door again. 'Miss Judy,' he says, 'can I borrow twenty-five cents? I'll pay you back next Sunday, promise. I've got a new pastor that gives numbers in his sermons. I'm sure to hit and I'll pay you back.'"

"Oh, I've heard that one before."

"So had Mommy. 'Rob,' she said, in her schoolteacher voice, 'turn around right now and go home. I'm not giving you a penny.' Rob turned to go again. He even made it to the elevator. But then he came right back just as we were closing the door. 'Miss Judy,' he said, 'you real nice, Miss Judy. You think I could take you to dinner sometime, Miss Judy?' And his hands still up like this, holding that invisible wall. And now Mommy just can't take it anymore. 'Dinner!

You just asked me to borrow *twenty-five cents*! Where you gonna take me to dinner? Street-corner hot dogs? Go *home*, Rob!'"

Tamara loved Pea's impression of her mother. A voice warmer than Pea's, but just as sharp.

"Did he ever take her out to dinner?"

"Nah, but would you believe, next week he hit the numbers!"

"No!"

"He did. Bought a fancy car and set himself up as a chauffeur on Sugar Hill. For all I know he's still doing it. He's probably getting drunk on better liquor, too."

They laughed again and then let it fade, let the crickets have their turn.

"Tammy," Phyllis said after a while. "Can I ask you a question?"

Tamara turned sharply. "What about?"

"That cough of yours . . ."

"It's nothing."

"And the hands. I thought they'd gone from me. I thought you'd found some way to take them away, but . . ." Pea picked up the bottle, drained it, and then launched it high in the air. It spun, end over end, before landing on its mouth in the dirt between them, perfectly straight.

Tamara took a deep and careful breath. Her heart hurt more than she could bear just now.

Pea put a light hand on Tammy's shoulder. "You didn't have to, whatever you did."

"I know."

"I'll do whatever I can . . ." Pea's eyes were bright, flashing green, distorted by water. ". . . to help you bear it."

The air was muggy and warm, the mulch she and Gloria had laid down the day before giving off a spicy ferment that grew more agreeable the more champagne she drank. Perhaps the smell was what had lured the first fireflies of the season out of their hidden spaces to dance among the tiny green shoots on the roses' spindly limbs and then rise stately, on a wave, into the strait between Pea's eyes and her own.

"Don't . . . don't imagine I'm some kind of martyr. I just realized I couldn't outrun it," Tammy said, keeping her eyes wide until the fireflies stained her vision with the negatives of their flashing yellow song. "I couldn't outrun who I was."

"Was she so bad?"

"No. But she wasn't so good, either."

Pea lifted a hand and held it before her so the fireflies could sway around it ponderously as an old drunk.

"Oh, but when she danced!" Pea said, her voice almost as soft as the buzzing of fly wings.

Pea poured the last of the second bottle into Tamara's glass. She pulled her old lighter from her pocket, considered, and then put it back.

"Why didn't you get rid of it?" Tamara asked. "When you found out?"

She regretted the question immediately. It came close—too close—to their unspeakable shore. Pea blinked. She looked up at the sky. "I tried," she said. "There's no doctors here to do it, certainly not for a colored woman. So I went to a rootworker outside Poughkeepsie. When I came back Dev was half-mad, he'd gotten some tale from Alvin. We were desperate for each other. He was sure I'd been fucking Bobby Junior of all people. And the next morning I drank it and vomited it right back up. I think she just decided to stay."

Phyllis smiled down at the mountain of her belly and the baby kicked in response. "I don't regret it. She makes me remember who I was, before."

"Before the hands?"

"Before I went back."

Tamara wasn't sure what this meant. She didn't ask; in that moment Phyllis looked more angel than saint.

She drank down her glass.

Pea said, "Dev wrote, you know."

Till all my human hungers are fulfilled . . . What would he say, when he learned of her choice? Or had the baby already dreamed it for him?

Tamara snorted. "I won't steal it this time. Promise."

She didn't need to know what else he might have told Pea, alone on the other side of the ocean and so afraid. It was over now. They were all safe. She had made sure of it.

Pea met her eyes. Fireflies swam between them, flashing slow heartbeats. From the river came a chorus of crickets, legs pumping with invisible fury: a song, a song, a scream.

12

It was late morning when Walter's Packard pulled in front of the house. They watched him come from the garden. He must have been driving all night.

Phyllis stood up to see him, stood up all by herself. Then she turned around. She faced the river, not Walter's slow walk. He had blood on his cuffs.

Tamara understood, then, what Phyllis had seen immediately.

She moved to block him. "Don't say it." She didn't think he heard her. "Wouldn't they have told us?" she tried, but of course Walter would know before anyone, his back-channel sources would have contacted him the second the casualty reports came over the wires. For a terrible moment, she wanted it to be Clyde. This couldn't be happening. She had taken the curse! She'd turned aside the fury of the hands!

"What happened?"

Walter never looked at her, but he said, with that great stillness that was equal to his anger, "From what I could piece together, he was sent on a suicide mission. A cover for the real attack. Expendable, they said."

She choked, but the roots wouldn't let any air pass, their rage was a mirror of her own. Walter held her up, thumped her on her back, never looked away from Pea. Tammy coughed until she could breathe again. She straightened.

There seemed to be a faint outline at Phyllis's back, though the sun was so bright that day she could never be sure. The shape of a man, broad shoulders and long fingers that lingered at her waist.

He was saying something, but Tamara couldn't make out his words. Only the murmur of a current against a rock, a tone she had heard before, and loved.

Phyllis tipped her head back, exposed that long neck to the touch of light. She reached into her pocket, pulled out a cigarette and then her old lighter. She ran her thumb over the circle scratched into the metal. She thumbed the catch and brought the flame to her face.

A soft trickle of water dripped down the porch slats beneath her feet and onto the earth.

"That means it's yours," she whispered. "It's time, sweet Pea."

They took her to the hospital in Hudson. The liquid falling between Phyllis's legs turned pink as a sunset and she wandered like an ancient between the corridors of past and present, dream and reality. Walter took the turn to the emergency entrance in one smooth rush that pressed them hard against the back seat leather. A pair of nurses rushed out of the door when they saw the silver Packard but they paused when Walter climbed from the front seat.

Phyllis breathed heavy against Tamara's collarbone. Her eyes were wide, her pupils blasted, but she blinked when Tamara called her name.

"Come on, sweetie, let's get you inside, all right?"

Walter had come around to open the passenger-side door. He pulled it open and bent for Pea. The two nurses—joined now by a doctor and a few others with a gurney—peered around Walter's bulk. One of them met Tamara's eyes and gasped.

"Oh," she said. "Oh no, I'm sorry—"

Walter turned around with Phyllis in his arms. The gathered crowd stepped back as though he were carrying a gun. Tamara climbed out behind him. She'd had vague notions, in the midst of their frantic rush to the hospital, of playing the easiest game, now that they had such extreme need of it: a pregnant white woman with her Negro maid, easy as you please, let us in, this woman needs medical attention urgently! But standing beside Walter and Phyllis before that gaping crowd, she faltered. Facing this wall of well-heeled, professional whiteness, she had a flash (so vividly that in later years she would recoil at the mere mention of the dentist's name) of Marty's foreshortened horse's heads and their marching rows of commercial-white teeth.

"We don't accept colored patients here," the doctor said, shortly. "You'll have to leave. Try Poughkeepsie."

Tamara glanced at Phyllis, who had roused herself enough to look around. It was easy to see where they'd gone wrong: her hair was loose, floating around her head in thick, fuzzy curls. She was pale from pain, but unmistakably high yellow, golden from the spring-time gardening. Her stained plaid housedress didn't speak to these people's notion of whiteness any more than her bare feet did. They'd had no time!

"The lady is white," Tamara said, haltingly. Even now, the words stuck in her throat.

The nurse who had first seen her pursed her lips. "Dr. Nolan," she said in a stage whisper, "I grew up in Virginia, and I know a nigger when I see one. She might be half-caste, but she's a nigger all right."

Phyllis started laughing. She laughed so hard that she started leaking again, and this time it wasn't rosy, it was red.

"She needs a doctor," Walter said.

The doctor hesitated. It was a hanging moment, the inhale before the clapper hits the bell, a second whose memory would return to her in dreams for the rest of her life—and what is that space, if not where the hands have always lived? When one group tries to grind out the existence of another, to enslave them for generations, to pretend to give them freedom while forging a dozen new kinds of chains, to kill their children and cite the inevitable meanness of their condition as justification, and not a most deliberate result— when the scales of justice have been so grossly weighted in the favor of those who have almost everything and who eye with deadly jealousy that meager portion which eludes them, where else might one fight back but in the spaces, the inhales, the numbers?

The doctor shook his head. "Go. We don't want any trouble with you people, but we'll call the police if we have to."

Walter's arms twitched, as though he would put down Phyllis to reach for his gun.

"Leave it, Walter," Pea said. She sounded so tired. In all the time they had known one another, Tammy had never heard her so tired.

All that power they'd collected between them, all that cowing strength. Saint's hands, an oracle's deck, a mobster's gun. Useless, useless. *This* was power. Jack of diamonds, running milky hands through thinning hair, going home to dinner that evening, drinking a scotch to relax, and never once thinking: *I killed a woman today.*

Much later, when it was over, she sat alone in the kitchen after the baby had cried herself to sleep, and she read Dev's letter.

Pea—

There's so much I can't tell you that I think they'd prefer I not tell you anything. I'm safe, and healthy. The danger isn't as much as it could be, though they try their best. I suspect you're in much more.

I know you think you have failed the hands. But their demands always exceed what we're capable of giving. Forgive them. Forgive yourself.

You are like a goddess with Durga inside you, a creature inscrutable, with four holy hands that reach into our future and our past. I dream of her, growing and moving in that fluid which is to her a universe. Pressing against its limits the way the best of us do, entirely unaware of how she hurts you.

I dream of our house by the river. Of a stubborn, wild little girl with her hair bound in thick dark plaits that have caught bits of grass and dandelion fluff. There is mud on her hands and knees. She hunts fossils and tells stories over bones. She will live half in the present and half in an unformed future, she will see her own death and face it as she faces the muddy current of the March river. She will know too much about us and out of love protect us from it.

This is battle: Men speechless with terror, expelling their consciousness in grunts and prayers and last cigarettes. They cloud the air but don't linger like the gun smoke, which comes later. It is the moment before the breath that could be your last, when you shit your pants and keep running across the line. Or drop where you stand, felled by terror a second before the bullet. It is screams and blood and death, of course, but it is mostly the sharp cold of the last moment you will ever feel the cold. Fighting in spite of it.

When men go into that thinking that they don't deserve to live, then they die. I deserve to live. You deserve to live, Pea. You deserve that more than anyone, no matter what you've done. What they call a labor is a battle, maybe the purest kind.

Tamara has her cards, and yes, they are a kind of power, but they aren't the only one. They predict the future, but they don't decide it. Whatever they have told you, don't bow to it. If there is such a thing as destiny, it can be changed. It can be fought.

Fight, Pea. If we die, let it be screaming, not with a bullet to the back of the head because we hid behind the line. Fight, Pea. I love our daughter more than I should, more than any logic can explain, and she doesn't yet exist apart from you, and I am telling you to fight her, our sweet Durga, if in entering this world she tries to take you from it—

And if she does, or if one of those bullets finds its mark on me, please believe, Phyllis—we are connected by more than this love or this lifetime. When we return to the wheel of life, you and I, we will find one another again and again, seven lifetimes and seven lifetimes more, until the colonized and the enslaved and the abused will rise up with the holy strength of the gods behind them and, together, we will make it right.

Your
Dev

Tamara lifted a knife, one of the rusted ones from the garden. Why not? She'd been wondering since she stumbled from Poughkeepsie's colored hospital with bloodstains on her dress. (A dry laugh in one of Pea's last moments of lucidity: "You made a bargain with them, maybe I can too.") Tamara tossed Dev's letter in the air. Then she speared it to the wall in one uncanny throw.

Tamara left it there and walked outside. She sat on the porch steps that led to the garden. The evening breeze slid down the bare skin of her arms like velvet, holding a lingering warmth from the cheerful spring day, already passing. The sweet pea vines were starting to put out flowers, and the watermelon as well. The earth beneath them was freshly mulched, a comfortable red-brown, mixed with ashes.

She lost sight of it momentarily, her thoughts caught up in a familiar eddy, a ritual rehearsal of events that could not make the ending come out right.

They had made it to Poughkeepsie by noon. Pea had lost so much blood. She sometimes knew Tamara, and sometimes mistook her for Gloria, or her mother.

"There's a reason, you know," she had gasped at one point near the end, "a reason they gave us the hands. They want us to fight, Mommy! I'm not going to stay up here, just taking it!"

"That you never did, sugar," Tammy had whispered.

She turned away from that memory and fought to find a better one. For the rest of her life, this would be her charge: to remember how they had been, for the sake of that dreaming child upstairs. Tamara looked at the garden, limned in blue and orange like a kiln fire, and recalled the last night she had spent with Phyllis.

They had slept outside, slept under the stars like Tamara had as a child, and held one another's hands, and talked, and tended their silences. In the morning Phyllis had got down on her knees and pulled her rusted knives out of the earth. Then she tossed them to the side with the weeds.

Tamara knelt beside her in the dirt.

Up the hill from the river, they could still hear it murmuring, laughing, speaking in the rushed conversation of the dead, who can't be understood.

Now, Tamara looked down at the garden and was unsurprised to see her: Phyllis sprawled among the watermelon vines like an ellipsis, her great belly shining in another day's sunlight. Tamara could see her so clearly, she could count the freckles on her shoulders. Her scars. Her stretch marks. Her yellow hands dipped brown in clean earth.

"What are you?" Tammy asked.

Pea looked straight at her. "A light."

Phyllis went into labor that night. She found no gentleness there. She fought like an angel, like a saint, like a Harlem girl with policy slips in her garter and luck in her hands. She'd make something of herself one day. She knew it.

What good was a dream, they always said, if you didn't play the numbers?

ACKNOWLEDGMENTS

A novel is always a community effort, for all that only one name appears on the spine. Over the last seven years, I have received help, support, and encouragement from countless friends, colleagues, and institutions that pulled me along and held me up during this journey to complete this novel of my heart.

I am endlessly grateful for my friends who read multiple drafts, helped me talk through knotty philosophical problems, and just let me vent when nothing seemed to come together. Thank you April Anderson for loud-ass conversations about historical philosophy and the legacy of trauma in our community; Amanda Hollander for hours-long venting sessions and charmingly pedantic attention to detail; Tamar Bihari for reading the first and last drafts and all the emotional support in between; Sonali Dev for her expert eye regarding Dev's perspective; Delia Sherman for an early read and an incisive analysis of the tricky third part; Justine Larbalestier for wading through the earliest draft and encouraging me to the end; and my decade-plus all-star writer's group, Altered Fluid, in particular Sam Miller, Eugene Myers, David Mercurio Rivera, Kris Dikeman, Rick Bowes, N. K. Jemisin, Matthew Kressel, K. Tempest Bradford, Kai Ashante Wilson, Lilah Wild, Devin Poore, Paul Berger, Kiini Ibura Salaam, and Rajan Khanna. I remember the first time I went to a convention with you guys after I joined the group; I felt as though I'd won the lottery.

Although I began this thoroughly New York triptych in New York City, I wrote most of it in Mexico. It was my life-changing experiences here that inspired me to go back to the original story and expand it precisely as I had dreamed of and dismissed before. I've spent six years here writing and rewriting this book. I'm indebted to cafés whose names I've forgotten in San Cristóbal and Veracruz; Mexico City's inimitable anarchist bookshop/café and counterculture social hub, Marabunta; Café Negro, with its picture window right along Coyoacán's main drag, where I would people-watch as I wrestled with my own characters for hours on end.

What came out of those intense years in cafés was a novel that approached my vision but still fell critically short. I kept trying—having my brilliant agent, Jill Grinberg, in my corner gave me the confidence to take the risk. She and her colleagues helped nurture that initial draft into something genuinely good. Even so, it wasn't until we were able to connect with Miriam Weinberg and Tor that *Trouble the Saints* truly came into its own. Miriam is that unicorn of an editor who will actually take the time to make a book do what it needs to do—the kind that had martini lunches with their acclaimed-but-temperamental writers in the '40s, except with more editing and less drinking.

I thank my sister, Lauren, as always, for her company and kindness in untangling the tricky knots of our lives. Thank you for keeping me grounded. I'm indebted to my parents and extended family for their stories. Y muchas gracias, querido Isma, por acompañar una historia que solo podías apreciar por medio de traducción y conversaciones intensas de noches de mezcal.

Why do certain characters stay in your head while others wither? There is certainly some complex psychology at play, but I am fortunate to have all of you in my life; you allowed Phyllis and her friends to flourish and me to tell their story while I've been figuring out my own.